Praise for the work of R. GARCÍA y ROBERTSON:

"Vivid and entrancing . . . García y Robertson skillfully persuades the readers to suspend belief."
Publishers Weekly

"Fine storytelling . . . Original and brilliant."
Roger Zelazny

"Extraordinary . . . A genuine and excellent novel."
Locus

"Intelligent . . . Vivid and swift-moving . . . Holds the reader's attention throughout."
Washington Post Book World

"R. García y Robertson's is a new and very special voice, blending the fantastic with the actual and letting us read history with a new and brilliant lens."
Jane Yolen, author of *Sister Light, Sister Dark*

Other AvoNova Books by
R. García y Robertson

THE SPIRAL DANCE
THE VIRGIN AND THE DINOSAUR

ATLANTIS FOUND

R. GARCÍA y ROBERTSON

Portions of this work have appeared in somewhat different form in "Seven Wonders," *Asimov's Science Fiction* (December 1995) and "The Moon Maid," *The Magazine of Fantasy and Science Fiction* (July 1996).

This is a work of fiction. Names, characters, places, and incidents either are the product of the author's imagination or are used fictitiously. Any resemblance to actual events, locales, organizations, or persons, living or dead, is entirely coincidental and beyond the intent of either the author or the publisher.

AVON BOOKS
A division of
The Hearst Corporation
1350 Avenue of the Americas
New York, New York 10019

Cover art by Jean Pierre Targete
Published by arrangement with the author
Visit our website at **http://AvonBooks.com**
Library of Congress Catalog Card Number 96-97093
ISBN: 0-380-78678-8

First AvoNova Printing: April 1997

For my wonderful daughters
Anneke and Erin

Part I
Pillars of Hercules

Gibraltar

In the beginning all was formless Chaos, then sea and sky divided, and the Daughter of Ocean danced naked on the deep . . .

—*Apollonius of Rhodes*
The Voyage of the Argo

"Welcome to BC boys and girls." Johnny Love kicked open the hangar deck hatch with his heavy jump boot, exposing a circle of predawn sky the color of unpolished silver. Spray hurtled at him through the open hatchway. "Watch yer asses gettin' out."

Sauromanta snickered. Crouching, she waited her turn at the hatchway, one of her bows digging into Jake's back. During mission prep she had picked up essential bits of English—words like "boys" and "ass."

Jake Bento swung his legs through the hatch into damp gray air, peering down at the heaving sea. As soon as his adhesive boots broke contact with the *Argo*'s hangar deck, the world seemed suddenly lighter. More expansive and precarious. Ready to fly off without notice.

Green-black waves broke over Jake's target a dozen meters below, the tiny humped deck of the submarine *Thetis*, rising and falling in the swell. The shadowy hull of the *Argo* curved above him, blotting out tarnished silver sky. Her turbofans strained to maintain position above the minisub, so Jake's team could transfer without getting dunked or drowned.

A quick mental chronometer check showed three minutes and six seconds till dawn—04:45:14. First Day of Summer, deep in the Second Millennium B.C. More than fifteen hundred years before the birth of Christ. Twenty thousand years before Jake himself would be born. The coast of Bronze Age Europe lay just below the watery horizon, out where the sun was already up.

Two klicks to the southeast a high-prowed wooden boat wallowed in the long Atlantic rollers, her hull appearing and disappearing amid foam-capped slopes and deep glassy green valleys that marched from horizon to horizon.

"Step clever," Love advised.

Jake nodded, concentrating on his target. Aside from Sauromanta—too hopelessly young and brave to know better—everyone had been in an advanced state of nerves since passing the last portal. The minisub's deck looked minute, half-awash and sinking in the swell, and his compweb had already come up with five ways he might make a fool of himself. Thanking his augmented anatomy for the vote of confidence, Jake reached for the nylon ladder dangling like a trapeze line from the hull of the *Argo*.

Reached and missed. A wet salty gust shoved the *Argo* sideways, whipping the ladder away. Stifling a squeal of panic, Jake lurched forward, full of unwanted momentum. He lost his balance on the hatch combing, a sick here-we-go sensation seizing his gut.

"Shee-it." Johnny Love lunged across the open hatchway, snatching at Jake. And coming up empty.

Jake pitched past him, about to have a cold bath in the Bronze Age Atlantic—if he did not break his neck on the sub's deck. One hell of a fine start, moments into the mission and already headed for disaster. His compweb computed trajectories, predicting a wet landing.

Miraculously he jerked to a stop—no longer falling, impossibly suspended. Dumbfounded, Jake hung head down, staring at wave tops ten meters away. The horizon heaved wildly, while the ocean swung overhead, watery chaos dancing above a steadily brightening sky.

Looking back up his leg, he saw his adhesive boot stuck fast to the hull. Sauromanta's blond head grinned in the hatchway, having a grand time admiring his antics. She had caught hold of his boot by the toe, sticking it to the airship, utterly blowing any hope Jake had of impressing her with his aerobatics.

Love seized the dangling ladder, shoving it at him. "Quit showin' off. Take the fuckin' ladder."

Feeling a first-rate idiot, Jake grabbed a rung, telling his boot to release. Sauromanta let go of his toe, and the Bronze Age righted itself. Light violet sky swung back atop gray waves throwing ragged strands of foam.

He clung half a meter beneath the hull of the *Argo*, getting his bearings. The Iberian coast still lay sixty klicks beyond the northeast horizon. Below him, the deck of the *Thetis* heaved in the surface swell, three kilometers of water lying under her keel. The empty Bronze Age boat bobbed a couple of klicks to starboard, drifting south and east in the Canaries current. Seconds tumbled toward sunup.

The compweb and navmatrix grafted atop Jake's skull made sure he was never lost. Dazed, confused, and demoralized—but never lost. He always knew the exact point-instant causing him trouble.

Gingerly he descended until his no-slip boots gripped the minisub's deck. Waves lapped his toes. He had done it, touched down in the Bronze Age. Sort of.

Pale silvery light spread rapidly along the eastern horizon. Sixty-three seconds till sunup. So far so good. Not that they had gotten all that far.

Sauromanta swarmed easily down the ladder to stand beside him on the pitching deck. She was an out-timer, perfect for the mission, nearly a local, a sturdy teenage Amazon, born a thousand years hence on the Great Sea of Grass. A blond barbarian with sky-blue eyes and hair as gold as summer wheat, dressed all in animal skins. She wore tooled cowhide boots, stag-skin pants, a red-leather riding jacket, and a lynxskin cap. A Saca battle-ax hung from her belt. Two bows and a quiver banged against her back.

Jake found her shockingly lovely. A wild demure Artemis in skins and leather. Mistress of the Hunt. Death goddess with a girl's disarming smile. Endearing in a dangerous way. It was hardly the moment for such thoughts, but facing trouble twenty thousand years from Home did not automatically turn off the baser emotions. Jake made himself think of Peg. His fiery red-haired Peg, whom he would marry in the far, far future. With Peg for a wife, he hardly needed entanglements. Keep to the task at hand.

Sauromanta held the ladder for Love. Another out-time volunteer.

John Butler Love was as black as she was light, about ten years older, but born two thousand years after her. (He'd say, "Listen up Grandma," when he wanted to make her mad.) He wore an open flak jacket, baggy paratrooper pants, and an olive-drab tunic with a 101st Airborne "Screaming Eagle" patch on the sleeve. LOVE CHILD was neatly stenciled above the visor of his crash helmet.

It said a lot, that when Jake selected his away team he took no one from his own time.

Despite differences in sex, age, and race, Jake's mission companions shared a sense of cool defiance. Still in her teens, Sauromanta was out to see the universe. Love was a misplaced child of war. Two and a half tours in Nam, plus a peek at the future, had him missing things "normal life" never supplied. Both put a studied swagger into their acts, flaunting casual deadliness. Sauromanta had her Saca battle-ax and pair of bows. John B. Love had his flak jacket with JOHNNY BE BAD scrawled across the back.

Love grinned. "You looked damned slick in them sticky boots. Damned slick."

"I'll get you a pair," Jake promised.

"Can't wait. You was one cool-lookin' honky hangin' by that boot."

"Glad to hear it." Anything to entertain. Jake told the main hatch to open, his navmatrix merging smoothly with the sub's onboard systems. *Thetis* was hardwired to obey him. "Let's look at that boat."

Having the adhesive boots, Jake was last in, pausing for a moment at the hatch, pleased to have gotten this far. 04:48:20. The red orb of the sun broke the horizon, right on time. Hopefully a good omen. Water surged over the deck, pulling at his ankles, cascading through the open hatch into the sub. Pumps sucked it back out of the bilges, throwing out fountains of spray shot with tiny rainbows.

Normally first dawn in a new age meant a celebration. When he and Peg first got to the Mesozoic, ancient rock anthems played in his head. "Break on Through (to the Other Side)" and "Light My Fire." Both by The Doors. He had greeted the first full day in the Uppermost Cretaceous with *Dawn Symphony*—completely orchestrated. Jake liked to move to music.

But today the sea provided all the rock and roll he needed. The microamps in his middle ear were silent, straining to pick up the slap of waves and the cries of sharp-winged gulls. Any sense of triumph was tempered by knowing that for once he was not the first. The original *Atlantis* team had made it here ahead of him, along with three STOP backup teams.

Only none of them ever returned.

All four teams were gone. *Finito*. An airship, a pair of power-assisted sailplanes, three STOP hovercars—with friends of his aboard—all swallowed up by the Bronze Age. Utterly erased, without an *adieu*. Or a reason why.

A sobering thought. The Bronze Age was not supposed to be that rough. Beyond that dawn horizon lay something tougher than anyone expected.

Back when the Faster-Than-Light agency, FTL, had a lock on the past, Jake had helped plan the *Atlantis* expedition. He had been Faster-Than-Light's star field agent, fresh from triumphant success in Hellenistic Egypt where he had gotten the Cleopatra interview. When things went sour he had been at the portal, acting as STOP liaison for FTL. With *Atlantis* seriously overdue, the Special Temporal Operations team went in, prepped and ready. And did not come back. Neither did their backup.

Crisis time. Panic replaced concern. Higher-ups frantically caucused. Autoprobes showed no problem with the portal, no sign of surprises in the anomaly. Special Temporal Ops had only one other team prepped for the Bronze Age. Nobody had seen a situation that required more than two STOP teams. The third team had been a redundant precaution. Now it was all they had left. Jake briefed a fourth team on the Bronze Age, while STOP sent its third and last team in. They did not come back.

STOP could not keep feeding people into the portal. FTL ordered the anomaly sealed, and the Bronze Age mission abandoned. By then Jake had the fourth STOP team thoroughly briefed, and would have led them in himself.

That was all in the bad old days, before Jake and Peg broke

the Faster-Than-Light monopoly. Success in the Mesozoic opened the way for independent expeditions to the past. FTL had used guile, subterfuge, and sabotage to hold on to their monopoly, until Jake beat them hands down. Returning twice from the Mesozoic had made him too big for FTL to touch.

But there was still the Bronze Age. Unfinished business waiting behind a sealed portal.

Jake had demanded, and gotten, an independent attempt to penetrate the Bronze Age. A completely new expedition, bigger than the original *Atlantis* expedition, and using a different portal—absolutely free of FTL interference. Faster-Than-Light acted anxious to be left out, as did anyone with a sense of self-preservation. Four straight tragedies tagged the Bronze Age as a death-wish assignment, fit only for hopeless volunteers and dedicated mental cases.

Four straight tragedies also turned Jake's habitual caution into clinical paranoia. Which was why he had the *Argo* hull down below the horizon—with nothing in sight for hundreds of square klicks but watery wilderness and an empty wooden boat. And why he meant to approach the European coast unseen and underwater. Fear was his best friend. And he aimed to be one hundred percent wary. Not just listening to his paranoia, but humoring and nurturing it. Making sure nothing final and humiliating happened to him.

He gave *Argo* the wave-off.

An answering wave came from the forebridge, then the airship swung slowly about, headed west. Bearing TWO-SEVEN-ZERO.

No further signals passed between them. No fond *adieus* over the comlink. Jake did not plan to leave electromagnetic fingerprints. A single microwave burp would broadcast their presence in an age struggling to perfect the messenger pigeon. So long as the airship hugged the surface of the sea, hiding behind the earth's curvature, there was little chance of being detected. No Bronze Age satellites looked down from orbit—Jake had checked.

Argo would meet a series of dawn rendezvous at three-day intervals two hundred kilometers to the west, hiding behind the horizon. If Jake did not return in twenty-one days, what to do next would be Captain Wasserman's headache.

But Jake meant to make one of those rendezvous.

He surveyed the bright eastern horizon. Polarizers on his corneal lenses let him sweep past the sun on high magnification, without so much as a blink.

Nothing but water, sky, and an empty boat. There might well be nothing out there. Nothing but Pharaoh's Egypt, Homer's Troy, and the Babylon of Agum the Conqueror. Bronze Age despots, settling differences at spearpoint. Plus Cimmerians and Hittites. Gods and heroes. Snake-haired Gorgons, the Golden Fleece, the Labyrinth, and Lost Atlantis. Or so the myths said.

At the moment Jake pegged his paranoia on one solid fact. Four highly equipped expeditions had disappeared trying to penetrate the Bronze Age. And three of them had gone in expecting trouble. Those teams could have succumbed to something natural. Like portal slips. Or mass attacks of time psychosis. Just four bad throws of the cosmic dice. All in a row. The odds against that were merely astronomical.

Four teams were gone. All else was frantic guesswork.

Time to get going. Jake entered the minisub, telling the hatch to close, ordering *Thetis* to dive. Silent scuttles sucked up the water that came in with him. Descending the ladder to the command deck, he had the sub level off. Exact depth and pressure readings lurked in his compweb—ready if needed. Continually updated.

Hand valves, switches, blinking readouts, and cushioned bulkheads crowded the minicontrol space. Semicircular pressure hatches led to fore and aft cabins, both detachable, doubling as escape pods. Easy effortless illumination came from everywhere and nowhere. Hip to hip with Sauromanta, Jake inhaled an intoxicating mix of wet leather on bare skin, acutely aware of the unconscious power she exerted. Sauromanta stood out, in a crowd or at a distance. Up close she took his breath away. Had it been right to bring her? He obviously needed her—only moments ago she had saved him from a morning swim. Besides, the problem was in him, not in her.

Never having been in a submarine before, the young Amazon seemed equally excited. "This ship sails underwater?"

"We are underwater."

Blue eyes widened, sizing him up. Home period's technology impressed her—making Jake appear somewhat wondrous as well. Nice, if disconcerting.

Love had never been in a submarine either. But what airborne trooper could be much impressed by a midget swabbymobile?

Thetis impressed Jake, with her sonar-absorbing hull, silent fusion reactor, and propellerless drive. Powered by seawater, she could cruise forever with just a whisper of current sliding over her hull. Or she could sink down to the cold black realm on the silent ocean floor, protected by kilometers of pressure no normal weapon could withstand.

He had designed *his* Bronze Age expedition around the sub—a piece of equipment the lost teams had lacked. Giving his paranoia free reign, Jake bypassed the established Eurasian hyperlight portals, making an end run out to sea, using the Midatlantic portal between Florida and Bermuda. A feat in itself. The Midatlantic portal had never been pushed so far back. Notoriously balky, the Florida–Bermuda Temporal Anomaly was infamous for spontaneous transmissions—more known for sending hapless locals on unplanned trips to the Stone Age than for serious attempts to penetrate new periods. But Jake had navigated it. (Hold the applause.) Now he meant to make maximum use of surprise—99 percent of the game in submarine operations.

He extended the whip-thin periscope. Its fish-eye lens projected a 3V image onto the control room bulkheads. Jake, Love, and Sauromanta seemed to be standing under open sky with water lapping around them. They had all the advantages of an open conning tower, and none of the discomfort, with only a tiny antenna showing.

Looking happily about, Sauromanta took deep excited breaths, saying to Love, "You can smell the sea!"

"Right, girl. She's fishy."

They closed in on the wooden boat bobbing in the waves, a simple double-ended craft, built like a Celtic *curragh*, but with wooden sides instead of skins. Rough-hewn oak planks fastened with pegs and hemp. A single pole mast inscribed circles in the dawn sky. A long top spar, wrapped in sailcloth and bound with rigging, lay alongside a pair of sweeps—real oars, not paddles. Whatever happened to her crew had not happened under oars or sail.

Love lifted a meaningful eyebrow. Jake shrugged. "Wind

and current are from the north. She might have drifted down from Finisterre or the Bay of Biscay."

"Could have been pirates," Love suggested. "She's pretty well stripped."

"No anchor stone. No cable," noted Jake. "Could have come adrift while the crew was ashore." Either way, he meant to make use of this Bronze Age *Marie Celeste*. Telling the *Thetis* to take the boat in tow, he turned east, toward the Iberian coast, ordering the galley to whip up meatless eggs Benedict.

Love sniffed. "Flash frozen yeast steaks an' lemony eggs—Yum."

Jake dished it out. "Most important meal of the day. It's better than low blood sugar for breakfast."

Sauromanta thanked the gods, then thanked him. Daughter to a Royal Scyth hetman—who raised her like a son—she never thought of helping with meals, except to hunt for the pot. But she smiled as she took her serving, touching his hand, a bit of warm contact that scrambled his memory banks.

Jake reminded himself that he and Peg were only precariously married. Sitting Bull had tied the knot, in 1857, The Winter When Ten Crows Were Killed. And a Hunkpapa marriage was pretty much what you made it—Sitting Bull himself was married nine times, but never liked having more than two wives at once. If something happened between him and Sauromanta, would Peg really care? Peg was a scientist, a paleontologist, her mind fixed firmly in the present, or the Mesozoic. Happiest when the present *was* the Mesozoic, putting the two halves of her personality in sync.

Breakfast odor faded, and Jake noticed a new smell, neither wet nor fishy—the green dusty scent of land over the horizon.

Landfall came on the second. A dark mass appeared, like a low black cloud bank—perfectly matching file images of Cape St. Vincent—the southwestern tip of the Eurasian landmass, a great blunt triangle jutting into the Ocean Stream. Jake's navmatrix had taken him from twenty thousand years in the future, through the Bermuda Triangle, then by airship and submarine to the nearest point in Europe. Mostly at night, without missing a nanosecond. Another excellent omen.

The Portuguese coast looked utterly abandoned, ragged hills and black rocks tumbling straight into the sea. Hoping to see people, Jake cut across the Gulf of Cadiz, drawing level with Gades. Probably the oldest Atlantic seaport, Gades was inhabited in every historic period until the Greenhouse Meltdown. An ideal spot for getting a look at his unwashed ancestors. Anchoring the boat to the tow cable, he took the sub in.

"How's about shore leave?" Love suggested. Submarine travel was already wearing thin.

Jake agreed. "Gades would be the place."

He had gotten his airship training aboard the *Graf Zeppelin* in the last decade of the PreAtomic, flying for Lufthansa on the South America run, with stopovers in the south of Spain. In those days Gades had become Cadiz, the "Dish of Silver"—white as a mirage, with terraced roofs and naked dancers, connected to the rest of Spain by a golden spit of sand. Jake would stay at the Continental or the Gran Victoria, doing his drinking at the Cerveceria Inglesa, spending Nazi reichsmarks on bullfights and flamenco dancers.

Bronze Age Gades was a very different place—not yet the "Fenced City" of the Phoenicians, just a pair of settled islets, the larger of the two sporting a wooden temple and a stockaded keep. Red-haired cattle grazed along the beach. The sandspit to the mainland lay in the far future.

Jake's corneal lenses zoomed in on a religious rite in a tall grove of trees. Women and girls filled the grove, some naked, some stripped to the waist, wearing snaky Gorgon masks and body paint, keening in an unknown tongue. Priestesses held wriggling snakes before a megalithic three-stone altar, offering up the first ears of summer grain. High-pitched chanting carried softly across the water.

"Extra fuckin' weird." Love shook his head. "*National Geographic* for white folks." He glanced at Jake. "How's she look in cinemascope?"

Jake owned it was a sight. Exotic. Certainly eye-catching. But hardly out of place. Sauromanta took one look and said it was bad luck. "Something men should not see."

Bad luck or not, seeing people made the Bronze Age seem more real, touched with the thrill of discovery. At the same time it drove home the immensity of the task ahead. A whole world lay spread before them, crammed with strange gods and wild peoples. Intricate. Practically endless. They could hardly search it one farmstead and settlement at a time. At best they could stay mobile, moving through the landscape as fast as a sub and airship allowed. Alert for anything out of place. Always in transit. Always a moving target.

Taking the minisub back out to sea, Jake picked up the wooden boat and headed south, aiming to give Cape Trafalgar plenty of sea room, making a cautious approach to the Strait of Gibraltar, the great gateway to the Mediterranean.

Boredom descended. Love listened to Billie Holiday's "Long Gone Blues" on a pocket recorder. Sauromanta sharpened already keen arrows. Jake fixed and served lunch—crepes à la Florentine—but that did not take up near enough time. Even a dangerous mission in an exotic locale got tedious when there was nothing to *do*. Not liking to go stale, Jake decided to have a hands-on look at the boat they were towing, telling the sub to surface.

Nothing extraordinary turned up. Beneath the sweeps and sails lay a cargo of tin ingots, and a wooden box full of sand and ashes that had held the ship's fire. Plus a stone mallet and lumps of black caulking pitch—but no personal effects, nothing to show where the boat had come from. The three of them stood in the empty boat, listening to waves lap the hull. "Spooky," Love ventured. "Damned spooky."

Jake shrugged. "Maybe they jumped overboard when they saw the *Argo*."

Spooky or not, the little ship was a godsend. Enough to make Jake believe in old-time sea gods. Or dumb luck. Now they could make a landing without creating a scene by coming ashore in a very out-of-period submarine. No sense starting myths about sea monsters disgorging passengers.

Love hefted a lump of tin, "Maybe these poor Bronze Age bastards—"

Before Love could finish, Jake's compweb flashed a warning. No alarms or bells. Just a swift readout showing an unexpected spike in the electromagnetic spectrum. He yelled, "Get to the sub."

Love dropped the lump of tin and leaped past the boat's high prow, onto the sub. Paratrooper boots skidded on the wet deck, but he caught the open hatch before going overboard. Jake landed right behind him, half-dragging Sauromanta, shouting, "Down the hatch." *Allegro*! *Mach schnell*!

Love vanished into the sub. Jake followed, sliding down the

ladder's sides, ignoring the rungs, telling *Thetis* to crash-dive. Sauromanta came down on top of him, her boot on his neck, landing them in a heap on the command deck. Water cascaded over them. The hatch slammed shut.

"That's my face you're puttin' your foot in," came from beneath the pile.

Jake moved his boot, shouting, "Flood forward!" He hated being right. Having his paranoia confirmed. *Atlantis*, and the three STOP teams sent to find it, had not fallen victim to some uncharted time warp. They had stumbled onto something high-tech and sinister—that was now reaching out for them.

Buoyancy tanks burst open in a roar of bubbles. With hydroplanes down hard the sub surged ahead, reeling out cable to keep from capsizing the boat. Jake kicked open the hatch to the forward cabin. Foam poured over the transparent bow. "Get forward," he shouted. "Get the nose down."

They tumbled into the forward cabin, jamming themselves against the see-through bow. Sauromanta landed atop him again, looking surprised but not scared. Jake at least knew what to be terrified of. Pulse pounding, he pictured the spark of an ASW missile falling out of the sky. The splash as it hit water, releasing its torpedo. Then the explosion, and the green surge of sea filling the sub, drowning and choking.

Lion Man

Huddled in the transparent bow, Jake held the forward hydroplanes hard down. Bow heavy, her trim tanks flooded, the minisub dived. Water bubbled up to cover the last tiny bit of sky. Jake leveled off, not daring to raise periscope, listening for the telltale throb of a homing torpedo.

Nothing. Waves ceased to lap the hull. Surface sounds vanished. The mad moment faded. *Thetis* plowed silently through green salt water, a few meters below the surface. Love turned down Billie Holiday, still singing the blues in his pocket. "Cool. Can you do it again?"

Sauromanta looked about, awed by the flow of water. Shafts of sunlight filtered down, making tiny motes gleam against the dark green sea.

Jake reran the spike in his head. "I picked up electronic scatter."

Love gave him an "Oh, really" look. No one liked to say out loud a guy had freaked, panicking at the hint of contact.

But Jake had not freaked. Overdramatized maybe. Hitting the alarm button hard. But he'd had a nasty start; that made it utterly essential to be submerged. They had brushed against an active radar system. Something with no business being in the Bronze Age. No more than Jake did anyway.

Unreeling the long stern antenna, a buoyant filament lying flat against the waves, he had his compweb scan frequencies. Masking out solar interference and cosmic background, isolating the signal. "It's from a point source to the south and east, on the African shore. The north face of the Jbel Musa, between the Atlas foothills and the sea. Ground-hugging radar on a standard STOP frequency."

"Which don't make it friendly." Love had a veteran copter pilot's hated for invisible fingers reaching over the horizon. And he had too often seen "friendly" equipment turned against him. In Nam it had been a national pastime.

Jake told *Thetis* to project the source, tracing lines of sight and laying down horizon circles. "No chance now of running the straits. Too dangerously narrow," he decided. "Only a dozen klicks at the choke point." Really good backscatter radar—like STOP used—could detect wave disturbance and wake turbulence, even from submerged movement.

But Jake did not need to run the narrows. Not when there was a better way. "Time to take to the boat. *Thetis* can sit on the bottom while we have a close-in look."

That meant humping it to the straits and beyond; going up against the unknown with nothing but sidearms, "sticky boots," and his augmented anatomy. But active radar had the bad habit of tipping its hand too early—and surprise had to be worth something. Jake did not mean to blow his advantage. No need to tell anyone that a fifth team from the future had arrived.

Transferring to the boat, he told *Thetis* to lie on the bottom and wait.

Sitting in the crude wooden boat, watching choppy little waves close over the minisub, Jake had done his best to blend in. He wore an embroidered tunic, Persian pants, and a bronze sword. All gifts from Alexander the Great. The sword was looted from a shrine in the Troad, having supposedly belonged to the Trojan hero Hector. His wool cape had been worn by Julius Caesar, or so Cleopatra claimed. Only his neural stunner, medikit, rations, climbing gloves, grapple line, and adhesive boots were drastically out-of-period.

Love had thrown a woolen poncho over his flak jacket and

crash helmet. And Sauromanta never deigned to disguise herself. They were set to show their act to the Bronze Age.

But first they had to master the boat. Fortunately wind and sea were with them, both coming from the starboard quarter, with the coastline falling away to port, promising an easy run down to the straits. South of Cape Trafalgar they took turns with the sail and steering oar. Love's pilot training showed, and Sauromanta was unskilled but willing. By dusk they were battling sleep and boredom instead of the darkening sea.

Volunteering to take the night watch, Jake stood out from shore, pointing the ship at Africa. Love gratefully turned in. With the restless energy of youth, Sauromanta stayed up to spell Jake at the steering oar. When it was her turn, he showed her to how to hold a southerly course, having her look over her shoulder at their wake—a straight track agleam with phosphorescence, aimed back at the European shore. He could feel every point where their bodies touched.

"The stars have changed," he told her. "Precession has shifted true north over toward Alpha Draconis." Thuban, Alpha Draconis, a white giant two hundred light-years off, was the north star on which the pyramids were aligned.

She spotted the star at once. "That is Ladon, the Dragon that Hercules killed in the Garden of the Hesperides. The Dragon that guarded the Golden Apples."

Draco, snaking through the northern night, stood for all the dragons in myth and history, from Tiamat of the Sumerians, to Fafnir in the *Nibelungenlied.* But Sauromanta would pick the dragon Hercules killed—that muscle-bound son of Zeus was her people's first ancestor. The Father of the Scyths. Sauromanta had a pair of fancy embroidered pants showing him mating with the Snake-tailed Mother.

She quoted Apollonius of Rhodes:

The serpent Ladon, Lybia's son,
Stood watch while the Hesperides sang,
Till Hercules struck him dead,
By the trunk of the apple tree.

Her father kidnaped scholars to teach her the classics. And Homer was as familiar to her as bending a bow. But it was Jake who introduced her to Apollonius—born a century after her. He had given her a copy of *The Voyage of the Argo*. She was showing him she had already memorized it.

Jake felt touched. Sauromanta had a schoolgirl's pride, and a savage sense of honor, always valuing his gifts, never hiding it if she felt slighted. Peg was absolutely honest—even hypercritical when she saw the need—but she came from a civilized era that had learned to leave things unsaid.

Sauromanta asked, "Are the stars different on Mars?"

"Not really." It always amazed her that he had been born on Mars. Now Jake wished he had taken her there. But mission prep had been hectic—he had not even taken her beyond the lights of Megapolis. Maybe he had not trusted himself with her alone on a starry night.

"Time makes the difference. Our north star is Vega." He pointed to Alpha Lyrae on the far side of Hercules—a tremendous blue-white giant only twenty-six light-years away. "Vega's a terrific system, fully terraformed ages ago." Jake meant in his own time. He described Vega's huge habitable zone and handcrafted worlds. The Pleasure Grottos of Erato. Mardi Gras on Thalia. Clio's virtual landscape and Living Archives. Galatic rotation had the whole solar system headed that way—toward Vega and Hercules. It was the future's future.

When they shifted positions she lay down beside him, her head resting against his thigh. Blond hair spilled into his lap. He wished he had the courage to lean down and kiss her. Sauromanta stared ahead at the purple African night. "Can they see us? Even in the dark?" She did not sound afraid, merely curious.

Jake nodded. The signal was stronger than ever, scanning the wave tops, probing the boat. "But all they'll see is the wake of a wooden boat with a cargo of tin. Someone taking advantage of a fair wind and a starry night to run south to the straits."

"Yet still you are afraid?"

"Afraid? Me?" He grinned at her. "I should hope so. I just fancied it might not show." He did not mind *looking* brave, wearing Caesar's cloak and a bronze sword. Hell, in her eyes he wanted to be a hero. But something in Sauromanta demanded the truth.

"You see forever. You hear the slightest sound. You travel

through the ages and to the stars. Yet you fear what will happen to us now, and on the morrow."

"Too true," Jake admitted. He was afraid even to touch her.

Despite endless precautions, Jake suffered gnawing doubts. Some created by the slipperiness of post-Einsteinian space-time. Whoever disposed of the previous Bronze Age expeditions might easily come from the future. Jake's future. Their technology might make *Thetis* look like this wooden boat. Still worse, they might *know* ahead of time what steps Jake would take. A faster-than-light universe was fundamentally unfair—making it his *job* to be scared.

The four lost expeditions had contained heroes aplenty. Jake meant to give himself more than the usual half-millimeter margin of safety. Aiming to be as cautious as possible, without completely flipping out or succumbing to a fatal fit of nerves.

Sauromanta turned to face him, taking his free hand in both of hers. Normally she moved with a natural grace, but this action had all the awkward sincerity of youth.

"You must never be afraid," she told him.

"Never?"

She held her hands flat, with his in between, as if in prayer. "Only the happy gods live forever. Our short lives are what we make them. So why live them in fear?"

Why indeed? They had not so much as kissed. Just doing some semi-innocent stargazing. But already Sauromanta had that woman-in-love conviction that Jake could be improved. Remade into something better than he was. Maybe. Women two and three times her age had tried—with mixed success.

"I have a job to do," he reminded her. "Dying bravely won't get it done."

"Trust me." She pressed her hands tight against his. "I'll see we succeed." Sauromanta was set to match her bows and ax against whatever the future had to offer. And not out of ignorance either—she had *seen* the future.

"I do trust you."

"Really?"

"Absolutely. You and Love are the only ones I trust." They were orphans out of time, utterly unconnected to any futuristic conspiracies. He had recruited them both. From fourth-century B.C. Persia, and twentieth-century Laos. "You have no reason to betray me. And you are someone I would want at my side. Or at my back. Especially if things turn scary.''

Satisfied she had his trust, she lay down beside him, warm and solid. She was soon asleep.

Looking down at her sleeping face, he felt finally safe to stroke that torrent of silver-blond hair. Jake felt happy as a poet on opium just sitting beside her. Sauromanta was the soul of honor, strong and honest. And all she asked for was trust. Clearly not the sort of woman you tackled on a whim.

Besides, he had learned something from his first night in the Mesozoic—a lively bedtime farce staring Jake, Peg, and a wandering triceratops herd. Don't be in such a hurry to bed a team partner that you get trampled in the rush. More than ever he wished Peg was with him, to keep him grounded. And make Sauromanta less of a temptation. But Peg was a paleontologist—not a skill demanded by the mission profile. There were no dinosaurs in the Bronze Age.

Every so often he would rest his eyes and brain, letting his compweb keep watch while his navmatrix held the heading. Not until after midnight did he turn eastward, into the straits, to face the dawn. Wind and current were now behind him. The electromagnetic emissions from the African coast were like a beacon, cutting through the darkness, sweeping the straits. Someone was keeping an anxious watch.

At dawn he woke the others. The sun rose up over the flat shining expanse of the Mediterranean as they approached the two great stone pillars marking the entrance—Gibraltar, the Mount of Saturn to the north, and Ceuta on the African shore. The Middle Sea opened up ahead of them, growing brighter and broader in the morning light. As if some invisible Hercules were pushing the continents apart, making room for them to enter.

Jake put over to port, to beat his way into the Bay of Algeciras, in the shadow of Gibraltar. He meant to swing around and come on the Jbel Musa listening post from the Mediterranean side, where they are apt to be less alert. He also hoped to pick up some rope and an anchor stone, as well as any word to be had about events on the African side.

The Bay of Algeciras sparkled in the dawnlight, a flat sheet of water stretching out toward the Rock of Gibraltar rearing up on its narrow peninsula. A small fishing village nestled in the lee of Cape Canero, facing the Rock. Farther inland a square fortified settlement stood atop a pine-clad hill. Olives and vines covered the lower slopes.

Two ships lay at anchor in the bay. One looked to be Phoenician, with rounded ends and a tall mast topped by a crow's nest. The other looked Atlantean, with a high sharp prow and stern. Both were anchored well away from shore, along with a flotilla of smaller craft—fishing smacks and the like. The beach itself seemed abandoned, aside from some tiny dugouts dragged up on the sand, and a single ship careened on its side, having rotting planks replaced.

Hiking the gain on his corneal lenses, Jake noted that the ships in the harbor were jammed with sailors, eyeing the beach from a safe distance as though they feared some plague ashore. The Phoenicians wore ankle-length robes and thick curly beards. The Atlanteans were more lightly dressed in kilts and codpieces, with clean-shaven faces and bare chests. Their dark hair hung down in long oiled locks. Bright necklaces and wrist bangles flashed in the sunlight.

Jake let the boat run gently aground. Sand hissed under the keel, and Love looked at him. "Shall we go ashore?"

"Not yet." Jake could hear the Phoenicians talking like something was about to happen. He wanted to know what.

Without warning the wooden gate on the walled settlement banged open. A procession emerged. Pipers, cymbalists, horse chariots, black bulls, and warriors with spears came winding down the hill headed for the shore. Drums beat. Acrobats cartwheeled toward the beach. People swarmed behind the parade like bees on a mating flight.

At their head rode a priestess in a gilded chariot, pulled by men dressed in bullhide, with horns on their heads. She wore a pleated robe with a silver belt, and had her long dark hair tied in a sacral knot. People threw grain at her golden car. Behind her walked three jet-black bulls with long gilded horns, led by high-stepping priestesses in great flounced skirts. Jake's flamenco dancers and fighting bulls had arrived.

Behind the bulls strode the biggest man Jake had ever seen decked with flowers. Mostly daisies. Bright yellow sun's eyes, rayed by white petals. Two meters tall, and nearly as broad, the man moved among the women and musicians like an old-time titan. His arms were as thick as Jake's thighs, his legs like temple pillars.

Beneath the daisy chains he wore a wool chiton and a crude lionskin cloak, fashioned from a single pelt, claws and all. The tail hung down between his huge legs, knotted in the middle. Head and jaws formed a hood, framing his bearded face with sharp white teeth. Across his shoulders he carried a brass-bound club.

A two-wheeled chariot rattled along behind him, loaded with armor, its charioteer a beardless boy about Sauromanta's age.

Priestesses led the three black bulls to a simple slab altar, singing to them in some strange tongue. Jake's compweb—set to translate every known Bronze Age language, from Ceremonial Hittite to New Kingdom Egyptian—instantly announced, NULL FILE.

The priestesses were not singing in Hittite, Egyptian, or anything in between. Ninety percent of the spoken languages in any new period were bound to be unknown. Still it bothered Jake. He was used to being better than the locals at their own language. Microamps let him hear what was being whispered in proto-Phoenician on a ship halfway across the harbor. But he could not understand these women just down the beach.

The man in the lionskin planted himself before the bulls, saying,

> *"Poseidon, Horsetamer, and Earthshaker,*
> *Give me safe passage over your seas,*
> *And to the African shore."*

This was better. Jake's compweb immediately recognized a prayer to Poseidon in Mycenaean, the proto-Greek language underlying Linear B. A lucky turn. Jake had someone ashore he could talk to. Someone who might help lay hands on an anchor.

Finishing his prayer, the lionskinned giant swung his club, sending flowers flying, braining the middle bull. A tremendous backhand caught the second bull behind the eye socket, breaking his skull. The third bull bellowed and pulled at his ropes, threatening to jerk the priestesses off their feet. The brawny executioner brought his club down between the gilded horns. The last bull crumpled.

Flower petals rained down on the dead beasts. It happened so fast—3.7 seconds according to Jake's compweb—that the last bull was down before the first stopped thrashing.

The odor of blood and bullshit wafted across the water. Love shook his head. "Beats the show at Burger King."

One more reason vegetarianism had swept Jake's Home Period. Sauromanta seized his arm as if she meant to speak, but kept silent. Maybe she did not want to disturb the ritual. Poseidon was a patron god of the Royal Scyths.

The priestesses lit a fire at the altar. The lion man knelt down, catching some of the bulls' blood in a gold cup. Turning toward the sea, he poured a blood libation to Poseidon.

Then the boy in the chariot handed down a longsword with a leaf-shaped blade. The lion man used it to disembowel the largest bull. Cutting himself a hunk of warm liver, he began eating even before the god. As he chewed, he surveyed the bay, the boats, and the big rock beyond.

Behind him, priestesses cut ceremonial thigh slices, wrapping them in fat and burning them for the god. Sprinkling wine on the flames. People carved the rest of the meat into small pieces, sticking them on bronze roasting spits. Spreading out blue-dyed fleeces, they settled down to eat.

"Beach blanket barbecue." Love said it in English, but the lion man caught the words and turned to look.

Shouldering his club, he strode straight toward them, splashing through the surf and seizing the bow of their boat, his fist fitting easily around the stem post. Without a by-your-leave he began to haul the boat and crew higher up onto the beach. As the keel grated firmly in the sand, he let go, spit half-chewed liver into the surf, and looked up at Jake. A lock of dark hair hung down from under the lion's upper jaw onto his forehead. His eyes were light amber, like a lion's.

"It is by Poseidon's will that you brought this boat," he announced in booming Mycenaean. "I am Hercules, son of Zeus, and I must get to the African shore."

The Golden Apples

Every man turned to mighty Hercules, begging him to take command . . .

—*Apollonius of Rhodes*
The Voyage of the Argo

''Did the man say Hercules?'' Love had zipped through Mycenaean in mission prep, adding it to English, Universal, and a smattering of French, Spanish, and Vietnamese. He had a quick, keen, unaugmented mind—the kind that took you from college ROTC to steering a helicopter in an alien culture, half of whose people shot at you.

''That is what the man said.''

Love scoffed, ''Don't be pulling my putter.''

Jake was also having a hard time believing the translation. But this had to be him, as big and brash as the myths claimed.

''Of course it's him.'' Sauromanta's eyes were alight, her lips parted in excitement. ''Mighty Hercules, true son of Zeus, with his dauntless lion-heart.'' Her words were from Homer, her ultimate authority on things mythical. She was seeing her people's first ancestor. The Father of the Scyths, consort to the Snake-tailed Mother. Maleness incarnate. Jake was already jealous.

Hercules strode back to the altar, congratulating Poseidon for being so prompt with a boat and crew.

Jake saw small use in arguing. A beach full of very excited

people *expected* him to take Hercules aboard. Disappointing the throng could be dangerous. Hercules' honor guard had long spears, round bullhide shields, and wicked curved swords. Half-grown boys strutted along with them, wearing deadly-looking slings as headbands or loincloths.

He could hear Phoenicians aboard ship in the harbor laughing up their embroidered sleeves, glad to have Hercules latching on to him instead of them. Algeciras harbor would soon be open for business again.

Finishing his devotions, Hercules had the boy charioteer drive his horses down into the surf. He began to unload armor from the tail of the chariot, tossing it up to Jake and Love.

"Take care," he warned. "These are gifts from various gods. Father Zeus gave me the shield with the serpent heads around the boss. The bow is Apollo's. The cuirass comes from Hephaestus, or mayhap Athene. They are utterly unbreakable, but I won't have them mistreated."

Unbreakable wasn't the word. Jake showed the breastplate to Love. "This is composite sandwich armor."

"No lie. Seen armor-piercing shells bounce off this shit." Nothing in the Bronze Age was going to scratch it.

The bow was compound metal and fiberglass. Whatever "gods" had armed Hercules had gone all out. Somehow Jake had to get this heavenly arsenal to the labs aboard the *Argo*—it could easily tell him who or what they were facing.

He called down to Hercules, "Where are we headed?"

The godson bent down, washing his sword in the surf. "To Africa. To visit the Garden of the Hesperides."

Jake furiously considered how this might fit into his plans. All thought of ditching the arrogant demigod had vanished as soon as he saw the armor. And the brash godson promised to be excellent cover. With Hercules barging about, swinging his club, who would look too closely at the boat that brought him?

Hercules held up his sword. Gold serpents twined down the blade. "A gift from Hermes," he declared.

"And worthy of a god," Jake agreed. The blade looked to be tempered steel, certainly not bronze. "But what we most need is an anchor and cable." Not a load of holy armor.

Hercules barked orders. Men vanished into the fisher huts, returning with coils of rope, and rolling a huge stone grooved about the middle. Hercules tossed the rope to the young charioteer, who scrambled aboard. Seizing another hunk of liver, he heaved the huge anchor stone onto his shoulder, then hoisted himself aboard. "Let us be off. I mean to be in Africa by midmorning."

Up close, his muscles seemed too perfect to be the product of exercise—looking suspiciously like he had been raised on steroids. People plunged into the surf to push them off, singing as they shoved the boat out into the bay. Hercules set down the anchor stone, sitting himself atop it, basking in applause from the beach. "People fuss over me wherever I go."

No doubt. These folks seemed particularly glad to see him go. Love and Sauromanta hastened to raise sail, before anyone else barged aboard. With the wind still strong from the west, Jake made for the east entrance to the bay, aiming to pass right beneath the Rock.

Sauromanta sat down next to the boy charioteer. Love settled in across from Hercules. The demigod tore off a bloody hunk of liver, offering Love a bite. "It's still warm."

"Hey, I believe. I *saw* you brain and butcher him. But they got me on one of those low-carrion diets."

Hercules ate it himself, happily watching the Spanish shore dwindle. He launched into a story about the last time he was in Spain. "I came to fetch the Cattle of Geryon. Great lovely shambling beasts, with long red hair and curving horns."

Hercules told how he had lifted the cattle from King Geryon of Tartessus, who lived beyond the straits, where the Guadalquivir emptied into the Ocean Stream. Or rather *had* lived. Hercules had been forced to kill King Geryon, along with the king's three sons, his chief herdsman, and a wondrous two-headed watchdog.

He committed this larceny and multiple homicide on behalf of his cousin, Eurystheus, High King of Mycenae. The High King had no claim to the cattle, but was in the habit of sending his muscular cousin off to lift or kill all manner of famous wonders. (If only to keep Hercules away from Mycenae.) Giant boars to fetch, stables to clean—it made no matter to Hercules. The harder the better.

"In eight years and a month, I performed ten labors the like of which the world has never seen. But King Eurystheus discounted the second and fifth, claiming Iolaus helped me kill the Lernaean Hydra, and that I took payment for cleaning the Augean Stables.''

Iolaus introduced himself, saying he was Hercules' nephew as well as his charioteer. ''I was less than nine when we fought the Hydra,'' he declared loyally. ''Hardly a bit of help.''

Hercules gave them an I-told-you-so nod. ''And I got nothing for cleaning those stables, though King Augeas promised a tithe of his cattle. Eurystheus just envies me for getting more women. And for being half a god.''

He heaved a heavy sigh, saying, ''We are cousins. And if it were not for my foster mother Hera, I would have been High King.'' Hercules acted as though being cheated by strangers and kinfolk was just the way of the world. ''Once the thought of such treatment drove me to savage fits of rage, but I have learned to hold my anger.''

''We're *all* happy to hear that,'' Love told him. No one wanted Hercules going berserk in a small boat.

''Now the Dung Man demands I bring King Eurystheus the Golden Apples of the Hesperides.''

''Dung Man?'' Love did not totally trust his Mycenaean.

''Copreus, the High King's herald,'' Iolaus explained. ''Ever since Hercules brought back the corpse of the Nemean Lion, the High King has been afraid to let us into his keep. He built a bronze box to hide in when Hercules is about, sending out Copreus, the Dung Man, in his stead.''

Iolaus sounded proud. How many teenage boys lived in such dangerous company that they were barred from the Lion Citadel?

''So where is the Dung Dude sending you *now*?''

''Dung Dude?'' Hercules had trouble following Love's mix of English and Mycenaean.

But Iolaus had an ear for languages, having spent his formative years wandering to world's end and back. ''To Africa. To Hera's divine garden. The Garden of the Hesperides, where the Horses of the Sun are stabled.''

''To pluck apples from Hera's golden tree.'' Hercules rolled his eyes as if to say, what-will-they-ask-next.

Love looked dubious.

''The tree of the Golden Apples is Mother Earth's wedding gift to Hera,'' Sauromanta explained. ''It is in her sacred garden, tended by the Hesperides, and guarded by the dragon Ladon.''

Hercules seemed to see her for the first time, ''You are an Amazon?'' She smiled and nodded. ''Wonderful. I very much want a woman to have spirit. And I have small use for law myself.'' Greeks considered Amazons to be outlaws against men and nature.

''I fuck when I please, and fight when I must,'' Hercules explained. ''Though gods and men often take it amiss.''

Sauromanta indicated she had heard as much.

''Furthermore, I have not had a woman since late last night. After we get the Golden Apples, we must certainly fuck.''

She took it as a compliment. Despite a tomboy upbringing—and her panoply of pants and weapons—Sauromanta was all woman, very much enjoying male attention. Especially from a demigod.

''Amazons go wild for me,'' Hercules confided. ''It's my muscles.'' He flexed chemically enhanced biceps. ''When I came to fetch Queen Hippolyte's girdle she was in a fever to get it off. We had great sport, and it was the merest mischance that I killed her afterward.''

He seemed prone to such awkward accidents. But Sauromanta was not worried, or put off, acting like she could handle him. Jake was not so sure.

Hercules glanced up, seeing the gnarled face of Gibraltar sliding by to starboard as they exited from the east side of the bay. ''Why are we headed east?'' he sounded suspicious. ''Africa is south of us.''

Jake pointed out that the boat's shallow keel and big square sail were costing them a lot of leeway.

Hercules snorted. ''If the wind won't serve, get out the sweeps.''

Jake, Love, and Sauromanta hastened to take in sail and lower the mast. Hercules shifted to the center of the boat, unshipping both oars. ''Don't try to match my stroke. You will only unbalance the boat.'' He began to row at a steady relentless beat, devouring the distance between them and Africa.

Rowing reminded him of the long pull up the dark swirling Hellespont in search of the Golden Fleece. ''By the time we reached Propontis the Argonauts were so tired I was rowing on my own, sending shudders through the ship. Until I chanced to break an oar. When I went ashore to cut another, Calais and Zetes treacherously talked Jason into leaving me behind.''

His tale, however, had a happy ending. He caught up with the traitors at Tenos, killing Calais and Zetes, though they were twin sons of the North Wind—and faster than greyhounds. ''I made a fine barrow for them, marked by a pair of pillars that nod when the North Wind blows.''

Half of Hercules' stories ended with him being forced to provide a fine burial mound for some friend, family member, or luckless stranger. Jake feared that the boat might not be big enough for the five of them, and hoped he never had to go up against Hercules. His neural stunner gave him the edge, but only if he struck first.

With Hercules at the sweeps they made excellent time. Once they cleared Ceuta, the southern pillar, the Atlantic west wind died, replaced by light offshore breezes. They raised the mast and coasted comfortably the rest of the way.

Hercules pulled the boat out of the water onto a beach south of Ceuta, some twenty klicks north of Cape Negro. Love leaped out, triumphantly scooping up sand. ''Mother Africa.''

He let the bit of beach slide between his fingers. ''You know, I have *never* been here before. Been to Nam, Laos, the future. Been to fuckin' Mars, an' Bangkok. But never Africa.''

Jake had been to Africa a lot, mostly in the nineteenth century and the Mesozoic. ''So how does she look?''

''Damn beautiful.''

The beach itself was blazing hot, and god-awful empty, but the hills beyond were green. Oleanders along the creek beds gave way to rhododendrons and aromatic shrubs higher up. The Bronze Age climate was clearly warmer, and wetter, at least in North Africa. Overgrazing and timber cutting had not yet spread the desert. The heat, the dense greenery and flowering shrubs reminded Jake of his first trip to Hell Creek in the Latest Late Cretaceous. Which made him miss Peg. At least he did not have to worry about tyrannosaurs at every turn.

Hercules ordered Iolaus to wait by the boat and keep watch over his heavenly hardware. He meant to take only his club, bow, and quiver. Shouting, ''Let's go,'' he set off.

It never occurred to Hercules that any of them might have business of their own in Africa. He had never so much as asked their names.

Sauromanta fell in beside him. Jake looked at Love, saying in English, "What do you think?"

"Cross him, an' he'll turn into Quasimodo with an attitude."

By now Hercules' method was plain. He went right for what he wanted. If he needed anything on the way. Food. Lodging. Directions. Passage to Africa. Or simple companionship. He walked until he found someone, then demanded it.

"Then let's tag along," Jake suggested. And maybe give him the slip later . . .

"Makes no difference." Love gave him a sideways glance. "I'm here to see Africa."

They set out after Hercules, headed north and west, in the general direction of the Jbel Musa, and the listening post. As soon as they left the beach it seemed they were already in a terraced garden. Vine-covered slopes were dotted with lime, olive, and apple trees. Flowers bloomed amid grape arbors and fountains of pure running water.

And there were animals everywhere. Gazelle grazed on stubble fields. Apes scampered through scented fruit trees. Africa was like an endless, exotic, open-air deer park and aviary, stocked with bright birds and chattering monkeys.

Love hummed "Back in the Boonies Again," clearly happy with what he was seeing, hearing, and smelling. Catching up with Hercules, he asked, "Why don't you just tell the Dung Dude to stick it where he came from?"

The demigod frowned, unsure of his meaning, and not having Iolaus to translate.

"Like why are you doing these labors?"

"It is my penance."

"What for?"

Hercules looked askance at Love. "You are an Ethiopian?"

"No way. Born in Detroit. You know, Motown."

"Where is that?"

"Michigan."

Hercules seemed wounded. "I would think they knew of my curse, even there."

"Man, there is *a lot* they don't know in Michigan. Most

folks in Flint could not find Mycenae on the map."

"You jest?"

"Sorry, we got some ignorant crackers back home. Especially in Flint."

"I killed my children," Hercules explained.

Love looked aghast. "God, that's horrible."

"Not all of them," Hercules hastened to add. "That would be impossible. Just six sons I had by a princess of Thebes. And a couple of bystanders. I'm not proud of it. I was mad at the time, and mistook them for enemies."

"Shit, that's sad." Love sounded like he meant it.

"I thought they were attacking me."

"Like a flashback? I seen guys back from Nam do the same thing. Sort of. I mean almost . . ."

"But I'm feeling much better now."

"Should hope so."

The first Africans they came on were children. Beaker-type pastoralists, grazing their goats alongside the gazelle. Dirty tanned cherubs in an earthly Eden. Breaking open his rations, Jake got out fiber bars, sweetened with fruit juice. Love helped hand them out, saying, "Cute kids. But I was kind of hopin' to see brothers."

"Africa is mother to us all," Jake reminded him.

"Right. Only she's more a mother to some. Brothers buildin' pyramids would have been nice."

So far the Bronze Age had been like a scrambled anthropology 3V, with Europe inhabited by bare-chested primitives, and Caucasian goatherds on the African shore.

More children crowded around, immediately recognizing Hercules. He got along famously with them, having barely bothered to grow up himself. His affinity for children was obvious—having chosen a young boy to accompany him on his labors and always being on the look out for nubile virgins.

Nor did the children show any fear of him. Or of Jake and his heavily armed companions. In an age when brigandage and blood feud were polite adult pastimes, these children seemed curiously immune to fear—tending flocks and talking freely to strangers, treating everyone as family.

Perhaps with reason. Primitive communities usually had strong taboos against child abuse. And Artemis, the deadly Maiden Huntress, doubled as a protector of children. Of his many crimes, the only one Hercules was roundly punished for was killing his sons.

A little blond Bo Peep with a suntan, offered Hercules a drink from her dipper. She directed the demigod to a shrine dedicated to the titan Atlas—a local sky god who held the heavens on his shoulders. The great mountains to the south were named for him.

Atlas's shrine was like a hero's tomb, cut straight into the hillside and dressed with stone slabs. Hercules bartered a bronze brooch and pin for a young goat, which he sacrificed. While Hercules communed with his fellow deity, Jake and his fellow mortals cooked the goat, listening to excited herdboys telling Hercules stories.

Children reenacted his killing of Antaeus, a troglodyte king from over the mountains to the south, who lived on the flesh of lions and wrestled strangers to death. So long as Antaeus could touch the Earth his strength was renewed. Each time Hercules threw him down, he bounced back, stronger than ever. But the boys showed how Hercules crushed Antaeus's ribs, then held him overhead until he was dead.

Hercules came bounding out of the tomblike shrine, happily announcing that Atlas himself had promised help. As soon as they had eaten the goat, he set out again, still headed for the Jbel Musa. Goatherds tagged along, laughing and playing their pipes.

The ground tilted upward. Sweltering afternoon turned to hot African twilight. Hercules strode past olive yards and pomegranate trees, happily saying how much he loved these marches to action, being out in the open air, enjoying exotic landscapes and enforced camaraderie from whomever he chanced to drag along. "Almost as fun as the battle at the end."

Night closed in as they approached the Jbel Musa. According to Jake's navmatrix the radar signals came from the seaward side of the rise. Hercules' search for the Garden of the Hesperides was leading them straight to the listening post. That was too pat to be a coincidence.

A cyclopean wall of undressed stone reared out of the darkness ahead of them. Jake's augmented memory contained no archaeological record of such a structure in this part of North Africa. But it could easily have been torn apart for building material at some later date. By the Berbers perhaps. Or the Romans. None of the children knew what lay beyond it. Locals were forbidden even to approach it.

Hercules turned to Jake. "Here is Hera's Garden. The apples grow on a tree in the center of the garden, beside a fountain. They are perfectly round, with a hot gold rind."

Jake nodded. They sounded a lot like oranges. But why was Hercules telling him all this?

"You must fetch the apples," Hercules informed him. "Atlas told me at his shrine not to go beyond the garden wall."

Jake was taken aback, having expected Hercules to go in swinging his club, while they hung back holding his bow and quiver. Was the mighty demigod scared? Or superstitious? Or just smarter than he looked?

He called his team into a quick huddle. Sauromanta looked eager. Love had big sweat patches on his fatigues. "We're going in alone."

"What's the matter?" Love looked over at Hercules. "Ain't Mr. Steroids coming with us?"

"It's against his religion," Jake explained.

Love laughed softly. "Mine too."

"But no one *asked* you."

Love shrugged. "Let's do it. There's no sayin', 'No' to this guy." Hercules might not be a god, but he was certainly a force of nature. Sauromanta was already stringing her bow. All set to go in.

"The listening post is on the far side of the mountain." Jake had his compweb rattle off map coordinates. "We need to get to the tree, bag a few apples, then go over the top and come down on the listening post from behind."

"What about opposition?" Love asked.

Sauromanta piped up, "The serpent Ladon guards the tree."

Love looked oddly at her. Ladon was the dragon they had seen in the stars on the run down to the straits. Clearly Sauromanta could not wait to meet the beast in person.

"A serpent?" Love shook his head and laughed. "No sweat. Let's go."

Having the adhesive boots, Jake went first. Shedding his cape, and pulling on his climbing gloves, he walked right up the wall, crouching at the top of the stonework. Microamps picked up the rustle of leaves, and night birds calling. Internal sensors swept the area inside the wall. No laser alarms. No sign of sentries, or roving stick-tights. Just hot darkness and the heady scent of oranges.

He switched his corneal lenses to infrared. Lanes of fruit trees appeared, converging on a central cool spot. Jake focused his microamps on the cool patch. Water splashed on rocks, indicating a spring or fountain. He pictured the golden apple tree standing beside it.

Jake let down his grapple line. Love swarmed up, followed by Sauromanta with her quiver and pair of bows. They balanced atop the wall while he shifted the line to the far side. Hercules called from the foot of the wall. "The apple tree is in the center, don't dally."

Right. Love went down first, with Sauromanta covering from atop the wall. A jerk on the line signaled for her to join him. She disappeared into the darkness at the base of the wall. Feeling the line go slack, Jake hauled it up. Looping it around his arm, he walked down the wall. They were in.

Crouched at the bottom of the wall, he got a clearer view of the garden. In front of him a lane between the trees ran straight toward the central fountain, a cool pulsing blotch of infrared. Something lay between them and the fountain, muffling the splashing, blocking out the lower couple of meters, keeping him from seeing the pool at its base.

He wet his lips, already dry with anticipation. The offshore breeze had been replaced by a night wind from the south, carrying the taste of the desert. "I'll take point," he announced.

Love nodded. "You got the night eyes, an' Dumbo ears."

"You take drag." Jake reached out and touched Sauromanta's arm, feeling warm, strong flesh beneath her linen shirt. "Keep me covered."

He slid out of the shadow into the lane between the trees. Microamps picked up Sauromanta's soft breathing about a meter behind him, but her boots did not make a sound. Jake focused forward. Still no trace of electronic detectors, just the radar scatter from the far side of the Jbel Musa. The garden nestled against its eastern slope.

The lane of trees ended abruptly halfway between the wall and the fountain. A head-high hedge of dwarf cypress blocked further progress. Jake worked his way around to the right, until he found a gap in the hedge downwind from the fountain. All that showed through the gap was more hedge, too high to see over.

Lying down, Jake stuck his head through the gap, looking left and right. A path ran between the hedges in both directions, turning abruptly in either case, so he could not see more than a few meters. A maze.

He reached back and tapped Sauromanta, who passed the signal to Love. They huddled. "I'm going in," he told them. "Back me with the bow." He nodded to Love. "Stay here and cover our rear."

"Hear ya." Love got out a gas grenade to go with his stunner.

"We'll go in, pick the apples, and get a closer fix on the signal. Then meet you back here."

Love nodded, flicking off the safety on his grenade. "Easy as shakin' drops off your dick. Just keep yer heads low, OK?"

You better believe it. Up to now, things had been frighteningly easy. No sentries. No watchdogs. Absence of opposition gave Jake's paranoia free rein. *Anything* could be waiting under the apple tree.

His navmatrix made short work of the maze. He crawled slowly in, letting his compweb compare the paths to all known Bronze Age maze patterns. None of them were that sophisticated. In minutes he found the right path to the fountain. He signaled to Sauromanta. "Two rights, then a left. The apple tree should be about twelve meters beyond the last gap in the hedge."

She nodded, her bow bent, an arrow nocked. She was helping Hercules with his labors—seconds away from grabbing the golden apples. Sauromanta had been waiting for this all her life. Jake wished he was half as prepared.

They went in. The center of the maze was just as Jake had pictured it. In the middle was the fountain. Beside it towered a broad-leaved tree with golden fruit on its branches. The signal source was on the far side of the Jbel, facing the sea—right in line with a hillside shrine.

But there was something he had not counted on. Beneath the tree was a huge heat source. Body temperature and elephant-sized. Until that moment it had been masked by the coolness of the fountain. Now it started to move, rising off the ground, so that its main mass was a couple of meters in the air. This odd elongated heat profile was instantly familiar.

Jake spun about, telling Sauromanta to run. She looked shocked, but obeyed, headed for the gap in the hedge.

Branches rattled behind them. Jake looked back. Rearing over the fountain was an old familiar face, or rather two of them, etched in infrared. It was *Tyrannosaurus rex*, king of the theropods.

For a frozen second, Jake thought he had to be seeing things. The great carnosaur's outline was unmistakable, with its massive hips, huge chest, tiny forelimbs, and long tail. A giant eating machine, thrust forward in a horizontal stance, powered by tremendous three-toed legs, all balanced by several meters of tail.

But this Bronze Age tyrannosaur had *two* heads. Two pairs of meter-wide jaws. Two batteries of saw-edged teeth. Twice the killing power.

Both heads turned toward Jake, glaring ominously, like a double hallucination. For all the good his stunner or Sauromanta's arrows would do, they might as well throw apples. Even the most overprepared paranoid would not have come here equipped to tackle a tyrannosaur.

And Jake knew from past experience that he had not a hope in hell of outrunning one. The twin-headed brute charged, roaring in stereo.

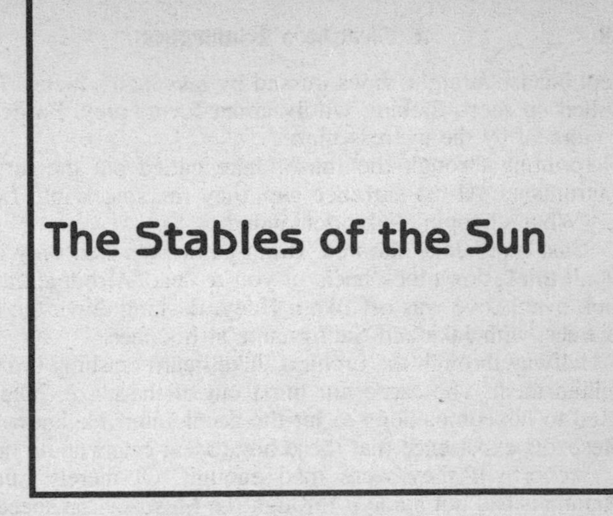

The Stables of the Sun

Horrified, Jake saw his own handiwork turned on him. He was the one who opened the Hell Creek portal to the Mesozoic. He and Peg had brought back the first *T. rex* DNA. Now someone had used it to produce a two-headed tyrannosaur, doubling the beast's terrifying ugliness. Something Jake never dreamed of doing.

But two heads aren't always better. Thanks to gene-splicing, oddball animals were common in Home Period. Jake had *seen* all kinds of two-headed carnivores, including a cobra. One head always dominated. On the cobra the dominant head went for big game, like rats and cats. The lesser head struck at mice, bugs, and whatnot. Once Jake had seen them fighting over a sparrow.

Frantically he quizzed his compweb. Which one?

The compweb did an immediate time-motion analysis—offering a 3-D factoring of the relevant data—RIGHT DOMINANT.

Ignoring the graph, Jake grabbed Sauromanta and dodged left into the maze.

The left head snapped at them, but the tyrannosaur's body

kept headed straight. Jaws missed by less than a meter. *T. rex* pulled up short, looking wildly about for its prey. Baffled for a moment by the cypress maze.

Sprinting through the maze, Jake called out the turns to Sauromanta. At the entrance gap, they ran smack into Love.

"What's happin'?" he demanded.

"Just run," Jake shouted. Blind panic was their only hope. Don't think, don't look back, or you're dead. Airborne training took over. Love was off like a Huey, dashing down the lanes of trees, with Jake and Sauromanta at his heels.

Halfway through the orchard, Jake heard crashing branches behind them. The carnosaur burst out of the maze. Jake hollered to his companions to hit the accelerator. He knew from Mesozoic experience that these huge meat-eaters could outrun a racehorse if they were mad enough. Or merely hungry. Mammals had not made it through the Mesozoic on speed and endurance.

The cyclopean wall came curving up in front of them, cutting off their escape.

Jake hit the wall running. Adrenaline and adhesive boots let him sprint right up it, using muscles he did not know he had. At the top he turned, unreeling his grapple line, throwing the free end to Love.

The airborne trooper leaped like an outfielder going for a fly off the wall, catching hold of the line. Sauromanta was a step behind, feet and hands scraping for holds in the masonry. Love reached back for her with one hand, yelling, "Grab on, Grandma." She seized Love's arm in a circus grip, hand to wrist.

Braced by his adhesive boots, Jake heaved on the line, hauling them both up. As they reached the wall top, he glanced up. And gasped in terror. The tyrannosaur towered over him, trying to figure out which head to bite with.

He froze. His only chance was to let go of the line, and leap down on the far side of the wall. Dropping Love and Sauromanta at the carnosaur's feet. Too bad for them, but still the only sensible alternative. It was let go, or be eaten.

But Jake found he could not get his hands to release, no matter how hard he tried. Friendship would cost him his life.

Suddenly, both heads snapped back. The tyrannosaur swayed dizzily, then stumbled. Holding tight to the line, Jake watched the monster collapse in slow motion. Falling sideways, the carnosaur hit the wall, then slid casually to the ground.

Resting back on his adhesive boots, Jake helped Love get atop the wall. Together they hauled up Sauromanta.

The paratrooper grinned, "Love those sticky boots."

"I promise I'll get you a pair."

A voice called to them from behind and below. "Quit sitting there talking. Go get the apples."

Jake looked over his shoulder. Hercules stood in the darkness at the base of the wall, holding his bow. "What's keeping you?" the demigod demanded.

Jake peered back into the garden. The tyrannosaur lay stretched out along the wall, both heads still, its tail beating feebly in the dirt. As he watched, the tail lashing ceased.

"Get going," Hercules insisted.

Telling his boots to let go, Jake dropped down alongside the dinosaur. The beast was as dead as the Mesozoic. He quickly found the cause of death, two arrow shafts lodged in the beast's twin throats. Some shooting. Over the wall and in the dark. Hercules was as good as he claimed with a bow.

Jake withdrew one of the arrows. It had a hypodermic head.

Love called down from atop the wall, "Is he dead?"

"Seriously so."

Sauromanta dropped down, eyes alight. Hercules, and the Garden of the Hesperides, had lived up to her expectations. "This is Ladon, the child of Typhon, though he only has two heads." She said it as though she thought he should have more.

Actually it was a Late Cretaceous theropod that someone had reworked. But Jake let her live the myth.

Love leaped down to land beside them. "What a sight. How come he keeled over?"

Jake showed him the hypodermic arrow. "Probably some quick-acting organic poison."

Love knelt down, examining the left head. Measuring a huge saw-edged tooth against his hand. "Where could something like this come from?"

"From the future. My future." Jake had seen Home Period's tyrannosaur herd, grown from DNA he and Peg brought back. All were newly hatched, and knee high, running around on a game preserve like a pack of killer turkeys. None had an extra head. This monster had been produced years later, somewhere in his own future, then brought back to the Bronze Age. But by whom?

Hercules called from beyond the wall. "Get the apples."

"Sure thing," Love yelled back in English. He turned to Jake. "Let's get going. Before his immenseness loses his cool. An' before they miss their watchdragon."

Jake saw the sense in that. They might be in and out before the opposition knew what was afoot.

They headed back through the orchard into the maze. When they reached the huge fruit tree by the fountain, each of them plucked an orange. On the far side of the tree was another tomblike shrine, a shaft leading straight into the Jbel Musa—in line with the signals coming from the seaward side.

Jake put his finger to his lips, and they entered. Love lit a small flare, so he and Sauromanta could see. The slab-sided passage led to an oval chamber housing an oracular shrine, with a simple stone altar in the center. Atop the altar lay the remains of a fresh sacrifice—bird feathers and black bloodstains. Behind the altar a triangular opening led deeper into the mountain, connecting with a corbeled passage supported by stone pillars.

Curled at the base of the first pillar was the skeleton of a warrior, wearing a boar's-tooth helmet and lying atop a bronze sword. "Doesn't look like an ordinary burial," Jake decided. "More likely a voluntary sacrifice, guarding whatever lies ahead."

"A volunteer?" Love sounded unbelieving.

"It happens," Jake assured him.

"Damn. Must have been a marine." As he stepped over, Love gave a swift salute.

Jake took the lead, going on ahead of the light. If he ran into anything, he wanted it to be in darkness, where night vision gave him the advantage.

Not even night vision could save him from what happened next. The floor was flagged with large, flat stones. Some long, some short, showing no particular pattern. As he passed the middle of an extralong one, the stone suddenly started to pivot.

His compweb screamed a warning, but it was too late to step back. He plunged into darkness.

His adhesive boots saved him. The stone, balanced on a central pivot, swung completely around, becoming the ceiling of a concealed pit. Jake found himself standing head down in utter darkness, held in place by his boots.

He could hear bits of gravel hitting the floor below. From the time of fall, his compweb concluded the pit was ten meters deep. Far enough to stun or kill him if he had not been wearing sticky boots.

Standing, upside down, wondering what to do next, Jake heard Love calling to him. Cautiously tapping on the stone.

By bending his legs, Jake managed to reach up and grip the rock with his climbing gloves. Fingertip pads adhered to the stone. Using the butt of his neural stunner, he pounded on the ceiling.

An answering rap came from overhead.

He beat out a coded message. "D-E-E-P P-I-T. U-S-E R-O-P-E."

Love acknowledged. "O-K."

As the answering rap faded, Jake heard far-off singing. He cranked up his microamps. The song was high-pitched and eerie. He could not make out any words, but his compweb calculated it was getting closer. Someone meant to inspect the trap.

Jake straightened up—still hanging by his boots. There was no time to wait for Love to move the stone. He had to find a hiding place before whoever was coming arrived.

Gingerly he told his right boot to release, taking a hesitant step. The boots supported him. He strode swiftly along the ceiling until he came to a corbeled rock wall. Grabbing the wall with his climbing gloves, he told the fingertip pads to grip, then transferred his boots one at a time from the ceiling to the wall.

Clinging like a four-legged spider, he looked for a place to hide. The singing got nearer. And the pit below began filling with light. Jake quickly spotted the source of the illumination—a side tunnel three-quarters of the way down the wall to his right, in the same direction as the singing. Whoever was coming to check the trap was bringing a light.

Aside from that tunnel the chamber was almost completely bare, with no other side passages, or convenient outcroppings to hide behind. As swiftly as he could, Jake edged his way over to the section of wall directly above the side passage. Resting his boots on the lintel over the passage opening, he pressed himself flat against the wall. Anyone coming through the opening would have to look directly overhead to see him. Not perfect, but the best he could do on short notice.

The singing drew nearer. So did the light. He could now see that the floor of the pit was covered with rows of bronze spearheads, standing point up, reminding Jake of the myth about Jason sowing the dragon's teeth in a sacred field. Rows of spearmen had sprung from the furrows, the points of their spears emerging first. Were it not for his boots, Jake would have been impaled on the points. Dead or slowly dying.

The singing stopped. A woman's head stuck out from the passage beneath him, looking down at the pit. She had red hair, only it was long and straight, not short and curled like Peg's. She looked from side to side, obviously searching for the body that should be lying speared and bleeding in the pit.

A second woman stuck her head out. She had straight white hair and was holding a torch—not a firebrand, but a sort of glowing wand, bright as a burning flare.

She lifted the light to illuminate the entire chamber. Seeing nothing, the two women looked up to check the ceiling trap. Jake plastered himself back against the wall.

Normally they would have had no trouble seeing him, less than a meter above their heads. But the white-haired woman held the bright flaring light at the level of his toes. The light shone straight in their eyes, making him invisible.

Jake's polarizers cut in, letting him clearly see their puzzled upturned faces. They had clean sculpted features, thin and ageless, way too computer perfect—not very Bronze Age at all. Biosculpt made future faces overly neat and regular. Something you did not see in the past. Aside from children, locals often had lumpy, lined, or pox-scarred features, adorned with crooked teeth. Hercules himself had a very bad overbite. And half a little finger missing.

Seeing nothing, the heads withdrew, along with the light. Singing began again, and the bright light began to disappear back down the passage.

Jake could not let them get away. The light in the passage was fading fast, giving him no time to reconnect with his companions. He meant to follow the women. If he came to a fork or a side tunnel, he would just have to leave some sign for Love and Sauromanta.

Carefully, he lowered himself over the lintel. The passage had a high corbeled ceiling. Clinging to the apex, he crawled along upside down, avoiding any further floor traps, following the singing light.

Every so often the two women would look back, as though they could not believe there had been no one in the trap. Each time, Jake flattened himself against the stones. The white-haired woman's light kept them from seeing him, clinging to the roof of the passage.

Thirty meters into the tunnel, they came upon a third woman, equally slender and ageless, with long dark hair. The first two women sang a greeting. The dark-haired woman sang in response. Then they all looked back together.

Jake wedged himself into the sharp angle of the corbeled vault, wishing they would give up and get going. They could not see him, but if the women waited long enough, Love and Sauromanta were bound to come blundering down the passage.

The black-haired woman had her hands cupped together, as if she were carrying something. Raising her hands to her lips, she sang into her cupped fingers. Suddenly she opened her hand and a slender long-tailed bird flew out.

The bird circled the light, then flitted off down the passage toward Jake. The white-haired woman lifted her light higher, sending its beam deep into the darkness.

Damn! This was it. The bird was being sent back to check the passage.

Sure enough. The little bug-eater flew straight down the tunnel to within a meter of where Jake lay clinging to the roof. Then it darted from side to side, giving off a sharp cry, that went, *cu-cu-cu cucucu*, just like an old-time cuckoo clock.

Instantly the white-haired woman doused her light. Utter blackness filled the tunnel. Above the cuckoo cry, Jake could hear the swift patter of women's feet fading down the passage.

He had been spotted. With no reason to keep clinging to the ceiling, Jake told his boots to release. Dropping to the floor, he dashed after the fleeing footsteps. He meant to give the weird trio no time to escape. Or prepare another trap.

The tunnel sloped downward, letting him pick up speed. His

microamps strained to keep track of the footfalls, using their echoes to test the passage for pits and obstacles.

The floor beneath him flattened out. The women's footfalls were getting closer, and rising higher, which meant the passage tilted up again. The women had crossed the flat stretch, and the slope beyond was slowing them. Jake put on a burst of speed. In seconds he would be up with them.

His compweb shouted another warning. Jake hit the brakes. Too late. Something was falling from above. He threw himself sideways, expecting it would be a stone or deadfall.

Instead a heavy net of bronze links landed on him, pulling him to the floor. He struggled to get up, but the net bore him down. It was big and weighted at the edges.

Footfalls and cuckoo cries disappeared into darkness, replaced by a more ominous rushing headed his way. Water was streaming down the tunnel.

Down on all fours, struggling in the net, he felt the first splash of water on his hands and face. Swiftly the wet surge covered his feet and knees, rising up toward his thighs and elbows. He tried to stand, but the net was way too heavy. And the dip in the tunnel was rapidly filling with water. In seconds it would be over his head.

Thirty-three seconds to be precise. His compweb made swift work of that simple calculus problem, matching the observed rate of inflow against the estimated volume of the passage.

Jake heaved at the net, but the heavy bronze links bore him back down. Twenty-seven seconds. Water was up to his hips and waist.

He heard loud splashes. A light appeared. Then Love was in the water beside him, splashing and cursing, pulling at the net. "Get up. Get up. You dumb Martian cracker. How'n the hell did you do this?"

Jake fought to get up, but the net was heavier than both of them, and Love was standing on one end. Fifteen seconds. The water was up to his chest. Fortunately, the higher it rose, the more sloped passage it had to fill.

Love heaved harder, pulling at the links. Above the rush of water, and Love's curses, he could hear the ring of steel against stone. Sauromanta was back in the passage, swinging her Saca battle-ax, attacking the net where the water was shallow. Bronze links flew each time she brought down the ax.

Crude carbon steel cut through the thin bronze like it was butter.

Holding his breath, Jake ducked down, worming his way toward the hole she had made. When he got to where the passage sloped upward out of the water, she stopped swinging, and reached through the rent, grabbing Jake by the collar, pulling him up. Jake pushed with his feet, while Love pulled back on the net.

His head came out the hole, then his shoulders. Finally he wriggled free, and lay gasping on the sloped stone passage, the still-rising water lapping at his legs. His heart beating fast enough to loosen his teeth.

Love dragged him to where the tunnel leveled out. There they all sat and watched the dip fill with water. As Jake expected, the water did not flow into the main passage, but stopped where the stone began to slope down, forming a pool that blocked off further progress.

Love stood up, happy to call it a night. "Charlie used water traps like this in Nam. Keeps out gas, an' unwelcome callers."

Jake wasn't ready to give up. "I'm going back in."

Love looked askance. "You got water on the brain?"

"Probably. But I've got to see this through." He didn't fancy going back in the water, but his compweb calculated the tunnel was swimmable. He had them on the run, and retreat signified weakness. A go-for-broke assault could sweep them up before they recovered. Time to chuck his paranoia. He had not come this far—across the straits, through a spiked pit and dinosaur-infested garden—just to be turned back by a brush with drowning. They would have to do better than that.

"Can you swim?" he asked Love.

"Not if I don't have to. I'm a sinker not a floater."

"You won't have to swim much." Jake clipped the climbing line to his waist. "I'll go first. You can just swarm along the line after me."

Love snorted. "Don't make me sorry we saved you."

There was no help for it. Love had to be the one to go. Sauromanta was a plains dweller, only recently introduced to large bodies of water. She could stay behind and belay the line. Too bad Hercules' religion kept him from being there—he would have made an excellent anchor.

Drawing his neural stunner, Jake hyperventilated vigorously, emptied his lungs, then dived into the dark pool. Black water engulfed him. He bumped against the sloping tunnel roof and kicked off, forcing himself down. Pressure stabbed at his ears. Again he hit the submerged roof. Again he kicked off. When his compweb told him he had reached the flat bottom of the passage, he struck out for the far side, blood roaring in his temples. By the time he got to where the tunnel tilted upward, his lungs were bursting. Pressure slackened. But what if there was no opening at the far end. What if . . .

He burst into open air, still holding his stunner, ready for whatever. All he saw was more black passageway. He lay on the cold wet stones, heart pounding, blood singing in his ears, feeling the line tug at his waist. Seconds later, Love came sputtering up beside him, flare in hand.

"Need a moment?" Jake asked.

"Hell no," Love shook water out of his eyes. "Go for it. They ain't payin' us by the hour."

They weren't paying them at all. Home Period had a moneyless economy. Jake took the lead. Tired of being the perpetual point man, he wished Love could take the next trap.

The passage ended in a wooden door, slotted to take a brass key. Love pulled the pin on an anesthetic grenade, while Jake used the stiff end of his grapple line to lift the latch. He eased the door open.

The room beyond was empty and in disarray. Cedar chests stood open. Robes and linens lay where they had fallen. An amber necklace lay broken on the tiled floor, surrounded by loose beads. A long scrape on the mosaic tiles showed something heavy had been dragged off. "Looks like they are leavin'," Love suggested.

"Let's catch them before they do."

The drag marks led through a bare hall with a hearth in the center. Predawn light filtered through a pillared entranceway. With the light came a loud familiar whap-whap-whap. Growing in volume, blowing in debris.

Love called out, "Chopper." Dashing across the empty hall, he took cover behind the left entrance pillar. Grenade in one hand, his stunner in the other. Jake followed, flattening himself against the opposite wall. Wind and dirt whipped through the entrance, spreading grit over the flagstone floor.

Jake nodded encouragement. Love stuck his head around

the pillar. "They're lifting off," he shouted. Keeping low, Love slid into the broad doorway. Jake slipped in behind him, happy to be slack man for once. Outside he could see a flat landing pad. A VTOL with counterrotating jet rotors was lifting off from the pad. Love took aim at the cab.

Bam! A sharp crack sounded overhead. Jake's motion detectors shouted a warning.

Leaping up, he dived at Love, hitting the paratrooper from behind, a perfect body check, propelling both of them through the door onto the leveled pad outside. Love pitched into the dirt, with Jake half atop his legs. His stunner shot went wide. "What the fuck . . ." he demanded.

Before Love could finish, a stone portcullis dropped out of the slotted alcove above the door. The multiton slab slammed down where Love had been kneeling. Another second and he would have been mashed to bloody jam beneath it.

Jake swung his stunner around and fired. Too late. The VTOL was airborne, showing only plasti-metal underside, shielding anyone inside. He lay watching as the VTOL headed east, disappearing into the dawn. Soon all he could see was the twin halos cut by the jet-powered rotors.

His compweb confirmed the make and model. It was your standard fiery chariot from the future—a STOP hovercar. The STOP teams sent to find *Atlantis* had been equipped with three of them. The telltale radar signal went with it, merging with the sunrise static.

"Thanks for the shove." Love slapped him on the back. Sitting up, he carefully slid the pin back into the grenade.

Jake turned to look at the slab. Completely filling the doorway, it must have massed ten tons. Scorch marks on the bottom showed that it had been released by explosive charges. Not only had they nearly been crushed, but the temple entrance was now closed for good. To rejoin Sauromanta they would have to hike around the mountain and enter through the garden.

Hyperboria

Sauromanta did not see the least mystery in what had happened. "The Garden of the Hesperides is where the Horses of the Sun are stabled." It made sense for the sun god's chariot to head east at dawn. That was where the sun was. And the three women were the Hesperides themselves, the Nymphs of the West, Hespere, Erytheis, and Aegle—whose names meant Dusk, Scarlet, and Dazzling Light.

Jake filed away this mythical explanation. East was not only the direction of dawn, it was also the way to Greece and Atlantis. Where *Atlantis* had been headed.

Right now, he had to get Hercules and his armor to a rendezvous with the *Argo*. Having missed the hovercar, Hercules' high-tech weapons were the only physical proof that things were not as they should be in the Bronze Age. And Jake already foresaw a skeptical reception back aboard ship.

Hercules insisted they stop off at Gades. There the local kinglet wined and dined them like visiting gods, slaughtering several of his red shambling cattle. He hosted them in a timber-pillared hall, with a thatched roof, an open hearth, and a footing of rough stones supporting the wall posts. The sort of hall Hrothgar used to entertain Grendel.

The kinglet—named Belcharon—was big and balding, with broad shoulders, crooked teeth, and upcountry manners. His jeweled girdle and gold arm rings held enough bullion to open a bank—but that was just for show. His chief joys were wine, women, and watching his hounds fuck.

Gades was the exact spot where Hercules killed King Geryon of Tartessus, as well as his three sons, his herdsman, and his wondrous watchdog—at the same time abolishing Geryon's hated cattle tax. Immediately making Hercules a local folk hero. Until his visit Gades had been under the thumb of Tartessus, the great tin emporium on the Guadalquivir.

He had left with enough loot and hangers-on to establish a Mycenaean colony at the mouth of the Tartessus, modestly naming it for himself. And with the death of Geryon and his sons, Tartessus had reverted to female rule. Geryon's daughter, Queen Erytheia, had to contend with the new colony of Herculeia; inhabited by the usual mix of exiles, escaped slaves, and light-fingered adventurers who followed Hercules about. She had neither the time nor inclination to bully Gades.

Fresh-faced young women served them dark fruity wine in big beaker cups, half-fermented grape juice that stained anything it touched. Jake could see how every day was a holiday for Hercules, every meal a feast. The harper sang of his deeds, embroidering old lies, and inventing new ones—tacking on verses about the Golden Apples, and the killing of "Ladon." Who now had three heads. Jake, Love, and Sauromanta did not make the musical version.

Sauromanta came to the feast-cum-concert in her favorite pair of fancy pants, silk pajama trousers showing an over-endowed Hercules mating with the Snake-tailed Mother. Hercules spotted the pants, and immediately offered to prove that the exaggerated manhood depicted was more than artist's imagination.

And when the torches were lit and the drinking got serious, Hercules disappeared with her, headed for a private orgy in the temple Gades had built to honor him.

Just as well, thought Jake. What healthy young Amazon wouldn't pick a demigod over a hopelessly human, badly harassed, and sometimes married time traveler? At least a contraceptive injection kept her from getting pregnant on the job.

King Belcharon seized Jake's arm, nearly upsetting the

wine, saying in slurred Mycenaean, "Look, he's about to stick the bitch!"

Jake was taken aback, until he realized the drunk kinglet did not mean Sauromanta and Hercules. Two of the king's prize hounds were furiously making puppies under the table. Belcharon was in heaven, able to drink *and* watch his dogs fuck.

His own mate was Aphrodisias, a dark-eyed Spanish beauty as slim as her lord was squat, with long black lashes and aristocratic features. The Lady of Gades reached over to steady Jake's cup. *She* had seen the look on Jake's face when Sauromanta left with Hercules.

Her lord dressed like Conan gone to drink, but Aphrodisias wore a long embroidered robe, a single elegant sweep of fabric falling from neck to ankle. And Jake knew what lay underneath. The last time he had seen his hostess was during his "look in" at Gades. She had been kneeling stark naked in an intoxicated trance, wearing nothing but a writhing python. He felt like Peeping Tom, confronted by a real-life Lady Godiva, married to a drunk barbarian, but still Sacred Queen to her people.

Married might be too strong a term. She eyed Jake over his wine cup as freely as he had looked at her from the minisub. Consoling him in a throaty whisper, "The best goes to the gods. But mortals may still please each other." If Jake were willing.

Both Belcharon and Geryon were descended from northern Beaker-folk—bronze-working chariot warriors and herdsmen, who had come out of the Spanish Mesta several generations back. (Being cousins had not made Geryon's cattle tax any more popular.) They had intermarried with the original coastal inhabitants—Mother-worshiping, matrilinear, megalithic tomb builders. Royal monogamy was a novel innovation among folks used to seeing shepherd-kings and priestess-queens picking bedmates as the need arose. Neither partner seemed intent on taking this new notion to extremes.

Seeing Jake's downcast look, Belcharon waved his cup to indicate several women seated around them. "Help yourself; no hero should go to bed unhappy."

Jake thanked him for the sentiment, but declined, saying he would just as soon sleep alone.

Startled, Belcharon quickly corrected himself. "Of course, you're a Hellene. You'll be wanting a boy instead. Take a pair of stable lads and make a night of it. Enjoy yourself." The alcoholic kinglet just wanted everyone to be happy.

Jake tactfully explained that he had a wife somewhere far away, and would just as soon sleep alone.

Belcharon declared that a far-off wife was a poor excuse for not having fun. Aphrodisias also seemed disappointed. Presently she disappeared with a stalwart young warrior from her honor guard. Her husband happily went back to watching the canine orgy under the table. Jake reached for the house red, wanting very badly to be drunk. At least for tonight.

Runners were sent to Gibraltar to fetch Hercules' horses and chariot. While they waited, Jake toured the sights, seeing Geryon's tomb, the mainland settlements, and of course the new-built temple for Hercules, with its miraculous spring that flowed at ebb tide, and ebbed at flood tide. Over a thousand years hence Julius Caesar would visit this same temple and stand before a statue of Alexander the Great. Realizing that he had done nothing memorable at an age when Alexander had already conquered half the known world, Caesar immediately returned to Rome to enter politics.

Jake felt strange, standing there a thousand years ahead of both would-be world conquerors, wearing Caesar's cloak and a sword given to him by Alexander.

And like Caesar, Jake ached to be doing things. But all he seemed to be doing in Gades was steering clear of Sauromanta, who was having a wild, glorious time with Hercules. Which was fine, so long as Jake did not have to watch.

"Grandma's got a boyfriend," Love noted. "Is that hurtin'?"

Jake shrugged. "I'll live." Or so he hoped.

"It's all in your head," Love reminded him. "This place ain't exactly sufferin' a pussy shortage." Jake shook him off. He did not want *sex*. He wanted Sauromanta. Sort of. If it weren't for . . .

Hercules' horses came, making it time to depart. Sauromanta led the besotted demigod down to the beach, while Iolaus loaded the chariot and horses onto the boat. The horses were gifts from Poseidon and not in the least spooked by water.

Jake sailed the somewhat overloaded boat out to a rendezvous with the *Thetis*. Which dragged them over the horizon to meet the *Argo*.

Hercules was not awed or frightened by either the *Thetis* or the *Argo*. Or if he was, he hid it well. All he said on seeing the *Argo* was, "Is Hera here?"

"Why should she be?" Jake asked.

"Because her ship looks like that."

Atlantis and *Argo* were near identical sisters. So it sounded like Hercules had seen *Atlantis*—in the hands of a goddess no less. Hera Queen of Heaven, his foster mother. But the sighting could not be absolutely certain. All airships might well look alike to an illiterate demigod.

Jake signaled the airship to lower a sling. Airships had to be stripped down to fit through a hyperlight portal. Neither *Argo* nor *Atlantis* had a beam-me-up capacity. Seconds later he was swinging in the bright sunlight, being hauled up onto the *Argo*'s hangar deck. A sub, a boat, Hercules, Iolaus, Love, and Sauromanta waited below, along with a two-horse chariot.

McKay the bosun swung him aboard. "Welcome back. Been souvenir hunting?" He had seen the chariot.

Chief Larsen was there, along with Doc Hathaway and two of the women from Special Temporal Ops, Emiko, the team commtech, and Morning Star, the Apache-Pawnee scout. All craning their necks to get a look at the boat below.

Swaying on his feet from the lift up, Jake was happy to be wearing adhesive boots. He told McKay, "Bring 'em up." Adding, "Leave the boat, but be careful with the horses."

Chief Larsen wanted to know what the hell horses were doing hundreds of klicks out in the Atlantic.

"A gift from Poseidon."

McKay shook his head dolefully. "Been hittin' the local hootch pretty heavy?"

"An occupational hazard," Jake admitted. "Just humor the big guy, or he'll tear the place apart."

"What big guy?" Larsen squinted out the sunny hatch, trying to see through the glare off the sea.

"His name is Hercules."

"Right." McKay rolled his eyes.

Jake told his boots to release, heading for the forebridge to see Wasserman. McKay and Larsen were really crack riggers.

They could deal with it. You had to be at the top of your field just to set foot aboard the *Argo*. Their complaints were the usual joking competition between support crews and field agents. Coming in always required a kidding. Showing up with a mythical demigod and a two-horse chariot begged for outright abuse.

Lights went on ahead of him. Doors dilated. He told the cargo lift to take him to the midline slidewalk—happy to be back in the normal world. Where objects obeyed him. Where the ship did the work. And computers did the thinking. Moving passageways swept him up, depositing him on the forebridge.

Wasserman's greeting was brisk as a sea breeze. Cool and aloof, he looked more like a clipper master than an aviator—reminding Jake of a beached U-boat skipper who served aboard the *Graf Zeppelin* on the Rio run. He was a hands-on commander, haunting the forebridge when the ship could be run as easily from his cabin.

With him were three women. Keane, his first officer. DePala, the young helmsmate on duty. And Dianna, the STOP commander. Maybe it came from having Hercules on the hangar deck, but he could not help seeing Nymph, Maiden, and Death Goddess.

The moment seemed overly dramatic. Normally the whole *Argo* would have experienced everything that had happened to the contact team. Communications silence was not standard procedure. Far from it. Talk and telemetry usually put the contact team on an electronic tether. Support personnel sat around rerunning the action in 3V, flashing inane suggestions out into the field.

Instead Jake had to condense nine days of misadventure, sight-seeing, and debauchery, into a semicoherent story before an increasingly incredulous audience. He hit only the highlights. Landfall. The electronic scatter. Leaving the sub. The run down to the straits. (No mention of stargazing with Sauromanta.) Algeciras Bay. The sacrifice on the beach. Hercules. And his heavenly armor. Crossing over to Africa. The Garden of the Hesperides and its two-headed tyrannosaur. The "Hesperides" themselves and the listening post. (No mention of nearly being spiked and drowned.) And the escape of the STOP hovercar.

That was the first forty-eight hours. The remaining week—two days spent beating out of the straits, plus four days partying at Gades, then the rendezvous—were all summed up in a sentence or two.

By that time Wasserman wore the same look Chief Larsen had given him when Jake ordered the chariot horses brought aboard. Keane, his number one, tried to stifle her grin. DePala, the helmsmate, busted up at her post. Only Dianna, the STOP commander, seemed indifferent. Even bored.

"You're bringing a *local* aboard?" Wasserman looked panicked for once, reminding him of the need for utter secrecy, implying Jake had put *his* ship at risk.

"I've promised him passage to the Eastern Mediterranean." Actually Hercules had demanded passage. Jake had just steered him toward the airship. "His armor needs to be looked at. We did not get much from the listening post. What we saw there was locally produced—or plundered from our STOP teams. His armor wasn't sent by us." Or made in the Bronze Age either.

"But why bring him?" Wasserman acted like separating Hercules from his weapons was the simplest task imaginable.

Keane offered a compromise. "Perhaps we could keep him under sedation?" She was younger than Wasserman, but with a worldly-wise air. Jake often wished their roles were reversed, with her in command, and Wasserman as her second.

Jake shrugged. "Knock him out if you want. Just so long as I'm not there when he wakes up."

Dianna scoffed. "You can't possibly be afraid of him." The STOP commander was a young blond Amazon, every bit as brave as Sauromanta—but more forbidding. Sauromanta could be soft when she wanted, but Dianna had cold, classic biosculpt features. A face that could be beautiful on a woman, but equally handsome on a man.

Jake eyed her evenly. "He's sufficiently scary. If you plan to do him dirt, you'd better be sure he's dead."

In a matter of hours Jake had seen Hercules row from Europe to Africa, search out the semimythical Garden of the Hesperides, and kill a two-headed tyrannosaur inside the walled garden. Leaving him in condition to come after you was divinely assisted suicide. Calais and Zetes, late sons of the North Wind, could not outrun his vengeance.

Wasserman snorted. Keane looked semiappalled.

Jake, Wasserman, and Dianna shared a nebulous equality of command. Home Period did not produce hard and fast lines of authority. Everyone aboard the *Argo* was a volunteer. Leaders all had overlapping spheres of authority. Wasserman ran the ship. Dianna had her STOP team. Jake's sphere was field operations. By hoisting Hercules aboard, Jake had breached Wasserman's sphere, bringing a loud, obnoxious, and deadly part of the outside onboard the *Argo*.

But in a very real sense this was Jake's mission. More than Wasserman's, or Dianna's, or anyone else's. And so far he'd succeeded. He had gotten them to the Bronze Age intact. And he had turned up a STOP hovercar from one of the lost expeditions. And Hercules' armor might tell them more about who they were up against.

In theory Wasserman and Dianna could outvote him. Even have Hercules heaved overboard. But there was a strange coldness between them, as if *Argo*'s captain and STOP commander were somehow jealous of each other. They seldom deigned to cooperate. Which made Jake more than ever the leader—the one holding the mission together.

He proceeded to present his plan for penetrating the Mediterranean unobserved. "We have to give up on the straits. Too narrow. Even if they don't replace that listening post they are bound to be looking that way. We can't just bull our way in without tipping our hand."

Dianna eyed him evenly. "Don't you think we are overrating the opposition?"

"Perhaps." Jake still planned to give free rein to his paranoia. "But there is no reason to throw away strategic surprise."

Wasserman grunted agreement. Dianna might be eager to come to grips, but he worried about his ship. "So how do you propose to get in? The Hellespont?" That was the back door to the Mediterranean. *Argo* could release *Thetis* into the Black Sea, then the sub could go through the Bosphorus and Hellespont into the Mediterranean.

"Still too easy to spot a sub." The Bosphorus and Hellespont were even narrower than Gibraltar. "But we can go in by way of the Nile."

"Aha." Wasserman's eyes lit up. "The seasonal floods."

Jake nodded. "Water is rising right now above the first cataract. In a month or two the river will be in full flood, spreading out over the valley. By the time the flood reaches the sea it will be hundreds of klicks across, filling a maze of channels." *Thetis* could hide in the turbulent river, letting the current carry it right out into the Mediterranean.

Wasserman liked it. Dianna didn't. "It means hanging around Ireland for a month and a half, waiting on a river."

"We'll need that time to set up the base camp. And I want to slip into Britain and reconnoiter." Jake did not mean to sit around. All evidence pointed toward the Eastern Mediterranean and the Atlantean sphere. That was where *Atlantis* had been headed. And where Hera supposedly held sway. Plus the fleeing hovercar had headed east. But Britain was tied to the Middle Sea by the tin trade. "Sometimes it's easier—and safer—to get information at a distance."

Dianna snorted. "Hauling some hugely muscled demigod along?"

"If he'll come." Jake did not *need* Hercules, but it hardly seemed smart to leave him behind.

"I still consider him a serious breach of security." For once Wasserman agreed with her.

Jake was tempted to tell them how much more manageable Herc had become since Sauromanta started sleeping with him. That would hardly appease Dianna. Special Temporal Operations always felt field agents were too intent on teaching the locals fancy ways to fornicate.

But Wasserman just wanted Hercules out of his sight. One 3V look had been enough. "Give him minimum contact with the crew. And keep him away from anything half-sensitive."

Jake promised to do his best. All this talk of Hercules was making him nervous, anxious to dash back to the hangar deck, to see what damage the demigod had done. At any moment Hercules could come bursting onto the bridge, demanding a turn at the helm.

Thanking Wasserman for the prompt pickup, he ducked out, headed for the midline slidewalk.

When he got to the hangar, he found Hercules safely enjoying the morning. His chariot was aboard. And McKay had fixed up a makeshift stable for Poseidon's horses, between the *Thetis* and the STOP team's hovercar. Love had seen Hercules' heavenly armor hustled off to the STOP lab for "safe-keeping."

All that remained in the water was the wooden boat. Jake bade it good-bye. The boat no longer fit his plans. It had been a gift of the sea. Now it was back in the Ocean Steam a couple of hundred klicks from where they had found it.

He took Hercules on a tour of the ship, carefully avoiding the forebridge and STOP quarters. Zeus's son was impressed by the great gas cells, moving walkways, and the cloud-flecked view from the upper deck. Jake asked Hercules how this ship compared to his foster mother's, hoping to get a positive ID.

"Hera never lets me come aboard her ship," Hercules admitted, actually sounding beholden to Jake.

Too bad. Hercules could not confirm that Hera's ship was the *Atlantis*, something Jake very much needed to know.

The tour ended up in the crew's quarters along the keel, where Sauromanta deftly installed the demigod in her cabin. Jake fetched food and wine. By the time the door cycled shut, Hercules was pawing at the Amazon's embroidered trousers. What was inside them ought to keep him entertained until they got to the Irish base camp Wasserman had selected.

Jake stood grimacing on the slidewalk, wishing he were the one with his hand in Sauromanta's pants. While she laughingly helped him open the merlot. What had Aphrodisias said at the drunken party in Gades?—"The best goes to the gods."

He retreated to his cabin, finding it depressingly spare. His living space could be programmed for a dozen configurations, and he chose the simplest, a futon, and a low cupboard doubling as a table. The cupboard was bare, and the futon showed no sign of having been slept in.

Jake had avoided 3V completely. Some crew members had their "cabins" in the high Himalalyas, or in the Bahamas. Wasserman's was on the ocean floor.

Lying back on the neatly made bed, he tried to forget about Sauromanta, dwelling instead on the excellent chances of finishing up this mission dead, maimed, or insane. The *Argo* was supposed to be his island in the sky. Safe and secure. A bit of Home Period brought to the Bronze Age, stocked with autodocs, gourmet rations, enhanced sensors, and enough neural-chemical firepower to anesthetize Pharaoh's armies. But being back aboard made him uneasy—with no solid idea why.

Which scared him, right down to the soles of his sticky boots. Scared him more than two-headed tyrannosaurs, mysterious singing nymphs, or murderous demigods with hypodermic arrows. Putting his paranoia in overdrive.

He had been way happier in the field, facing the paranormal with a team he could trust. Which brought up Sauromanta. Bringing his problems full circle.

A voice asked through the door, "Are you decent?"

"Sad but true."

The cabin was sealed, but Keane thumbed the lock and entered. All doors opened for the first officer. Sitting down on the cupboard-cum-table, Keane told him, "Dianna has gone over that high-tech armor, and concluded it was manufactured aboard the *Atlantis*."

One more sign the *Atlantis* was in enemy hands. Jake stared at the ceiling. "So what does that say to you?"

"That we're in deep, deep trouble." A flat chilling statement coming from Keane, who never made snap judgments.

"How so?" He lay on the futon, waiting to hear her reasons. Jake trusted Keane. More than Dianna. More than Wasserman. He had in fact handpicked her. Wasserman had more or less come with the ship. STOP had insisted on sending Dianna. Jake had picked Keane to balance them out, but she was merely Wasserman's second. Not for the first time, Jake wished Keane commanded the *Argo*.

Keane spread her hands palms up. "We've ruled out the simple stuff. It's not a portal slip, or a case of mass time shock, or some natural accident, like landing in the middle of the Atlantis eruption. Our own equipment is being systematically turned against us. Otherwise, we don't know anything more than those three STOP teams did."

And look what happened to them.

"It's unnerving," Jake admitted. "But we are not dead yet."

Keane gave a gallows laugh. "Dianna sure does not think so." Dianna did not seem worried in the least. *She* wanted to head straight for Atlantis. To get to immediate grips with whoever, or whatever, was waiting there.

As STOP team leader, it was Dianna's duty to defend the ship and back up the contact team. Brushing aside local opposition. Which made him very much wish he trusted her more. She had Sauromanta's violent energy, but it was channeled and controlled, not just thrown back at life. Jake could never see her having a fling with Hercules.

"What do you think of her?" he asked.

Keane considered. "As a STOP commander, or as a person?"

"Both."

"She's young, and inhumanly efficient. Shot up through the ranks at STOP. Another ambitious, brilliant overachiever, with a certifiable death wish."

"Right. Otherwise why would she be *here*?"

"As to her personal life." Keane shrugged. "You know her as well as I do." There was unspoken subtext to that answer. Keane was same-sex oriented. Dianna's sexuality was a mystery. She clearly had small use for men. The whole STOP team was a woman's team with a female team leader and assistant leader. The only men were Dowar, the team heavy-weapons tech, and Doc Hathaway, the medic. This was intentional, done to balance an expedition that was otherwise testosterone heavy, with Jake heading the contact team and Wasserman commanding the *Argo*.

Jake wanted to hear that Keane had gotten a glimpse of Dianna's human side. That they might have made love was too much to hope for. Keane's current lover was DePala, the young helmsmate on the forebridge who had laughed at Jake's labors with Hercules. But Keane might have known more than he did about Dianna's private life. Might have, but did not.

"There is something asexual about her passion," Keane decided. "I've seen it before at STOP. Warrior to the core."

(Love liked to put his doubts about Dianna in simpler terms—"The bitch's got a smile that will chill yer ass.")

Keane grinned. "She absolutely hates what's happening between your Amazon and the Hunk from Hellas. Hates it and wants it stopped."

"Good luck." Jake laughed. He doubted that Dianna and her whole team could pull Hercules off of Sauromanta.

"She's taking it worse than you are."

Jake groaned. Great. An hour aboard ship, and his problems were already in plain sight. That was why he preferred the field. Picking certified geniuses for an expedition meant you ended up with a ship full of know-it-alls.

Keane got up to go. "Guess we just keep doing our jobs."

"And watching our backs," Jake added.

He did not feel better until they sighted Land's End on infrared sensors. Wasserman timed his approach to pass over the Irish Sea at night. There was an active tin and amber trade between Cornwall and Tartessus; if a ship spotted them, word could reach the Mediterranean before they did. Hibernia Base itself was deep in the Emerald Isle—in what would become Tipperary. Any word filtering out would be so much Irish malarkey.

Dawn revealed green woodland stretching over the hills and far away. A cleared space surrounded a settlement of roundhouses ringed by an earthen bank. Irish poured out to greet them. They had their hair tied in elaborate knots, and wore ornaments of beaten gold—great crescent collars called *lunulae*, as well as gold torques, hairpins, and arm rings. Their bodies were painted with circles, chevrons, spirals, and triangles. Ship's computers had built up a dictionary of the local dialect, but Jake needed no translation to know that the Irish were singing, Hallelujah!

Doc Hathaway blamed himself for the reception. "On our first visit I went around curing whatever ailed them. Giving them immunities to all the common infectious diseases. Now they think we are gods."

Jake nodded. It was hardly possible to be anything *but* gods in the Bronze Age. Flying about, granting wishes, and curing diseases automatically made you divine. However much you might protest.

Hathaway, a staunch Baptist-Rationalist, was embarrassed to have his patients worshiping him. Other team members weren't so picky. Bronze Age Ireland was a green Eden. Religious warfare and foreign domination lay in the far future. Setting up base camp called for blasting a clearing in the endless forest, and felling trees to build *Argo* a titanic wooden hangar. Making them look even more wondrous in Irish eyes. Off-watch personnel were welcomed into people's homes and hearts. Lovers and bedmates were theirs for the asking. Who wouldn't want a god in the family? Or a god's child?

Jake had seen it all before. But it was heady stuff for STOP team members, and an airship crew, who had never stayed long among locals. Even Dianna went seminative, hunting the great-antlered Irish elk with a spear and bow. Only Wasserman seemed totally immune, hardly ever leaving the ship.

Hercules was in his element. Coupling with the local colleens, eager to go with Jake to Salisbury Plain—"to see Apollo's great temple." This was Hyperborea, the Land Behind the North Wind. Adventuring here could only add luster to his already inflated reputation. Besides, Herc plainly suffered from wanderlust, and loved showing up the High King by *adding* to his labors. Being able to say, "Here are your Golden Apples. I toured Hyperborea and World's End on the way home. Anything new in Mycenae?"

A week after landfall, Jake, Love, Sauromanta, Iolaus and Hercules set off for the coast. Two of the women came with them, a rigger's mate named Tyler, and Emiko, the STOP team commtech.

It was near to High Summer. Happy to entertain important strangers, locals feasted them through Tipperary and Kilkenny, butchering their small hairy cattle and brewing big vats of Irish beer. Offering up platters of parboiled beef. Or roasted elk ribs in heavy gravy swimming with fat.

Emiko, a petite Buddhist, had to subsist on rice and ship's rations, plus any roots or berries that came with the meat. Fortunately it did not take much to sustain her. And she acknowledged her host's hospitality by playing tunes on her communicator. Sometimes she backed up the local harper, matching harmonies, complementing melodies, filling in gaps with counterpoints and jazz variations. Other times she played alone, quick jaunty tunes that set everyone dancing, or throbbing wordless pictures of air, of light, and of the sea.

By now Jake's compweb had a grip on the local preliterate, pre-Celtic language. But there was hardly need to talk. It was summer. They were guests. This was food. Music said the rest. Communities handed them from one to the next, sending someone along to see they were well received.

When they reached the coast at Wexford, Jake saw faience beads and Baltic amber, evidence of a trading net stretching from Sweden to the Nile. Here Hercules bullied a tin trader into giving them passage across the Irish Sea, promising to put in a word to Poseidon as payment. Fortunately the fellow was on his way to Cornwall in ballast. One look at Hercules and the tin trader decided he would be doing himself a lucky turn by dropping them in Wales.

A storm caught them halfway across. (So much for Herc's pull with Poseidon.) And they arrived at St. David's Head drenched and seasick. Hercules was heartless, saying they must set out immediately for Salisbury Plain. He alone did not seem to mind being pounded about in a small boat.

They marched through Dyfed until they came to the River Cleddau. There a big flat-bottomed barge decked with summer flowers was drawn up near the river mouth, waiting on the tide. Jake asked where they were headed. The captain's name was Biton, and he solemnly explained that his was a holy barge, bringing a huge stone to Apollo's sanctuary. "The god has ordered his sanctuary rededicated. This is the last stone."

Hercules brushed aside the captain's objections, saying, "This is Apollo's work. He meant this barge to be here." Captain Biton looked dubious—but he had come to collect Apollo's holy stone, not to risk bloodshed with pushy strangers.

"Tell him I am the god's half brother," Hercules insisted. "Show him my bow." The god-bow cinched it. It was fiberglass and steel, with Apollo's gold sun disk on the laser sight. No Bronze Age mortal could have made it.

They trooped aboard. The stone lay in the bottom of the barge, lashed to a sledge, a big igneous slab of blue dolerite, spotted with feldspar, from the sacred quarries of Prescelly. Jake's compweb estimated it massed a couple of tons.

The tide lifted them off the river sands, and the crew poled out of the estuary, then set sail, rounding St. Govan's Head, making for Carmarthen Bay. It took three days to skirt the coast of Dyfed and Glamoragan, then work their way up the Bristol Channel and across the Severn estuary to Avonmouth. They poled up the Frome, past the sacred springs at Bath. There locals hauled the barge overland, nine and a half klicks to the River Wylye. Then the barge took them down the Wylye and up the Avon, past Old Sarum—a beautiful haunted landscape, cut by tall banks and wooded along the rivers. Through gaps in the trees Jake could see grassy uplands dotted with ring forts and burial mounds.

They docked on the east bank of the Avon, where the river makes a big curve around Amesbury Down. Here, too, people were waiting, set to haul the stone the final three kilometers to the sanctuary.

Hercules made an immediate commotion, insisting that he be alone in the traces. He was the god's half brother and offered to brain anyone who objected.

The crowd was completely taken aback. They had come down to the Avon expecting to find a stone. Instead they faced a lionskinned stranger four cubits tall, wielding otherworldly weapons and claiming to be a brother to the sun. Lifting the sledge onto greased and polished rollers, they let him pull.

God or not, Hercules had the eye for a grand entrance, slowly emerging from the line of trees along the Avon. Breaking out onto the grassy bottom beneath the sanctuary. Bent by the weight of the stone, muscles bulging, he wore nothing but his lionskin, using his chiton to pad the traces. Ahead, beyond the black-topped burial mounds, the sanctuary appeared on its rise, a circle of colossal gray sarsen stones, topped with massive lintels.

A great flock of Britons followed behind him, for none would walk in front of the stone. Sauromanta strode beside him, her light bow strung, holding her moon-shaped shield. Iolaus carried his club, bow, and quiver. Emiko rode atop the sledge, playing her communicator. Jake, Love, and Tyler brought up the rear, keeping between them and the Britons, ready with their stunners to smother any sign of trouble.

As Hercules crossed Stonehenge Bottom, ascending the Avenue, Emiko struck up *Also Sprach Zarathustra*, softly at first, then louder, and louder, until it echoed off the stones. Masses of Britons drawn up at the sanctuary stood in stunned silence. Hearing the otherworldly music. Seeing a single man striding up from the Avon hauling the stone alone.

Then they started to cheer. Shouting blessings and throwing flowers. Becoming so drunk with religion that Jake and his team had to help with the rollers to get the stone into the sanctuary. As they passed the Heel Stone, word went round that this was a godson, half brother to Apollo—sent by the god to put the last stone in place. People dropped to their knees, thanking the sun that was by now low in the west, setting beyond the Long Barrows.

Jake had feared Hercules' muscles would tear or his bones might crack, but he set down the traces, acting only moderately tired. More than ever, his strength seemed chemically assisted.

Bonfires burned and drums beat. Naked painted bodies leaped before the flames in time to Emiko's music. Great tubs of beer were set out. And there was wine to be had as well. The mild Bronze Age climate encouraged vineyards even in Britain's misty isles. Another mad summer night was in the making, with these Britons bent on putting the wild Irish to shame. Turning partying into a religion.

Jake wandered among the stones—something that became hard to do in later times—seeing Stonehenge in pristine condition, with the last of the Welsh bluestones fresh from the quarry. Greeks believed the stones were Medusa's victims. The Gorgons, whose glance could turn men into rock, were supposed to live in Hyperboria, surrounded by weathered standing stones.

Jake's favorites were the sarsens that made up the mighty trilithons, ten times as massive as the bluestone they had brought, yet ground to a gentle eye-pleasing taper. Mortised, tongued, and grooved to fit together, using only the simplest of tools—stone, sand and water, bronze, blood and sweat. All aligned to astronomical observations so precise that they would only work at this particular north latitude. Which was why the huge stones had to be hauled out onto this soft chalky plain in the first place.

People once supposed Stonehenge had to be built by the Phoenicians. Or Egyptians. Or that engineers from Mycenae or Atlantis must have shown them how to set the stones. But the first sarsens were older than Phoenicia. Older than the pyramids. And the only help they got from Mycenae was having the High King's cousin haul the final stone the last three klicks from the river.

Jake ran into Captain Biton. The barge master was hoisting a wine jug in honor of his last journey up the Cleddau to the sacred quarry. "I will never again haul such a holy cargo. The sanctuary will be complete."

"Who could think of adding to it?" Jake could not imagine what the place needed.

"Only the god." Biton drank to the luck of the sun. By now the god had set, leaving a golden smear above the trees.

"Let's hope he is happy."

The barge pilot handed him the jug. "He seemed pleased when he came at midsummer, seeing his plans taking shape."

Jake stood with the jug halfway to his lips. The sun god here? Really? Did he come in human form?

Oh, yes, Biton assured him. The god had been there in the flesh. As real as Hercules. He used a local name, but he clearly meant Apollo-Helios, the sun incarnate. The god had arrived on the solstice and stayed for a fortnight, overseeing the work, while lying with the local virgins.

"He left only a week ago. And now he sends us his brother." To Biton, Stonehenge was the mystic center of Hyperboria, accustomed to heavenly comings and goings.

Jake took a swig from the jug, saying he was sorry to have missed seeing the god-on-earth.

"You can still see the signs of his visit." The tipsy barge pilot tried not to sound condescending; he could not help living at the center of the cosmos.

Biton led Jake away from the stones, out onto the grassy bottom. The sounds of celebration fell to a low drumbeat surging round the bonfires on the plain. He pointed into the fading light, "There are the marks left by his chariot."

By bright northern-summer twilight Jake did not need night vision to make out a dish-shaped depression in the grassy bottom—clear and sharp as a crop circle—ringed by a wider area where the grass was wilted and blown flat. He immediately recognized the marks. A STOP hovercar had landed here, sat on its hull long enough to crush the grass, then taken off.

Out of Africa

Two of the three lost hovercars were accounted for. ''Apollo'' had been visiting his sanctuary on the same day that Jake discovered the backscatter beyond Gades, well over a thousand klicks to the south. STOP hovercars were miraculous, but they usually were not in two places at once. Jake could imagine him coming over the horizon on Midsummer's Day, backed by a dawn light show.

But it looked as if they had caught whoever was playing Apollo off guard. The pseudo–sun god would hardly have hung about Salisbury—sighting stones and instructing virgins—if he knew someone from the future had raided his African stables. Now was the time to slip into the Eastern Mediterranean via the Nile, and hopefully locate *Atlantis*.

Leaving Hibernia Base, Jake had Wasserman swing in a wide arc over the Atlantic, headed for Africa. When they drew level with Gibraltar, he took *Thetis* for a quick look in. There was no backscatter. No sign that the listening post had been reestablished. Or they might have just turned off their radar.

Jake had *Argo* swing even farther south, crossing the African coast at night—a thin sliver curve of surf separating dark land from black sea. Dawn found them headed east over the shifting dunes of the Grand Erg Occidental. Ahead lay the flat white expanse of the El Djouf, the great salt desert.

Sauromanta joined Jake on the forebridge, eager for her first look at the Sahara. It felt odd to stand beside her, pointing out sights, answering questions. Just like old times. Hercules had not changed her attitude in the least. She was friendly as ever, smiling whenever she saw him, happy when he had time to talk. Jake was the one who felt awkward.

And he had to admit she had done a splendid job of keeping Hercules in check—leading him around by his cock. He had not made trouble. Or molested the other women. Aside from sleeping with Tyler during the mass orgy at Stonehenge. Neither woman seemed to mind sharing him. Hercules was certainly happy.

Jake was odd man out. He kept reminding himself that was okay. He had things to do. A goddamn a mission to run. But it was hard when Sauromanta was right beside him, as excited by the desert as she had been by the sea.

They stayed clear of the caravan routes, going through the Adar and Air, passing south of the Tibesti Massif. The Bronze Age Sahara was not nearly as desiccated as in later days, showing wide patches of veldt. Jake saw families of elephants and a lone giraffe. They passed the sea of dunes bordering the Nile, crossing three-quarters of a continent without being seen by anyone. Desert turned to grassland. Herds of gazelle bolted beneath them, fleeing from the airship's giant shadow.

"Look, lions!" Sauromanta spotted them, not needing augmented vision to pick out the great cats. A pride on the move. Too bad this was Wasserman's ship, and the mission was so demanding. Back in the Mesozoic Jake and Peg had spent days shadowing big carnivores, moving when they moved, going aloft to make love when they rested.

"When are we coming down?" Sauromanta wanted to mix with the scenery.

"Soon," Jake promised. Though not before dark.

Ahead lay the Dongola Reach, the great sweep of river between the third and fourth cataracts of the Nile, hundreds of klicks of river and savanna forming the heart of Egyptian Nubia. Love came forward for a look. Spread out before them were the black and brown kingdoms and queendoms of eastern

Africa, filling the Great Rift Valley, wedged between desert and the sea.

Love rattled off the names for Sauromanta. "To the south, over the mountains is Punt. Then comes Ethiopia, Kush, Nubia, and Egypt. Too bad we don't have time to do this right."

"Like working our way down the Nile, visiting them all?" Jake suggested.

Love nodded, his gaze never leaving the horizon. That was what a mission was supposed to be, a look-see into the past. The entire Bronze Age was mostly unexplored territory. Every klick they flew over was history unrolling below them. Instead of learning from it, they were slipping unseen into the Mediterranean. Playing tag with unknown forces.

A dark green line appeared at the far edge of the gold-green savanna. "That's it." Love leaned forward. "The line of the Nile." Keane had seen it, too, turning the airship to parallel the river—staying high and up sun, where they could not be seen from below. "Damn." Love licked his lips. "Wish we could get closer."

"We're gonna be in it," Jake reminded him. He meant to be in the river before morning.

Keane put up a magnified view on the 3V. A long, narrow oasis appeared, stretched along the silvery river, dotted with palm groves and flooded fields. The river had risen, filling the low spots, narrowing at the gorges. On the far bank Jake spotted Kawa, and the caravan route to Napata. A hundred klicks farther north they drew even with the third cataract and the island fortress of Tombos, built by Thutmose I, who went into "valleys my ancestors had not known, which the wearers of the vulture and the serpent diadem had never seen"—extending Egyptian control past the fourth cataract and the great Bend in the Nile.

It was dark by the time they reached the "Belly of Stones," the long stretch of islands and white water forming the second cataract. The *Argo* crossed over to the east bank and plowed on through the night. Finally they passed the first cataract, leaving Nubia and entering Egypt. From here on the flooded river was fully navigable, giving the minisub ample room to maneuver. Love happily ran an equipment check. "Land of the pharaohs at last."

The moon was down. Under pitch-black cloud cover they

descended on a deserted stretch of river north of Elephantine, feeling their way down to the water's surface, using night glasses, infrared, and ranging lasers. Wasserman had not so much as warmed up the navigation radar since arriving in the Bronze Age. Hyenas chuckled in the darkness. Jake waited at the hangar deck hatch as *Thetis* was swung out and lowered into the dark river. STOP team members crouched around him with black lights and shock rifles. On croc watch.

Jake went first. ''Watch out,'' Love warned. ''Or next time we see you, you'll be comin' out a croc's ass.''

A drenching rain came down as Jake descended the nylon ladder, knowing that at any moment a croc could come blasting out of the black river at 50 kph. Jaws agape.

Ever since the Nile first carved her path to the sea, Nile crocodiles have been waiting for anything, or anyone, unwary enough to enter the water. Or just saunter along the bank. The biggest Nile crocs were seven meters long and a couple of meters thick, the nearest thing to dinosaurs in human times—until Jake and Peg started bringing back tyrannosaurs. They dined on humans as a matter of course, taking them down in seconds. Gone for good. It happened every year, especially in flood season when the Nile overran its banks. This time of year the lower river was one long meat aisle stocked with warm tasty humans.

His boots touched the black slippery deck. He told them to grip, holding the ladder for Love. As the airborne trooper descended, Jake stepped back. Sauromanta was next.

Without warning, the sub flipped suddenly sideways. The deck rolled over, plunging Jake into rain-pocked water.

His first thought was ''Croc!'' He tried frantically to swim, expecting cold scaly jaws to close on him.

But his legs would not kick. He thrashed with his arms, unable to move a millimeter. The reptile must already have him by the feet. He flailed about, immobilized, his head underwater. Lungs aching for air. Crocs liked to drown their victims, then eat them at their leisure.

His compweb yelled at him, ''BOOTS—RELEASE!''

Of course. His adhesive boots were stuck to the capsized hull. No wonder his legs would not work. He told his boots to release, trying once more to kick.

This time he swam. But did not get far. Something huge,

soft, and immensely powerful struck Jake from below, lifting him clear out of the water. He sailed through the rainy air, catching a fleeting glimpse of the *Argo*'s dark bulk overhead. Then he landed with a splash. Nile water closed over him again.

Jake fought his way back to the surface, sputtering for breath, getting a mouthful of rain. He barely had time to take a gasp before something big and menacing bore down on him, throwing up a tremendous bow wave.

Croc? No, hippo! A huge male massing a couple of tons came ripping toward him, mouth agape, bellowing horribly to show off murderous knifelike canines. Each self-sharpening ivory tusk was razor-sharp and thick as his wrist. Somehow the hippo had mistaken the minisub for a rival. (Maybe they had come down in the middle of its harem.) Having disposed of *Thetis*, he was after Jake.

Hippos are not the hapless clowns shown in kids' cartoons. What looks like blubber is solid muscle. Nothing takes on an adult male hippo—not lions, not Nile crocs—nothing but another hippo. Their mating battles are splashing bloodfests, often ending with a maimed or dead Don Juan.

His compweb estimated closing speed at 50 kph, warning that his stunner would be useless. Adding the somewhat irrelevant observation that hippos killed more people than rhinos or rogue elephants. It advised—"PLAY DEAD." Not easy to do while failing in the rainswept Nile sputtering for breath.

With the enraged hippo almost on top of him, he heard the zap-crack of a shock-rifle and smelled ionized air. The hippo kept coming.

Another zap-crack, and the beast struck him, colliding softly. Already asleep.

He could hear Love calling to him from atop the minisub, which had managed to right itself. Swimming around the sinking hippo, Jake called back. Love answered, sounding relieved, "If yer done playin' with the hippo, we need a hand unloading."

Emiko was at the hangar deck hatch, a shock-rifle cradled in her arms. Being a Buddhist and vegetarian did not stop her from being a dead shot.

Suffering from a badly dented demeanor, Jake crawled out of the river to lend a hand unloading.

By dawn they were done. The rain stopped. *Argo* headed back over the desert toward Hibernia base. The sub lay concealed on the river bottom, awaiting orders. Still drenched, Jake got a fire going. Love paced about, ready to be off.

The hippo had drowned, bloated, and risen to the surface. Crocs were feeding on him, making hideous slurping sounds as they ripped off hunks of flesh, bolting them down whole. Others gathered, attracted by the spectacle, sunning themselves on the banks and sandbars, yawning while tickbirds picked their teeth. Jake felt bad for the hippo, and Emiko had to feel worse. But it was the beast's own fault for taking his love life so seriously. A mistake Jake strove to avoid.

Hercules was out hunting with Sauromanta while Iolaus saw to his chariot and horses. The plan was for them all to go into Elephantine together. Jake wanted to talk with the locals, getting a feel for what they might face downriver. Love wanted to *see* Egypt, and not just through a 3V periscope.

Neat, simple, hopefully easy. But Jake had on his crash helmet, and a plasti-armor vest beneath his tunic, for safety's sake. Just getting the sub into the river had been more of an adventure than he needed.

Iolaus announced that the horses were hitched and ready. They all boarded the chariot and set out after Hercules. It was cramped. The light chariot, built to carry a boy and a demigod, was loaded down with Jake, Love, Iolaus, and Hercules' heavenly armor. But Poseidon's horses were strong, and the track along the bank was firm. Neither Jake nor Love wanted to miss a chance to ride in a real war chariot.

The sky cleared and the day heated up. With the river rising over its banks it was hard to tell the water from the haze. Hills hovered in the near distance ringed by silvery moats that might be real, or mirage.

Rounding an elephant-sized termite mound, they came on Sauromanta, standing in its shade, holding Hercules' bow as well as her own. With her was a group of bushmen—naked golden brown nomads with peppercorn hair. Everyone was excited. The bushmen had semierections, but that was more or less normal. They talked rapidly at each other in a language of clicks, snaps, pops, and lip smacks. Jake hiked up the gain on his lenses.

Hercules was half a klick away, roaring through the canebrake, chasing something. He cut right. A huge boar broke cover, heading squealing off downriver. With Hercules hot on his heels.

In an amazing bit of broken-field running the demigod caught up with the boar, cutting him off, driving him into the nearby mud flats. Mud slowed the big pig. In a moment Hercules was on him, seizing the boar by the tusks and tossing him. Stunning the beast with his fist, Hercules tied its legs together with the rope he used for a belt.

"Sign that cracker up." Love laughed. "The NFL *needs* him."

Hercules came trotting back, the boar slung over his shoulder, basking in the click-cheers of the bushmen. He tossed the bellowing pig onto the tail of the chariot, and they headed south toward the Elephantine ferry.

Elephantine lay at the end of a long island just north of the first cataract. A tall stela on the east bank marked the ferry slip. Graffiti proclaimed the glory of the ram-headed god Khnum. The caravan route south around the cataract was protected by a massive mud-brick wall to the east, and a string of island forts along the river. But most of these defenses had fallen into decay since Thutmose I conquered all of Nubia, down to the borders of Kush. In fact Elephantine had gotten so civilized that the ferry captain absolutely refused to take Hercules' hog-tied boar aboard.

As Hercules tried to shoulder his way up the gangplank, Egyptians leaped fully clothed into the Nile, frantic to avoid contact with the pig. Frowning, Zeus's son called for his club.

Sauromanta saved the ferryman's life by suggesting they sacrifice the pig to Artemis, Maiden Goddess of the Hunt.

Setting up a slab-stone altar, they said their prayers, and slaughtered the big squealing pig. Hercules ate the liver raw, then flayed the carcass, cutting the flesh into long strips, which he salted and laid out to dry, saying he would finish curing it when he got back from Elephantine. It was safe to leave the meat lying by the dock; no Egyptian would so much as touch it.

He promised the head and tusks to Sauromanta, saying he would make her a helmet out of them. "I am handy with hides," he boasted, showing off his lionskin cloak. "This is from the Nemean Lion, whose skin was proof against bronze or stone. Which forced me to strangle him, though it cost me a finger.'' He held up his left hand, showing the little finger bitten off at the first joint.

''Since the skin is proof against bronze, I used the beast's own claws to cut and dress it. I've often thought I would make a marvelous seamstress.'' Sauromanta seemed to bring out his feminine side.

Leaving Iolaus at the ferry dock with the chariot and horses, they boarded the ferry for Elephantine in the best of moods. Love put a Hendrix tape in his pocket recorder, saying he was happy to be seeing Egypt at last.

''Try not to be shocked,'' Jake advised.

Love laughed. ''After two tours in Nam. A visit to the future. An' a year in Flint, Michigan. I ain't easy ta shock.''

Sauromanta smiled. She had never been to Flint, Nam, or Elephantine, but she knew Egyptians.

Elephantine had long been the last outpost of Egyptian civilization, the jumping-off point to the unknown. Gateway to the Heart of Darkness. But since Thutmose I pushed Egyptian rule past the fourth cataract, Elephantine had become just another sleepy provincial town on the Upper Nile, living off traffic shuttling around the first cataract.

Currently Elephantine suffered from a plague of frogs, brought on by the high Nile. Thousands of little baby frogs that hopped about, perpetually underfoot. The market street droned with heat and flies, backed by the low jangle of an electric guitar coming from Love's pocket recorder. Jackal-nosed dogs lapped at muddy puddles, snapping up tiny amphibians.

Women jammed the market stalls. Jake saw tall black Kushites, short brown Hottentots, and lanky Hamites offering little dark pygmies for sale. The main shade missing was white. Hercules and Sauromanta stood out with their pale skins, her blond hair, and his light amber eyes. And a month in Britain had cost Jake his Martian tan. Only Love blended in.

Fat black market women, sitting on three-legged stools, hawked wares from the south, ivory, ostrich fans, leopard-skins, and giraffe tails. They called out to Johnny Love. He looked questioningly at Jake.

''They are inviting you into the shade for a beer and a fuck.''

"No shit?" LOVE CHILD gave his crash helmet a sorry shake. "Tell them I appreciate the thought, but it is damn early for anything but a beer."

A thin little fellow in a breechcloth scurried out of a palm-frond stall, setting out pots of pale brew. To be sociable Love turned down the Hendrix tape and took a seat at the women's table. A matron half his height and twice his weight leaned over. She felt the material of his flak jacket, then fingered the gold stud in his ear, murmuring drunken endearments in Egyptian.

"What's she saying?" Love whispered.

"She thinks you are cute, with your stork's legs and strange soft armor."

"Well, thank her. An' tell her she's built like a major appliance herself."

Jake switched to Egyptian, and the woman laughed merrily, slapping the plank table, making the frogs jump. Jake translated. "I told her you said she had the hips of a pregnant hippo."

Love looked unbelieving. "An' she *liked* that?"

"Sure. Thunder thighs are sexy here. She can wrap her calves around a man, squeeze him dry, and squirt out babies. Egyptians are big on babies. Just ask her husband at home, or her lovers in the garrison."

Fermented mash floated atop the warm beer. Love's would-be paramour showed him how to suck down a whole beer pot through a hollow reed. "She says she can do the same for you," Jake told him.

"God damn. She's a double helping, that's for sure. Tell her a gentleman don't mess with married women that outweigh him."

"They don't care. This is village Egypt. Women run the markets, while men stay home and weave. Greeks call Egypt 'the land where men pee sitting down, and women pee standing up.' "

"Don't have 'er demonstrate." Love cocked his head. "What about the skinny dude servin' beer?"

"He's gay. Homosexuals help with the marketing, and are highly prized as sons."

"Go on," Love scoffed.

"Sure. A mother with a gay son has a gold mine. He'll do

a girl's work, and never leave her for another woman.''

''God, what a zoo!'' Love laughed nervously. ''Folks in Flint will *never* believe this. Why are they set on having me?''

Jake nodded toward Hercules. ''They figure we're Greeks. No Egyptian would kiss a Greek, much less fuck one. Greeks eat cows and pigs, and don't bathe enough. Egyptians wash several times a day, circumcise their men, and only eat bull-meat. They won't even use a Greek's knife or drinking crock—unless they know it's clean. Egyptians are big on clean—even invented the condom. These women won't touch us. But you could have the lot of them.''

''An' the skinny guy, too.''

''It's up to you.''

Love shook his head. ''At least they're clean.''

They *were* freshly washed—glossy black skin stretched over bulging flesh smelled of nothing but beer. Jake was fresh from his midnight dip in the Nile, but Hercules was not nearly so well scrubbed. And the scents Sauromanta rubbed on her body were no substitute for a bath or two. The women totally ignored the Amazon. A thin, unwashed blonde in drag could hardly be called competition.

All at once the Egyptians looked up. Jake looked, too. Men had come into the market. More men than Jake had cared to see. The squad of Nubians on duty in the market were being reinforced by a band of veteran *menfyt* ''strong arm'' infantry.

Love saw them, too. ''Looks like a full company.''

''The ensign's standard says it's the 'Bull in Nubia' of the Corps of Amun.'' A company of line infantry was all Elephantine needed in the way of troops. Someone had turned out the garrison. Jake hoped it wasn't for them.

The soldiers marched straight over to where they were sitting. They were big men, mixed Nubian and Egyptian, armed with spears, axes, and cowhide shields. Their ensign had a zebra-striped shield, and a sickle-shaped bronze ''khopesh'' sword, instead of an ax. The rear ranks had bows.

''What the fuck do they want?'' Love had his stunner out, nervously fishing for a gas grenade, trying to look innocent about it.

''Nothing good.'' Jake assured him. He glanced over to see how Hercules took it.

The big fool had been into the beer, and was absolutely

beaming. Fortunately he was unarmed, aside from his club. His sword and bows were aboard the chariot down by the ferry dock. Seeing Jake's concerned look, Hercules' drunken grin widened. "My escort has arrived."

"Your escort?"

"Pharaoh has heard that I am in Egypt, and sent an escort."

Pharaoh resided in Thebes, three hundred klicks downriver. It was impossible for him to have heard anything. Jake tried to explain that Pharaoh was not like King Belcharon of Gades, or Hercules' cousin at Mycenae—living almost on their own borders, surrounded by the only real town in the kingdom. Pharaoh's writ ran from Kush to the Euphrates, or so the Thutmosids claimed.

Nonsense, Hercules retorted. He had arrived at the border of Egypt, and here was his escort. Pharaoh had heard Hercules was here, and meant to pay homage.

"Which of you killed the pig?" demanded the ensign. He was clearly trying to decide between Jake and Hercules. "White skin and male," must be all he had to work with.

"What's he want?" Love demanded.

"He wants to known who killed the pig."

Love swore softly. "An he's havin' trouble tellin' his honkies apart."

Seeing the ensign's confusion, Hercules hit his chest. "Me, me! I am Hercules. The one you've come for!"

Jake let Hercules have the credit. If it had been left to him, the boar would still be grunting in the canebrake, instead of salted and drying by the Elephantine ferry.

"You killed it?" The Egyptian's eyes narrowed.

"Yes, me." Hercules hit his chest. He knew no Egyptian, but he was sure the man meant him.

"And hung its remains by the Stela of Khnum?"

"It's me. How many times must I tell you?"

Jake shot a tense look at Love. "He's broken some local taboo." Khnum was Elephantine's ram-headed god. Egyptians were serious about what they offered up. Cows were neither eaten nor sacrificed. The ban on pork was lifted only at midwinter. Even a bull or ram had to be passed on by a priest, who wrapped a paper seal around its horns. Offering the gods an inferior cut of beef was an impaling offense.

The ensign gave a sideways nod. "You must come with us."

Jake translated, trying to make everything sound friendly. "They beg you to go with them."

"Of course." Hercules stood up.

Love stayed seated, saying in English, "Let him go."

"I can't," Jake replied. He nodded at Sauromanta. She, too, was on her feet, not sure what was happening, but unwilling to abandon Hercules.

"Shit."

"Come, Pharaoh awaits!" Hercules insisted.

Jake knew they weren't headed to see Pharaoh, but still hoped to avoid a fight. He got up, taking a British gold button out of his tunic and tossing it onto the table to pay for the beer. The women praised him to Khnum, saying this generous Greek and his cute friend could drink with them anytime. If they survived their problems with the law.

Love smiled to the ladies and stood up, grenade and stunner ready. The troops closed in around them like a living box, then they tramped off through the plague of frogs.

Jake expected to be taken to see the governor-general of Elephantine, but instead they were marched down to the docks. Large empty ships lay at anchor. Elephantine was a major turnaround point, as far up Nile as seagoing ships could go. He recognized several oceangoing cargo ships—the type that Queen Hatshepsut would sent to Punt—and a fancy traveling ship with red sails that would have suited the viceroy of Nubia.

They were hustled aboard the traveling ship, much to Hercules' delight. "Pharaoh has sent a better ship than the High King ever sailed in."

He was less pleased by the delay in getting off. First Iolaus had to be fetched from the ferry dock, along with the chariot and horses. As the team was loaded aboard a cargo ship, Jake could hear intense negotiations at dockside between the ensign and the ship masters. Pharaoh had, of course, "sent" nothing. The traveling boat was at the governor's disposal, but the cargo ships were ordinary merchant ships, awaiting cargoes from upriver. The ensign had to offer a bounty to get him and his men to Thebes, the royal capital. A place Jake would not have minded visiting—under far different conditions.

Love liked the look of things even less than he did. ''Where are we headed?''

''Thebes.''

''Well ain't that grand.'' It probably would be, but not the way Love meant. ''Look, I got a sick sense about this.''

''So do I,'' Jake admitted.

Love nodded at Hercules, happily surveying the traveling boat. ''Biceps brain does not know the danger he's in. He's had pussy more times than we've pissed. It messes with your mind.''

''Probably,'' Jake agreed. ''But I can't just abandon him.''

''Why not?'' Love demanded.

''Because *she* won't.'' He meant Sauromanta.

''And you are still half-stuck on her. Promise me, if we get out of this, you'll get professional help.''

''Believe me. I think we can handle this.''

Love laughed. ''Oh, I believe you. You just ain't always right.''

The Egyptians came to an agreement, then shoved off. The trip was tense and expectant. Hercules kept going on about the great reception Pharaoh had planned. As proof, he pointed out the splendid fittings aboard the traveling ship, which had a two-story deckhouse with dining couches and sleeping lofts.

Nursing a bad case of nerves, Jake considered punching a distress call through to the *Argo*. STOP trained constantly for just this sort of emergency. Dianna's team could come get them with a minimum of fuss. A dose of anesthetic gas and the troops aboard would not know what had happened.

But communications silence stayed his hand. He had told Wasserman he would send a coded signal once he had found *Atlantis*. A call now could reveal their presence, making the mission a thousand times more dangerous. And worst of all, Hercules was the cause. Him and his pig sacrifice. If he called for STOP, Dianna and Wasserman's worst judgments would be confirmed. Somehow he had to handle this on his own.

The trip downriver took two tense days. Nile crocodiles nosed in their wake. They spent the final night anchored near enough to see the lights of Thebes burning on the east bank.

Dawn came. A shaven priest moved among the crew of the traveling boat, reaching into the dark river, sprinkling each man with sacred Nile water, intoning a morning prayer to mother Isis. The helmsman on the high stern lifted his kilt, peeing contentedly into the golden brown water. It was that kind of morning—bright and lazy, sparkling with promise.

On the east bank the entire Corps of Amun lined the temple docks, ready to receive them. Not a full-sized corps, just four thousand infantry and five hundred chariots, about the equivalent of an infantry brigade with light tanks attached—but damned impressive nonetheless. Chariot horses stamped and snorted. Dawnlight flashed on massed spearpoints. Jake could pick out the officers by their ostrich plumes and leopardskin shields. Hercules was happy to see such a worthy escort.

They went ashore, led by the ensign from the ''Bull in Nubia.'' Hercules strode briskly, with Iolaus bringing his club, bow, and quiver. The rest followed more cautiously, stunners ready. Sauromanta's rapid-fire bow was nocked.

The Corps of Amun opened ranks to let them mount the steps of a great riverside temple. Jake recognized the temple of Amun at Karnak, though it did not yet have Grand Pylon Gate and the Hypostyle Hall that the Ramsesids would add. But it was still an impressive pile, greater than any cathedral, a walled complex of gates, shrines, grand halls, and colonnades, surrounding an inner sanctuary the size of a sports arena.

All dedicated to Amun, the Invisible Creator. A god so great that thousands of years later people would still pay unconscious homage to the ''Hidden One'' heading the Egyptian pantheon. Every Christian prayer ends with a corrupted version of his name, ''Amen.''

They went through a series of massive pylon gates, then through the vast Hall of Records, built by Thutmose II, to keep track of state archives and temple booty. Finally, they entered the Sanctuary, a huge inner shrine dominated by a great raised altar.

Here Jake got a real surprise. Pharaoh was there. No mistaking it. He wore the double crown, signifying his rule over Upper and Lower Egypt. Jake recognized Thutmose II, a frail version of his warrior father. Doomed to die young and suddenly, presumably from disease. Beside him at the altar was a great pregnant goose of a priest, wearing the tall crown of the High Priest of Amun—the most powerful cleric in Egypt. This seemed to be a great commotion over a single pig.

Hercules marched up to the altar. Attendants anointed him with oil, then bound his head in a fillet—the type used to mark a bull for sacrifice. Too late, Jake saw just what honor they had in mind for Hercules. The big dumb demigod hopped up onto the altar, letting them bind his hands with scarlet cord.

Jake had nothing saved up his sleeve for this moment. Hercules seemed mesmerized by the ceremony. Dianna's STOP team was far beyond call. Two fresh companies from the Corps of Amun had followed them into the sanctuary. The portly High Priest led his minions in prayer, then called for the sacred ax. Attendants handed it to him. He raised the great double-headed blade over Hercules' neck.

Queen of the Nile

By the life of Pharaoh, you shall not leave this place unless your youngest brother comes . . .

—Genesis 42:15

The bright bronze double-ax descended. Jake had his stunner out, his compweb locking on target.

Hercules beat them both. With a shrug he burst his bonds, sitting bolt upright—spoiling Jake's shot at the High Priest. He caught the ax haft in his hand, the blade bare centimeters from his throat.

Nanoseconds tumbled in Jake's compweb. No one breathed. No one moved. Everyone stared at Hercules and the High Priest. Both were now gripping the ax. A packed shrine stood paralyzed by surprise and indecision. Pharaoh. Priests and prophets of Amun. Ladies of note. Lords and flunkies too numerous to mention. Court musicians. Two companies of the Corps of Amun. Love. Sauromanta. Iolaus. And Jake, unsure now whom to shoot.

But not Hercules. Wrenching the ax from the High Priest's grip, he leaped to his feet atop the altar. He split the High Priest's skull with the ax. At the same time, with his left hand, he seized Pharaoh by the throat.

Leaping down from the altar, he began swinging the ax. Gleefully hacking his way through the lesser priests and attendants, using Thutmose II as a shield. Acolytes lifted their skirts and ran screaming toward the door of the shrine. Frustrated archers, afraid to fire at Pharaoh, turned their bows on Hercules' companions.

Down on one knee, Love returned fire, aiming at the first rank of the "Lion of Amun." A line of *menfyt* collapsed on the stone flags, sleeping peacefully through the pandemonium.

Forced back by the press of bodies, Jake tried to cover Sauromanta, seizing a dropped shield as arrows winged toward them. Love had his flak jacket, crash helmet, and wool cloak, but Sauromanta wore no armor. Jake held up the shield to cover her. Flint-tipped missiles thudded into the cowhide. Sauromanta had her heavy bow out, returning their fire, sending steel-tipped arrows ripping through hide, linen, and flesh.

An officer sprang at her from behind, wielding his sickle-shaped sword. Jake let his compweb lock on target and fire. Augmented anatomy allowed him to shoot one-handed from the hip with absolute accuracy. The officer went down, dropping his *khopesh* blade at Sauromanta's feet. Seeing the man fall, she flashed a smile at Jake, then went on shooting.

Having routed the unarmed priests of Amun, Hercules plowed into the packed ranks of archers, still holding Pharaoh before him. They could not fire without puncturing Thutmose. Panic spread. Bowmen ceased firing and joined the rout.

Hardly an Egyptian remained standing in the shrine. Hercules hurried the last of them out the door into the pillared Audience Chamber beyond. The main doorways of the temple were all in a line, forming a single straight passage, from the Inner Sanctuary, through the Audience Chamber and the Hall of Records, out into the sunshine. The final doorway framed dun-colored Theban hills, and the blue sky beyond.

Brushing past Jake, Hercules burst through the Sanctuary door, dropping Pharaoh, determined to chase every living Egyptian out of the temple, and then take on the entire Corps of Amun.

Taking careful aim from behind his shield, Jake shot Zeus's son in the back. Hercules toppled forward. Flint-tipped arrows and bronze spears had bounced off his lionskin cloak, but a jolt from Jake's stunner brought the demigod down.

Seizing the dropped bronze sword, and the officer's leopardskin shield, Sauromanta ran to cover her fallen hero, standing over Hercules like a lioness protecting her cub.

Firing past her, Jake and Love cleared the Audience Chamber, driving the Egyptians back into the Hall of Records. Jake pointed to the far door, yelling to Love, "Secure that entrance."

Tossing a gas grenade through the entrance, Love positioned himself beside the doorway, firing at anyone left standing.

Jake glanced about. All the rooms were windowless. He ordered his compweb to recall all observed entrances and exits. The Outer Hall had several entrances aside from the main one. The grand pylon leading into the Hall of Records was flanked by smaller portals, used to shuttle people in and out during processions. But the Audience Chamber had only the main entrance. Other doors led into robing chambers and the like. A quick look showed they were empty, with no Egyptians cowering in the corners.

That left the Sanctuary itself. His compweb recalled one small door behind the altar, that probably led to the temple treasury. With any luck they had only a single entrance to watch—the one Love was covering.

Jake had to check the Sanctuary and that door behind the altar, but first there was Hercules to deal with. Sauromanta still stood over him. Iolaus was on one knee, trying to wake him, but having little luck. Jake bent down and told his medikit to administer an antidote.

Hercules snapped awake, ax in hand, leaping up so fast Jake had to jump out of the way.

"Where are they?" He brandished the bloody ax, looking for heads to bash.

"Routed," Jake replied, trying to emphasize that the fight was over. And for the moment they had won.

Hercules smiled, cleaning his ax blade on the skirt of a dead Egyptian. "I abhor human sacrifice. And gave them every chance to desist on their own." Hercules, who obeyed no laws and swore no oaths, did not mind mending other people's manners. It was one of his minor pastimes.

Jake asked him to relieve Love at the doorway to the Hall of Records. Since that was the post of most danger, Hercules happily obliged, hefting his high-tech bow and calling for arrows. Iolaus went with him, to hold his ax while he skewered overrash Egyptians.

Sauromanta stood leaning on her new leopardskin shield. The *khopesh* sword that had nearly killed her dangled loosely in her hand. She must have guessed what he had done to Hercules, but all she said was, "You saved my life."

"Really? How many times until I've paid you back?"

She laughed. Slipping her left arm out of her shield, she leaned over, put her hand behind his head, and kissed him. Not a sisterly kiss either, a long tongue-twisting one that Hercules must have taught her. "Thanks," she told him. "I've missed our times together."

"Me too." Seeing her there, breathing softly, skin slick with sweat, as alive as ever—thanks to him—Jake dearly missed the Sauromanta he used to talk and flirt with. Who was not the god's chosen one.

Love came walking up, shaking his head. "There's some lot of angry Egyptians outside."

"I'll bet." Jake did not have to stick his head into the Hall of Records to know there must be archers at the far door. Hundreds of soldiers were probably packed into the Outer Hall.

Instead he went the other way, from the Audience Chamber into the Sanctuary. The scene in the inner shrine beggared description. Bodies lay scattered over flagstones slick with blood. Most of them—including the whole front rank of the "Lion of Amun"—were merely stunned, but others had their heads bashed in, or steel arrows through their throats.

Love surveyed the litter of slumped bodies, smashed urns, and broken flutes. "Beats Beirut on a bad day."

They went first to Pharaoh, lying where Hercules had dropped him. Getting out his medikit, Jake hoped Thutmose II could be revived quickly enough to help talk them out of this. Pharaoh was lying faceup, without a mark on him. His own people had held their fire, and Hercules had not struck him. But that did not stop him from being stone dead. Even futuristic medicine was not bringing him back.

"Is it him? Is that Pharaoh?" Love demanded.

Jake nodded. Never an imposing figure, Thutmose II looked especially nondescript lying dead, without his wig or double crown. Just a frail, bald little dark-skinned man, with the life choked out of him.

''Damn. I *very much* wanted this dude to be alive.''

''Hercules must have strangled him, while using him for a shield.''

''Right.'' Love had been doing a slow burn ever since they boarded the boat at Elephantine, now he boiled over. ''Herc the Mad Honky had to kill the one dude that might have gotten us out of here. This is *not* how I meant to spend my time in Egypt. I could still be sippin' beer through a straw with those ladies in the marketplace.'' He lifted an eyebrow, giving Jake a knowing nod. ''Who is lookin' *way* better by now.''

Jake admitted as much.

''Instead, this ax-murdering psycho has got us playin' Butch and Sundance with the whole damn Egyptian army.''

''Half the Egyptian army,'' Jake corrected him. The Corps of P'Re was posted a thousand klicks downriver at Heliopolis.

''Well the other half is gonna be hot-footing it this way when they find out what we done to Pharaoh.''

Not at all unlikely. Jake could not deny that their chances of getting out of this had just taken a serious nosedive. He, too, had wanted Pharaoh to be alive. He had hoped to strike some sort of deal with Thutmose. Instead they were trapped in a windowless stone temple, with only one exit, surrounded by irate Egyptians. But it was hardly his fault. If Pharaoh had not been in such a lather to sacrifice Hercules, none of this would have happened.

He told Love, ''Let's go see where the door behind the altar leads.'' To get there they had to pass the High Priest, who was in even worse shape than his master. But Jake had not expected to find him breathing.

The door behind the altar did lead to the temple treasury, a large windowless room stuffed with offerings to Amun. Gold god statues, crystal bowls, silver-studded furniture, ivory footstools, bales of frankincense and spices, jars of perfumed oils, ebony boxes, and aromatic woods, all piled higher than Jake could reach. Sitting amid this Pharaoh's ransom were two Egyptians who had somehow escaped the carnage in the shrine—a tall thin priest and a slightly built boy. The priest looked scared. The boy defiant.

Jake tried somehow to set them at ease, saying he would

not hurt them, and just wanted to know who they were. So far he had not hurt *anyone*. He had even *saved* Egyptian lives by stunning Hercules. Despite all appearances, he and Love were pretty much innocent bystanders in the fracas.

The Egyptians were not buying it. The boy bristled. The man replied that he was a Lector Priest of Amun. "And this is my pupil . . ."

Before he could finish, shouts, yells, yelps of pain and a pair of war cries came from behind them.

Jake spun about. His microamps fixed the commotion at the far end of the Audience Chamber. He and Love sprinted back through the shrine to see what was happening.

Leaping over sleeping soldiers and Pharaoh's body, they burst out of the Sanctuary in time to see a bloody skirmish in progress. Pandemonium in the pillared Audience Chamber. Hercules stood squarely in the main doorway, bellowing defiance, facing a determined wedge of Egyptians charging behind a wall of shields. More Egyptians poured out of a robing room, pressing back Iolaus and Sauromanta, who were about to be brought down by sheer weight of numbers. How could things have gone so bad, so fast? Where had all the Egyptians come from?

Love slapped him on the back, yelling, "Pick 'em off. I'll play thumper."

Jake dropped to one knee, firing at the Egyptians closest to Sauromanta. Hercules would have to look out for himself.

Love began throwing anesthetic grenades. He tossed the first one into the robing room. Then he threw two perfect strikes past Hercules into the Hall of Records. Egyptians collapsed. The charge crumpled, and the Corps of Amun retreated.

Sauromanta slammed the robing room door shut, trapping the knockout gas inside. Pounding from within slackened. Then ceased. Egyptians lay strewn about the Audience Chamber, some dead, some sleeping.

"What happened?" Jake demanded.

Sauromanta nodded at the door she was holding shut. "All of a sudden they burst at us from two directions. They must have tunneled through the wall into the robing room, then timed their attack to coincide with a charge from the Outer Hall."

Love stared at the robing room door, appalled to have the

Corps of Amun burrowing through the walls. "Damn. These suckers built the pyramids. They're gonna tear this temple down around us in no time."

Jake did not doubt it. He took a look down the long corridor that led through the hallways and down to the Nile. He saw only dead or stunned Egyptians, but archers had to lurk behind the pillars.

His motion detectors buzzed a warning, "INCOMING. ONE-EIGHTY." Which meant right behind him.

He ducked sideways. A spear flew past his ear, thudding into Love's back.

The spear sliced through Love's wool cape, but the bronze point did not even dent his flak jacket. It did, however, make him mad. Love spun about. "Who threw that?"

There were not many options. In the shrine doorway stood the Lector Priest, looking terrified, and his pupil.

"Damn you." Love stormed over to them, the spear still dangling from his back. "Stop trying to kill us. I can *see* you wantin' to sacrifice Hercules. Half the Bronze Age wants a whack at him. Hell, I'm mad enough to sacrifice the sucker myself. But *we* have done nothin'."

It is hard to know what the Lector Priest made of this, since Love's tirade was in mixed English and Mycenaean. But the priest was scared enough to start squealing in Egyptian.

Turning to Jake, Love jerked the spear out of his cloak, pointing it at the priest. "What's he sayin'?"

"He says he did not throw it."

"Right." Love threw the spear down in disgust. "I was all set to *enjoy* Egypt. You *know* I was. But this place is as bad as Nam. They are all the time tryin' to kill you, and you don't know a word they're sayin'."

"I don't think he threw it."

"That's what they *always* say. I didn't do it—it must have been Charlie. Charlie put the *punji* stakes in the trail. Charlie rigged the grenade in the shithouse."

"No. I think the boy did it."

Love turned to stare at the slight lad standing beside the priest. The boy glared back, supremely defiant. Though he could not understand Love, he heard the priest's protests.

"I threw the spear," he declared. "By the Ka of my dead Father-on-Earth I will kill you all. I am Thutmose III, Son of

Amun, Pharaoh of Upper and Lower Egypt, Lord of Nubia, Kush, Canaan, and Syria. Bow down dogs. Plead for a pleasant death.'' He folded his arms, waiting for them to obey.

The priest threw himself prone before the boy, but there was no rush to imitate. Love looked back at Jake. ''What did the kid say?''

''He says he is Pharaoh, and he threw the spear at you.''

''Right.''

Thutmose stamped his foot. ''Bow down I say. In this very temple Amun anointed me. Bow down and obey.''

''And he wants us to bow,'' Jake added.

''Tell him I ain't got the time.'' Love took the spear over to the robing-room door, jamming the point between the door and the wall, bracing the butt against a joint in the flagstones. A flimsy lock, but at least the door would not come flying open.

Leaving Iolaus watching the main door, Hercules strolled over, seeing the priest on the floor, asking what was happening.

''Bow down before Pharaoh,'' Thutmose insisted, ''or I will have you gutted and spitted on sticks like pigs at midwinter.''

''He says he is Pharaoh.'' Jake left out the part about turning them into Yuletide pork.

''What else did he say?'' Hercules could tell he was not getting a full translation.

''I am the son of Amun. I will have you dogs flayed alive, and your squealing carcasses fed to the crocodiles.''

This time Jake was forced to give a full translation, fishing for his stunner in case Hercules took offense. They could not afford to have him throttle this Thutmose, too.

Before Jake could act, Hercules dropped his bow and snatched up the boy, hugging him to his chest. Smiling absurdly he shouted to Jake, ''Tell him we are brothers.''

Thutmose yelled, ''Tell this brainless barbarian to let me go.''

Given the choice, Jake translated for Hercules first, ''The brainless barbarian says you are brothers.''

Thutmose rejected any possible relationship to ''filthy foreign slime.'' Jake translated, no longer afraid Hercules would brain the boy. Hercules seemed to have taken a liking to the lad. Perhaps it was his love of children.

Tears rolled down the demigod's cheeks. "Tell my little brother that I hate most of my family, too."

Struggling in the grasp of the demigod, the young Thutmose continued to deny any conceivable kinship to "gutless Greek gutter-spawn."

Hercules laughed. "Ask if he is truly a Son of Amun."

Jake put the question to the pint-sized Pharaoh.

"Of course I am, you gibbering ape. Amun came into my mother's bed, disguised as my father." This was the polite fiction that allowed Pharaoh to be both son-of-god and of an earthly father. More than a thousand years later, when Alexander the Great became Pharaoh, it would be as son of Zeus-Amun—not Philip of Macedon.

"So it was with me," Hercules had Jake assure him. "Zeus came to my mother's bed disguised as her husband, King Amphitryon of Troezen." Amun, the Invisible Creator, was the head of the Egyptian pantheon, the equivalent of Zeus. In later times they would be worshiped together. "We must be immortal half brothers; otherwise, we are merely our father's sons."

It made an insane sort of sense. If they were both sons of Zeus-Amun, they had to be half brothers. Thutmose was not in the least convinced, but Hercules was hard to argue with, even in translation. The boy was barely half his size. And kicking and struggling only amused the man who had lost a finger strangling the Nemean Lion.

At last the boy gave in, calling him brother. "But I still hate you, and will kill you!"

"Of course. No brother of mine would be fool enough to forgive his enemies." Hercules kept smothering him with affection, which made little Thutmose furious.

Jake and Iolaus began to clean up the place, dragging the dead and stunned Egyptians into separate robing rooms. Jake was pleased to find there were only a few of the former and a lot of the latter. But any way you looked at it, this had been a busy day in the Bronze Age. And it was not yet noon.

Love and Sauromanta watched the main entranceway and the room the Egyptians had breached. Every so often an arrow would come flying through the doorway from the Hall of Records. But so long as you kept a stone pillar between you and the door, there was not much chance of being hit.

Hercules made a game of shooting back, trying with signs to coax Thutmose into playing. Offering to give the boy archery lessons.

"But they are my subjects," the boy Pharaoh complained.

As he hauled dead and comatose Egyptians about, Jake's microamps listened for more digging. What he heard instead was footsteps, sandaled feet walking purposefully toward them. Mixed with cries of, "Make way, make way," coming from outside the temple.

Jake looked up at Iolaus over the dead Egyptian they were dragging—it was the heavyweight High Priest, and it took two of them to move him. "Someone's coming."

They both glanced at the long corridor that led out of the temple and down to the Nile. The cries got closer, "Make way, make way," was mixed with, "Don't shoot. The Cretan is coming. Make way for the Ambassador from Atlantis."

Archers in the Hall of Records took up the cry, calling through the door to them, "Barbarians, don't shoot. The Atlantean Ambassador is coming to talk."

Jake told Hercules to hold his fire; they did not need another regrettable accident. Then he called out in Egyptian, "Send him in—alone."

The archers outside laughed. The sound of sandaled feet drew closer, climbing the temple steps. Brown hair topped by a tiara appeared in the doorway. Jake saw why the Egyptian archers had laughed—the Atlantean ambassador was a woman. He should have known.

A young woman, too. Her face appeared in the doorway. She had luminous brown eyes and smooth tanned skin, not as dark as an Egyptian, but browned by the sun. Her smile showed white, even teeth. Shoulders appeared, then her body. She was wearing a short sleeveless jacket belted at the waist, above a long silver-flounced skirt that hid her sandaled feet.

Head high, she strode into the temple, brown eyes looking straight ahead, ignoring the bowmen cowering behind the pillars, oblivious to the signs of carnage. She was tall for a girl—taller than Sauromanta, taller than Jake for that matter—but probably no older than sixteen. Her hair was tied in a priestess's sacral knot.

As she came through the door into the Audience Chamber she nodded to Hercules. He lowered his bow and looked her over. Youth and beauty had charms to soothe the savage demigod. Seeing the High Priest lying between Jake and Iolaus, she addressed the corpse in flawless Egyptian. ''Poor Busiris, your passion for sacrifice ends with your own. Hope that the gods below appreciate all the souls you have sent them.''

She switched to Mycenaean, ''I am Anneke, Maiden Priestess of the Atlantean Embassy. I was sent to speak to Pharaoh Thutmose II.''

Love shrugged. ''Go on. He's lyin' down in that robing room. But talk loud, Hercules interfered with his hearing.''

She nodded solemnly, turning to the young Thutmose, she bowed, ''Hail, Pharaoh, Lord of the Nile. Atlantis offers condolences on the death of your Father-on-Earth, and congratulations on your ascension to the double throne.''

Thutmose acknowledged her homage. ''Any messages for Pharaoh may now be delivered to me.''

Anneke sighed, ''My message was a private one, from the Queen to her husband. Alas, it cannot be delivered. However, Atlantis would be happy to offer her services as peacemaker.''

Thutmose snorted. ''We have no need for peacemakers. In due time I mean to have these barbarian dogs butchered.''

Anneke bowed again. ''As Pharaoh wishes.''

Switching back to Mycenaean, she asked politely, ''Do the barbarian dogs have anything to say before they are butchered?''

Jake desperately wanted to talk, hoping somehow to end this siege short of calling in Dianna's STOP team—totally blowing their cover. But he did not mean to talk in front of Thutmose. Or Hercules either. He answered heartily, ''Before we are butchered, let me show you the treasure of Amun. It's an eye-opener.''

Ambassador Anneke smiled. Sauromanta had not seen the treasure either, so the three of them trooped through the Inner Sanctuary to the treasury, leaving Love in charge of the Audience Chamber—with orders to call for help if the Egyptians attacked. Or if Herc went berserk.

The two young women were delighted by the treasure pile, trying on silver necklaces and gold headpieces studded with lapis and amethyst. Anneke answered Jake's questions, as they sniffed rare unguents, perfumed oils, and jars of sweet myrrh.

''Why did they try to sacrifice Hercules in the first place?''

he asked. It seemed such an insane undertaking, like climbing Vesuvius to chuck rocks down the volcano.

"Oh, that was Busiris's, the High Priest's idea. And he has paid nicely for it. Years ago a Cyprian seer named Phrasius predicted Egypt would be invincible if they sacrificed a stranger every year. To be clever, Busiris started by sacrificing Phrasius. Then every year he found an excuse to execute some hapless foreigner. When Hercules showed up at Elephantine, slaughtering pigs in public, it must have seemed like the gods had sent him." Perhaps they had.

Anneke added thoughtfully, "I have never understood the urge to kill—it seems so ghastly. But being barbarians, I suppose you are used to killing."

Jake tried to explain that during the whole battle in the temple he had taken care not to kill anyone. In fact, he wanted to get out of this without another death.

Ambassador Anneke approved his attitude. Holding a carnelian necklace up to her throat, she asked Sauromanta what she thought. Sauromanta said the blood red necklace looked beautiful against Anneke's brown skin. "You have perfect coloring. Bold colors make me look pale."

Anneke smiled. "My little sister has blond hair and blue eyes. When she was born, I thought she was the most beautiful thing in creation."

She set down the necklace. "Now what shall we do about this mess?" Anneke did not mean the treasure of Amun. "I must first know who you are and what you want."

Jake shrugged. "Hercules you must have heard of. Iolaus is his nephew. Sauromanta comes from the Great Sea of Grass. Love and I come from distant lands." That pretty much covered Mars and Michigan. "What we want is to get out of Egypt."

Anneke nodded. "That can be done."

"How?" Jake was eager to hear, but not sure how much he could trust this breezy teenage ambassador.

"You must agree to leave empty-handed, taking none of this treasure with you. To steal from it is death-cursed."

Sauromanta quickly set down a pearl bracelet she had been fondling. Jake swore he did not want a single sequin, death-cursed or not.

"And you must not kill anyone else."

Jake promised to try. It was hard to answer for Hercules, who was apt to leave bodies wherever he went.

Anneke said that sounded good. "May I speak freely?"

"I suppose so." They were in a treasure vault, behind meters of stone and mud brick, surrounded by half the Egyptian army. Jake could hardly imagine a place more private.

"If you repeat anything I say outside these walls, diplomacy forces me to deny it."

"Of course. Everything here is *herkos odonton*." Greek for secret—literally, "behind the hedge of teeth."

Anneke shook herself, as though she were happy to throw off her diplomatic cloak. "I am glad you suggested talking here, away from young Thutmose. Though he would not stoop to learning a tongue as foreign as Mycenaean, I would hate to talk in front of him. He is a horrid little monster. If he ever *really* becomes Pharaoh, it will be a black day for Egypt and her neighbors. And if I believed in killing, I would *pay* Hercules to throttle him, instead of teaching him to shoot."

Jake could, of course, see into the future, and knew that the boy would one day be Pharaoh. Ambassador Anneke and Thutmose III were barely into their teens, but the next generation's battle lines were already drawn. If this tall girl lived to womanhood, she would have her hands full thwarting the budding Egyptian Napoleon. Jake wished her luck.

"If you mean to live, you have much to barter with," Anneke suggested. "You have young Thutmose. You have Pharaoh's body. Also the treasure of Amun. And just beyond that entranceway is the Hall of Records. If you dragged the treasure into the Audience Chamber, broke open these casks of precious oils, and set the place on fire—you could kill the heir presumptive, deny Pharaoh his body in the afterlife, desecrate Egypt's greatest temple, bankrupt their most powerful priesthood, and destroy a mountain of papyrus tax receipts."

The gold would merely melt, but the perfumed oils, priestly robes, ivory furniture, aromatic woods, bales of incense, tiger skins, and Indian cottons would make an expensive bonfire. Jake was not about to *do* that, but it sounded devastating.

"Of course you would burn yourselves up as well. But it still makes those outside nervous. The Corps of Amun swears it will retake the temple, but they have been saying that all morning. Short of tearing the place down, they show small sign of getting in. Sorcery, they say, is stopping them."

"We have a demigod on our side," Jake reminded her.

Anneke nodded. She had *seen* the carnage Hercules had wrought. For the moment, the Corps of Amun had as much chance of hacking its way through the Great Pyramid, as it had of getting past Hercules.

"What is more, you hold the balance of power in Egypt."

Hard to believe, but Jake was happy to hear it.

"The Queen and Pharaoh were great-grandchildren of Queen Ahhotpe the Unifier, whose sons expelled the Hyksos from the Delta." The Hyksos were Semite nomads who brought bronze weapons and horse chariots to the Egyptians. "Their grandmother was her daughter Queen Ahmose-Nefertiry." Like all Atlanteans, Anneke traced descent only on the maternal side. Paternal grandparents hardly mattered anyway, since Queens and Pharaohs were presumably fathered by Amun the Invisible. "But their Father-on-Earth was a general named Thutmose, who married the Queen's daughters to make himself Pharaoh, laying claim to all the lands from Kush to the Euphrates. Clearly absurd, but he had the army to back his fantasies, invading Nubia and Palestine before the Mother grew bored and called him Home." None too soon in Anneke's opinion.

"As often happens, he tried to pass this shaky empire to his son. But Thutmose II was weak and sickly." Which to her showed the absurdity of father to son succession. Who could know how a son would turn out?

"Nubia rose at once, but Thutmose quelled the rebellion with mass executions. Backed by Busiris's cult of killing foreigners for luck. When Queen Hatshepsut opposed him, Thutmose fathered that horrid little boy on the goddess Isis." Jake could see Anneke disapproved of gods and goddesses bringing their sex lives to earth.

"Isis is too busy to mother him. Instead he was raised by soldiers to be the bloodthirsty little brat you've met, believing the whole world is Egypt's rightful prey."

Jake quoted from a typical Thutmoside victory stele:

"Trample on the Dwellers in Asia,
Set Mitanni to trembling,
Trample on Nubia, on Kush, on Lybia,

Bind the Sand People in slavery,
Trample on the Western Lands,
Let Crete, Cyprus, and the Islanders,
Fear Pharaoh, as they would a jackal or crocodile.''

''Exactly,'' Anneke grimaced. ''But Hercules has decapitated the whole imperial faction. Thutmose II is dead. Busiris is dead. And their army is disgraced. Whoever walks down those steps with young Thutmose in hand holds the keys to Egypt.''

''And who would you have take him down those steps?''

Anneke did not hesitate. ''Queen Hatshepsut.''

''If she did, would she let us go?''

''If it is put to her properly.'' Anneke appeared fully prepared to do that. ''Right now the reins of state are lying loose. Hatshepsut is backed by the Steward Senenmut, and Inebny the Treasurer—wars are expensive. And she has her own candidate for High Priest now that Hercules has opened up the post.''

''Will she be able to sway the rest of the government?''

''Turn young Thutmose over to her, and she will *be* the government.'' Anneke clearly relished the idea of having the obnoxious little Pharaoh-to-be frog-marched down the temple stairs by his stepmother.

Jake considered. He had to trust her. She held the keys not just to Egypt, but to Atlantis as well. He needed entry into Anneke's world. ''If I do as you say, I need something in return.''

Anneke nodded happily. ''Name it.''

''I want you to arrange for our safe passage back to Elephantine.'' Just getting out of the temple was not nearly good enough.

''Of course. All of you must leave Egypt, and soon. Queen Hatshepsut cannot afford to have her husband's killers hanging about. However useful they may have been.''

''Done,'' Jake decided.

Anneke had a final look at the treasure, shaking her head. ''How sad to bury such beauty behind stone.'' Then she took her leave.

Jake and Sauromanta were left alone. He watched the Amazon try on various trinkets for the last time. Her favorites were the carnelian necklace, and a gold-and-lapis headdress, with ivory chains dangling from it, each loop carved to link with its neighbors. "Do you think I look beautiful in this?"

Jake smiled. "You'd look beautiful in a goatskin."

She laughed. "I *know* that. But would I look beautiful dressed as a lady?"

"Yes."

"Really? You barely treat me like a woman." She set down the headdress, taking a last look around.

What could he say? Jake came from an age where male gallantry was out-of-date. Besides, Sauromanta's habit of swinging a battle-ax when upset did not invite coy flattery. "You are very much a woman." Albeit a young and dangerous one.

"Good." She tossed her head, flicking her blond ponytail like a filly slapping at flies. "Sometimes, Jake, you never seem to notice." How strange to hear her use his name. Something she almost never did.

Before the shadows in the Outer Hall had moved the length of a pillar, Anneke was back, bringing with her Queen Hatshepsut, granddaughter of Ahmose-Nefertiry, God Wife of Amun. A dark woman dressed in splendid robes, with deep searching eyes, looking strong, willful, and ambitious. With her came Inebny the Treasurer, and Hapuseneb, the new High Priest, to see that Amun's hoard remained intact.

Everything went as Anneke had foretold. The Queen of the Nile, with her unwilling stepson at her side, led Hercules out of the Temple of Amun, to where his chariot was waiting. No one tried to stop him. The Corps of Amun had been replaced by a horde of women and girls—professional mourners hired to grace the occasion, weeping for all they were worth. And at the dock was the Atlantean Ambassador's own traveling ship, ready to take Jake and company back to Elephantine.

Atlantis

The trip back to Elephantine was much more to Jake's liking. For openers, Hercules was not with them. The demigod saw no reason to backtrack. He had his Golden Apples, his chariot, and Poseidon's horses. Having made a sizable dent in Upper Egypt, he and Iolaus turned north from Thebes to see what damage could be done downriver. Almost everyone was glad to see him go. Egyptians were ecstatic.

Jake, Love, and Sauromanta were the only guests sharing the plush accommodations aboard Anneke's ambassadorial traveling ship. Anneke's position *required* her to travel first-class. Egyptians expected foreigners to be rich and generous—otherwise, why were they here? So her traveling ship had to make the Viceroy of Nubia's look like a garbage barge. Stem and stern were carved into giant lotus blossoms, and it took a pair of thirty-oared boats to pull them upriver. The two-story deckhouse was adorned with a life-size mural of Cretans bearing gifts to Pharaoh. To remind the Egyptians how forthcoming Atlantis could be.

Inside the deckhouse was thoroughly Atlantean, painted in bright pale colors like the interior of a seashell. Friezes of flowers and dolphins danced through the cabins. Anneke had an ornate strongbox for her valuables, and a small water closet with a flush toilet and a wooden seat. Diplomacy obliged her to live in such opulence—but she plainly embraced the necessity.

Her crew was Cretan. Black-haired, tanned men in kilts and codpieces, wearing jewelry and broad leather belts, served her guests. Pouring fruit juices from crystal pitchers into dainty eggshell cups thin as fine porcelain.

Anneke apologized for her youth. "I have been a Maiden Priestess since I was nine. Serving overseas is part of my training. And my age puts the Egyptians off guard. They think we Atlanteans are hopelessly frivolous, hardly worth being watched or killed. If I had been a man, they never would have let me into that temple. Or let me be alone with the Queen."

She ran over her plans for Egypt. With Hatshepsut as Queen-Regent she looked forward to peace in Canaan, and a trade alliance between Egypt and Atlantis. Egypt could maintain a loose claim to Gaza, Joppa, and Armageddon, but so long as Pharaoh had no war fleet, Tyre, Sidon, and Byblos would be independent. And the only ships Hatshepsut wanted to build were for trade with Punt. Jake could see Anneke was enthralled with the notion of a three-sided trade alliance between Atlantis, Egypt, and Phoenicia, spreading peace and plenty throughout the Eastern Mediterranean.

"What about the boy Napoleon?" Love had seen enough of Thutmose III to know the boy was itching to march on someone.

"Right now he is Pharaoh in name only, with his stepmother as Queen-Regent. In a year or so . . ."

Anneke did not need to finish. Clearly Hatshepsut meant to declare herself Pharaoh as well, coruler and regent for life. Nowhere was the Bronze Age split between male and female rule more dramatic than in New Kingdom Egypt—running right through the royal marriage bed. The Thutmoside males were would-be conquerors, bent on extending Egyptian rule from Kush to the Euphrates. But in a matrilineal society, they had no claim to the throne unless they married their mothers, daughters, and sisters—women who were largely content to see Egypt unified, prosperous, and at peace.

And right now the women had the upper hand. Thanks to

Hercules. Thutmose III would have to wait a long time before he could lead an army, or sit on the throne alone.

But one day he would. As much as Jake admired Anneke, and sympathized with her schemes, he knew her plans were doomed. As doomed as Atlantis. One day Thutmose III would lead his legions into Palestine, to do battle on the plain of Armageddon. The Bible told him so. Seeing the future could be no fun. Just ask Cassandra.

"Is he really the son of Isis?" Jake had to know what role the "gods" played in this.

"All too true." Anneke sighed. "Isis-Aphrodite visited Pharaoh's harem, presenting him with a son. Making no end of trouble." Not surprisingly the boy had gotten things exactly backwards—his mother was divine, not his father. Hercules was his cousin, not his half brother. But Thutmose III very much wanted to be a son of Amun.

"Strange choice for a goddess." Love did not sound like he believed it. "Thutmose didn't seem much of a stud."

"Not so odd if you have the morals of a she-goat in heat." Anneke acted as if this was mere fact, not in the least blasphemous. "Aphrodite's sole task under Heaven is to make love, and she takes it seriously. Besides, Pharaoh begged for a son by her, praying night and day. It was the only way he could have a divine heir." A queen merely had to let a god into her bed—a king had to find a goddess willing to bear his child. Another natural advantage of matriliny.

"Maybe his prayers moved her. Or she liked how Egyptians bow and scrape before a goddess-on-earth. Aphrodite usually goes for virile young huntsmen. Look at Adonis. She absolutely flipped over him." Anneke plainly did not approve of Isis-Aphrodite making a religion of sleeping around.

Love struggled to get a handle on Bronze Age theology. "You don't talk like you exactly worship her."

"I fear and respect her. What woman wouldn't. Displease her, and she has the power to make you fall insanely in love with a donkey."

Love smirked.

"Don't laugh, I've seen it happen. She could do it to *you*. But we don't worship her, or any of the Olympians."

"Why?" Jake sensed Anneke might be a willing ally against the gods-on-earth.

"They are more than mortal. And have the power to kill us all. But if we worshiped that, we would be worshiping fear. My mother taught me to worship life—even if that means accepting death. To us, Artemis and Hera are manifestations of the Mother. And Zeus is her child. But Apollo is merely a mouse demon. And Ares is an abomination."

She said it with the unquestioning conviction of youth. How many of Anneke's elders were ready to deny gods they did not like? Not that Jake considered these pseudo-Olympians to be gods. Their taste for high-tech toys was a tip-off. What use would the *real* sun god have for a STOP hovercar?

Out-time visitors often ended up as deities. Sometimes you could not help it—as in Ireland. It was too complicated to be anything else. A lot of locals did not like being lectured on post-Einsteinian physics. To the Crow and Lakota Jake was He-Who-Walks-Through-Winters, a messenger from the Great Mystery. In twelfth-century Cambodia he was The Shatterer of Worlds, an avatar of Shiva—but in medieval Cambodia anyone of importance had to be at least a demigod.

And this was the Bronze Age. When God himself would come down for an occasional heart-to-heart with Moses, saying, "You shall have no other gods *before* Me." Acknowledging there were lesser gods that Moses might bow to in a pinch.

"Do they really have the power to kill us all?" Jake asked. Whatever STOP weapons these gods stole were mostly nonlethal. But perhaps the Olympians had powers he did not know about.

Anneke stared at Jake as if to ask where he had been for the last several centuries. "Atlantis has been at the mercy of the Olympians ever since Zeus seized the Shrine of Callisto."

"Which Shrine of Callisto?"

"You truly come from far away."

Jake nodded. Twenty-first-millennium Mars was a ways off.

"It is the Shrine of the Maiden on the slopes of Callisto, above Atlantis. From time out of mind this shrine protected Atlantis from the fury of the volcano." Callisto, the Beautiful One, was a goddess name, given to the volcano overlooking Atlantis. In part it was an attempt to placate the goddess, in the same way the Furies are called the Gentle Ones.

"When Zeus first seized the shrine, the island shook to its

roots. Atlantis was leveled, along with the Labyrinth on Crete. Both have been rebuilt, bigger than ever. But the shrine was never restored. Zeus is all that sits between Atlantis and Callisto.'' The calamity was generations old, but so terrible that it seemed current—even to a teenager. Anneke clearly considered Olympian ''protection'' just a deferred death sentence. Unless the Maiden returned to her shrine, Atlantis was doomed.

Jake thought at once of the myth of Callisto, the maiden huntress seduced by Zeus. Hera and Artemis turned Callisto into a wild bear, which Zeus hurled up into heaven. That was myth. The history behind it was sufficiently frightening. At a date still in dispute, the volcano Callisto was going to explode with such violence that people would later call her Thera, the Wild Beast. Blowing the city of Atlantis into the stratosphere. Bits of it would come down as far off as Greenland and California.

These gods-on-earth had a good racket going, which begged to be busted up. But that was not Jake's job. He was here to retrieve what was left of the original *Atlantis* team, plus the STOP teams sent to find them. And the Olympians were bound to oppose him—making Anneke a natural ally. Jake just had to be careful what he promised. He could not save Atlantis. Or keep Thutmose III from becoming a midget Mussolini. But he could put the Olympians in their place. Or so he hoped.

''There is a chance we could help each other,'' he suggested.

Anneke laughed. ''You have already aided me admirably.'' Or at least Hercules had, by tilting the balance of power in Egypt.

''Not just here,'' Jake explained. ''But in the Aegean as well.'' The Aegean was the heart of the Atlantean sphere.

Anneke saw at once where the conversation was headed. ''I can do nothing openly to oppose the Olympians.'' They were much too dangerous and vengeful.

''We don't need anything openly.'' This was another case of *herkos odonton*, something kept behind the teeth.

''What do you need?''

''A ship. One that can get us secretly to Atlantis.'' Once Jake had slipped *Thetis* into the Mediterranean they could use the ship to scout out Atlantis, keeping the minisub in reserve.

A larger version of the plan he used to penetrate Gibraltar.

Anneke considered. "That can indeed be done." She promised to make arrangements in Elephantine.

Next morning, Jake found Sauromanta atop the deckhouse, standing alone at the starboard rail, staring out over drowned fields at the long desert escarpment bordering the Nile valley. Hercules was atop that escarpment, headed for the oasis of Siwa, to hobnob with his heavenly father at the oracle of Zeus-Amun. The same journey Alexander the Great would make a thousand years hence. If they wanted, they could check on his progress—Love had planted a passive transponder in his chariot chassis.

"Miss him?" Jake asked.

"How could I not?" She smiled over her shoulder at him. "He is a god."

"Really?" How seriously did she take the notion of gods-on-earth?

"Well, maybe only half a god." She laughed. "Out of bed he was rash, opinionated, quarrelsome, and shortsighted. A man through and through."

"What about in bed?" That was what worried Jake.

She lifted an eyebrow. "You'd be surprised."

Jake did not doubt it.

"He can be brutal, it's true. And no doubt he has mistreated women. But what man can deny that? Yet at other times he is quite tender and caring. And eager to please. Very much like a woman might be . . ."

Sauromanta was not the least bit shy. Just infuriatingly honest. Jake asked, and she told. What was there to hide?

"Did my sleeping with him disturb you." She sounded truly concerned.

"Not in the least," Jake lied, then swiftly changed the subject. What about Anneke? How did she feel about her?

Sauromanta smiled wide. She *loved* Anneke. "She has courage. Look how she marched into the temple, setting right the mess Thutmose and Hercules had made." Even an Amazon could be impressed by that bit of daring peacemaking. "And style as well." Sauromanta waved to indicate the traveling boat. Such luxurious accommodations were bound to impress someone brought up by a dung fire in a skin yurt.

But would she be willing to battle the gods on Anneke's

behalf? Or Jake's? They had come to the Bronze Age not knowing what the stakes would be. (Jake had not even been sure they would *get to* the Bronze Age.) Now they were up against people posing as gods. The gods. The ones Sauromanta prayed to.

Blue eyes stared back at him, candid, clear, and innocent, framed by golden hair. "I came to be at your side. Nothing has changed that. Not Hercules. Not anything."

"Even if we have to face the wrath of Apollo?"

"Even then."

He believed her. Sauromanta took religion seriously, but it did not cloud her sense of justice. If she saw an Olympian doing evil, she would fight it. Of all the Greek deities, the one her people held in highest esteem was Hestia, the virgin goddess of the hearth and family. Upright, honest, and charitable. Hestia never fought except in defense of home, women, children, or supplicants. A curious choice for the warlike, wandering Scyths. But just the goddess Sauromanta would honor.

Jake asked Anneke to let them off at night, in the same hippo-infested stretch above Elephantine that *Argo* had visited.

Ambassador Anneke loaded them with parting gifts, gold trinkets, frankincense, a roll of silver wire, and bolts of fine Egyptian wool and linen. Then she asked, "Do you know where Rhacotis is?"

"A fishing village above Lake Mareotis?" Jake had been there more than a thousand years later, in Cleopatra's day.

"In ten days time a Carian trading vessel will dock there. Tell the captain that you are the ones he has come for. He will take you to Atlantis. And return you to Rhacotis."

Jake thanked her. Anneke accepted, saying, "It is nothing to what I owe you."

"Not really." Jake worried about dragging Anneke into conflict with pitiless opponents, who might take hideous revenge against her and her people.

But the young diplomat was determined to pay her debt. "The Egyptians call us *keftiu*, which means Cretan, since Crete is Atlantis's greatest isle. And lies closest to them. But I am neither Cretan, nor Atlantean. I was born on the mainland, in Greece. My mother is Head Nymph at the Shrine of the Isthmian Maiden at the narrowest part of the Isthmus of Corinth. If ever you are in need, come to her and say I owe you a service. People always bring her their problems. Common folk call her a goddess.''

Jake thanked Anneke again, hoping he never needed such aid. How sad it was that if everything went well, he would never see Anneke again. But if you don't like long good-byes, you have no business going faster-than-light.

The minisub slid easily down the river's main channel, past Thebes and Abydos, deeper into Egypt. It was a measure of how much more African Pharaoh's kingdom had become that Thebes, the Thutmoside capital, was three times closer to Nubia than it was to Memphis and the pyramids.

Seeing village after village, sitting atop their *tels*, like islets in the flood, was a reminder of just how African the entire Mediterranean Bronze Age was. The Nile valley made Mother Africa the Middle Sea's most populous shore—a nearly inexhaustible source of wealth and people. It had been that way ever since the first African hominids left to settle Asia and Europe.

Jake arranged for them to pass the pyramids at sunrise, taking the minisub in close to the pale line of monuments. Floodwaters let *Thetis* ride right up to the edges of the funerary compounds.

Dawnlight touched the tallest pyramids, descending meter by meter, turning the flat eastern faces into giant blazing white triangles of Tura limestone—throwing the rays of Holy Ra back toward heaven, while sleeping villages still lay in shadow. Slowly the light descended, turning Mother Nile into a silvery sheet, filling the valley floor. A sight worth coming centuries to see.

The parade began south of Memphis with the ''Bent'' Pyramid of Sheferu, and then the monuments to Amenemhet II, Sesostris III, and Pepi II. Then came the gleaming White Wall of Memphis, crenellated and indented. North of Memphis was the Saqqara group—Userkaf, Sekhemkhet, the Step Pyramid of Zoser, and the Sacred Bull Cemetery, with its priests' houses, schools, and sanatorium. After that came Abu Sir.

Then there was Giza. On a high plateau at the edge of the desert stood the Great Pyramid of Cheops, the Sphinx, and the lesser pyramids of Chephren and Mycerinus, ringed by satellite pyramids, mastaba tombs, mortuary temples, and gold-sheathed obelisks—a shining city of the dead, peopled with lizards, priests, embalmers, and beasts of sacrifice.

All scaled to colossal proportions. The Great Pyramid alone had two million multiton stone blocks, aligned on a cosmic axis to within a tenth of a degree. Nothing in the Bronze Age compared to it. Stonehenge had only a hundred-odd stones. The Great Wall of China and the pyramids of Mexico were not yet begun. But the Great Pyramid had already stood for ten centuries. A wanderer out of space and time—just like Jake.

Morning turned to noon and afternoon. Giza sank beneath the dunes. By nightfall Jake was negotiating the Delta, headed out to sea. The minisub left the Nile through the Rosetta mouth, one of those end-of-the-river channels like the Gates of the Mississippi—fingers of land thrusting far out into the Mediterranean. Staying well below the surface, steering by arclamps, Jake followed the flat alluvial plain down toward the seabed, then coasted through cold, still depths along the sea floor. Near Rhacotis the seabed began to rise again. Jake followed it upward.

Rhacotis was a sleepy fishing village and customs post, perched atop a limestone ridge separating Lake Mareotis from the sea. On one side lay Mareotis, a seaside swamp infested with hippopotami and river pirates. On the other side lay one of the finest harbors in the ancient world. Egyptians made no special use of it, since it was not connected to the Nile, and faced away from Palestine, their only overseas possession. But Rhacotis was perfect for what Jake and Anneke intended—a backwater aimed at Crete and Atlantis.

And it was the future site of Alexandria, the world capital of the Hellenistic Age. Alexander the Great founded nineteen cities from Africa to India. (With characteristic modesty he named seventeen for himself, one for his dog, and one for his horse.) But his first and greatest Alexandria would be here.

Love looked down the sweltering market street—the future Sarapis Boulevard—paved with sacred cow patties. Flies whined in the wet heat. "Needs work. A *whole* lot of work."

Jake took his teammates on an imaginary tour of the city-to-be, walking down Canopic Street, the wide avenue that would bisect the city, describing the parks and *palaestrae*, the baths, canals, and floating villas. Jake had seen it all centuries later when he came to get the Cleopatra interview. (Not surprisingly, the best loved, and longest remembered Greek ruler of Egypt would be a woman.) His compweb reeled off the sites of temple squares, hippodromes, and the Jewish Quarter. Dust puddles marked the future location of the Great Library.

At the head of the cow path that would become Argeus Boulevard lay the harbor, dotted with fishing smacks. Riding at anchor—near the palace peninsula Caesar and Cleopatra would defend against an army—was the ship Anneke had promised. A twenty-oared trading galley, its sternpost topped by a *labrys*, the double-ax standard of Caria. Caria, at the eastern end of the Atlantean sphere, lay so far from Egypt or Greece that the ship would not likely be traced back to Anneke.

Her captain—a dark wiry Carian with a game leg—stumped over the sand to greet them. He wore a plain tunic and a wide-brimmed hat, inviting them aboard in a laconic accent, confusing his Mycenaean consonants—saying "Jag" for Jake, and totally mangling "Sauromanta."

Jake took an instant liking to the old salt, who exuded the leather-skinned competence Jake looked for whenever he had to trust his luck to wooden ships and fickle seas. Leaving the minisub hidden at the bottom of the western harbor, they boarded the Carian ship, ready to get their first look at Atlantis. The trading galley was a tightly built example of mortise and tenon construction, with a single mast, a tall curving stern, and a narrow deckhouse aft. Crawling out of the anchorage under oars, they passed a sizable islet, and a string of offshore rocks. Sauromanta quoted from Book IV of the *Odyssey*:

> "There is an isle in the open sea before Egypt. Men call it Pharos . . ."

Pharos was the future site of the towering Lighthouse of Alexandria, which would mark the entrance to the Grand Harbor—a pillar of smoke by day, and a fiery beacon by night, visible a hundred klicks off the Egyptian coast. Pharos was also the spot where Menelaus and Helen would be stranded on their way home from Troy—supposedly the home of nymphs, and the Old Man of the Sea. All Jake saw were seals basking on the pebbled beach.

The Carian captain headed east along the African coast, toward the queendom of Cyrene. From there—where the sea passage was shortest—he planned to stand out for Crete.

Jake could at last relax a bit, trusting the Carians to get him to Atlantis, a run they had made many times. *Thetis* was hidden in a safe anchorage. No longer having Hercules with him, he need not worry about the demigod taking drunken offense and stamping a hole in the boat. Or slaughtering the crew. The sea voyage could be a minivacation. So long as he kept an eye out for vengeful gods. Plus the usual dangers of storms, reefs, wreckers, pirates, and whatnot.

Dusk found them anchored in a barren African bay, where the crew went ashore to spend the night. Jake stood for a while at the deckhouse rail, staring at watch fires ashore—then decided to call it a night. A light showed in the space curtained off for Sauromanta. He scratched on the cloth. Her voice invited him in.

She was sitting on her cot, brushing her gold rope of hair by the light of a tiny oil lamp, a simple indented lump of clay with a wick floating in the tallow. Maybe it was the play of the lamplight, or the prospect of heading out onto Homer's wine-dark sea, but seeing her made him think of goddess shrines, altar fires, and burning cities.

He took the brush from her hand, saying, "Here, let me do it."

She gave it up with a smile. Jake started to brush, but her jacket hung open. The shining curve of her breast provoked a pang of lust so sharp he could barely wield the brush.

Sauromanta must have sensed it. She looked up, staring into his eyes. Never shirking from anything. Not him. Not Hercules. Not even the gods. This is what he got for bringing along a girl who was so goddamn unafraid.

Her courage was contagious. Without much thinking about it, he kissed her.

The kiss began as a brush of lips. But then her lips parted, and their tongues met, licking and sliding. He smelled the perfumes Scyths rub on their bodies—cypress, cedarwood, and frankincense.

Their lips unlocked, and she laughed. "I've been wondering when you would do this."

"Now you know." What else was there to say?

He thought of Peg. And the task ahead. And the dangers

they faced. But he could not let go of Sauromanta.

"Don't be afraid," she whispered. "Trust me."

He relaxed, letting go of his fears for the future. "I have always trusted you. Since the first time we talked."

She grinned. "In the camel court of that caravanserai on the Royal Road east of Nineveh."

Jake smiled. His compweb conjured up the scene. He could smell the burning cow dung, and hear ghostly post riders galloping past flapping rag tents, carrying word that Alexander was across the Tigris in force. For once Jake could see his own future with absolute certainty. Over a thousand years from now—on 24 September 331 B.C.—he and Peg would have a typical married spat. Then he would storm out to sleep with the camels. "You came up to say someone had tampered with my bag."

Her eyes dropped, and she hid her face. "I lied to you."

"No. My compweb has your exact words." It was one of those moments you never erased. "You said someone moved the bag and took its tags. That was true. You just did not say that *you* had done it."

"It was to get your attention," she admitted.

"I'm glad you did." Until that moment she had merely been the tomboy daughter of the Scyth hetman they were traveling with. And she ended up saving his life—for the first time—the next day, during a mad brush with Alexander's Paeonian Rangers. From then on he owed her. And kept on owing her. Sauromanta proved invaluable throughout the whole Alexander misadventure, helping to rescue Peg from Alexander's harem, salvaging something out of a thoroughly bungled expedition. When it came time for the remnants of the team to depart, there was a space open, and Sauromanta snapped at the chance to see more of space-time.

"You remember everything." She looked wonderingly into his eyes.

"Only when I want to. That night was special. I remember every word. How you looked. How you acted. How your hair smelled of horse dung."

"Did you find that horrible?"

"No. Just different."

Sauromanta slid off her stag-leather pants and pushed up

his tunic. It was always strangely convenient to make love in an era where men wore skirts.

When they were done, he lay with her head on his chest, listening to the creak and groan of the ship riding at anchor, feeling the alternating warmth and coldness of her breath. Soft hair in his face smelled of sex and spices. She was asleep and happy. He should have been, too. Sauromanta was young, tough, and casually, almost offhandedly, sexy. Loving, too, when she cared to be.

But what was he going to say to Peg? The sometime "Mrs. Jake Bento." Well at least he did not have to worry about that now. That was the beauty of nonsimultaneity. Once you negotiated a faster-than-light portal, here-and-now was wherever you bobbed up in the time stream. Nothing else existed. No Peg. No marriage. No Home Period. No hyperlight civilization. Mars, his birth world, was a dead husk waiting to be terraformed. Pretty sad if you thought about it.

Next morning Sauromanta was bubbling and happy, honing her weapons and shooting him happy glances. Looking over the sea toward Crete.

Love greeted Jake with a grin. "It's good to see Grandma's gettin' laid *real* regular. Puts her in a good mood."

Jake shrugged. "We all got to do what we can."

"More better, baby."

It took two weeks of rowing to reach Cyrene, fighting headwinds and the slow counterclockwise current of the Eastern Mediterranean. So far as Jake was concerned, it should have taken ten times as long. Or better yet, they could have kept going past Cyrene, west along the coast of Libya, looking for the Isle of the Lotus Eaters. It was the happiest two weeks he ever had—in the Bronze Age anyway.

When they tired of lovemaking aboard ship, he and Sauromanta spent nights ashore. Stargazing beside a beach fire. Rising early to stalk lions by dawnlight. Not to hunt them, just to get close to them. Sauromanta had an affinity for the big cats—"I was a lioness in another life."

He could believe it. She would shake her long tawny hair, then stretch out naked on the sand, studying their antics. One morning they awoke to find that the pride they were stalking had doubled back, to lie down around them. It was Sauromanta's favorite moment in the whole trip.

Other mornings he would be wakened by her rubbing bare buttocks against his groin, imitating the come-hither nicker of a willing mare. Reared among horses, the Amazon's sex education had begun with seeing mares mounted in the spring. She would whinny as he slid into her, pressing with her hips for a perfect fit. Contraceptive implants kept him from getting her in foal.

Queen Cyrene feasted them when they arrived on her coast. Seeing Sauromanta was the only woman, the Queen naturally assumed she was in charge, treating Jake as a bedmate-interpreter. A sort of male Sacajawea, handy for conversation and pleasure—but hardly leadership material. Through him, the Queen invited Sauromanta to stay as long as she wished. Even join her Amazon bodyguard.

Politely refusing, Sauromanta pleaded pressing business in Atlantis, and they stood out to sea from Cyrene, headed for Crete.

The crossing from Cyrenaica over to Crete was the longest sea voyage they faced. But they got a boost from the same prevailing west wind that forced them to crawl along the African coast. With the wind on her port quarter the galley made a quick pleasant crossing under sail. Dolphins danced ahead of them, standing on their tail fins to lift out of the water, peering curiously over the gunwales at a tiny bit of humanity afloat on endless sea.

Homer's wine-dark Aegean is enclosed on three sides by Europe and Asia. The open southern end faces Africa, and is sheltered by a natural breakwater—a series of long narrow islands, the largest of which is Crete, the "Great Goddess Island."

The southern spine of the island rose straight out of the sea before them, formed by the peaks of a sunken mountain chain—wild and cloud-wracked, slashed by chasms, covered by deep green cypress forests. Goats with great curving horns clung to cliff edges and perpendicular trails. It was hard to believe Crete is close enough to Africa for bananas to grow.

The galley made landfall east of Cape Ram, then clawed her way round the cape under oars. The promontory was shaped like a ram's head, with its long rocky muzzle dipping down to drink. Curling strata formed the beast's nostril, eye, and horn. Beyond Cape Ram, the Cretan coast turned north toward Greece, into the teeth of a rising north wind.

Ahead lay a yawning double gap in the Aegean's island breakwater, between Crete and the south coast of Kythera. Ninety klicks of open sea—divided in half by the small thin island of Antikythera. Here Atlantic cyclonic storms, blown through the Pillars of Hercules, met boreal winds howling off the Balkans. Northerly squalls hitting the Kythera Gap could drive a fleet of ships all the way to Africa. As would happen to Ulysses, Menelaus, and Helen of Troy.

Jake spotted mastheads in the harbor at Korykos, an islet off the northwest tip of Crete. Ships were huddled there, waiting for the north wind to slacken. Korykos harbor was called the Leather Sack, after the leather bag used by Aeolus, the Keeper of the Winds.

For a week they shared the anchorage with a half dozen Atlantean round ships, a Mycenaean state *triakonter*, and a pair of Phoenician trading galleys, loaded with dyes, tin, and Egyptian glass. As long as the north wind blew, they formed a floating village, trading and partying back and forth. Then the winds turned westerly, and they went their ways—the round ships headed east along the north coast of Crete, the galleys striking out for Kythera and the European mainland.

Land dipped out of sight. The galleys were strung in a line, with the Mycenaean *triakonter* in the lead, and the heavy-laden Phoenicians falling behind. Jake, Love, and Sauromanta leaned on the starboard rail, staring out across the Cretan Sea, toward the central Aegean. Atlantis was out there, and beyond that, the Asian mainland.

Jake asked Sauromanta what she saw.

"Home." She nodded to the northwest. She did not mean it literally. The view was all waves and whitecaps. But Jake knew what she meant.

His navmatrix confirmed the direction, correct to within a couple of degrees. Sauromanta had a rock-solid grip on space-time. Beyond Atlantis. Across the Aegean. Beyond the Bosphorus, and the Black Sea, lay the grassy steppes of Eurasia. Sauromanta had been born there by the banks of the Amazon, a broad winding river that came to be called the Don.

"You can't go home again." Love said it softly in Mycenaean.

"Why?" She looked curiously at the airborne trooper.

"Don't work. Tried it once. Went back when my hitch was up, and the war was over. Found my mama dead, and my little brother grown up and gone away. Tried living with my sister in Flint—but I couldn't hack the bullshit. Gettin' cheap service in expensive places. Not after seeing the future. No way."

He turned his back to the rail, talking about the far future as though it were long ago. "Goddamn FBI looked me up. After all the time hearin' what an *outstanding* job we did in Nam—and how proud they wuz to have us back—I am here to say the MPs were not one fuckin' bit proud to find my black face on the streets of Flint. Not when I was very much MIA in Laos."

Love laughed. "Only they dithered too long decidin' on charges. I was sure enough AWOL. But desertion did not seem to fit—not when my unit was well-known to be wiped out. What was I gonna tell 'em? That I got snagged by a UFO?"

"How did you get here?" Sauromanta vaguely knew Love was recruited from a war zone. Just like her.

"The Airborne was thrown into this *absolutely* brilliant operation. Lam Son 719. Supposed to be a gook-vs-gook show in Laos. No grunts involved. Not in the ground game anyway. We were the passing attack. Flying ARVN into layers of flak—12.7mm, 37mm, 57mm. Whatever Mr. Charlie had handy. And when you were hit, you went goddamn down. Onto the ground, orders or no."

Leaning back against the rail, he closed his eyes, to help picture the scene. "Our firebase was overrun. And my chopper went down—with the copilot and door gunner dead. Leaving me real damn alone. Until I heard a whir overhead. Thought it was a Jolly Green Giant coming to get me."

Only it was a STOP hovership, homing in on a time-slipped expedition to twelfth-century Burma, that had become badly tangled in a twentieth-century war. Love took an active part in the ensuing firefight between Special Temporal Ops and a full battalion from the 308th NVA Division. Rather than leaving him for the NVA, STOP wafted Love up along with the team out of Burma.

Jake had *been there*. But he was not sure how much Sauromanta got, hearing it half in English and half in Mycenaean. There being no good proto-Greek equivalents for "gook," "door gunner," and "Jolly Green Giant."

Enough of the flavor got through for her to go wide-eyed. "Wars in the future must be wondrous."

"Hell no." Love opened his eyes, laughing at her. "You'd hate it. Fighting a war you can't win, in places people claimed did not exist. Drive you crazy, Grandma."

Love shook his head, like he was amazed *he* had been there. "An' gettin' some from a Huey is awful antiseptic. Compared to swingin' ax, an feelin' it go *chunk*. Don't look to see me goin' back."

Sauromanta saw the disadvantages.

"I lost a lot of interest when I landed in the future. Found out Nixon's 'secret' plan for winnin' was to give in and go home. It don't always do ya good to know what's gonna happen."

She nodded. And she had to know the Sea of Grass beyond the Bosphorus was not really her home. In the Bronze Age her people barely existed. The first ancestor of the Royal Scyths was just learning to toddle around the yurt—a boy fathered by Hercules while driving the cattle of Geryon to Greece.

The crossing took two days, with the night spent anchored in the lee of Antikythera. Kythera harbored an Atlantean settlement, the oldest in the islands, facing the Greek mainland across the Kythera channel. The Carians docked there, resting up from their row, drinking, debauching, and waiting on the winds.

The town was typically Atlantean, happy and bustling, with a port market that made Elephantine seem tame and sleepy. Energetic bare-breasted women, wearing open embroidered jackets and great flounced skirts, sold wares from all over. Baltic amber. Egyptian linen and Arabian spices. Local pottery with Atlantean motifs, wheeled toys, and live monkeys with their fur dyed blue.

Jake bought Sauromanta a carnelian necklace, like the one she had admired amid the treasure of Amun, paying with a piece of the silver wire Anneke had given him. At least he could not be accused of buying gifts to seduce Sauromanta. That had already happened.

He rented a sunny upper room overlooking the port, and enjoyed the novel experiment of making love to Sauromanta in a normal bed, instead of on a cot or sand dune. Morning light poured through a wide window across from the bed. Through it, Jake could see Cape Malea, the southeastern tip of Greece, his first look at the European mainland since Gibraltar.

After a day's rest, the Carian captain drove his crew out of the alehouses and the temple of Aphrodite. Everyone boarded ship and set out again. Beyond Cape Malea lay another stretch of open sea. The normal coasting route was to sail north, along the east coast of the Peloponnese, sometimes as far as Cape Sounion in Attica, then backtrack toward Atlantis, sailing down the line of the Cyclades. But a steady west wind gave them the option of heading straight for Melos in the southern Cyclades.

Turning their backs on Cape Malea, and the European mainland, they sailed east, deeper into the Atlantean sphere. The Carian captain made a fair crossing, heading straight for a landfall on Melos, using only the sun and dead reckoning.

Dawn revealed the southern Cyclades spread out before them, island after sunny island set in a china blue sea. They were now totally in Atlantean waters—from here to the Asian mainland. Whatever direction they sailed, they would find peaceful island communities, with a mix of religion and races, trading and visiting, tied together by the sea.

On Melos the commercial port was all Atlantean, though the galley captain claimed the first settlers had been Carian. Jake and Sauromanta strolled past market stalls, where women with long black hair, dark eyes, and narrow waists offered fish, fruit, and carved crystal for sale.

Even with Sauromanta at his side, Jake found the open-fronted jackets and rouged nipples distracting. The Amazon teased him, saying she was surprised he "even looked at a woman dressed in skins and leather."

At a dressmaker's shop Suaromanta stripped down to try on Atlantean outfits. The women in the shop delighted in fussing over her, combing and fixing up her yellow hair, letting Jake get the full effect. No one seemed the least afraid of nudity. Not the naked children. Nor the men in codpieces. Nor the gay, laughing women who delighted in Sauromanta's strong young body, saying, "Look, she is blond even there."

Jake bought the dress and jacket for more silver wire and seven grams of frankincense.

Narrow cobbled streets rose up from the port market, winding round irregular blocks of flat-roofed houses. Kitchens, baths, and storage rooms occupied the ground floors. Living and sleeping quarters were upstairs. People called to each other from upper windows, or sat on the roofs, speaking to neighbors across streets and open courts.

That night she wore the dress and necklace, and they made love in a cheery little rented room with dolphins and porpoises painted on the wall. She laughed and lifted her skirt, climbing atop his hips, taking his hands to her breasts through the open jacket. Lamplight shone on her happy face. Dolphins danced in her flickering shadow. The whole trip seemed like a pleasure cruise—or a honeymoon-cum–shopping expedition—not at all like a serious recon.

From Melos the run down to Atlantis ended in a slow row south across a last patch of blue enamel sea. Hours passed. The day grew hotter. Melos and Ios sank down behind them. A warm south headwind stirred the heat. Jake's navmatrix ticked off each passing klick, giving him a constantly updated ETA.

Minutes dwindled. Jake drifted to the bow, finding a spot behind the high prow. Love came with him. Sauromanta joined them. She was back in her Amazon jacket and hide pants, but she still wore the necklace he bought her.

Jake scanned the cloudless sky. Then he saw it, low on the horizon, a small dark column rising from the sea. It grew in his augmented vision, getting denser, darker. "There it is," he announced.

"Where?" Love looked intently, staring where he was staring. A call in Carian came from the masthead. The crew had spotted it too.

"Dead ahead," Jake pointed.

Love sighted along Jake's arm. "You're right, there she is." Sauromanta saw it, too. A vertical smudge on the cloudless horizon, best seen out the corner of your eye.

Through his corneal lenses it took on shape, becoming a pillar of smoke. "No way that's an island," Love declared.

Sauromanta agreed. "It's too tall."

Love looked at Jake. "So what *is* it?"

"It's a volcanic plume."

They watched in silence as the thread of smoke grew taller,

slowly widening at the base. "That's the top of the cone," Jake added.

Soon they could clearly see a miniature smoking mountain, sitting on the horizon. The south wind kept rising, becoming a sirocco, blowing the plume their way. Love breathed softly. "Imagine living under that."

Jake shook his head. "I can't."

"Look at the sucker smoke. She could blow anytime."

Sauromanta sounded solemn. "To live there is to put yourself in the hand of the Goddess." And what the Goddess gave, she could instantly take away.

As the smoking mountain grew, the plume seemed to recede, becoming less menacing compared to the mass of the mountain. But Jake knew that was an optical illusion. What awed him was not a wisp of smoke, but what that smoke signified. Here was a volcanic fissure, a weak spot in Mother Earth's thin crust. Beneath their feet was a huge sea of molten rock—larger than all the world's oceans—compressed by hideous pressure, working constantly on that flaw in the crust. At any time the crust could give, blowing that mountain and everyone on it to oblivion.

And it would blow. That was the one indisputable fact about Atlantis. One day the island would go up in an explosion three times bigger than Krakatoa. Bigger than all the nukes ever exploded. Scattering ashes around the world. There was nothing anyone could do about that—least of all Jake. He just aimed not to be there when it happened.

A white gleam appeared halfway up the peak. He had his lenses zoom in. Sitting on a shoulder of the smoking mountain was a white-columned portico. According to Anneke, this was the Maiden Shrine the Olympians had seized. Something Jake very much wanted to have a close look at. Too bad it sat on such an iffy spot.

Not that the place *looked* bad. The lower slopes of the volcano were so lush and green, Jake could see why the mountain had been dedicated to Callisto, the Beautiful One. Atlantis radiated a sense of doomed beauty, like a maiden that must in time grow old and die.

The island itself appeared, then gleaming tiers of city. Temples and houses rose row on row, extending back toward the lower slopes of the volcano like seats in a huge amphitheater.

Jake was astounded. This was just the port of Atlantis, and already it looked bigger than Babylon. Bigger than any known Bronze Age city. A giant mole lined with houses divided the harbor in half, anchored to a massive sea temple. Towering lighthouses marked the harbor entrances. Jake could see cargo ships at anchor, and fishing smacks working their nets in the lee of a lighthouse.

A cry came from the masthead, ''Ships to starboard.''

Jake spun about. Two long black shapes were standing out from the green coast. There seemed to be a lot of coastal traffic, but these weren't coasters coming to trade. Or shrimpers out to sell their catch. They had the look of warships—coming on fast.

He cursed himself for gawking at the sights when he should have been keeping watch. Focusing his augmented vision on the ships, he saw they were *pentekonters*, fifty-oared war galleys. Greek ones. Jake recognized the sun disk and laurel on their bow posts—sacred to Helios-Apollo.

He glanced toward the helm. The galley was already coming about. The captain had the steering oars hard over. Carians were letting out sail. Jake hurried back to the stern, telling the captain he wanted to keep clear of these warships.

The Carian dismissed his concern, confusing his Greek consonants and gender. ''Mistress Jag, they have not a slug's chance of catching us in this sea.''

By coming about, the captain had put the south wind on their port quarter. The *pentekonters* were showing no sails, and having to battle the heaving swells. With a stiff wind blowing, the merchant galley could easily exhaust the warships' rowers, then disappear at dusk.

The gap-toothed helmsman grinned over his shoulder at the long cranky *pentekonters* wallowing in the whitecaps. ''Look at 'em. Cryin' an' gnashing their teeth!'' He called out to the *pentekonters* in Carian, ''Go weepin' home ta Papa Apollo. You rosy-cocked, cattle-herding, boy-fucking Greeks!''

But Carian taunts soon turned sour. As Atlantis dipped down on the horizon, the sirocco died. The galley's huge mainsail boomed and flapped, then hung limp. Making it the helmsman's turn to weep. Waves magically slackened. The *pentekonters* came skimming over the glassy swells, like a pair of angry scorpions. Crimson oar blades flashed in the sun.

Running was pointless, and would merely leave the galley's oarsmen too tired to defend the ship. Sailors swung the main-yard around, using helmets and leather buckets to douse the sail with seawater, turning it into a sodden barrier against arrows and fire pots.

Love unshipped a big bullhide shield from its waterproof case. "Think it could be pirates?"

Jake shook his head. "Not likely this close to Atlantis." Privately, Jake feared things worse than pirates. Seeing Apollo's sun disk on their standards had him spooked.

Love shouldered his shield. "Whoever it is, we got ourselves a pissin' contest with a pair of *pentekonters*."

The Mouse God

Who made this feud? It was Apollo, son of Leto and Zeus.

—*Homer,* Iliad, Book I

The *pentekonters* came over the hot oily swell, decks dark with armed men. Sinister painted eyes, half-submerged by bow waves, glared from above the rams, alive with evil intent. Jake listened numbly to his compweb rattle off percentage chances on selected outcomes: maimed, crippled, drowned, or dead.

Unenviable choices. Jake hated battles. Even minor skirmishes in backwater periods where the methods of mass destruction were charmingly underdeveloped. He wished he was working some safe, sane time period—like the Late Neolithic, attending fertility orgies and teaching the locals to brew beer.

Crash helmet, plasti-armor, and Sauromanta's leopardskin shield were proof against primitive projectiles—but self-defense was not sufficient. Somehow the crew and passengers had to hold the galley against four times their numbers. Despite a well-publicized knack for art and poetry, Greeks often did ghastly things to prisoners—like cutting off their thumbs or throwing them overboard. Slavery could be the kindest fate awaiting the unwary stranger.

Bending down to buckle on a pair of greaves, Jake saw a thick line of breakers boiling up to starboard—as if a virgin reef were surfacing, spreading white water between them and the warships.

Incredible. Impossible really. His compweb had them in the open sea, with close to a kilometer of water under the keel.

The *pentekonters* bore down on this foam barrier, red oars dipping eagerly, ready to ride over the reef—but never actually reaching it. The line of breakers kept ahead of the warships, outpacing professional rowers.

Jacking up the gain on his lenses, Jake saw the reef separate into hundreds of leaping, splashing, gray-black bodies. A shoal of dolphins was making the sea boil, blowing white plumes of spray. He had never seen these playful sea mammals act so frantic—as though spooked by something below. Sharks perhaps, prowling after the warships in search of an easy meal.

"Let's git some." Love slapped Jake on the back and headed for the bow. Jake jealously longed for Love's fluid grace under fire. Love was lucky. In Laos he had seen worse. Much worse.

At arrow range, boarding parties crowded into the sterns of the *pentekonters* to raise their bows—the Greeks did not aim to sink their prize, merely wanting firm contact. Jake hurried to take position beside Sauromanta atop the deckhouse, covering her with the leopardskin shield.

She had her big distance bow drawn back to her ear, Scythian style. Greeks drew their bows only far as the chest, and assumed Amazons amputated a breast to shoot. A silly notion. Sauromanta let fly, sending an arrow thumming toward the nearer *pentekonter*. She could outshoot any Greek alive, without needing a mastectomy.

Her shaft caught an officer in the throat as he turned to encourage his men. Jake winced. That would only make the Greeks madder. She could empty her whole quiver and hardly reduce the odds against them. Their only hope was to turn them back when they tried to board.

He glanced anxiously at the Carians crouched behind the gunwales, clutching boarding pikes. Armed with riphooks and daggers for close-in work. Their captain, holding a shield and wearing his broad-brimmed hat, braced them with lurid tales of Greek atrocities. He finished with a plea to "send the pirates home on their shields." Meaning feetfirst.

Leaping dolphins parted. Sauromanta switched to her

lighter, rapid-fire bow—taking her last shot at point-blank range. Jake grabbed the deckhouse rail. With an appalling crack, a *pentekonter* slammed into the galley's starboard bow.

The deckhouse heeled drunkenly. Timbers shrieked. The ram rode up the thick wale at the galley's waterline. Boarders rushed forward behind a wall of shields, bringing down the ram, embedding it in the galley's side, turning it into a bridge.

Johnny Love leaped up to the forecastle to greet them. Crouched behind his big bullhide shield, he aimed his neural stunner under the rim, raking the legs of the boarders. The front rank collapsed. A couple hit the ram and bounced overboard, headed straight for the bottom, pulled down by bronze armor and paralyzed limbs.

Jake felt bad about that—they had not come all this way just to drown the locals. But such were the perils of piracy.

Sauromanta turned her fire on the second *pentekonter*, which aimed to grapple with the galley's stern. Jake rotated with her, assailed by slings and arrows, keeping his shield between them and the enemy. Sling pellets zipped by his ear with a Doppler whine, as Greek Davids tried to make his helmet ring.

Behind him he heard Carians cry, ''Fire!'' A horrible shout to hear aboard a wooden ship. Desperate Greeks were pitching fire onto the forecastle to harry the defenders.

Love would just have to deal with that. Jake had other worries. Arrows arched down to quiver in the deckhouse roof. He felt a flood of concern for Sauromanta, fighting in only her lynxskin cap. She was young and strong, able to trounce him at hand-to-hand combat, but still he feared for her. He had brought her here. And making love had made him feel *more* responsible. The idiotic personal sense of invincibility that Jake drew around himself in dire moments did not extend to her. He could well picture himself sobbing over her body.

A javelin thudded into Jake's shield, jarring his teeth. Making the threat here-and-now, without a spare moment for useless imagining. Beneath a rain of darts, the second *pentekonter* banged into the galley's stern. Grapples snaked through the air, biting into the deck. Carians slashed at the lines with long-handled scythes, as Greek sailors drove daggers into the galley's bulwarks to use as footholds.

Too bad Herc was not there to greet them.

An ugly mob of Greeks bounded forward behind locked shields, shouting their paean. Corneal lenses showed bearded faces, some set and glowering, others fearful, or fixed with lunatic grins. The line of spears had big leaf-shaped bronze blades, sharp as cleavers, and set to fillet him.

Time to take action. Jake flicked the safety on an anesthetic grenade, lobbing it gently onto the *pentekonter's* forecastle. The grenade hit, bounced, and skidded into the open thwarts, landing among the oarsmen. Goddamn gutter ball.

His second bowl was a strike, lodging against the low forecastle rail, spewing anesthetic gas, laying an invisible barrier between the ships.

Boarders crumpled into a comatose pile in the bows, shields and spears askew, taken out like tenpins.

With a heartfelt hurrah, Carians cut the grapple lines. Using their oars to shove the warship off. The *pentekonter* made a halfhearted attempt to come about and try again, but Jake could see the grenades taking effect. Oars slumped or missed stroke as gas spread through the packed hull, putting rowers to sleep.

Sauromanta drew her ax and leaped down from the deckhouse, bounding over the oar benches to help out Johnny Love. Jake dashed after her, shield in hand. Carians huddled in the bilges gave a cheer. Sauromanta at full stretch was a stirring sight.

But by the time they got to the blackened forecastle, the fight there was over. And the fire was out, smothered by wet cloaks and buckets of sand. Wielding heavy bronze axes, the Carians cut the ram free from the shattered bulwarks.

The Greeks backwatered—no longer eager to tackle a ship defended by invisible forces. For Bronze Age seamen, divine intervention was a daily thing, and this galley clearly had potent gods on her side. Carians yelled insults at the retreating Greeks. Not a sailor on the galley had been scratched, aside from one born fool who broke a toe by dropping his shield on his foot.

Jake stood drenched with exertion, barely believing the battle was over, and the Greeks beaten back. All he had to show for it was a bad sweat. Love grinned at him, eyes alight, "God damn. For a moment there it was all happenin' in Cinemascope. *Definitely* number one!"

Seeing Sauromanta, Love shouted, "Damn, gal, don't tell *me* that wasn't number one!"

He said it in English, but the Amazon grinned back.

Leftover adrenaline *did* give the world a "great to be alive" dazzle. Sun and sea sparkled. Even the dolphins looked delighted, leaping and cavorting, turning cartwheels against a lapis sky, a heaven so blue it took Jake's breath away.

Smack in the midst of his adrenal rush, Jake saw a gray shape break the surface. It slid out of the glassy sea, dripping foam and scattering the dolphin summer Olympics. He stood rooted, recognizing the rounded hull and antenna-cum-periscope. It wasn't a whale, or a magic reef, or some unrecorded sea monster. It was the *Thetis*. Water cascaded off the curved deck, glittering in the sun.

Love swore softly, "Shit, I purely do *hate* surprises."

They had left the minisub back on the Egyptian coast, hiding in the west harbor at Rhacotis. To have it appear now, no longer under their control, meant serious trouble. The fix was in. At very least their cover was completely blown. The opposition knew about them, and their sub. And was all set to use *Thetis* against them.

Sauromanta's eyes narrowed, and she shifted her ax.

Love looked over at him. "Man, this is fourth and long. Time to special team 'em. Punch S-T-O-P."

Jake had a sick sense it was much too late. But he thumbed his communicator anyway, sending out a Mayday. They could at least warn Wasserman that something had gone horribly amiss. The signal went out, a compact scrambled summary of the situation. But Wasserman would need many hours to get there from Hibernia Base. In the meantime he would not even bother to acknowledge Jake's distress signal, for fear of giving his own presence and position away. Until the *Argo* actually showed, they were on their own.

The *pentekonters* hove to. Far from being beaten, the Greeks were only waiting for their own divine backup to take a whack at the galley.

Jake's compweb sounded a warning, "CRAFT APPROACHING FAST. BEARING ONE-THREE-ZERO."

He spun about. A bright spark was headed their way, coming from the direction of Atlantis, skimming the wave tops. Fiery rotors whipped up circles of spray, accompanied by a familiar whine of turbines. A STOP hovercar.

Love whistled. "Make that fourth and *very* long."

Odds against them mounted rapidly. Jake wondered what hope they had of holding out until *Argo* arrived? His compweb rattled off probabilities that translated out as, "Not much."

As the whap-whap of rotors grew louder, *Thetis*'s cargo hatch slid silently aside, leaving a yawning gap in the gray hull.

Dogs tumbled out of the gap in the hull, leaping from the sub into the water. Ugly brutes with red ears, flat disk eyes, and steel jaws. Seven were gray, one spotted, and two particolored. Big paddle-shaped paws propelled them furiously toward the galley.

As they came on, Jake's compweb tried to calculate where such creatures could have come from. Claws and jaws looked like chrome steel, but their bodies seemed to be some sort of duro-plastic, light enough to float.

Just when it seemed that things could not get any more surreal the hovercar dipped down, the roar of rotors rising to blank all other sounds. Amid the howl of propwash, a naked sun-bronzed young man leaped out of the hovercar onto the deck, holding a bow and quiver. His limbs, muscles, and torso tapered perfectly—the sculptor's ideal of the male form. Tall and honey blonde, with a long impudent penis swinging from its yellow nest. He wore arm rings and a soft gray mouseskin cap. Wild unshorn hair danced in the whirling propwash.

But his face was what shocked Jake, sending his estimates of survival into an alarming nosedive.

"Shit," Love shouted over the propwash. "Where have we seen that self-satisfied smirk before?"

The golden god in the mouseskin cap looked exactly like a male version of Dianna, the *Argo*'s STOP commander. Either a cosmic coincidence, or a sure sign that help would not be on the way.

Telling his compweb to lock on target, Jake tried his stunner. No effect. His compweb swiftly diagnosed the problem. Dianna's look-alike wore a disrupter on his arm, nullifying the neural charge. Standard STOP equipment. Jake, Love, and Sauromanta all wore them, along with nasal gas filters—to keep your own side's weapons from knocking you out in a melee. Locals, even handsome godly ones, weren't supposed to have them.

The dogs from the sub hit the side of the ship, climbing the bulwarks on chrome claws.

Carians scrambled for safety. Their lame captain, caught in the front rank, could not limp out of the way. Steel jaws closed on his legs, arms, throat, and belly, all ripping at once. He barely had time to shriek before being torn apart. Red rags of flesh and still-twitching limbs landed on the deck beside his broad-brimmed hat.

Sickened, Jake watched the Carians throw away their pikes and riphooks, falling to their knees before the naked bowman, prostrating themselves. Calling him Helios-Apollo, groveling for mercy.

Love looked over his shield rim at Jake, saying nothing. He had seen enough lost battles to know they were beaten. Jake just tried to keep his own shield between Sauromanta and the dogs. His stunner had failed to take down Apollo and was bound to be just as useless against the plasti-steel dogs.

There was a thump as a *pentekonter* swung back alongside. Greeks scrambled aboard. This time the Carians made no move to stop them.

Nor did Jake. He had sent off his call to Wasserman. All he could do was hang on until help arrived—if it was even coming. Seeing that Phoebus Apollo was a male double for the mission's STOP commander did not bode well for future rescue. His compweb quoted appallingly small odds of coming through this alive.

Without warning, Sauromanta stepped forward. Hefting her ax, she shouted, "Mouse Dung, call off your dogs." Apollo had begun his career as a Delian mouse-demon, one of Zeus's innumerable bastards.

The blond god strummed his bow, searching idly through his quiver, asking the Amazon, "What death do you want?" The quiver held a more varied assortment of Hercules' hypodermic arrows. Their feathers formed a rainbow array. "Red arrows are for heart failure. Yellow ones carry plague and fever. Black gives you instant stroke. Gray is for paralysis, one scratch and you'll waste away on your back."

Sauromanta snorted. "Put away your poison arrows. If I must die, let it be fairly, by your own hand."

The blond god laughed. "I am Phoebus Apollo. There can be no fairness between gods and mortals."

Jake seized Sauromanta's arm, trying to drag her back behind the shield. "Don't. He'll kill you."

Her blue eyes flashed. "And giving in will save us?" She had him there. The Greeks had no Geneva Convention. Rape and slavery were standard treatment for pretty young prisoners—male or female. Sauromanta had no desire to live on as some Greek's bedmate and domestic drudge.

Jake let go of her arm, slipping the shield off his shoulder, handing it to her, feeling helpless.

She took the leopardskin shield, at the same time drawing him closer. "Trust me to win," she whispered. Then she kissed him, long and on the lips. He felt her living warmth in his arms, her tongue in his mouth, and smelled the spices on her skin—for what looked to be that last time. Then she let go.

She turned to Love. He had scooped a fallen spear off the deck. "Take this," he told her.

Taking the spear in her shield hand, she reached up with her right, pulling his head down to her lips, kissing him, too. When she let go the airborne trooper's face looked grim. "Fuck, gal, watch yer ass. He's gonna try an' trick you."

She smiled up at Love. "I know." Shifting the spear into her right hand, she turned to face Apollo.

The god laughed. "A pity to make dog's meat out of such a pretty bitch."

Jake watched Apollo make light of the contest, handing his bow and quiver to a Greek, borrowing a brass-studded corselet, a pair of sharp spears, and a bronze-backed shield. If this nonchalance was meant to intimidate Sauromanta, it failed. She stood waiting, grimly amused.

When he was ready, Apollo stepped forward, hefting one spear, holding the other in his shield hand.

Sauromanta knelt for a moment in prayer, calling on the goddess Hestia, head of the Scythian pantheon:

Hearth Maiden,
Protector of Women,
Guide my spear,
Accept my Sacrifice.

Humble this Mouse-Demon,
Who claims to be a God.

Then she sprang lightly to her feet, her leopardskin shield before her, looking as grave as a priestess at the altar. Greeks and Carians backed off, giving the Amazon and the Mouse God room to work.

Horrified, Jake watched them dodge and feint on the narrow deck. Apollo's two spears gave him two casts to Sauromanta's one—but the Amazon had her ax for infighting. She advanced slowly, waiting for the god to use his extra throw. Apollo jabbed playfully from behind his heavy shield. Greeks shouted insults at the girl, waving their weapons to distract her. Sportsmanship had yet to be invented.

Suddenly the Mouse God threw, fast and brutal.

Sauromanta leaped sideways. The spear sailed past, ripping clean through the deckhouse to stand quivering in the sternpost. Had she tried to block with her shield, she would have been dead.

Apollo's miss silenced the Greeks. Advantage had shifted. Now it was spear against spear, but Sauromanta had her ax as well, a double-edged chopping tool, perfect for such confined quarters—able to take off a wrist or sever a tendon. The Amazon could risk a throw. If she missed, her ax could still get under Apollo's guard. The Mouse God had hang on to his spear, having neither sword nor dagger.

Sauromanta feinted twice, and then threw, lunging forward, putting all her strength behind the throw.

Apollo's countercast caught everyone off guard. No one expected him to give up his last weapon.

Sauromanta flung up her shield. The spear ripped through the leopardskin front, and the layers of bullhide behind, cutting her shoulder strap, carrying away her lynxskin cap, nearly taking off her head. She rolled onto the deck, losing her shield, but coming up alive.

Her own throw had been stopped by Apollo's shield, but that hardly mattered. The Mouse God was disarmed.

Love gave a hoot of triumph. Jake gripped his stunner, hardly daring to hope.

Sauromanta's faced remained set. Capless, she shook blond

hair out of her eyes, dancing forward, determined to close. Her ax cut soft circles in the air.

"Get him," Love hissed. "Don't fiddle with the fucker."

Apollo grinned inanely over his shield rim. Jake could hardly understand his good humor. Apollo had only his shield and fancy armor, against an agile young woman and a sharp steel ax—able to cleave bronze and bullhide like butter.

But Apollo acted like he had the advantage. Lifting his head, the Mouse God called out. "Father Zeus, aid my arm."

His right arm went behind his shield, then made a dramatic flourish. A slim steel javelin appeared in his palm, chrome-plated and needle-sharp. Before Sauromanta could recover, he threw, shouting, "Uncle Hades, take this bothersome bitch."

Sauromanta had no reason to expect a throw, no chance to dodge. The shaft caught her full in the stomach, piercing her jacket, a hand's span of bloody point protruding from her back.

Flung backwards by the impact, Sauromanta skidded across the deck. She landed gasping at Jake's feet, bent double, clutching at the shaft in her middle. Bright red blood poured over the deck.

Part II
Sea of Grass

The Gods Themselves

Do not hope to equal the gods. The immortals are one race, those that walk the earth are another . . .

—Homer, Iliad, *Book V*

Jake gave an anguished shout. Telling Love to cover him, he knelt over Sauromanta, going to work with his medikit. She was unconscious, in deep shock, sinking fast—dying. One hand clutched the steel spear in her midriff.

Strapping the medikit to her arm, Jake ordered an antishock injection, then did his best to disinfect the wound. Careful not to move the spear, he managed to staunch the flow of blood. Tears rolled down his cheeks as he struggled to keep her alive ignoring armed Greeks, hideous steel-jawed dogs, and the death-dealing god.

The medikit reported massive internal hemorrhage, demanding she be moved at once to an autodoc. So far as he knew, there was only a single functioning autodoc in the entire Bronze Age—the one aboard the *Argo*, headed this way from Hibernia Base. Hours away at best. Maybe days.

Love stood over him, covering them both with his shield. Apollo, the supposed God of Healing, looked on, amused by Jake's efforts. Jake told the medikit to do without the autodoc. "Stabilize her condition, you bioelectronic lamebrain, or I'll smash you into microchips."

The medikit flashed back, "NULL PROGRAM."

He looked up at Apollo. "Do something."

Apollo smirked. "She chose death."

Jake wept in terror and frustration, watching her indicators sink. Sauromanta slipped rapidly away. She needed a miracle. Something, anything. But it had to be *now*.

Love shook Jake's shoulder. "Look, man! It's the *Argo*."

Jake looked up, hardly believing it—but there was the airship. Nosing down from the north, coming in low, like some heaven-sent hallucination. There was no way Wasserman could have gunned it all the way from Ireland in answer to his call. *Argo* had to have been already on the scene—hull down, just below the horizon.

Dumbfounded, Jake did not question how this could have happened. Sauromanta now had a ghost of a chance. If the STOP team hit the scene fast, smothered the opposition, and spirited the wounded Amazon up to the ship.

As he watched, *Argo*'s hangar doors opened and ultralights tumbled out, their parasails blossoming in midair. It was the STOP team coming down fast. Apollo was in for a rude surprise.

Instantly Jake was on the comlink, shouting, "MEDICAL EMERGENCY! ARMED OPPOSITION!"

Emiko answered him, "Identify opposition."

"All around me," he replied. "Two warships, armed Greeks, and ten mechanical dogs. Plus *Thetis* in enemy hands. Sauromanta is down, dying. Fix on my position."

"Fixing on you," Emiko replied. Help was hurtling toward them. He could see the ultralights shifting formation, bringing Doc Hathaway out of the center, pairing him with the leader.

But that was not near enough to save Sauromanta. They had to get her aboard the *Argo*. "Get the goddamn hovercar going," Jake demanded.

As if in answer to his call, the hovercar shot out of the hangar, roaring into action. Miracles were happening—seemingly on order—but everything had to break really right . . .

Jake had his compweb estimate chances. Hopefully the hovercar could cut through the opposition, and make a pickup, covered by the STOP team. It might work. It had to.

As the hovercar drew level with the team, it banked.

"Don't slow," Jake shouted.

The hovercar did not answer. Instead it continued to bank, careening toward the descending ultralights. Jake watched in horrified disbelief as the hovercar hit the rear of the formation, shattering parasails, sending team members tumbling toward the water.

"TRAFFIC EMERGENCY," Emiko shouted. "Pull up, Dianna."

The hovercar did not pull up. Instead it banked and twisted, methodically using its jet-driven rotors to chop at the ultralights, swatting them down one by one. Ripping through the formation, the hovercar turned back to get those it had missed. Jake heard Hathaway curse as his ultralight was hit. The medic who might have saved Sauromanta could not save himself.

Emiko, the last one in the air, did not wait to be hit. She calmly announced she was bailing out. Jake saw her separate from her craft, still several hundred meters up. She spread her arms to slow her fall—then tucked as she approached the water. She hit with a splash, amid a rain of debris.

Apollo laughed and snapped his thumb. "Get her."

Two of his dogs dived overboard, swimming swiftly toward the point of impact. Jake saw Emiko surface, her crash suit inflated. She looked to be conscious.

"Look out," he shouted. "Two dogs headed your way."

"Thanks," she replied, without even a sputter. Emiko had incredible presence—especially after seeing her team ripped to shreds. She started to swim, making for the galley. Where else was there to go?

Before she was halfway, the dogs caught her. There was a gasp and sputter as the dogs pulled her under, then dead silence on the comlink. In a matter of minutes four women and two men had died. An entire STOP team wiped out.

Almost. One member remained alive. The *Argo*'s hovercar swung low over the ship, hanging on its propwash like a deadly dragonfly. Jake braced himself for more horror. The last act in a cruel drama—when the god comes down on a machine and bodies litter the stage.

Dianna leaped out. No longer wearing her STOP suit, she was dressed in a saffron hunting tunic with a red hem, and she carried a silver-moon bow and a quiver full of deadly rainbow arrows. Seen together, her face was absolutely the same as Apollo's—both had the same beautifully sculpted looks and wolf brown eyes. Only Dianna's hair was longer, hanging loosely down her back. There was hardly a hand's span of difference between them in height.

"Welcome, big sister." Apollo pecked her on the cheek.

Then the god strode over to where Jake sat with Sauromanta. He made a short mocking bow, then reached for the steel spear. "This, I believe, is mine."

Jake held tight to Sauromanta. "Damn you, leave her alone." Drawing out the spear would finish her.

Apollo tut-tutted. "I only want what's mine."

"It will kill her."

"She chose death." He reached for the shining spear.

Jake rose to stop him. In one swift movement, Dianna drew a gray-fletched arrow, nocked it, drew back, and released.

Jake's compweb rang a warning, but he had no time to react. The arrow hit him in the thigh, seeming to sprout suddenly from the flesh above his knee.

His leg buckled. He sprawled forward, unable to rise. He could see and hear, but not move a muscle. One leg lay across Sauromanta, who felt alarmingly cold and limp. He tried to twist about, to see the medikit on her arm.

Love shouted from somewhere above him, "Damn you, Dianna."

"I am Artemis," she replied icily. "Address me as a goddess."

"Bitch. I don't care if yer fuckin' Snow White."

Jake's compweb reported another incoming arrow. Love pitched forward, landing on the far side of Sauromanta, a gray-fletched shaft in his calf.

Apollo whistled up the pack. "Drag them to the chariot."

Red-eared plasti-steel hounds bounded up, seized Love by the flak jacket, and started to haul him toward the aircar.

Apollo stepped over Jake, planted a sandaled foot on Sauromanta, and grasped the javelin. He yanked it out. Jake felt her body convulse with the pull. The medikit screamed a warning, then went silent. She was dead.

"Toss her overboard," Apollo commanded.

Dogs dragged Jake across the deck to the hovercar. Apollo picked him up, tossing him atop Love, who was lying paralyzed on the floor of the car. All Jake could think about was Sauromanta. How alive she had been. How brave and honorable. How full of love. And he had brought her to this. A useless death. Her strong, beautiful body tossed into the sea. Joining Emiko and the others. Even his own imminent demise did not bother him half so much.

Apollo leaped aboard the hovercar. Producing a square of silk, he wiped Sauromanta's blood from the javelin. Jake saw that the weapon was made of small segments, each progressively slimmer, ending in a needle point. Apollo twisted the base segment—the weapon collapsed neatly into itself. He was left holding a small silver baton, which he tucked into his corselet.

The Sun God bent down, relieved them of their neural stunners, then disappeared forward. The hovercar took off.

Jake lay atop Love, staring at nothing. Fiery arcs from the rotor blades cut through his field of vision. Beyond them he saw only vast, colossal emptiness. On the far side of the uncaring sky lay a universe that had no Home Period. No Peg. And now no Sauromanta.

His compweb insisted on spouting meaningless data. Course estimates. Altitude readings. A huge object approached, identified as the *Argo*. He ignored it. He was beaten. The gods had triumphed over love, beauty, and honor. Only physical paralysis kept him from sobbing.

The gray hull of the *Argo* appeared, blotting out the sky. The hangar deck yawned wide, swallowing them up. Rotors stopped with a thump. They were aboard.

He was dumped out on the deck, along with Love. Inertial sensors told him the airship was turning, and accelerating, heading on a new bearing—THREE-FIVE-ZERO. Almost due north. Not that it meant much.

His compweb sounded a warning, accompanied by the click of chrome claws. The dogs reappeared. Steel jaws dragged him across the hangar deck and into a storage locker, then let him drop—alongside Love. He heard the click of the dogs' claws retreating. The door cycled closed, and the locker went black.

Black but not empty. Behind him, someone was sobbing softly. There was a scraping shuffle. His compweb warned him that a person was approaching.

His arm lifted. Someone strapped a medikit to it. There was a soft stab of pain, spreading antidotes and stimulants through his system. He could move again. But he didn't. He stayed limp, not caring to respond, seeing nothing but blackness.

Whoever had strapped on the medikit shook him, whispering, "Jake."

A woman's voice. Tyler, the rigger's mate who had slept with Hercules, was trying to wake him. He turned to look, seeing tear-stained features etched in infrared. Tyler was not the one crying—but she had been. She squeezed his arm. "It's so good you are alive." Jake did not agree. But he could tell by her voice *she* really meant it.

Tyler moved over to where Love lay. Soon he was stirring, too. "What's happening out there?" Tyler whispered.

Love snorted, "Woman, you don't want to know."

"That bad?"

"Worse."

"What about the STOP team."

"All dead. Unless you count Dianna. Only now she's a goddamn bitch goddess with a bow."

"She killed Keane," Tyler told him. "Shot her when Keane tried to stop her from taking over."

Jake recognized the sobbing in the rear of the locker. It was DePala, the young helmsmate who had been Keane's lover. Jake's heart went out to her, knowing *just* how she felt.

"What about Wasserman?" Love demanded.

"We haven't heard from him. Not since he gave orders to head for Atlantis."

"What about Chief Larsen and the bosun?"

"They were both taken at the same time we were."

"Shit, seems like they made a clean sweep." With the possible exception of Wasserman, the entire crew of the *Argo* was killed or captured, as well as the STOP team. Dianna/Artemis had done most of it. Maybe she was a goddess.

Jake's inertial sensors told him *Argo* was slowing. The door cycled, and the locker flooded with light.

Tyler blinked. Her face was not only tear-stained, but was also smeared with blood. So were her hands. Sauromanta's blood. Jake's arms were covered with it, and she had gotten it on herself when she put the medikit on him.

Love looked grim. Tears still rolled down DePala's cheeks.

Jake had expected to see Apollo sneering in the doorway. Instead a naked boy stood waiting. Perhaps the most beautiful youth Jake had ever seen, with clear blue eyes, frank sensitive features, firm tan skin, and soft downy pubic hairs. As beautiful a boy as Apollo was a man. He held a long-stemmed *kylix* cup.

"May I help?" he asked, looking wide-eyed at the blood.

No one answered.

He held up the cup. "Is anyone hurt? I have water."

Tyler took the cup. "Yes. Please. Water would be wonderful."

Jake pulled himself to his feet. Something stank outside. Wafting in from the hangar deck was a musty compound of fresh urine and stale sex, mixed with the worst crotch odors of men and goats. Jake stumbled out to meet the smell.

The boy helped him, saying, "My name is Hyacinth. Are you wounded?"

Jake shook his head. Hyacinth seemed a shade regretful not to be tending a battle wound.

Waiting outside on the hangar deck was the source of the foul odor, a weird compound creature. From the legs up he was a man, bare-chested, with dark matted hair, a spade beard, and curling horns on his brow. From the hips down he had the legs of a large black goat, with shaggy hair and cloven hooves. A stubby tail sprouted above his hairy buttocks. One of the most bizarre pieces of biosculpting Jake had ever seen.

With him were the plasti-metal dogs, stilling any faint hopes of escape.

Hangar doors stood open behind the goatman in a vain attempt to air out the hideous smell. Jake could make out thin clouds, blue sky, and islands ahead, lying like puzzle pieces on the blue-green sea.

The women came out behind him. Tyler, still bloody and tear-stained, half supported the sobbing DePala.

Goat Legs grinned, spreading his hips to reveal a stupendous erection. "Would either of you ladies have something to fit this?"

Hyacinth nodded toward the goat man. "Meet the Great God Pan." His tone indicated he did not consider Pan much of a god at all.

Two tall blond women came up. They looked to be Hyperborean, with blue face tattoos, like Jake had seen in Britain. Hyacinth introduced them as Hecaerge and Opis, telling them to take charge of the Tyler and DePala. "Bathe them. See that Pan does not break in on you."

Pan sneered at the boy. "Beastly little fag. Just because you are afraid of pussy, must you spoil it for everyone?"

The Hyperborean nymphs hustled the women away. Hyacinth himself led Jake and Love to a decontamination shower on the hangar deck. Pan trotted behind on his goat legs, blackguarding Apollo for putting a pansy in charge of the ship. "How's a real man supposed to exercise his cock around here?"

Hyacinth ignored him, helping them with the shower, asking what the battle had been like. "Was there much of a fight?"

"Too much," Love told him. "More than you want to know."

The boy nodded soberly. "I suppose so. Luckily Apollo does not let me see such things." He sounded less than half-convinced, but had the good grace to shut up. Bundling up Jake's bloody clothes, he laid out a fresh tunic. Love was not giving up his fatigues and flak jacket.

Jake watched the bloody outfit go down a disposal. The last bit of Sauromanta had been washed from him. She was gone.

The boy led them to the midline slidewalk. Pan came, too, bringing the pack. As they approached the forebridge, Hyacinth whispered, "Be careful. Artemis is back. Don't do anything to anger her. She is kind to children, but hates grown men. A Boeotian prince once saw her bathing in a stream—she had his own dogs tear him apart." Hyacinth seemed happy not to be fully grown, still able to appeal to Artemis's good side.

Tyler and DePala joined them on the slidewalk, dressed in fresh chitons. They went in together.

The Unheavenly Twins were waiting, posed against a sweeping backdrop of sea and islands—the nearest land was a light brown irregular squiggle lying on the sea. Jake's navmatrix instantly identified Delos, Apollo's home isle, nearly due north of Atlantis. He could make out Mount Kynthos and the Sacred Harbor.

Just offshore Jake saw the outlines of a sunken temple. A small twenty-oared galley passed right above the undersea shrine, headed for the harbor mouth.

Artemis fixed immediately on the women, pointing to

DePala. ''That one is a virgin. Entitled to my protection, unless you have raped her already.''

DePala glared, showing how little she valued Dianna's protection.

Apollo shrugged. ''I've been busy, big sister.'' According to the myths, Artemis was the older. As goddess of childbirth, she helped deliver her twin, bare minutes after she herself was born.

''Has he touched either of you?'' Artemis asked.

Tyler said he had not.

''He's forever trying to fuck my maidens. He knows I hate it, but he has the looks. And licking ambrosia off his godlike prick makes you immortal. Some girls are tempted.''

She smiled at DePala. ''But I doubt we'll have that problem with you.''

DePala muttered that she would rather die first. The only words Jake had heard her speak.

''That's the spirit.'' Artemis applauded.

Whoever these people were, they took their roles seriously. Apollo was every bit the son of Zeus, even more full of himself than Hercules. Pan played the leering satyr to perfection. Artemis/Dianna acted cool and deadly.

Jake did not doubt that Artemis and Apollo were true twins, born brother and sister, showing the same quick, active temper, and complete self-absorption. Without that natural bond they would have been enemies. Apollo was a poser, urbane, inventive, very male, and highly sexed, ready to spread his seed far and wide. Bisexual, too, if Hyacinth was his boy toy. Artemis was his near opposite, elemental, willful, almost sexless. Like Keane had said, virgin to the core.

Apollo looked at Jake and Love. ''And these two?''

''They are not part of the flight crew,'' Artemis told him. Apollo, God of Wisdom, did not appear to be all-knowing. His sister was still bringing him up to speed on the *Argo*.

Pulling the recorder out of Love's pocket, Apollo thumbed a switch. Bessie Smith began singing ''Beale Street Mama.''

Apollo smiled. ''Music. One of my best inventions.''

Pan grinned. ''Right beside buggery.'' He was not taking Apollo's claim too seriously.

Apollo stuck the recorder back in Love's pocket, still playing. ''Perhaps they have uses,'' he suggested.

"I doubt it." Artemis looked at Love. "Would you serve us faithfully?"

Love snorted. "No can do, Madame Nhu."

"Madame who?" Apollo looked puzzled.

"He is mocking you." Artemis made it sound like sacrilege.

Apollo looked coolly at Love. "Be wise, and show respect. You are our prisoners."

Love snapped back in English. "Yea, but we aim to escape. You'll *always* be assholes."

His tone needed no translation. Apollo gestured to Artemis. "Take them."

The *Argo*'s former STOP commander turned to Jake, with an exasperated look, dropping her goddess guise. For just a moment, she seemed to be the old Dianna—cool, calm, and professional. "No doubt you think me cruel."

"No doubt," Jake replied. Inhuman was nearer the mark, but she would probably consider that a compliment.

"You'll never know how much it cost me, pretending to be mortal, swallowing insults and orders. But that is at an end."

She looked at Love. "Luckily for you, we are landing at Delos. It is a sacred isle—my brother's birthplace. No other births are allowed there. And no *deaths*."

Delos sounded like Jake's kind of place. Giving them a one-stop reprieve.

"Take them back to their hole," Artemis decided. "I'll dispose of them when we get to the mainland."

Pan whistled up the steel-jawed pack. Artemis looked admiringly at the plasti-metal dogs. "What wonderful animals. Better than the hounds that tore Prince Actaeon apart."

Pan instantly offered up the pack. "Here, they are yours." God or not, Pan respected her silver bow. He would taunt Apollo—but was happy as Hyacinth to get on Artemis's good side.

She smiled her thanks. "If only I can somehow get the smell off them."

Artemis's new pack dragged Jake and Love back to the hangar deck. A half dozen blue-tattooed Hyperboreans were there—big British savages armed with bows and bronze axes. They helped stuff Jake and Love back into the locker. The door cycled closed, leaving them alone in blackness. Bessie Smith softly sang the blues in Love's pocket—"Baby Have Pity on Me."

Miletus

Miletus was mighty—long ago.

—*Greek proverb*

Jake sat in darkness, feeling twenty thousand years out-of-date. His attempt to crack the Bronze Age was as big a disaster as the previous four. Bigger even. He had more warning, more time to prepare—yet he had done every bit as badly. From the moment he arrived here-and-now, the ''gods'' had been playing with him, waiting patiently, then casually springing their trap. Swatting down a crack STOP team like so many mosquitoes. What had Gloucester said in *King Lear*? His compweb supplied the lines: ''AS FLIES TO WANTON BOYS, ARE WE TO THE GODS; THEY KILL US FOR THEIR SPORT.''

Only he had killed Sauromanta. As sure as if he had thrown the spear—putting her in a time and place where death was her only out.

He did it by letting his guard down, acting like a lovestruck idiot on a slow boat to Atlantis. Making love and enjoying the scenery, when he should have been expecting the unexpected. If he had resisted temptation and stuck to his task, Sauromanta could still be alive.

''You're missin' her, aren't you?'' Love sat in the dark, reading his mind.

He did not answer.

"You're missin' her. I can tell."

Jake stayed silent.

"Louder please."

Still no answer.

"Git yer shit straight. She would not be wantin' us to give up."

"Let it rest," Jake whispered.

"Well she wouldn't."

"Shut up."

"Damn." Love shifted position in the dark. "I wish she were here instead of you. Damn it, I purely do. She would not be moping in a corner. Not her. She was a fighter. She'd be aimin' to be gettin' 'em back."

Jake looked over at him. Love's black skin shone in the dark on infrared. "We agree on one thing."

"What's that?"

"I wish she were here instead of *you*."

Love laughed. "That's it! Get mad. Get stoked. Get even."

Right. But how? Getting out of the locker would not be so hard. Then what? Take on the Unheavenly Twins, and their dog pack bare-handed? Escape would not be easy. Even if they got off the ship, Delos was a very small island. Smallest of the Cyclades. There was nowhere to run to. What would they do? Steal a boat? Hijack the *Argo*? Make a swim for it?

Better to take advantage of the Delos stay of execution and try to escape at the next stop. Besides, that gave him an excuse to sulk.

"Lookit, life just took a big shit on us. Right?"

"You could say so."

"Well don't fret. We'll make it. God'll think of something."

Sure thing. Jake knew he was not up against real gods. Apollo and Artemis had been all too human. So was Pan. The horns, hooves, and goat legs were simple skeletal grafts. Not even as hard as growing a two-headed *T. rex*. Creating that god-awful odor was the tricky part. But not being gods did not make them pushovers. They had played him to perfection. Using Jake as neatly as if he had been a local—to be tricked, lied to, then discarded when no longer needed.

Jake had seen gangs from the future before—slavers and

antique dealers out to loot the past, cheerfully posing as gods or wizards. This was something far more dangerous. Dianna had joined the team in Home Period. So STOP itself was thoroughly infiltrated. Wasserman was probably in it, too. No wonder they were aghast when he brought Hercules aboard, avoiding him like herpes. He would have recognized the "gods" at once—and being Hercules, would have broadcast it immediately.

Jake tried to limit contamination by excluding the old FTL organization—but all the time the gods had been snickering up their sleeves. Letting him get all the way to the Aegean before grabbing everything he had brought. Jake's "rescue" expedition had been a huge, heavenly shopping trip.

When he was not beating himself for his stupidity, Jake was reliving his misspent life. Total recall meant he never had to be bored, or lonely. All the best bits were on file in his compweb. Like the first time he made love with Peg, halfway up a giant sequoia in Mesozoic New Mexico, with an *Alamosaurus* shaking the tree. Or winning at high-stakes poker on a Mississippi riverboat, with Mark Twain turning the cards. All the bad, embarrassing parts were edited out. Like the stupendous airship crash that landed them in that sequoia. Or the gang of Arkansas river rats that collared him after the card game. Virtual love. Virtual sex. Exciting stuff when you are being kept in a dark hole on skimpy rations with a clay pot for a toilet.

Only his memories of Sauromanta were too painful to be replayed.

Whatever business Apollo had at his birthplace took the better part of a month. They lifted off late on the twenty-eighth day of their incarceration. And *Argo* surprised Jake by heading almost due east. Bearing ZERO-EIGHT-EIGHT. Directly away from Greece, headed for Asia. Jake's inertial detectors picked up occasional turbulence and variable headwinds. Landfall was just before dusk, local time.

Love felt the airship settling down. "Where are we, laser brain?"

Jake listened for the snap of grapples. "Best estimate is that we crossed the coast south of Miletus. Can't be too far inland; we bucked headwinds the whole way."

"So what do you think?" Love eyed the hatch nervously.

Delos was history. At any time the hatch could open and they could be hauled out and killed.

"I'd say it's a good place to get off."

"You're forgetting we got to get through that door."

"I'm not forgettin' nothin'." Jake gave the ship several hours to quiet down. Then he slid over to the door and listened. The hangar deck sounded empty.

His compweb merged easily with the electronic lock. All onboard systems were hardwired to obey him—a fail-safe measure Jake had built into *Argo* and *Thetis*. First he ordered the lock to shut off its alarms, and continue to transmit a CLOSED signal. Then he ordered the door to cycle.

Light flooded the little space. Love was grinning. Jake hardly recognized the hangar deck. Apollo had redecorated, turning the hangar into a spacious atrium with a sandy floor and a sky-blue ceiling.

Port and starboard bulkheads were decorated with matching frescoes showing the horses of the sun being hitched to their chariot at dawn, and brought into their stables at dusk. The decontamination shower had become a fountain, with a life-size statue of Apollo, done in stiff Egyptian fashion, holding his bow and tortoiseshell lyre like Pharaoh's crook and flail. A thin stream of water spouted from his bronze penis to splash in a mother-of-pearl basin.

Despite the new decor, the place still smelled badly of Pan. "Pew," Love whispered. "That Pan dude could use some aroma therapy."

Jake had toyed with the notion of taking over the ship. But going up unarmed against Apollo, Artemis, and that murderous dog pack seemed like an overelaborate form of suicide. Even in his depressed state escape seemed more prudent. And since the STOP hovercar was not there to steal, they would have to hump it.

Jake put his finger to his lips, nodding toward the rear of the hangar. An access hatch led to a maintenance tunnel just beneath the keel slidewalk. He did not mean to use any of the regular hangar exits, which might easily be guarded.

Telling the hatch to open, Jake wormed his way inside. He could hear Love behind him, complaining under his breath. "Couldn't find anything tinier could you?" Jake did not answer. He was too busy listening for what lay ahead. Nothing.

Just his own breathing, echoing off the far end of the tunnel.

Moving as fast as knees and elbows allowed, he squirmed the length of the tunnel reaching another access hatch abaft of the stern anchor. Letting his compweb merge with the lock, he eased it open, making sure it continued to read CLOSED.

Cold black wind whistled through the hole, smelling of pines and the sea. Setting his lenses for night vision, Jake stuck his head out.

Argo was about three hundred meters above sea level, tethered to the bare top of a knoll that sloped down to the sea. A footpath disappeared into the pines below. Beyond the trees he could see a natural harbor sheltered by a northern headland. Microamps picked up the splash of a nearby spring.

His navmatrix immediately fixed the location. They were on the northern coast of Caria, less than twenty klicks south of Miletus. The hill was named Didyma, and it had an ocular spring. To the north there was a Cretan colony at Kiliktepe, overlooking one of Miletus's two harbors.

He pulled his head back in. Love had caught up with him. Jake signed for silence. Pulling a safety line from its socket, Jake tapped his chest and pointed to the dark hole, indicating he would go first.

Love made an "after you" motion.

Jake swung out, twisting to bring his boots in contact with the hull—telling them to grip.

Apollo had taken his stunner, but missed his adhesive boots. Artemis had missed them, too—probably because they were not standard STOP jump boots.

Standing upside down on the hull, he walked over and shifted the safety line to the taut anchor cable. Taking hold of the cable, he told his boots to release, then scrambled down the hundred-odd meters to the ground. Love was right behind him, swarming hand over hand along the safety line, then letting himself down the cable.

They were free of the ship. Tapping Love on the shoulder, Jake pointed to the footpath. Love nodded and they set off. The steep dark trail twisted between pines and over deadfalls, meandering downhill. When it reached the bottom, the path forked.

Jake called a huddle. "The left fork heads toward Kiliktepe. The right one goes inland."

Love peered in both directions. "What's at Kiliktepe?"

"A Cretan colony. We might find a ship there that could take us to Egypt or Corinth." Jake wanted to somehow get to Anneke, or to her family in Greece.

"And inland?"

"Hill country. Upcountry Carians mostly."

"That good or bad?"

Jake shrugged. "Hard to say. They might shelter us. Or help Artemis hunt us down." The Lady of the Beasts was highly respected in these parts.

"Let's take ship for Egypt. I liked it there."

Jake motioned for silence. Something was headed their way. He upped the gain on his microamps.

Merde. He heard footfalls, and the click of chrome claws, coming up fast. Some diligent idiot must have checked the locker.

He told Love, "They are coming for us. We've got to split up and leave the road. Try to confuse them."

"Great. How are *we* gonna find each other again."

"One of should head for the north side of the peninsula. He can follow the north shore back to Kiliktepe. The other one can strike out into the Carian hills. We can meet back at the Shrine of the Isthmian Maiden." Anneke's mother was Priestess of the Shrine, and could help or hide them.

Love snorted. He did not like the odds of that happening. "Hell. I can't speak Carian. I'll take my chances in Kiliktepe. Tell 'em I'm a lost Egyptian. There's a woman in Elephantine who'd be happy to put me up."

Jake reminded him he couldn't speak Egyptian either.

Love laughed. "She'll teach me."

He slipped off between the pines. Jake doubled back along the path, then turned south, to lead them away from Love. That part seemed to work. Half a klick from the path he heard the sounds of pursuit coming closer. They were on his trail.

Jake took off down a gully, scrambling over a fallen log partway down the draw. When he reached the bottom he doubled back in his tracks until he came to the log. This time he climbed up it, lying down in some brush where he could not be seen. He heard dogs and people tearing down the gully.

Wriggling beneath the brush he came to a stream, running north and east, toward the River Meander. He waded downstream until he came upon a clump of willows overlooking the south bank. He used the willow branches to pull himself out without touching the bank. Leaping from rock to rock, he set off over bare ground, trying not to leave tracks.

He had done the three best things to hide his trail. He had changed direction, doubled over his scent, and left no prints—reversing his trail, confusing the nose, and concealing his tracks. Now he put on a burst of speed, hoping to be far away by the time they untangled his trail.

A couple of klicks to the south he came on another stream. He used this one to turn east, then he set off again at a run. Dawn was coming up ahead of him. He looked for a place to lie low, in case they mounted an aerial search at first light.

Scrambling up some loose scree, he found a root bole to hide beneath. Clean and dry, offering good overhead cover.

But just as he settled in, he heard the click-click of pursuit, coming across the rocks. How in the hell had they found him? Jake had no idea, but he knew he had better run. Luckily the scree slope ended in a rocky gully that did not make noise or tracks. He rabbited up it, hoping pursuit would pass him by.

And ran right into a woman with a bow. She was waiting at the end of the gully, while the dogs had circled around, driving him toward her.

Seeing a slim body, a blond head, and a silver bow—aimed straight at him—Jake stopped dead. Chest heaving, cornered and unarmed. He had been outthought at every turn, by a huntress who had read him like a clay tablet. First light filtered between the pines, falling on her face.

Jake expected to see Artemis staring at him over the arrow. Instead it was Sauromanta.

He could not believe it. But there she was, pointing a bow at him. Cool blue eyes studied him over the head of the arrow. A single blond curl fell down over her knitted brow.

Jake stepped forward, thinking she had to be some hopeful hallucination. A product of panic and exhaustion. Reliving the past had shorted his compweb, conjuring up a virtual mirage.

"Stop," she warned, pulling the nock back to her ear. It was Sauromanta's voice, soft and serious. Another step and she meant to let fly.

Jake stopped, still expecting her to vanish. "Sauromanta. Is that you?"

She looked puzzled. "You know my name?"

"Of course. It's me, Jake." He felt insanely happy, ready to run up and hug her. If she would put down that stupid bow.

"Jake?" She crinkled her nose in confusion. The bow did not waver.

"Yes. Jake. Don't you recognize me?"

"I know no men. I am a Maiden Huntress of Artemis."

No men? Not one? What a comedown for Herc. Jake's compweb flashed a warning. Voice inflection showed she was deathly serious. She really believed what she was saying. And she was a heartbeat away from releasing the arrow.

But her heart was beating. How that thrilled him! Making his own heart race. She looked as fit as ever. Dangerously healthy. Someone—probably Artemis—had countermanded Apollo's order to throw her overboard, hustling her to an autodoc instead.

Slowly Jake opened his hands, showing he was unarmed. "You must remember me." The caravanserai near Nineveh? The starlight run to the straits? Sex at sea? Shopping on Melos?

She stared at him. "I have been in battle. There was a blow to my head, clouding my memory. There are things I have forgotten."

"Well, I am one of them."

"Perhaps. But I am taking you back." She was serious. More so than usual. And she had no idea who he was. In fact she was set to perforate him if came a step closer. Her reconstructive surgery had included some sort of brain scrub. But memories were tricky, easier to suppress than erase. If she killed him, subconsciously she was bound to be sorry. As time went on it would trouble her—maybe really mess her up.

But of course by then he would be dead. Better play her carefully. He smiled wide. "By all means. Take me back. But let's talk a little on the way."

She eased back on the bow. "Do not try to trick me."

"No tricks," Jake promised. "I just want to help you remember."

The dogs came crashing up. Skidding to a stop. Jake tried to ignore them. He stood rapt, enjoying the familiar sound of her voice, the lines of her face, barely believing she was alive again. Totally ignoring the arrow aimed at his breast.

Sauromanta frowned. Telling him to turn around. Making sure he was truly unarmed. Jake did as she said, doing a slow carefree pirouette. "You know, I am *really* happy to see you alive. I feared you were dead."

"How glad can you be—I am taking you back to your own death."

"Maybe," he admitted. "But there are worse things than dying."

That struck a chord. For the first time she smiled, her wonderful warm Sauromanta smile. "You are right."

Careful to keep her bow bent, she marched him back to the airship. By the time they reached the hill called Didyma she was relaxed, enjoying their short time together, laughing at his strange jokes. There Jake found Love waiting for him. He, too, had been captured, run down by Artemis herself.

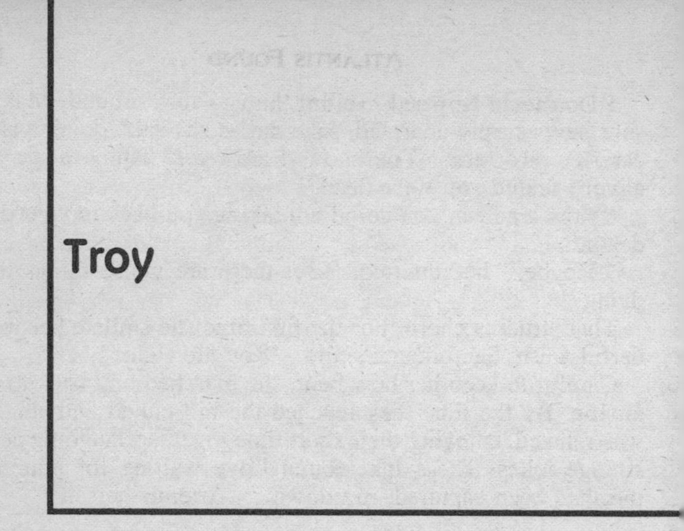

Troy

"You're happy now, aren't you!" Love was back in the dark locker, this time with two dogs outside the door. Jake could hear their chrome claws scrape on the hangar deck.

"Yep," Jake had to admit it. They had caught him, taken away his adhesive boots, and shoved him back in the hole. But Sauromanta was alive.

Love swore at him, "Fuck, what a fool!"

"You're the one who said you wanted her here."

"Sure, to help us get out. Not to be some zombie for them."

"She's not a zombie." Sauromanta just did not remember them.

"Not a zombie. Just forgetful? Get some fuckin' sense."

But Jake *was* happy. Recklessly so. Sauromanta was alive. The weight of having killed her was lifted. Somehow he and Love would get free again. And then . . .

"Listen, Shitkick, she ain't the same, you know."

"What do you mean?"

"I mean, you're thinking you can just waltz in, make the right moves, an' she's yours again. Right?"

Jake shrugged in the dark, "Maybe."

"Don't maybe me. I can tell."

"It's possible." The brain scrub did not seem to be drastic. While walking back to the ship they had talked about her family, and her childhood on the steppe. Only recent memories had been erased—and some bogus ones added. She "remembered" being dedicated to Artemis. But she was vague on when and where. That *darned* blow on the head . . .

Love could hardly believe what he was hearing. "Brilliant, really brilliant. She don't remember me. Or you. Or comin' here."

"True."

"Or gettin' laid by you an' Herc?"

" 'Fraid so." Artemis had managed to wipe out all adult memories of men and heterosex. Mentally restoring her virginity. Maybe physically, too. Biosculpt could correct anything. But she was still Sauromanta. Curious, friendly, honorable to a fault. Artemis had bridled at seeing her newly minted "maiden huntress" getting on so well with a male prisoner. Even a goddess doesn't always get her way.

"Just don't be takin' wild chances with her. She's dangerous as they come—an' then some."

Jake grunted in semiagreement. It was way too late not to be taking wild chances with Sauromanta.

Inertial sensors told him *Argo* was headed north, toward the Troad. Bearing THREE-FOUR-SEVEN. By noon they began to descend. He warned Love.

"Damn! Do wish we had gotten off at that last stop."

"We tried." Somehow Jake did not expect to die until he had at least seen Sauromanta again.

They were kept in the locker for several hours after the landing. His compweb could not decide if that was good or bad. Finally the door cycled. Light flooded the locker.

"Out," Apollo ordered. "Or we'll send dogs in for you."

Love went first. "Still yer same old nasty self."

"Hold your tongue, or I'll have it out."

Love helped Jake upright, watching Apollo stride off after Artemis and her Maidens. "Man, he thinks the sun shines straight out of his own ass."

Sauromanta was there, standing guard at the main hangar deck hatch, along with a pair of white plasti-metal hounds. Blood red ears tracked Jake as blue-tattooed Hyperboreans hustled him across the deck. Trying to act nonchalant, as he was frog-marched towards her—Jake greeted Sauromanta in Scyth.

He got an immediate smile and greeting, followed by a frown. Hearing him use her native tongue must have jogged suppressed memories.

As soon as he reached the hatch, Jake's navmatrix recognized the Plain of the Scamander—a flat brown-grass delta, dotted with salt marsh, sand dunes, and green lagoons, bordering a broad blue bay sheltered behind Cape Sigeum. The walled city looking down on the landing site had to be Troy.

Jake put on the brakes, pausing beside Sauromanta. He nodded at the city, ringing a high acropolis, quoting a line from Agamemnon's lament in Book II of the *Iliad*:

"Cruel Zeus deceived me, bowing his noble brow . . ."

Without thinking, Sauromanta completed the couplet:

"Saying I would topple the tall towers of Troy."

She turned to look wide-eyed at the citadel staring down on the plain. Troy looked very intact. In fact the Trojan War had not yet taken place. Agamemnon was not yet born. The great cyclopean walls he assailed were not even *built* yet. Homer would not sing about them for centuries. Yet Sauromanta had the whole Homeric epic in her head. Pounded into her as a child by kidnaped Greek tutors.

Before she could say anything, Hyperboreans pulled Jake through the hatch. But he meant to keep giving her things to think about, hitting at deep memories, which would not match her reprograming.

As he was hauled toward the city, Jake compared the Plain of the Scamander to his own memory. During mission prep he had gone over the ground at numerous prominent Bronze Age sites. In Home Period the blue bay no longer existed. Troy had ceased to be a port, pushed inland by the slowly advancing river delta. Even here-and-now there was no proper harbor, just a big sandy beach—long enough to accommodate the entire Mycenaean navy when Agamemnon came to call.

Horse herds roamed the shoreline. Jake saw corrals and paddocks belonging to Homer's "Horse Taming" Trojans. Also a hero's tomb, the resting place of Ilos, who gave Troy its other name, Ilium—and the *Iliad* its title.

Outside the low outer walls was a port market. Stalls offered spun yarn, local pottery, and bone fishhooks—as well as foreign wares, glass beads, and ivory game boards. Barter and gossip ceased as they approached. People stared, then abased themselves. Even in cosmopolitan Troy, it was not every day that gods, Nymphs, Hyperboreans, Maiden Huntresses, a pack of mechanical hounds, and an African captive appeared at the gate. Jake alone did not draw looks.

They passed quickly through the lower city, a warren of clay walls and thatched roofs, overlooked by the royal acropolis rising above on a terraced slope. The upper gate was flanked by a cult house and goddess images—idols set up in honor of the Maiden, Mother, and Crone. Showing why Homer called the place "Holy Ilium." The ruling dynasty was Cretan-Anatolian, worshiping the Triple Goddess above the male gods. Apollo was a Mouse God. Zeus a mere babe of the Mother.

Entering the upper city was like entering a new world. The narrow streets and noisy markets of the lower city gave way to stone-pillared mansions, with upper floors of wood and brightly painted plaster. Windowed roofs let in light and air. Temples filled the sky with incense and burnt offerings.

A wide paved roadway climbed the triple terraces toward the royal palace—a labyrinth of flat-roofed, columned halls surrounding the central megaron. They were led past a smithy and chariot shop to a ceremonial bath. Only after being cleaned and anointed were they taken to the main hall. With the sweat and dust of the lower city washed off it was easy to believe you were in another world, a lesser Olympus, inhabited by servants, royalty, and visiting gods.

Apollo and Artemis were waiting in an open court, beneath the perfumed sky. Priestesses dedicated Jake and Love like a pair of prize goats, offered up for sacrifice. They would be transported to Artemis's Shrine in the Tauric Chersonese on the Crimean Peninsula. And there sacrificed in some suitable fashion—the exact method being left to the bloody-minded Taurians.

Everyone seemed pleased. Artemis positively beamed. The

Trojans were relieved to get through a potentially dangerous divine visit at the cost of a couple of complete strangers—who did not even need to be done to death. That would be left in the competent hands of the Taurians. Only Sauromanta acted displeased, frowning and casting odd looks at Jake.

Hector's sword—presented to Jake by Alexander the Great—was ceremoniously turned over to the Trojans for safe-keeping. Which created one of those curious time loops. Hector was a Trojan hero, not yet born. Would he one day get the sword, and use it? And when Achilles killed him, would the sword go into the dead hero's shrine? To be looted by Alexander centuries later—then given back to Jake?

If so, who *made* the sword in the first place? Another mystery of faster-than-light travel. Bits of matter and energy sometimes seemed to pop spontaneously from space-time. But you could never be sure. The sword could be a copy of itself—beaten out by some Trojan con artist dealing in duplicate antiques.

You would never know, without expending the time and energy to track a sharp-edged piece of bronze through many centuries. One of those little puzzles the mind fixes on—to avoid dwelling on a newly announced death sentence.

Before taking leave, Artemis let slip a few last words in Universal, giving Jake a glimpse of Dianna—his sometime STOP commander. "You can never know how galling it was to get orders from you."

Jake shrugged. "I tried to be polite."

"Making it even more mortifying. Luckily a goddess can endure even male condescension. Of course I knew things would be put right in the end."

Artemis was plainly delighted to be back in her place, the willful Golden Daughter of Zeus, feared and worshiped by prince and slave alike. Mistress of Birth, Death, and Maidenhood—the things most out of male control. Not even Jake could ruin her mood. "That is why I am being merciful. The Taurians club their victims to death. Or in special cases behead them. Either way will be quick."

"As always, you are too kind." He thought about Emiko, drowned by dogs. Somehow he had to turn the tables on Artemis.

"You are hardly in a position to be impertinent," the goddess reminded him.

"I'm hardly in a position to be anything else."

Artemis laughed. "I won't pretend to miss you." She left, trailing her Maidens, brother, and dog pack.

One member of the goddesses' suite hung back. Sauromanta started to say she was sorry.

Jake stopped her. "Don't. Please."

"But we will not see each other again. There are things I must say."

"I just don't want the last words between us to be, 'I'm sorry.' " He so much wanted to touch her. To take her in his arms, and stroke her golden hair. To tell her how much he loved her. But that would only confuse her more. And he wanted just to set her at ease.

But Sauromanta meant to speak her mind. "I believe we knew each other once. That we were friends. And if I had not hunted you down, you might have escaped. Now you will die."

"Not if I can help it."

She stared at him with worried blue eyes. To wish him to escape was sacrilege. But she could not abide having betrayed a friend.

"We were more than friends," he told her. "Death cannot change that. You did what honor demanded." He was the one who had screwed up royally, dragging her on this doomed expedition. Letting the gods make a fool of him. Someday she *might* break through the reprogramming and remember. Then what had happened would hit her hard. He did not want her thinking she had killed him.

"Do me one favor," Jake asked.

"What's that?" She still looked conflicted.

"Leave with a light heart." And take my love with you. He did not say that last part—it would have been too much.

She was the one who touched him, reaching out to take his hand. "I will do that."

Then she let go, and was gone. Leaving a vast emptiness. Being beaten to death by Taurians was fairly abstract—and comfortably far in the future. According to his navmatrix, it was over a thousand klicks to the Crimea and the Tauric Chersonese. Through the Clashing Rocks and across wild seas.

Hercules had not even gotten halfway. Missing Sauromanta was immediate.

And she left in deadly peril. If her memories did resurface, Artemis would swiftly dispose of her. The penalty for a Maiden Huntress who had been with a man was to be hunted to death.

But to save her, Jake had to first save himself. No simple feat. Apollo and Artemis had taken his adhesive boots, and other out-of-period paraphernalia. Jake had only what was wired in him—his augmented senses, his compweb and nav-matrix. They would have to be enough.

The Trojans treated them grandly. A guest suite in the palace. Servants at constant call. Nothing was too good for those dedicated to Artemis. Oysters and sea urchin for breakfast. Ebony beds and Bebrycian slave girls at night. Love declared the service first-rate. "Would make a Bangkok hooker blush."

Jake did not indulge. They both knew the slave girls and servants ensured they were never alone. And the honor guard was meant to make them keep their appointment with the Taurians. In truth Troy was anxious to see them gone—only contrary winds kept them as guests in Ilium.

So Jake put his energy into scoping out escape routes, touring the walls with his honor guard in tow. The view was magnificent. Mount Ida towered behind the city to the east. To the west and south the Plain of the Scamander spread out toward the blue bay.

But on these three sides lay the lower city, and a second set of walls. Only on the north side did the walls drop straight down, into the marshy valley of the Simois. From there Jake could see the Hellespont and the European shore beyond.

A strong north wind blew into his face, so forceful that lamps could not be lit inside the citadel. Only the great hearths gave light and heat. This north wind was the wealth of "Windy Troy." Her blue sheltered bay was the most practical spot for waiting out the northerly winds that closed the Hellespont to northbound traffic—making Troy the toll keeper between the Mediterranean and the Great Sea of Grass.

So long as that north wind blew, they could not leave for Artemis's Taurian temple. Jake happily reminded himself that contrary winds could keep sailing ships from entering the Hellespont for weeks. Lord Byron spent seventeen days at anchor in the Troad, waiting on the wind.

In the meantime he looked hungrily at handholds in the stonework. They would not even need adhesive boots. The walls were easily climbable—rough, dry stonework, each course fitting into the next like limestone puzzle pieces. But they could not just ask their honor guard to hold the knotted silk bed sheets while they swung over the side.

Jake was standing on the north wallwalk when he got the call. A coded message came in clear as glass over his compweb, "POSITION FIX."

He responded instantly. His compweb was primarily a passive receiver, but had a limited capacity to send signals.

As he stared into the north wind, gripping the stone rampart, a second coded message came in. "UPDATE—6/21–NOW."

Someone wanted all relevant data from the first day they arrived until now. Jake dispatched the data at once. A quick synopsis of the expedition, from their first meeting with Hercules, to the present betrayal and crisis.

Jake waited on the wallwalk until dusk, but no further signals came in.

That night he had Love kick out the slave girls. "We got to talk." One look was enough. Love told the young women that getting laid nine nights in a row was against his religion—but be sure to see him in the morning. "What's happenin'," he demanded.

"Someone's contacted us."

"Who?" They had to carry on the conversation with a servant sleeping in a nearby niche, but none of the Trojans spoke any English.

"I'm not sure."

"Maybe Wasserman?" Captain Wasserman was the only expedition member still curiously unaccounted for. No one had seen him since Apollo and Artemis took over the *Argo*.

Jake shook his head. "They wanted a complete update. Things Wasserman would know."

"What about STOP?"

Jake shrugged. "It was not on a standard STOP frequency. And they are incredibly cautious. Short signals. Minimum contact. And a one-time emergency code." Uncrackable so long as you kept the conversation brief.

"Not exactly STOP style," Love agreed. A STOP rescue team would more likely come roaring in, relying on surprise and firepower to smother the opposition.

"It could be a trick." Defeat put an edge on Jake's paranoia.

"Right." Love did not think it likely. "What reason they got to trick us when they are set to club us to death?"

Jake admitted that was far-fetched. Artemis had been in on mission planning from the beginning. If she or Apollo wanted to know more, they would have strained Jake's brain aboard the *Argo*. Still he had held back, not implicating Anneke's family in his summary of events.

In the next week Jake got only one more short message. "SIGNAL IF THEY MOVE YOU."

But three coded calls gave him plenty to think about. If another team had arrived from Home Period, they were being very low profile—leaving him and Love to cool their heels in Ilium. Understandable, but immensely frustrating. Jake very much wanted to be in on the action, not sitting around waiting to have his brains beaten out.

It was Boreas who broke the impasse. The north wind dropped. Determined to be rid of their doomed guests, the Trojans immediately readied two thirty-oared galleys to take them to the Tauric Chersonese. Jake sent word at once, saying they were headed up the Hellespont. No signal came back.

By now a twenty-oared galley and a pair of coasters were waiting in the bay for the wind to drop. They would accompany the *triakonters* at least as far as Propontis, the Sea of Marmara. Jake and Love left the bay in the lead galley. The view was magical. To port the Aegean shone like a vast blue mirror, broken by distant islands. Imbros. Lemnos. And the peaks of Samothrace. To starboard the Hellespont poured out of the Narrows, a great rush of water forming a river in the sea. Fishing smacks harvested tunny and mackerel migrating through the straits.

Creeping under oars the Trojan galleys turned into the dark swirling Hellespont, bucking the current flowing down from the Black Sea, making slow, grinding progress as the rocky spine of Gallipoli slid by to starboard. By the time they reached the Propontis, the Sea of Marmara that lies between the Black Sea and the Aegean, the rowers were spent. The

Trojans sheltered in the lee of Mount Dindymum, a peninsula connected to the Asian mainland by a narrow isthmus. Supposedly inhabited by six-armed earthborn giants—until they were slaughtered by Hercules.

Jake saw no sign of them. Perhaps Herc got them all. He did see the original anchor of Jason's *Argo*, left as an offering to the Mother. And each day he diligently sent out a position report. Nothing came back. Whoever was out there was lying very, very low.

Love, for one, felt abandoned. "Did you get any fix at all?"

"Barely. The signals were mere blips. Somewhere to the north and east."

"Where we're headed?"

"Seems so."

"Fuck. We're bein' played with."

Jake nodded. "Used and abused."

In the Sea of Marmara the little coasters and the twenty-oared galley turned aside, exchanging cargoes of olive oil and Egyptian glass for wheat, tin, and dried fish. Only the big thirty-oared galleys would attempt to stem the Bosphorus.

Even the far-faring Trojans saw the Bosphorus as a great barrier, a natural limit to their world. The narrow strait carried the discharge of the huge rivers that fed the Black Sea—the Danube, the Dniester, the Dnieper, and the Amazon. When a north wind whipped the channel into full flood, the Bosphorus became a roaring cataract, sending ships whirling backwards into the Sea of Marmara.

Wild Thracians inhabited the west bank. The east bank was held by the Bebryces, enemies of Troy, whose kings enjoyed beating strangers to death with their fists. Artemis had set the Trojans no small task, telling them to take Jake and Love to Tauria. But she was not known for being easy to please.

With nothing better to do, Jake stood at the prow, watching the galley's progress. If the Trojans failed to stem the current, they would have to send their charges overland, dramatically increasing chances of escape.

The rowers would have had no hope at all, were it not for the countercurrents. The tremendous rush of water down the main channel created huge eddies along the banks, where the current slowed, and even ran backwards. To find the first backwater they had to cross over to the European side, angling in north of the Golden Horn, guided by the great promontory where Byzantium would one day be built.

The site of the golden city of Constantine, Hagia Sophia, and the Topkapi Palace, was currently occupied by savage tattooed Thracians. Jake spotted three of them watching from atop the promontory, in long wool cloaks, foxskin hats, and high fawnskin boots. Otherwise, they were stripped for battle, wearing only arm rings and body paint, carrying javelins and round bucklers.

One turned and disappeared, headed inland with the news that ships were in the narrows.

Jake's sighted the first countercurrent, a standing line of foam running along the Thracian shore. Rowers beat toward the faint mark. Veins bulged on their faces. Sinews cracked. Oars bent backward, besting the current by main force, heaving the ship over the line of foam.

The effect was magical. The current turned abruptly. Instead of a whirling southward torrent, banging against the ship, it became a flat northward drift. The galley shot forward, as if some giant hand that had been holding her back suddenly gave her a shove.

But to find the next countercurrent they had to breast the main current again, an angry rush of water, whipped by whirlpools and bobbing like the sea. All morning they rowed back and forth. Naked ship's boys ran among the rowers, giving them bread soaked in wine, fortifying them between bouts.

Finally they reached the Bebek Narrows, where Europe and Asia are only a klick apart. Past that choke point the Bosphorus opened up, and Jake could sense slow-rising swells beneath the keel. The feel of open sea ahead.

The Trojans heaved to in a tiny bay at the entrance to the Black Sea, resting and taking on water. The Trojan captain pointed out the Clashing Rocks, two huge stationary stones at the entrance to the Bosphorus. "Once they were a great menace, whirling about and crushing ships between them. Who knows, they may someday break loose again."

Trojans were full of such tales, believing the Bosphorus needed to be more terrible than it was, so as not to tempt the Greeks. Jason's voyage had shown they were right.

Beyond the Clashing Rocks lay the Black Sea, infamous for sudden squalls, summer fogs, and winter ice—the sea was called the "Traveler's Friend" in hope of placating its wrath. Just like the Callisto volcano was called the Beautiful One. The Trojans turned north, hugging the coast, like children clinging to their mother's breast. Which meant rowing against the counterclockwise current, and battling the prevailing headwinds. And they were still not halfway to Tauria.

But that was fine with Jake, who was in no hurry to get where they were going. He saw no sense in being on time to his own funeral.

Thracian hill country sank down, replaced by rolling steppe, inhabited by wandering Cimmerians—cattle-herding battle-ax people, living in moving wagon laggers. Many had never seen seagoing vessels, and vanished as soon as the galleys appeared, mistaking the ships for giant centipedes walking on the water in search of prey.

Finally they came to the wide mouth of the Danube, a broad hundred-klick delta, dotted with islands and split by rivers and streams. Halfway across, a wide front of gray clouds rolled out of the west, driving rain before it. With no hope of making shelter, the captain ordered his ships to heave to, dropping anchor off the marshy coast, hoping to ride out the squall.

The blue-black mountain of clouds rose higher, blotting out the land, then hurtling the sea at the helpless ships. Anchored with her stern to the storm, the galley pitched alarmingly along the whole length of her keel. Each new wave seemed about to swamp the ship. And each was followed by another, one every few seconds for hour upon hour.

By midafternoon, the stern anchor started to drag on the sandy bottom. Swinging sideways to the storm, the galley began to wallow as well as buck, taking on water faster than it could be bailed. It was just a matter of time before the ship rolled over, capsizing on her lee bulwark.

The captain had only one option, to cut the anchor lines and run before the storm. Carrying just enough sail to give headway, the galley plunged downwind, galloping like a frightened mare, burying her snout in the sea, then bursting back up, spraying foam as if she were frantic to breath.

At dusk Jake saw something horrific. One moment the sea was all towering waves, glassy whitecapped mountains heaving amid curtains of rain. Then the rain parted and there was the second galley, wallowing in the swell. Her mast gone, she gyrated wildly, like a thick black stick in the flood. Only men clung helplessly to this stick. Even at minimum focus Jake could see their faces. First he saw her full abeam. Seconds later he saw her stern rising up to show several meters of keel, her useless steering oars lashed clear of the water. She was bow on to him when he lost sight of her. He never saw that galley again.

On the second day of the storm, the wind slackened and the sky to the east cleared. Jake caught sight of a gray-peaked mass far off to leeward. Blurred at both ends, and attached to nothing, it seemed to hover above the storm, a hundred klicks to the east. He pointed it out to the captain.

The Trojan captain gave a wan smile. "The Tauric Chersonese. But I would not worry about getting there."

For most of the morning the mountains hung ahead of them, growing larger and clearer. Then they were blotted out by gray rain and a rising sea. The "Traveler's Friend" came pouring over the windward rail.

The second night was raging chaos. The galley's hull screeched and groaned in utter darkness, while black rain sang through the rigging. Exhausted bailers, who had gone without meals or rest since the storm hit, collapsed atop their buckets, falling asleep in the frigid water.

Jake and Love broke down and helped with the bailing, figuring the sea could kill them as surely as the Taurians. They bailed all night, working themselves senseless. Sleep and waking became the same. Unattainable abstractions. Replaced by an in-between state combining the worst of both. Never alert. Never rested. Always soaked and freezing.

At first light the storm receded. By dawn the rain ceased. Clouds lifted. Across the wind-whipped sea, Jake could see land ahead, the mountainous south coast of Tauria. The Trojan captain looked positively embarrassed. Jake and Love had struggled mightily to save his ship, when half the crew had abandoned hope. Now he was right where he'd said he would not be, about to deliver them up to death.

He laid the blame squarely on heaven. "It is the gods. They have plans for us we cannot know." It did seem as if Artemis had decided their delivery was taking too long, and blew them straight to Tauria.

Jake and Love stared at each other. Drained spirits and insane fatigue kept them from resisting.

The captain ran his ship into a deep harbor on the sharply indented Crimean coast. Dead-tired crewmen dropped into the surf, dragging the galley up onto the beach. Taurians came riding down to meet them, wearing tall felt hats, and carrying small powerful bows, their hideous tattooed faces smeared with grease, grinning at the exhausted crew like human ghouls.

It was a delicate situation. Taurians were headhunters. According to time-honored custom, anything washed up on their beaches was salvage. Ships wrecked on their coast were looted and torn apart for timber—the heads of the survivors decorated Taurian homesteads. Driven ashore by the storm, the Trojans fell somewhere between being chance guests and legitimate prey.

But the Trojan captain hit on a happy compromise. Presenting bronze pins and jars of wine to the Taurian chiefs, he offered up Jake and Love, claiming they were captive princes. The Taurians got their heads without having to fight for them. After some insincere pleasantries, Jake and Love were loaded aboard a cart, bound hand and foot, then trundled off for sacrifice.

The Taurians lived in huts thatched with sod, surrounded by the great herds of cattle that gave them their name. Stakes driven into the sod around each hut's smoke hole were adorned with blackened heads, cured by the smoke. The wooden temple of Artemis was a long dark hall with low eaves. Jake and Love were dumped in a dirt-floored antechamber, where polite Taurians fed them beef gruel, explaining in halting proto-Greek that they would be bathed and purified in the morning.

"At dawnbreak, priestesses will come and bathe on you. Being stripped, wetted, and rubbed. Please be erect for them."

"Sounds cool," Love admitted. "Make mine Egyptian."

Noting Love's request, the Taurians withdrew—having clearly learned their Greek from some victim with a sense of humor. When they were alone, Love whispered, "You hearing anything between your ears?"

"Not a word." Jake had diligently sent out position reports, but gotten no response.

"Damn. This trip is shapin' up ta be a big mistake. The Bronze Age ain't near as nice as she looked in the brochures."

Too true. Once more Jake felt fucked and far from Home. How did he get himself into such situations? Better yet, how would he get out? Numb from two days of storm, and a night of bailing, he sat loosening his bonds, and studying the temple walls—thick logs, caulked with clay. Nothing he could dig through. His bonds were a simpler problem. His hands were still slick from the sea, and he had the whole ride in the wagon to work on them. But before he could make any sort of break, he had to shake his terrible insomniatic fatigue. When he had his ropes comfortably loosened, he went to sleep.

His compweb woke him well before dawn, giving him plenty of time to finish undoing his bonds, and wrack his brain for an escape plan. So far the Taurians had acted lax and confident. Somehow he had to show them up.

Love was up, too, looking damned disappointed at the prospect of dying. ''Why can't Herc be here to brain the fuckers with their own club?'' Desperation had him missing the mad demigod who happily took on the Corps of Amun.

None of Jake's favorite tactics—fleeing, fawning, or feigning illness—seemed to fit the situation. And before he could fix on a plan, a lone priestess shuffled in, wearing crimson sacral robes embroidered with gold griffons, her face hidden by a gold death mask. She wore a jade headdress, made of flat plates held together by bronze links. The hair showing between the plates was red, reminding him of Peg.

As she knelt down in front of him, Jake worked his hands free of the ropes. He could reach out and grab her. But then what? He needed a way *out.* Or weapons to fight with. Not a hostage.

She lifted her gold death mask slightly, so he could see under it, whispering in Universal, ''Jake, don't say anything.'' It was Peg.

Peg

Jake had expected some supersecret STOP team. Instead, here was Peg, cool, clear-eyed, and giving orders. Her plan already in operation. Rigged out as a Taurian priestess, and telling him to shut up.

"What's happening?" Love whispered, whipping his hands out from behind him. He had already worked through the knots.

Peg nodded at the door behind her. "We're getting out."

"I was hopin' to hear that."

Jake had forgotten his own hands were free. Bringing them around, he seized Peg's arm, about to say how glad—and astounded—he was to see her. She stopped him, putting a finger to his lips. "Get your hands back behind you. They've got to think you are both still prisoners."

He and Love wound the ropes back around their wrists, holding the loose ends together. "Act cowed," Peg reminded them. "You're going to be bathed—but then clubbed to death. Try not to look the least bit lighthearted."

No problem. After a night of bailing, then being bound and hauled to the shrine, fed gruel, and forced to sleep on a dirt floor, it was not hard to act hangdog. There was a real drag in Jake's step. His tunic was a sodden wreck. He needed a hot bath, and a lot more sleep, just to feel fit for sacrifice.

A dozen Taurians lounged beyond the antechamber door, evil-eyed, leather-clad brutes armed with wicked little bows. Bowing tattooed faces, they touched their topknots to show respect for the red-haired priestess in the gold death mask. Peg hustled her prisoners past them, toward the inner shrine, where the goddess image sat on her pedestal. A small legless wooden idol, stained black with blood from centuries of sacrifice. Behind the goddess a low door opened onto a temple court lined by a bank and stockade.

Outside was a trough, where victims could be bathed, before being led back in to die. Jake looked for a gap in the stockade, but the only gate faced the town, and was guarded by an ugly pair of headhunters. Women in the court stopped their tasks, looking startled, then suspicious, seeing a strange priestess with the prisoners.

Using a wooden dipper, Peg poured wash water on Jake and Love, starting with their hands and feet. She whispered, "Get set to run."

A woman called out to Peg in Taurian. Jake needed no translation to get her meaning—she wanted to know what Peg was up to. He bent down alongside Love, his legs braced beneath him, like a sprinter at the blocks.

"Now," Peg hissed through her teeth.

With an alarming thud, the back half of the stockade collapsed in a cloud of dust and splinters. Women shrieked. Temple guards stared wide-eyed, then went for their bows.

Peg sped straight for the gap. Love was right behind her, followed by Jake. In seconds they were outside the stockaded camp. The shrine was built on high ground overlooking the harbor, backed by a deep, wooded ravine. Peg and Love dashed down the draw. Jake slid after them. A barbed arrow zipped over his shoulder, showing someone had gotten over his shock.

A fine start. But being free of the camp was just the first part. Soon Taurians would be ahorse, and howling for blood. Peg obviously had a plan, but it had better be good. They had no hope of outrunning headhunters on horseback.

Jake heard drumming hooves behind him. He glanced over

his shoulder. "Keep going," Peg shouted. Horsemen came clattering down the draw, waving bows and tufted lances, making a hellish racket.

Suddenly a huge figure dressed in a lionskin burst from the thicket. He fell on the lead horseman like a thunderbolt, swinging a brass-bound club and bellowing with delight.

It was Hercules. Shouting his paean, he lashed out with his club like Goliath in a lionskin, unseating the lead rider, and stampeding his horse back up the draw. The Taurians were even more taken aback than Jake. Horses reared. Stirrupless riders slid off their backs, into a hopeless tangle. Hercules happily knocked them on the head.

Seeing their leaders surprised, dismounted, and beaten to death, the remaining Taurians turned and fled. Dropping his club and drawing his bow, Hercules sent a flight of poisoned arrows winging after them, hurrying the Taurians along.

Peg pulled on Jake, telling him to "Come on." There was no time to watch the show.

At the bottom of the draw was a small cove. Waiting on the beach was a boat. Love leaped happily aboard. Jake helped Peg in after him, preparing to shove off. Hercules sauntered out of the draw, casually crossing the beach to the boat. Jake thanked him profusely, never having been so happy to see the homicidal demigod.

Love had lost any leftover ill feeling from their disastrous visit to Egyptian Thebes. "Way—to—go," he grinned. "Can't imagine *what* holds yer ears apart. But I'm damned happy to see you."

Hercules laughed, wiping blood and brains from his club. "You know how I hate human sacrifice." Just part of his heroic crusade to beat people into religious sense.

Not everyone appreciated his efforts. A horde of angry Taurians came pounding down the beach. Hercules put his shoulder to the sternpost and shoved them out into the bay. Then nearly scuttled the boat getting aboard. Taking hold of the oars, he vigorously propelled them out to sea.

Outraged Taurians drove their horses right into the surf, throwing tufted lances after the boat. Arrows hit the water on either hand. A barbed shaft buried itself in the gunwale, making Jake jump. But with Hercules at the sweeps, they moved briskly out of bow range. Screaming in frustration, mounted bowmen rode along the beach, shouting insults.

Jake relaxed back into his seat, nursing his badly banged nervous system. Taurians were superb horsemen, but their notion of proper seamanship was beating stranded sailors to death. He and Love could count themselves as saved.

He looked over at Peg, who had taken off her gold death mask and jade headdress. Sweat plastered red hair to her cheeks and forehead. Wrung out from having run more than a mile in heavy robes, she still looked absolutely stunning in the clear air with the sea behind her. He marveled aloud at the ease with which she had spirited them away.

Glad to be appreciated, Peg leaned over and kissed him. Which was good for a stab of guilt. What was she going to say about him and Sauromanta? When he got around to telling her—there had been nothing in Jake's mission update about sex and shopping with a member of his contact team.

Love leaned back against the gunwale, grinning. Waiting to see how this played out.

Jake took Peg's hand, feeling the need to hold her, to know she was truly there. "How did you do it?"

"The hard way." Obviously, she had no big team behind her. No STOP backup. Peg was a paleontologist. Not a field agent. Without a compweb or navmatrix, she could not even navigate a portal. Before teaming with Jake, the only time travel she had done was chipping into a bone bed.

"Are you braced for bad news?" she asked.

"Is there any other sort?"

"You've been gone for over a year."

Actually winter solstice was months away. He had been in the Bronze Age less than six months. Once you went hyperlight, the only time was trip time. Even the longest trips to the past took only minutes out of your life in Home Period. But Peg still thought in sublight terms. What she meant was, Jake had just not come back. (Unsettling news in itself.) And more than a year had elapsed between his leaving Home Period, and hers.

"When you did not come back, FTL pushed to reseal the portals. The entire Bronze Age is now off-limits—closed to traffic either way."

Right. The "gods" had collected their airship and sub, and used their connections at FTL to pull the ladder up after them.

They must figure they had milked Home Period for all the equipment they could get. Now they just wanted to avoid pesky interference from former owners.

"So how did you get around the seals?"

She laughed. "Technically, I'm in the Pleistocene."

Peg seemed very pleased with herself. Happy to be pulling off this cloak-and-dagger field-agent rescue—not at all concerned about being cut loose in the time stream. "We organized a Second Pleistocene Expedition, using the Rancho La Brea portal. FTL could hardly object to that." FTL already stood accused of sabotaging the First Pleistocene Expedition—they had to keep hands off the Second.

"We smuggled a Cold Sleep Chamber in, disguised as an autodoc. Crossing over the land bridge from North America to Pleistocene Europe, we set up the Sleep Chamber on the Bessarabian steppe, below the lower Dniester. I got inside and set the controls for the approximate time of your arrival here."

This was jury-rigged time travel. The sort they used to use on sublight trips to the stars. Sleep Chambers put people into suspended animation—for thousands of years if need be—then reanimated them at their destination. Only in Peg's case the chamber didn't go to the stars—it just sat on the Bessarabian steppe, waiting for the Bronze Age to happen. A desperate measure, offering undetected access to the Bronze Age—so long as no one discovered the chamber and opened it up.

"Hello—Sleeping Beauty," Love chuckled.

"So you are here alone?" Jake shook his head, amazed that Peg had taken such a long shot at finding him.

"There was only room for one."

Since awakening, she had been sitting on the steppe, monitoring electromagnetic frequencies, searching for some sign of Jake's expedition. "I picked up your Mayday from the Aegean. Also coded traffic between *Argo* and *Atlantis*. Onboard systems cracked the codes. When I heard you two had been dropped off at Troy, I punched a call through."

That was the position fix and update request Jake had gotten atop the wallwalk of Ilium.

"What about Herc?" Love nodded at the demigod happily plying the oars.

"Jake's update included the tracer attached to Hercules'

chariot. I spotted him headed west from the Caucasus, and caught up with him fording the Dnieper. As soon as I explained things, I had an apalling time holding him back. He meant to rout out the Taurians, burn their temple, teach them a lasting lesson. As a favor to me, he settled for a simple rescue.''

''Yea.'' Love shook his head. ''Hates to do things halfway. You should *see* the mess he made out of Egypt.''

At the harbor mouth, Hercules turned north, stranding the pursuing horsemen on the south bank. They would have to turn about and ride totally around the inlet to renew the chase on already exhausted horses.

Rounding a promontory, they put in at a small beach on the north shore. Iolaus was there, with Hercules' chariot and team. Hobbled nearby were half a dozen of the small Taurian horses. Hercules filled the boat with stones, sinking it to further confuse pursuit. He waded ashore, saying he had hardly had so much fun since the Garden of the Hesperides beside the Ocean Stream. ''Where we got the Golden Apples, and I killed that four-headed dragon. Or was it five? I never remember such things.''

''Let the bards supply the details,'' Jake suggested.

''Exactly.'' Hercules beamed.

Nightmare days followed, riding almost without rest, changing horses constantly. Hercules was determined to get off the Crimean peninsula before the Taurians came howling after them. When they reached the narrow neck connecting Tauria to the mainland, they saw only a scattering of horsemen in shaggy caps standing watch on traffic over the isthmus, looking north toward the mainland. Slipping by their fires at night, they escaped onto the Sea of Grass.

Morning found them on the green sweep of steppe, south of the Dnieper. Narrow-bladed grasses bowed and waved in the north wind from one end of the world to the other, broken only by solitary twists of wormwood or low patches of marsh. Great herds of bison, wild cattle, horses, and antelope drifted across the plain, stalked by lions and wolves.

That night Hercules celebrated with fresh meat and a hot meal, killing and cooking up several rabbits, and a big ground-dwelling bustard. ''I usually do not hunt little birds and rabbits. It is fine to kill fierce boars and wild bulls, or man-eating lions. But what harm do birds and bunnies do?''

Like Sauromanta said, he could be quite tenderhearted, doing the cooking and sewing without complaint. ''I would have made a wonderful woman—which I suppose comes from having fucked so many.''

As he cooked, Hercules told the whole circuit of his adventures since leaving Egyptian Thebes. ''I visited the Oracle of Zeus-Amun at Siwa, where Father spoke to me, wearing the fleece and face of a ram. Then I traveled the width of Asia, crossing the Caucasus Mountains. I had hoped to reach the far coast of Ocean, but all I found on the far side of the Caucasus was the landlocked Hyrcanian Sea.'' Hercules keenly wanted to claim that he had gone from one end of the world to the other. But India and China prevented him.

Producing a wine jar from the chariot, Herc proceeded to drain it, musing about all the people who had thwarted him. Hera, his foster mother, kept him from being High King. Calais and Zetes got him kicked off the *Argo*. Complete strangers took it amiss when he came to clean their stables, lift their livestock, or just slaughter some nearby wonder.

Seeing trouble on the way, Love tried to snag the wine jar. ''Hey, man, go easy on yer liver.''

But Hercules was not listening, saying, ''What I really need now is a good fuck. Nothing rounds out an adventure like a woman, or two. Fortunately we have one with us.'' He grinned drunkenly at Peg.

Alarms sounded in Jake's tired head. Peg was not Sauromanta, whose people *worshiped* Hercules. If he attacked her, there was bound to be a battle. Exhausted from the trek, Jake doubted that he and Love could easily overpower a fully armed demigod.

Hercules tried to excite Peg with stories of his conquests, telling how when he hunted the Lion of Cithaeron he took time out to deflower the fifty daughters of King Thespius. ''Though I sometimes fear I only lay with forty-nine, leaving one still a virgin. The drawback to mass deflowering is the tendency to lose count. You end up relying on a bunch of giggling virgins to keep track.''

Women always gave in to him, he explained. ''I never resort to rape. Once they see I am irresistible, they usually enter into the spirit of it. Or at least stop struggling.''

Well into his cups, Herc was having trouble telling myth from legend. The eight-headed Lernaean Hydra now had nine heads—one of them immortal. The fifty nights he spent with King Thespius's daughters became a single dusk-to-dawn debauch.

Only seconds away from her own debauch, Peg sat idly by the fire, her legs tucked under her, not looking in the least alarmed. Determined not to give Hercules an excuse for violence.

Love looked at Jake, mouthing the words, "Get ready."

Jake held up a hand, warning Love off. If anyone threw his life away defending his wife's honor, it might as well be him. And from what Jake had seen it was suicidal to deny Hercules anything. God or mortal. Mad or sober. Death followed him about as diligently as his High King's herald, the Dung Man. Hercules killed people in battles and single combats, in athletic contests and acts of larceny, or in simple drunken accidents. He killed to administer rough justice, and in contrite compensation for previous killings, also in fits of madness and chance encounters. And not just people. By his account he had killed lions, serpents, bulls, bears, and brazen-winged birds. Not to mention centaurs, Titans, Gorgons, three-headed shepherds, and six-armed monsters. If half of his claims were true, whole districts had been depopulated and many marvelous species turned to myth by his club and bow.

Lurching to his feet, the drunk demigod told Peg, "Come, let's do it in the long grass. Stars make the best bed canopy."

Seizing at her, he seemed to stumble. Pitching forward, Hercules ended up sprawled on the dirt. In the dark and firelight, Peg did not appear to have moved.

Hercules picked himself up, staring at her. Peg still sat idly on her knees, smiling.

Jake's compweb replayed the action, and recognized her response. *Suwari waza*, kneeling aikido. Low fluid movement, from a grounded position, forming a protective sphere almost impossible to penetrate by brute force.

Hercules sprang at her again. This time Jake's compweb cut the action down to slow mode. He saw her swivel at the hips, adding to Hercules' momentum, breaking his hold with her hands, and "helping" him go sailing into the dirt.

Seen at normal speed, in the half-light, Peg did not seem to do *anything*. It was as if Hercules simply could not touch her. Drunk and bewildered, but still bent on sex, he picked himself up and dived at her.

Peg leaned out of his way, catching hold of an ankle. Hercules cartwheeled past her, fetching up against his divinely sturdy chariot.

This time he did not get up, lying in a drunken stupor, loking bewildered. Soon he was asleep. Always the gentleman, Iolaus apologized, throwing a cloak atop his uncle.

Love applauded. ''Damn, remind me not to try an' rape you.''

Jake awoke early next morning, fearing Hercules might wake up enraged at being beaten by a woman. But Zeus's son got up fit and happy, making no mention of his attempts to ravish Peg.

Instead he held up an arm, announcing, ''Here's breakfast.''

Hanging from his fist was a huge dead cobra, as thick as Jake's arm, dangling down to the ground. Enough venom to kill an ox dripped from its fangs.

Hercules launched into another of his never-ending stories, telling how the cobra had foolishly crawled under his lionskin, looking for warmth. ''This viper did not know that I strangled cobras in my crib. When I was only eight months, or maybe a year. Two of them. Sent to kill me by some jealous god or goddess. My foster mother, perhaps. Or maybe my stepfather.''

Even when he was a toddler, Hercules' extended family had been trying to rid themselves of this monster.

He cut chunks off the cobra, sliding them onto a spit. When they were cooked, he offered Peg the first piece.

Being a vegetarian, she passed it to Love—who popped the bit of breakfast snake in his mouth and chewed. He grinned at Jake. ''Most important meal of the day.''

Several times Jake caught Hercules taking sidelong glances at Peg. Twice, he made sudden attempts to seize her. But the result was always the same. Peg would shrug him off, seemingly without conscious effort. He finally decided she was protected by some kind of spell.

They headed west, crossing the Dnieper at a marshy ford, then turned south after fording the Dniester, putting the first cold blasts of winter behind them.

On the Bessarabian steppe, they came upon Peg's Sleep Chamber. The time capsule was hidden by a mound of earth bulldozed to resemble one of the burial *kurgans* that dotted the steppes—only this *kurgan* ended in a plasti-metal lock. A blank untarnished surface that could not be so much as scratched by preatomic technology.

Which clearly impressed the locals. None of their ancestors lay in the make-believe tomb, but offerings sat beside the blank surface of the lock. A sheaf of grain, a horse's skull, a long hank of some clan enemy's hair.

Around the overgrown mound the flat wintery steppe stretched off in all directions, lonely and bare. The Second Pleistocene Expedition had picked a perfect spot for the pseudo-*kurgan*—between the long barrier of the Lower Dniester, and wide marshy mouth of the Danube. Close to Greece, the Aegean, and the Black Sea, but far from major trade routes or centers of habitation. No big cities would be built in the area until well into the postatomic. By then the chamber could easily be retrieved and the site cleaned up. A perfect one-shot entrance and exit to the Bronze Age.

Opening the capsule was like Christmas come early. Since the sea fight off Atlantis, Jake and Love had been callously denied the benefits of hyperlight civilization. Now the benefits were back in abundance. Medikits. Gourmet rations. A microstove, comlinks, heated shelters, and survival packs. Even rebreathers and a collapsible motor-kayak. Not knowing what was needed, Peg brought a little of everything.

Being Peg she had gone light on the weapons, only packing some plastic explosive—in case something heavy had to be broken open. But no gas grenades. And no neural stunners. A woman who could hold off Hercules with her bare hands saw no sense in becoming a walking arsenal.

Jake and Love were glad for what they could get. Stuffing themselves on double servings of *soufflé aux blancs d'oeufs*, with *timbale de chou-fleur* in a *sauce au cari*, they tried to decide what to do next.

Love nodded toward the Sleep Chamber. "One of you could go for the cavalry." A halfhearted suggestion. The chamber could hold only one of them. Who would it be? It could not be Love. A twentieth-century "local," Love had absolutely no pull in Home Period. Nor would Peg look much better, a paleontologist—supposed to be going to the Pleistocene—coming back from an unauthorized Bronze Age excursion. Besides, Peg had risked enough to get here. She was not going back alone.

Hercules gladly volunteered, eager to see the future. But they could hardly send him. Or Iolaus.

That left Jake, who had an absolute horror of the notion. This was *his* Bronze Age Expedition—what was left of it. How could he go Home defeated? Abandoning Peg and Love. What would he do? Ask to head yet another rescue operation?

Going back was no go. Which meant they had to somehow push ahead. But to where? There was really only one answer.

"We have to head for Greece, to the Shrine of the Isthmian Maiden," Jake announced. That was also the way Hercules was headed, and Jake still had hopes of making use of him. He was too big and powerful an ally to pass up. "Anneke's people are our best links to Atlantis. Somehow we have to penetrate the defenses Apollo and Artemis have drawn around that island."

Love smirked. "What do we do if we get to Atlantis?"

"Get back what we've lost. Free what's left of our teams. Then we will have them. The Achilles heel of these pseudo-gods is their need to plunder our technology."

"Some weakness," Love scoffed. "We're the ones freezin' our asses out on the steppe, while they're flyin' around in our airships and hovercars."

"If they had their own resources, they would not be robbing us and enslaving our crews."

Love eyed him evenly, "Don't just be desperate to get back with you-know-who."

"I mean to free the whole team," Jake replied. Not just Sauromanta. There was Tyler and DePala as well. Plus Chief Larsen, Bosun McKay, and anyone else left alive. "And to reclaim *Argo* and *Atlantis*."

Love laughed. "Nothing like askin' us to shit miracles."

"Stranger things have happened," Jake reminded him.

"Lately," Love admitted.

"So are you in?" Jake asked.

"Sure. It's kind of late to switch careers. Besides, I'm a connoisseur of lost causes. Did three tours in Nam, didn't I?"

"Two and a half."

"Right." Love had been MIA ever since Jake pulled him out of Laos.

That night Hercules built a bonfire beside the mock burial mound, sacrificing a wild auroch that he had dragged live and complaining to the spot. He prayed for a safe return to Greece while the big hairy bull bellowed in terror.

The savage spectacle ended with Iolaus turning the auroch on a spit, while Love taught Herc juggling tricks using the Golden Apples of the Hesperides.

Jake sat next to Peg atop the phony burial mound, staring out over the cold Sea of Grass, glowing in the circle of Herc's bonfire. The endless steppe made him think of Sauromanta.

"What did Love mean when he said, 'you-know-who'?" Peg could at times pretty much read his mind.

Jake sighed. "He meant Sauromanta."

"The young Amazon?"

Jake nodded. How many Sauromantas could there be.

"Your update said she was a prisoner of Artemis."

"My update did not tell it all."

Peg arched an eyebrow. "Want to fill me in?"

"Sort of." Jake was not looking forward to it, but now was as bad a time as any. "She's been brain-scrubbed. Turned into a Maiden Huntress."

Peg shook her head, "Poor girl. I liked her, you know."

"So did I." A little too much. "Anyway, the brain scrub is likely to wear off. And if certain memories return, Artemis will most likely kill her."

"Which memories."

"Memories of me. For one." The penalty for being with a man was death. According to the myths, Artemis herself had killed Callisto, the Huntress Zeus seduced.

"You mean you had sex with her?" Peg was a classical scholar—able to speak and read Homeric Greek and Mycenaean—well versed in the myths.

"Yea." So many times he needed his compweb to keep track.

"What about *him*?"

"Him who?"

"Hercules." Something in the man's style had alerted Peg.

"Him too." Jake admitted.

"And Love?"

"Not that I know of."

"And now she's in trouble." Peg sounded hurt.

"Are you mad?" Jake could not tell. Peg had strict principles, but they were *hers*. And often unpredictable.

"No, just sad."

"I admit, it does not look good."

"Why? Because some strong, brave young woman comes along, and you guys can't wait to get her in bed. And now she's in danger because of it. And you two are happily off somewhere else trying to bed other women—like me?"

"It was not *exactly* like that." Though the end result was awfully similar.

"How so?"

"I did not mean for anything to happen."

Peg laughed. "Like you did not mean for anything to happen with me. I haven't forgotten our first campfire in the Mesozoic."

Jake's immediate attempt to seduce Peg almost got them trampled by a triceratops herd. He protested, "It was different."

"How different? No dinosaurs?" Peg knew about the two-headed tyrannosaur.

"With *you* my intentions were purely dishonorable. I meant to fuck you as soon as I could."

"Really? What was wrong with Sauromanta?" Peg was teasing him now.

"Nothing." There was too much *right* about her. "But I was involved with you at the time." Actually not. Nonsimultaneity did not allow relationships at a distance. But Peg never thought in hyperlight terms.

"Was involved? You mean we are not anymore?" Peg was still toying with him.

"We are," Jake protested. "If you want to be."

"Well I came all the way from the Pleistocene to find you. That should be a hint."

Love's juggling lessons were a success. By the time Peg and Jake returned to the fire, Hercules was proudly showing how he could keep all three Golden Apples in the air at the same time. Jake pretended to be impressed—though it was nothing compared to the juggling *he* was doing.

They forded the Danube more than four hundred klicks

from its mouth—floating Hercules' chariot across. The Thracians on the far side were friendly. Sometimes overly so. One tribe talked to their gods by tossing pampered messengers onto the points of spears, promising eternal bliss. Declining that honor, they headed south through the Balkans, crossing over the Shipka Pass—already choked with snow. Then they followed the valley of the Nestos to the sea, once more reaching the shore of Homer's Aegean.

Hercules went at once to the Phoenician settlement of Abdera, near the mouth of the Nestos, which he had "founded." Or at least renamed—after a former companion, eaten by wild mares during his last trip through Thrace. There they were entertained royally, but had no chance of getting a ship to Corinth. Winter was full upon them. And treacherous Mount Athos lay between them and Greece—where Darius the Great's fleet was wrecked, and his men eaten by sea monsters.

Hercules hardly noticed the inconvenience. From here on, every meal was a feast and every night a party. At the end of the day Hercules would tell Iolaus to pull up before the most prosperous farmstead. Or some clan chief's keep. Leaping out, he'd pound on the door, informing his startled hosts they had guests. No names were asked or given. But who could mistake his lionskin and brass-bound club? Survivors of previous visits hastened to make him comfortable.

After dinner he would juggle his Golden Apples, telling tales of the Garden at World's End, life among the Hyperboreans, or exciting happenings at Pharaoh's court. No one felt cheated. Or if they did, they had sense enough not to show it.

He liked best the sororities of nymphs and priestesses, supported by temple estates. Bronze Age nunnery-cum-brothels, where a hero of his standing was always welcome. Still he assured his companions, "A night passed outdoors beats the softest of beds."

Past Mount Olympus, they descended the Vale of Tempe and entered Thessaly. There they were entertained by Caeneus, the Lapith, who had been a woman but now was a man, and Prince Admetus of Pherae—former Argonauts, who had sailed with Hercules in search of the Golden Fleece.

South of Phocis, they picked their way through the Boeotian Plain; avoiding Orchomenus, which Hercules had humbled in the service of Thebes. Then avoiding Thebes, where Hercules had murdered his children. "An unlucky place for me. And I do not care to meet with Megara, my wife."

Instead they went southeast through Thespiae, a happier place for him. There the people worshiped Eros, the god of erotic love, and Hercules had hordes of living children, including the fifty (or forty-nine) sons he fathered on King Thespius's daughters. Skirting Mount Cithaeron, they passed through the back door of Megara, and onto the bandit-infested isthmus. But even bandit lords feasted Hercules, draining their wine jars and stripping their winter larders in hopes of keeping him happy.

They ended their trek fit and trim at the Shrine of the Isthmian Maiden.

Bull Dance

There is a land called Crete, ringed by wine-dark sea . . .

—*Homer,* Odyssey, *Book XIX*

The Shrine of the Isthmian Maiden stood at the narrowest part of the isthmus, where the two halves of Greece come together. And both the Aegean and the Gulf of Corinth could be seen at once. The holy spring and peak sanctuary had long been sacred, offering fresh water and safety from club-wielding footpads. Anyone reaching the sanctuary was safe from mayhem so long as they clung to the altar stone. The temple compound came later, built to house a college of nymphs.

Nymphs drawing water from the spring saw Jake, Love, Peg, Iolaus, and Hercules approaching, and sent a child running ahead with the news.

Low stone walls circled the main shrine with dry stonework, about head high. Stock pens, sheepfolds, and a horse paddock surrounded the nymphs' residence, a combination cult center and cattle ranch.

The narrow main door was overlooked by the flat roof of the shrine. Not a proper gate and battlement, but it put intruders at a disadvantage. The isthmus was totally untamed. The nearest neighbor was Sinis, Pine Bender, who tied hapless travelers to a pair of bent pines. Then he let the trees spring back, tearing the victims apart, sacrificing them to the North Wind.

Hercules beat on the wooden door, and Jake heard light footsteps on the far side. A bolt slid back. The narrow door opened, and they were greeted by a small blond girl-child with blue eyes.

She invited them in, saying, "Enter," in a small solemn voice. "My name is Erin, daughter of Nausicaa. Your garments are not those of simple travelers. Perhaps you are royalty, or gods in disguise. Or merely mortals in outlandish garb. In any case, come grace our home."

Jake recognized Anneke's younger sister, the one colored like Sauromanta. It was uncouth to ask people's names and business before they had been washed and fed. And any well-set-up stranger had to be greeted like a god—just in case.

The door led into a small space penned in by stone walls and three similar doors. Erin opened the door to the right, leading them through a short stone passage past a kennel. Hounds leaped about, greeting and sniffing. From there Erin led them down a dogleg into a stable yard, past a paddock gate and hen yard. She was plainly taking them on a twisted path, winding through the walled enclosures surrounding the shrine. Jake's navmatrix detected false turns and doubling backs. A way of impressing guests with the size and mystery of the shrine. A homey barnyard version of the sacred labyrinths enclosing the great palace-shrines on Crete.

The final door opened onto a sunny rammed-earth court. Jake could hear bulls bellowing and smell their odor coming from the far side of a long stone wall. Kitchens and a well occupied the far end of the court. Drains ran underfoot. Windows looked down on them from above.

Turning the far corner, they came on an entrance hall, smelling of soap and incense. Women were waiting with warm water, towels, and oil. Erin bid them strip and be bathed.

It felt odd to disrobe in front of nymphs and children. Erin claimed to be eleven—and looked more like eight—but she supervised the whole bath, without a blush or an awkward look. Personally anointing Hercules with oil, she rubbed his muscles until they shone. To have a small girl, living in bandit country, bathing and anointing absolute strangers showed how totally different the Bronze Age could be.

Dressed in clean tunics, they were set down at a North African-style feast of flat bread, olives, dried fruit, figs, and hummus. Erin went about with a pitcher and silver basin, washing their hands and inviting them to eat. Only after being fed, washed, and thoroughly looked over, were they finally presented in the inner shrine.

After being herded through courts, passages, the bath chamber, then the small entrance hall, coming into the *megaron* was like stepping back into the open. Only in a new reality. A tall two-story colonnade looked out toward the peak sanctuary, framing blue sky and wild isthmus hills. Sunlight streamed between the forest of columns, splashing onto frescoes of flowers and butterflies, bringing the outside in, blending light, air, paint, and stone, in a mythic oneness of building and nature—hidden at the heart of the labyrinth. It was clear where Anneke got her sense of style.

The inner shrine, with its wooden goddess statue, lay in shadow. Framed in the last of the light, stood Anneke's mother, wearing silver sacral robes cinched beneath her breasts by a gold clasp of bees kissing. Black hair hung in long serpent tresses. Tattooed snakes twined about her bare arms. As Anneke said, she had the look of a goddess.

And like Anneke she was long-boned, dark-eyed, and dark-skinned. Almost Egyptian. She said her name was "Nausicaa, the Burner of Ships."

She called Erin to her. Though they looked to be total opposites—the girl being so small and fair—they stood not merely as daughter and mother, but also as novice and priestess. Erin gravely practiced for the day when she would stand in her mother's place, with daughters of her own beside her. Greeting Zeus-knows-who. Theseus perhaps, on his way to Athens.

Hercules displayed the Golden Apples from Hera's Garden at the Western End of the World, giving his name and lineage, and that of his nephew Iolaus. Despite months on the road, the hybrid oranges showed no sign of spoiling. Future fruit lasted forever.

Jake made the other introductions, adding that they had been sent to the isthmus by Anneke in Egypt. Nausicaa ordered up an immediate sacrifice of thanksgiving, happy to greet anyone having had contact with her distant daughter.

Men appeared, bringing in a heifer for sacrifice. At their head marched a muscular blond who had to be Erin's father, looking strong, compact, and sure of himself. Jake could see both halves of the family now—the dark Cretan, and the blond mainland savage. He was called *Wanax*, which meant king, but in this case was clearly more like nymph's consort. Like Pharaoh, *Wanax* was a title earned by marriage, not by birth.

With him were other men who'd managed to attach themselves to the shrine—coppersmiths, furniture makers, herdboys, and handsome ne'er-do-wells sharp enough to spot a soft billet. Welcome so long as they kept the shrine safe and the women happy. If they did not, the isthmus road offered ready replacements.

Matriliny and queenship helped make the European Bronze Age the era of the wandering hero. There was little to keep an ambitious boy at hope. Simple father-to-son succession remained a rarity. And absent fathers abounded. Gods set the standard, freely abandoning their offspring, making the primal family link mother-child. Hercules, Apollo, Perseus, and Theseus were all reared by their mothers.

Hercules remained extremely attached to his mother—his real mother Alcmene, not Hera, the foster mother he was named for—considering her a female paragon, the wisest and most beautiful of women.

Father-son relations were more often fraught with danger. Theseus's father tried to poison him. Perseus was put in a box as a baby and thrown into the sea. Zeus's father tried to eat him. Fostering was a common, and somewhat less violent alternative. Those who did come into their father's kingdoms often did it through murder and incest. Zeus and Oedipus killed their fathers—then made love to their mothers. To preserve father-to-son succession the Thutmosids regularly married their mothers, sisters, and daughters.

But more often heroes-in-the-making hit the road. Exiled princes. Footloose vagabonds. Beggars and godsons. Looking for monsters to kill, cattle to lift, or stables to clean, seeing what the world had to offer. And mostly what the world had to offer was women. Find that queen, princess, or nymph and you were set for life—so long as the two of you could stay together. Or until someone tougher came along. It was a world in which any boy could grow up to be Pharaoh, provided he found the right wife.

Women tossed scented wood on the central hearth, while the *Wanax* slaughtered the fatted cow before a courtyard altar. Though he wielded the poleax, Nausicaa made the offering. By the time the feasting and drinking was done, it was high morning, and the *Wanax* whistled up his pack, inviting her guests to go hunting. Love and Hercules accepted.

As soon as they left, Nausicaa dropped all pretenses, inviting Peg and Jake to a private *durbar*. She would not be much of a priestess if she had not already known who they were. Hercules was tolerated as a touchy guest of honor, but Nausicaa treated Peg as the true head of the party. Jake she included because he was Peg's "consort."

And because Anneke had written about him. From swineherd to High King mainlanders were mostly illiterate—but Nausicaa and her daughter used waxed tablets to send messages in the Atlantean script, Linear A.

"The family is deeply in your debt," she told them. "But nothing can be done about getting you to Atlantis until the sea lanes open in the spring. By then Anneke should be back. Doubtless she will have some idea. She usually does." Clearly they were Anneke's problem. A pair of priceless strays Nausicaa's daughter had picked up—and would be back in the spring to deal with. Until then they were guests of the shrine.

That night Nausicaa led them up the stairs, bare slender feet showing beneath her robes, keys to the shrine ringing with each step. Tattooed snakes on her forearm danced in the lamplight. At the top of the stair she unlocked a small bedchamber, inviting Jake and Peg to make themselves at home. The double couch inside smelled of must and incense.

Next morning, Jake awoke to find Peg's familiar form twined around him. Out the room's one small window, he could look over the mazelike walls toward the isthmus. Cattle lowed beneath them. Between the barnyard odors he could smell the sea. He and Peg had made love in the Mesozoic, the Pleistocene, on Mars, in Sitting Bull's tipi, on a Mississippi riverboat, and now in a Bronze Age shrine. A sixty-million-year span that never ceased to surprise.

They went down to breakfast hand in hand. Erin eagerly

served up a posset of cheese, barley, honey, and wine, looking as pleased as her older sister had been helping Hatshepsut mount Pharaoh's throne.

Love acted fit and happy, bolting down cold beef from a marble bowl. He beamed between bites. "These are *friendly* folks. Damn good to their guests."

Jake did not have to ask how Love had spent the night. His folding bed in the hall was still folded. Linens lay neatly stacked alongside it. "Especially the women folks," Love chuckled. "I ain't been so well taken care of since I left Troy. With no silly talk about clubbing us to death."

Jake nodded. From what he had seen the shrine was run by women and for women. Part sorority. Part family enterprise. Like a convent—with children—and without vows of chastity. Supported by lands and offerings, and protected by popular opinion, backed by the might of Queen Medea.

"Yep. I've hardly ever *seen* white folks so hospitable." Love chewed happily. "You don't see me missing Flint one little bit. Nor Nam neither."

Hercules was eager to go on to Corinth and carouse with Jason. Queen Medea's consort had been a penniless wandering prince when Hercules helped get him as far as the Hellespont. Now that Jason had made good, Hercules meant to bask in his gratitude. After that it was on to Mycenae, to show off the Golden Apples, rubbing his success in the face of the High King and his Dung Man.

Love decided to go with him. "We should split up. We'll be in Greece all winter. It's silly to all stay in one spot, where we can all be swept up at once. An' we need to keep an eye on Herc. A dude that big is *bound* to be useful." The demigod could be an amazingly dangerous oaf, but handy to have on your side.

"Herc's always collecting traveling companions," Love reasoned. "No one's gonna notice him comin' back from Egypt and the Barbary Coast with an African."

"You're from Michigan, *remember*?"

"What High King honky is gonna know *that*?"

"He wouldn't. But there might be Egyptians in court."

Love snorted. "Africa's a big place. I'll slip in a little jive Swahili. Let 'em think I'm Nelson Mandela."

"Don't double-talk yourself into trouble."

Love laughed. "Like we ain't in trouble already?"

The man made his point. Under Jake's sole direction, the expedition had gone straight into the ground. Love was lucky just to be alive. He could hardly do worse on his own. Nor would he be going far. Mycenae was only a couple of days away. The heart of Greece was a small place, where a dozen city-states lay within walking distance.

"An' I hear the Queen of Corinth is a sister. Women kept askin' if I was royalty. Aimin' to commit a little *lèse majesty*."

Jake grinned. "Living among demigods gets *real* addictive."

"Hey"—he grinned back—"don't I know it?"

Love took a pair of Taurian horses, a comlink, medikit, two spears, and a bullhide shield. Ready to take the Bronze Age by storm. His parting advice was, "Try not to do anything dumb-ass."

"I'll try not to." Jake was running out of things to do. Dumb-ass or otherwise. He had tried once to get to Atlantis, failing drastically. And all the equipment he had brought was now arrayed against him. Somehow he needed to salvage what remained of his expedition, beating the gods and the odds. But how?

Winter deepened. Erin took them on tours of the spring and peak sanctuary. The rounded top of the knoll stood bare against the sky, shaped like a maiden's breast, with the altar for a nipple. Erin pointed to two moon-shaped dents in the bedrock. "Those are hoofprints of Pegasus, the flying horse born from drops of Gorgon's blood."

Looking at the little priestess-in-the-making, Jake wondered what it would be like to grow up in this sacred spot, the golden daughter of a nymph, surrounded by myth and mystery.

From the peak sanctuary he could see the whole circuit of Erin's world. The Acrocorinth and Medea's citadel. The coast road. The two seas divided by the narrow isthmus. On one side lay the Aegean. On the other side lay the Gulf of Corinth, a great tectonic trench cutting Greece almost completely in half. A pair of wooden rails let ships be hauled from one sea to the other.

Peg made herself perfectly at home, getting on famously with Nausicaa and the nymphs of the shrine. She had an amazing ability to adapt to the situation at hand. Perhaps it came from studying dinosaurs all her life. Always fixed on a distant goal, Peg pretty much took the present as it was. Such blithe unconcern had gotten her to the Mesozoic and back—twice. How much harder could the Bronze Age be?

Jake was the worrier, always trying to angle his way around trouble. Never quite succeeding.

The shrine gave a grand feast at winter solstice, celebrating an early Christmas—more than a thousand years before Christ. Storehouses and granaries were thrown open. Those who came were sent home with gifts of new wine, bread, partridges, and winter pears. Another feast six weeks later marked the halfway point between solstice and equinox—Christmas and Candlemas. Yule and Groundhog Day.

Jake saw how the shrine fit into the moneyless Bronze Age economy. The countryside had no general market for grain or cattle, just private trading or periodic barter fairs. People producing for themselves fell into a cycle of summer-fall harvests, and winter-spring starvation. The shrine acted as a counterweight, stimulating production by demanding harvest offerings, then returning the forced savings in the form of public feasts, just when folks needed it the most.

Even in the dead of winter there was farming to be done—digging and pruning, planting winter crops, bringing in green olives. The shrine ensured that those who toiled also ate. Year-round, her looms and shops offered steady work for those with nothing to do and nowhere to go—serving as a safe haven for unwanted children and unattached women. A welcome alternative to the female infanticide popular in more "civilized" periods.

Anneke arrived as soon as the sea lanes opened, coming home in triumph, accompanied by an Egyptian flotilla. Five ships had taken her first to Crete, to Amnisos, then on to Atlantis, and Kenchreai, the Aegean port of Corinth. She told how Egypt had turned from war to trade. "Not just with us, but with Troy and the Black Sea—and south, around the Horn of Africa. Hatshepsut plans to dig a canal through the desert, to make Egypt the way station between Spain and India."

She was ecstatic to have Jake to share this with. Her sole disappointment was not having Sauromanta there at her hour of triumph. But the gods give, and the gods take away. "You will see her again,'' Jake promised. He only had to figure out how.

As for getting to Atlantis, Anneke had to scheme for that as well. She had arrived at the very start of the sailing season, because that was when the shrine maidens went into the pastures to Greet the Bulls.

Greeting the bulls meant seeing which—if any—of this year's bulls were suited for the Bull Dance. Anneke led the procession down to the meadows, tall and proud in tumbler's tight jacket and soft leather knee breeches. Maidens and youths trooped behind her, carrying sheaves of grain.

Jake and Peg went, too. Peg to participate. Jake to keep an eye on Peg. She was also dressed like a tumbler—but in stretch fabric, an electric blue torso suit that looked otherworldly amid the homespun wool and dyed leather.

The cattle were in the lower meadows, where the pastures blended into dunes and salt marsh and the tang of brine seasoned the breeze. Cattle lifters from the isthmus were forced to come farther, and go closer to the towns and coast road, then drive their booty back past the shrine.

Twice that winter the *Wanax* ambushed rustlers attempting to slip back onto the isthmus, retrieving the stolen cattle, and sending the surviving brigands to his wife to judge. Both times microamps and infrared vision led them right to the raiders, convincing the *Wanax* that Jake had the night senses of a leopard. Word had gone into the isthmus that the Maiden Shrine had uncanny defenders, letting Jake earn his keep several times over.

Bronze Age cattle reflected the various wild strains. So far Jake had seen the red shambling bulls of Spain, the lyre-horned cattle of Egypt, and the shaggy aurochs of the steppes. Now he was seeing the big piebald and pinto-coated bulls of Crete, magnificent beasts with great mountainous backs. Graceful curving horns sprang out of massive curly brows, sweeping up in an open U, with tips as sharp as bronze spearpoints. Backed by the full force of a charge, they could shatter oak planking, or drive right through a shield.

Anneke walked straight up to the nearest, holding out her sheaf of grain in one hand, and a lick of sea salt in the other. Peg went with her. Jake hung back, with little Erin at his side, plenty happy just to watch.

The bull took the grain and salt as his due. Several of his buddies came up to the line of smiling girls and boys, to see if they could get some, too. Never having been chased or beaten, the bulls had no reason to fear these happy treat-bearing humans. Even the isthmus robbers had gone for the cows, not wanting to try to herd home half a ton of trouble.

Without warning, Anneke slid around the horns of the biggest one and pulled herself up on his back. The beast snorted and stamped, trying to shake her off. She clung to the horns, like Europa riding Zeus, digging her heels into his hump. His fellows retreated, fearing they, too, might be mounted.

Bucking and snorting, the bull tried to toss Anneke off. Fanning out into a circle, the youths and maidens began to dance and dodge around the bull. Such bulls are wickedly fast, and can outrun a racehorse in a sprint, but the dancers drew him this way and that. Always presenting a shifting target.

From where Jake stood, it seemed insanely dangerous. But this was a rite of spring, leading to the midsummer Bull Dances on Crete and Atlantis. A dance sacred to Poseidon—the Mother's husband and patron god of the isthmus. So far as the maidens were concerned, the dance symbolized the sacred marriage, a mating of female and male principles that could not be consummated without risking blood and death. The boys seemed to take it less seriously, enjoying the sheer deviltry and adventure.

When the bull was played out, Anneke leaped off. Peg was there to catch her and the dance was done for the day. Girls and boys came back from the bull pasture happy and joking, doing handsprings and dance steps.

Nausicaa and her *Wanax* met their daughter at the edge of the pasture, leading Anneke to the sacred spring, where she was bathed and anointed. Celebrating a successful Greeting of the Bulls. Peg, too, was all alight, saying to Jake, "This is it."

"What's it?" He looked her over for bruises.

"How we can get to Crete and Atlantis."

Jake could see the conversation headed in a scary direction. Plainly Peg and Anneke had planned this ahead.

"When summer comes, Anneke and the best of the mainland dancers will sail for Crete. If they succeed there, they will go on to Atlantis. We can learn the dance and sail with them.''

''If we live,'' he reminded her.

''We'll live, silly.'' Peg brimmed with self-confidence. ''And no one will look for us among the dancers.''

''No one with any sense.'' The Bull Dance brought back memories of dodging taurosaurs on their second trip to the Mesozoic. A single angry taurosaur—a sort of big-headed triceratops—had killed or maimed half of the Second Mesozoic Expedition. That time Jake only had only been trying to extract his team; no one expected him to dance with the beastly behemoth.

That night they argued it out in bed. By dawn Peg had won him over. It was a way to get as far as Crete. Then maybe to Atlantis. There was even a divine goofiness to the plan, which held out the hope of success. And it was better than trying to beg another ship and crew from Anneke's family.

Happy with their choice, Anneke began teaching Jake more than he ever meant to know about bulls. ''Not one bull in twenty is fit for the dance,'' she told them. ''Most are too cowardly. Some are too savage. The trick is to find the few that are born to the dance.'' Having trained as a bull leaper on Crete, she knew bulls as minutely as teenage girls in other times and places might know breeds of horses.

''But every bull comes armed and angry to the dance,'' Anneke warned. ''Angry enough to kill. With a terrible temper and two stout horns. Never doubt that. But the bull is not afraid. He is out to teach you manners. Not fighting for his life.''

''He lets you take liberties,'' Jake suggested, ''so long as he is in charge.''

Anneke grinned. ''Exactly.''

This was what made the dance so different, and difficult. Jake had been to bullfights, where the bulls were goaded into fighting, then tricked to their deaths by the matador's cape and sword. But this was neither a fight, nor a trick, just daredevil acrobatics with a half-wild bull.

Jake went back down to the bull pasture, prepared to dance, or at least catch Peg if she was thrown. This time the bulls were more wary. Only a few could be tempted with gifts of grain and salt. Anneke laughed. "We have shown we cannot be trusted."

After several edgy passes, the lead bull—the one Anneke had ridden—snorted and stamped, bellowing defiance. There would be no joy riding today. A boy dashed forward, did a cartwheel, and tried to mount. But the bull caught him with the flat of his horn, sending him flying into a patch of salt marsh.

Still not satisfied, the bull spun about, aiming to skewer the youth.

Peg ran in, shouting to get the angry beast's attention. He stopped, turned, glared, then charged. Fast as she was, Peg could hardly outrun a charging bull. Instead she feinted left, then spun right. As he brushed by Peg reached out, laying her hand on the near horn, turning the bull's head around her, using his momentum the way she had used Hercules'. Anneke leaped up and down, yelling advice.

Once, twice, three times the bull spun around her, but could not touch her with his horns. He gave a disgusted snort and lumbered off, fed up with the dance.

Anneke was all over Peg, checking her for bruises, saying she was a natural. "I have never seen a beginner do so well." Jake could have told her that Peg feared nothing on four legs.

Peg was fine, but the boy who had been thrown had to be carried back to the shrine, with a twisted ankle and two broken ribs. Nothing their medikits could not handle.

That spring the medikits got a good workout. Youths and maidens were whacked, kicked, tossed, and trampled, during weeks spent in the bull pastures. Only one was gored, a girl who got a horn through her calf. Nausicaa was amazed that the medikit even took away the scar.

A few scrapes and bruises were the worst that Jake could boast of. He was only tossed twice. But on Crete and Atlantis it would be ten times as dangerous—trying to pull these tricks with strange bulls in narrow, paved courts, in front of shouting crowds. This was only practice. That would be the real thing.

Love came up from Tiryns, where he and Hercules had wintered. Herc was still not allowed within the gates of Mycenae. High King Eurystheus was determined not to succumb to one of the lethal "accidents" that dogged his demigod cousin. Love got a laugh out of Peg's plan to infiltrate Crete and Atlantis by way of the Bull Dance. ''Why not somethin' safe and sober? Like juggling cobras.''

Dancing in the bull pastures sounded way too bucolic to a Motown man. And it made no sense for all of them to go on this Cretan recon. It was better to have some reserve backup.

''Just keep close to Hercules,'' Jake suggested. ''We're going to need him down the line.''

''Hey. Me and Herc are real bros. I don't think he'd even brain me—unless he was drunk.'' Being Hercules' friend and boon companion was only slightly less dangerous then being his sworn enemy. Love would have been far safer with the bulls.

They got a grand send-off from Kenchreai, a small unwalled Atlantean trading station that served as the Aegean port of Corinth. Medea and Jason came down to bless the ship. As Love had said, Medea had black skin and long, snaky dreadlocks. There was plenty of Afro-Egyptian blood in the royal families of Greece, and Medea's birthplace, Colchis on the Black Sea, was an African colony flush up against the Caucasus Mountains. The Bronze Age racial mix included black Caucasians and tribes of blond Africans.

Jason stood a half step behind Medea, as befitted her consort. Wearing a wolfskin over his shoulder, he carried two bronze spears, and had one foot bare—just for luck. He perfectly embodied the mythic Bronze Age wandering hero, standing half-shod, spears in hand, behind his queenly mate. Already Jason seemed to find this boring. Jake sensed the same restless energy that had taken Jason to Italy, Africa, and Colchis, now aching to go to work on Corinth.

The ship that would carry them to Crete bore a black sail and bull's horns on the prow. She was a big double-ended, thirty-oared trading galley, with an awning aft and a deckhouse for the passengers. Nothing was too good for Bull Dancers on their way to meet the god.

Aided by a gentle west wind, they coasted along the Isthmus, past the tangled hills of Megara, putting in at Eleusis, and at Phaleron Beach, which served as the port of Athens. From there Jake could see the Athenian citadel atop the Acropolis rock. South of Athens lay twenty klicks of open sea, separating Sounion Head—Homer's ''Holy promontory of Athens''—from Kea, the westernmost of the Cyclades.

The Isle of Kea topped a seamount that was actually an extension of the Attic mountains. The galley put in at a narrow harbor on the northwest coast. A walled city sat on a promontory overlooking the bay, a mixed Mycenaean-Atlantean settlement, crowded with tall houses.

They had crossed over the invisible border into the Atlantean sphere. The Greek mainland had been a barbarous outback, overrun by bandits and robber barons. Within its walls, Kea was a warren of commerce, populated by masons, tanners, potters, gem cutters and perfume sellers. Peg and Jake toured the harbor town, climbing staired streets and stopping to rest on public benches.

Next day a north wind blew them straight down the line of the Cyclades, past Kythnos and Seriphos, to Melos, last stop before Crete. Rather than spend a night aboard ship, Jake looked for lodging ashore. Melos was filling up with summer traffic, and the only place he found was the same little room he had shared with Sauromanta. The one with dolphins on the wall. Lying awake that night, he smelled cypress and frankincense. The spices Sauromanta rubbed on her body. He wondered if the woman who owned the room had not washed the sheets.

But when he awoke he saw the linen was a new Egyptian pattern, part of Hatshepsut's export revival. The smell was in him.

Even with the north wind behind her, the galley took a day and a night to cross over to Crete. Dawn found them off the tall rocky coast. This time it was the north shore, not so bleak, sprinkled with port cities and white villages set amid lush green fields.

Crete began life as a primeval Eden, virtually uninhabited until the late Stone Age, her hills and mountains covered with virgin forests of oak, myrtle, juniper, fir, and cypress. Pears, quince, mulberries, and almonds grew wild for the picking. The first hunters to arrive found fat Cretan ibex so tame they could be taken by hand. Protected by the long sea crossings, "The Great Goddess Isle" had never known war or want. Her towns had no walls. Her people passed their time harvesting land and sea. Or crafting works of art.

If Atlantis was the head and heart, Crete was the body, home to more than half the Atlantean population. Birthplace of Zeus. And the Minotaur. Equidistant from Europe, Africa, and Asia, a link between Atlantis and the outer world.

Amnisos, the main port of Knossos, had a double harbor, separated by a rocky promontory crowned with houses. The western bay was a river mouth, teeming with barges and pleasure boats. Cobbled streets black with people wound down to meet the sea.

It made Jake sad (and nervous) to know that this idyllic peace would some day be ripped apart. Hidden below the horizon a hundred klicks to the north was the Callisto volcano, smoking above Atlantis. When Callisto blew, Amnisos would be leveled by the shock, then engulfed by the sea, obliterated by a *tsunami* of terrible proportions. A wall of water hundreds of meters tall would come roaring over the northern horizon, drowning anyone who chanced to survive the quake. Depositing harbor shipping several klicks inland.

There was nothing Jake could do about it. Trying to change that unpleasant bit of history would be as profitless as standing on the wharf and trying to hold back the tidal wave with his hand. But Jake believed in doing his bit. During airship training in Hitler's Germany, Jake told every Jew he happened to meet to get the hell out of the country. He got a lot of knowing nods and odd looks.

Right now, his job was to get in and out of Atlantis before any of this happened. He still felt queasy stepping ashore.

The happy throng that met them was clearly oblivious to the coming catastrophe. Seeing the black sail and the curving horns on the prow, they poured down to the docks, eager to see the mainland Bull Dancers. Dockworkers in kilts and loincloths, ladies carrying sunshades, potters with clay in their hair, all came cheering as the ship docked. Brown, white, and black faces beamed with anticipation, lit up by the dancers' piety and courage.

Jake shook his head. "They have already made us into heroes—and all we've done is arrive by boat. We'd better not disappoint."

"We won't." Peg was all confidence.

Jake was not so sure. He had hoped they might not have to do the Bull Dance. That they could just slip aboard a ship plying between the northern ports and Atlantis. It was not that he was afraid of the bulls—which he was—but that the Bull

Dance was not *essential*. Merely a cover to get them to Crete. If they could go on to Atlantis without actually tackling the bulls, so much the better.

One look at that crowd told him that was never happening. The dancers from the mainland were going to have to show their steps. Anything less would cause a religious riot. Jake, Peg, and Anneke were shuffled ashore, strung with flowers, then hoisted aboard sedan chairs with seats of red bullhide. The cheering crowd surged back into the streets of the town, carrying them with it, singing songs in Cretan, showering them with summer flowers.

A fine welcome. But the red bullhide Jake sat on was a reminder that a bull's horns were meant to draw blood.

They stopped above the port, at a sacred cave, dedicated to the Maiden Goddess of Birth and Death. There they were anointed with a sprinkle of blood from a bull sacrifice. Standing in the cool dark cave, flecked with bull's blood, with flower petals in his hair, Jake saw a grim irony. The Maiden of Childbirth was another name for Artemis. In Tauria, Peg had saved him from being clubbed to death by Bull Men to please Artemis—only to haul him to Crete to dodge real bulls in her honor.

A cart arrived to take them to Knossos, a small half room on wheels, with gold tassels hanging from the embroidered awning. Cushions were piled around a table decked with sweetmeats, candied fruits, and almonds. But the bullocks pulling the cart had red paint spiraled round their horns.

They set out on a slow ride to Knossos, jolting over grassy hills and flowery summer fields.

So far as style and comfort went, Crete was light-years ahead of the mainland. The road inland was lined with two-story country homes, flower gardens, and wayside shrines. Peak sanctuaries looked down from the heights. Every farm seemed prosperous. Harvesters in rolled headcloths stopped to applaud their progress. And there was never a wall or weapon in sight. No one feared being waylaid by bandit lords. Or being seized by Sinis, Pine Bender and offered up for sacrifice.

Jake began to see how the Bull Dance frenzy fit into all this. War, rape, and plunder were mass participation sports on the mainland. Here that violent energy was channeled by religious ritual. Heroines and heroes placed their lives on the narrow altar of the Bull Court—for the Goddess to take, or give back. Too bad Jake had to be one of them.

He asked Anneke if there was human sacrifice on Crete.

Of course, she said. "When we dance with the bulls we offer ourselves up, facing the Mother's Consort in one of his most dangerous forms. But we do not throw our lives away."

Hopefully not, Jake thought.

She pointed at Mount Juktas, "The Dead Zeus," rearing over the hills a dozen klicks to the south. "On the side of the mountain is a ruined shrine, too small for you to see from here."

Actually Jake's lenses locked right on the ruins, three oblong stone shrines lying crushed beside a fallen hall.

"When Zeus first seized Callisto, people tried to placate him, taking an unblemished youth and binding him to the Dying God's altar, like a sacrificial bull. A priestess gave a benediction, while a priest slit the boy's throat."

Judging by the ruins, Jake guessed the sacrifice did not take.

"As soon as the blood drained from the body, Atlantis shook to its roots. An eruption leveled that shrine, along with the Labyrinth, Knossos, and every city on Crete." The destruction was so vivid, Anneke talked as though she had been there, though it all must have happened long before her time. "We rebuilt the Labyrinth. We rebuilt the cities. But that shrine remains as the Goddess left it. The bodies inside were never reburied. Priestess, priest, and victim lie there on the side of the sacred mountain. Lest we forget."

On the mainland human sacrifice was so much a way of life, even Hercules could not stamp it out. Anneke clearly preferred the Bull Dance.

The dance was dangerous—no doubt about it—but free of intentional cruelty. No bulls died, except in sacrifice. And dancers set their own limits. In less civilized periods—like the twentieth century—Jake had seen bullfights that always ended in death. Death for the bull. Death for the picador's horse. And any matador who did not take the prescribed risks was hooted from the ring.

But that was a century of mass slaughter, with its atomic bombings, holocausts, and highway fatalities. Far behind the Bronze Age in many respects. In the early postatomic a large nation lost more people driving to work than the Bronze

Age lost in battle. When Love left for Nam he was statistically *safer* than if he stayed in Motown, with its car culture and murder rate.

They crossed over the divide, descending into the valley of the Kairatos. Jake saw the Labyrinth ahead, an immense temple-palace hundreds of meters across, built outward from the Bull Court. A true wonder of the ancient world.

Columned porticoes, gaily painted shrines, audience chambers, baths, treasuries, and private apartments covered thousands of square meters of hillside, forming a royal residence, cult center, and bull ring—all surrounded by formal gardens, lesser villas, and country manors. Which were in turn ringed by Knossos town, the religious capital of Crete. The ground floor of the Labyrinth alone had more than three hundred rooms. The upper floors were topped with flat roofs, decorated with great stone horns pointed at the sky.

But none of this was what caused Jake to instantly focus his corneal lenses. ''Look.'' Anneke sat up in her seat, alive with excitement, pointing at the palace. ''Hera, Queen of Heaven, has come to view the dance.''

Perched atop the highest roof, tethered to a tall wooden pillar, was an airship, a near sister to the *Argo*. But Jake's compweb immediately noted a dozen minor differences. She was the *Atlantis*, the lost flagship of the First Bronze Age Expedition. Supposedly in the hands of the goddess Hera—Hercules' foster mother, and Apollo's sworn nemesis.

Part III
God on a Machine

Labyrinth

Chances took a quantum leap. The *Atlantis* was here. So close Jake could *see* her. And clearly in running condition. But who was running her? Were any survivors of her crew aboard? How much original equipment was intact? And how could he get ahold of her? His compweb came up with a dozen different plans—none of them surefire.

Jake huddled with Peg and Anneke in the back of the oxcart, saying, ''I have to get aboard that ship.''

Peg studied *Atlantis* with her unaided eyes. ''Won't that be dangerous?''

''Probably,'' Jake agreed. But hopefully not impossible. Peg was utterly nerveless, facing the most appalling risks with matter-of-fact unconcern, often acting as if Jake had to remind her where the perils lay. He was the one with the wary compweb and paranoid sense of self-preservation.

Anneke cut in, ''There is a way.'' They both looked at her. ''It won't be easy,'' she added.

''Naturally,'' Jake nodded.

''With the Goddess here, the best teams will be taken into the Labyrinth, heaped with honors, then presented to Hera, Queen of Heaven. If we do well enough, we could be taken into the Labyrinth with them.''

Jake watched the Labyrinth and airship draw closer. Anneke's plan had some sharp angles to it. To be honored in Knossos, they had to do more than just survive in the Bull Court. They had to shine. Taking more chances with strange bulls. Shaving their margins. Taking risks to really amaze the Cretans. Not hiding among the Bull Dancers, but standing out.

If they succeeded—and survived—they would be housed in the Labyrinth itself, under the eye of the Queen of Heaven. That alone might be fatal.

It was hard to know how Hera related to Artemis and Apollo. In mythic terms they were enemies. Hera was Zeus's sister, raped and forced into marriage to legitimize his position as King of the Gods. Apollo and Artemis were Zeus's children by Leto, a demigoddess. Hera had reason to hate them all.

But how much could Jake rely on the myths? These were not *real* gods. Yet myths were often based on truth. There might be some rift in the opposition Jake could somehow exploit.

The oxcart lurched along the paved road, slowly ascending the valley of the Kairatos. "The Goddess is in all of us," Anneke added. "She is in the beasts in the woods. In the trees. In the wind that blows, and in the rain that falls. And also in Hera. To deny that is to deny life. But Hera is one of Her most dangerous forms. More deadly than a leopardess. She has the power to destroy. And to predict the future."

That Jake could believe—this pseudo-goddess was *from* the future.

Anneke let the seriousness of this sink in. Atlantis walked a fine line with the Olympians, honoring their power without worshiping it. "Even Apollo has the God within him. Just as a wolf does. Or as you do, Jake."

He thanked her for the honor.

Crowds filled Knossos town, as thick as bees in winter, buzzing with excitement, cheering the oxcart all the way through town. The bullocks hauled them up to a spacious caravanserai, separated from the Labyrinth by a small stream and a screen of tall cypress—housing for the dancers who did not have quarters in Knossos.

Dancers came out to greet them—Cretans, Atlanteans, and other Islanders, Trojans and Carians from Asia Minor, Libyans in goatskins, Lycians in feathered bonnets. Drawn from three continents, and speaking a dozen languages, they represented the entire Atlantean sphere. As well as adventurers from as far away as Spain and Babylon. Dark and light, male and female, all they had in common were athletic builds, a knowledge of bulls, and an overdeveloped death wish.

The caravanserai was too full for there to be any privacy. Peg and Anneke lodged together in the women's wing. Jake shared a small upper-story room with two Cretans from the eastern part of the island, a pair of Milesians, and a Canaanite from the Phoenician colony on Atlantis. No one complained about the crowding. Everyone's mind was on the bulls.

A few days later they got their first look. The festival opened with a running of the bulls. Poseidon's sacred herd was driven down from its pastures on the north slopes of Mount Juktas, through fields and orchards, past the caravanserai to the temple meadows along the Kairatos. A stunning sight. First came the great cloud of dust rising over the hills, then the carpet of running bulls, topping the last tree-lined ridge. A jostling stampede of waving horns and thundering hide—piebald and dappled, clay yellow, blue-black and brick red—pouring into Knossos town, toppling market stalls, snorting and bellowing as herdsmen funneled them down to the meadows.

They seemed twice the size of the mainland bulls, throwbacks to *Bos primigenius*, the Stone Age bulls of Europe painted on cave walls. The tallest were taller than Jake, as tall as Hercules. Hercules himself claimed to have tackled one, dragging the bull from Crete to Mycenae, to fulfill yet another of his labors. Jake could easier believe the stories of nine-headed Hydras or brazen-winged birds. But Hercules had insisted the isthmus breeds were descended from that bull. Nausicaa never stooped to contradicting a guest. Having seen how big the isthmus herds were, Jake merely suggested, "That must have been a lot of bull." Hercules beamed in happy agreement.

Eager dancers met the herd at the edge of town, dodging in among the leaders, dashing up alleys to escape. Cretans lining roofs and upper windows cheered their courage, gasping when the horns came too close. Two dancers were thrown. One trampled. Jake stayed clear, hoarding his luck for the dance.

Down in the meadows the herds were culled under the watchful gaze of the dancers. Priestesses marked how the bulls behaved in a strange pasture. Seeing which acted too scared or timid. And which seemed unnecessarily savage.

When the culling was complete, the dancers divided into teams. Jake, Peg, and Anneke stood together, scratching their names on a potsherd, passing it to the priestess in charge of the bulls. She put it in her pot. Three by three the bulls were announced, prayers were said, then the priestess rattled her pot and produced three curved clay shards—the teams that would face each set of bulls.

Jake added his own appeals to the priestess's prayers—saying yea or nay, depending on the quality of the bulls.

When their potsherd popped out, Jake could hardly believe their luck. Peg broke into a grin. Anneke jumped and giggled, "The Goddess is with us."

Two of their bulls were near perfect. One of them was the absolute best of the lot. A brick red beast, with a broad solid back, and horns that curved inward at the tip—less likely to gore. Sure they could do wonders with this bull, Jake mentally named him Rusty.

The second was a frost white giant with a slow, even temper, that Jake called Snowball. The chief priestess gave Anneke a garland of flowers to mark him with. As she approached, Snowball came forward to meet her, curious, alert, and active, but not aggressive. An excellent sign.

Anneke came back happily saying, "He accepts our sacrifice."

The third bull was not nearly so good.

Enoch the Canaanite returned to the caravanserai bitterly disappointed. Enoch had tight curly hair, and a dour outlook on life. Luck of the draw had put him in the fourth day's dance with Jake's team, facing the same three bulls. That night he and Jake ate together in the communal dining hall, decorated with a frieze of partridges and hoopoes.

Rusty and Snowball were fine by Enoch, but the third bull scared him. This bull had splayed horns and a touchy disposition. He had snorted and pawed, shaking off the garland Peg put on him. Stamping on the flowers. "A bull that will kill," Enoch declared.

Jake nodded, barely believing the priestesses had passed on

the beast. But he was a magnificent black monster—Baal incarnate. And the Bull Dance was sacrifice, never meant to be easy. Or safe.

He pointed out to Enoch that the odds were two to one against his ever having to face this Beast of Baal.

Odds did not comfort Enoch. "Three teams and three bulls means someone must face him." Jake admitted that was so. He just hoped it was Enoch and not him.

The midsummer Bull Dance lasted as long as it takes the moon to wax from new to full. On Crete the main dance was at Knossos. Lesser dances were held at Phaistos and Mallia, and in open courts and pastures all about the island. When the frenzy reached its peak, the Bull Dance moved to Atlantis for the last dances of midsummer.

Jake, Peg, and Anneke were on the tablet for the fourth day, along with Enoch's team, and another team composed entirely of Cretans. During the first three days they got to see some hair-raising stunts—double flips over the horns, handsprings and handstands on the bull's back. Showing how impossible it would be to impress the Cretans at their own game.

Dance day dawned fever tense. Tall billowing thunderheads towered over the Bull Court, heralding another long hot summer day. With a chance of thunder.

Jake was up at dawn, being bathed and curried, like a beast of sacrifice. By now he was used to being stripped and washed by women and girls. Atlantean society had a relaxed attitude toward nudity. Children ran naked. Women went about with breasts bared. Mother's caves and phallic pillars were accepted as natural manifestations of divine genitalia. Everyone *knew* what was under the public codpiece.

Washing guests was a bit of Bronze Age sex education, done in the home or shrine, under the Mother's supervision. Here-and-now the family was still everything—teacher, preacher, government, and lawgiver. Farming your kids out to professionals had yet to be invented. Jake had learned to relax and accept. Here is the male body, to scrub, rinse, towel, oil, and groom. Hot and cold water cascaded over him, women's hands washed and combed him, amid friendly laughter and coy jokes.

Thoroughly cleaned and primped, Jake waited by the caravanserai door, naked except for a loin guard crimped at the waist, and calf-length dancer's boots. Women wore the same outfit, along with necklaces and arm rings.

Crowds lined the paved processional way connecting the caravanserai to the Labyrinth. Every citizen of Knossos and all their upcountry cousins had come to cheer the dancers, to see them enter the Labyrinth. Jake heard the roar of applause as the women emerged, then he stepped into the sunlight with the men. With him were Enoch the Canaanite and the two Milesians. The rest of the men were Cretan.

The processional way led through the cypress groves, crossing the stream atop a stone viaduct. As the screen of cypress parted, the great temple-palace appeared. Wave upon wave of cheers ushered the dancers up the steps to the west entrance. From the tall-columned West Porch, Jake could see a sea of Cretan faces, black-haired and sun-bronzed, shouting encouragement. People had come from hundreds of square klicks to see and cheer *him*—always an intoxicating feeling.

None of these people would see the dance itself. Those who would witness it were already inside. This was the overflow. The Bull Dance was a religious ritual. Not blood sport or public spectacle—but sacrifice. Friends and strangers offering up their lives to keep off plagues and hard winters. But most of all, to placate the great earthshaking Bull Beneath the Sea, the god of earthquakes and tidal waves, whose wrath in times past had leveled every city on the island.

For a long while they stood on the West Porch, basking in applause, backed by brilliant frescoes depicting the peril and glory of the Bull Dance. Above them towered the huge western façade of the Labyrinth, with its indented porticoes and horned roof. Impressive, but uneven. In part because the grand façade was built around the *backs* of shrines and audience chambers, whose fronts faced inward—onto the Bull Court. And atop the façade, behind the fringe of stone bull horns, sat the hugely long airship belonging to the Queen of Heaven.

Finally the priestesses led them past the Bull Dance frescoes into the Labyrinth. Cheers faded behind layers of stone, replaced by the dancers' own footsteps, taking them deeper into the mystery.

The Bull Court lay at the heart of the Labyrinth. But the way in bent and doubled back on itself, spiraling round to enter the Bull Court from the other side. The entrance to the temple of Amun in Thebes was laser straight, drawing a direct line between Mother Nile and the inner shrine. The Labyrinth was intended to enfold you in stone, to disorient, bewilder, and astonish, recreating the twists and turnings of life.

Any mystic effect was lost on Jake. His compweb contained a detailed ground-floor map of the Labyrinth—a handy guide Jake would never have left Home without. The map was imperfect, pieced together from the ruins of Knossos. But thanks to his navmatrix Jake always knew where *he* was. And the map constantly updated itself based on incoming data, letting Jake know where each step had taken him, where each new turn would likely lead.

The final hallway turned left, then left again, suddenly opening onto the bright expanse of the Bull Court. Jake heard other dancers draw breath. Microamps picked up the leap in Enoch's pulse. But Jake was not surprised. Even an imperfect map could hardly miss something as big as the Bull Court.

Not surprised, but plenty awed. No foreknowing could possibly prepare him for his first look. The Bull Court stretched straight ahead under a blazing summer sun, a bare expanse of flagstones half as big as a football field. But instead of a stadium, the court was surrounded by a palace façade several stories high. Open porticoes, broad painted stairways, and red-columned shrines rose right up from the flags of the court, surrounding it on all four sides—as if the whole great temple-palace were turned inward, to look only on him.

And the towering façade was jammed with people, filling the galleries, standing on the staircases, lining the roofs. Priestesses, novices, eunuchs, and acolytes in animal masks, plus porters, clerks, children, guests, and hangers-on. The ability to "be there" was one of the main perks in a moneyless economy. The best seats went to the Ladies of the Labyrinth, temple priestesses sitting on cushions, wearing long, full skirts and short, embroidered jackets—backed by a sea of ordinary faces, craning to get a first look at the dancers.

As they strode two by two into the ring, Jake saw the Sacred Queen, standing stiff as a statue in her tall headdress and robes of state. Beside her was her young consort, naked except for a codpiece, with long flowing hair and graceful limbs—purposely made to appear smaller, standing bareheaded on a lower platform. This was the Minos, the Moon Child, chosen for a nine-year reign as Queen's war leader and bed warmer.

Since there were no wars on Crete, he was clearly picked more for bed than for battle. Rumor had it that this Minos had been a Bull Dancer, whose beauty and daring had charmed the Queen, lifting him up from the flags of the Bull court to the High Gallery and her private apartments.

The Tripartite Shrine on the west side of the court stood empty. So Hera was not in personal attendance today, meaning Jake had only the bulls to contend with. Which was good. The bulls were bad enough.

And they went first on the day's tablet. Enoch's team came second. But the order of the bulls would be determined by lot. Out of sight of the dancers.

Jake was glad to be first, when he felt fresh and confident. The crowd would be with them as well. Not jaded by previous performances. Following a good act is always hard. Coming on after a bad one even worse. They also got a clean two-to-one chance of getting the better bulls—Rusty or Snowball. Hopefully the Beast of Baal would fall to a later team.

Prayers were said, then the other teams filed back behind the barriers. Jake, Peg, and Anneke faced the bull door, alone on the court, except for the catchers. These catchers were all Cretan, seasoned bull herders and ex-dancers, whose job was to catch the dancers as they came off a leap. Or draw the bull away if there was trouble.

Jake stood staring at the Bull Gate, fifty meters away. Peg on one side of him, Anneke on the other. Dancers entered from the south. The bull came from the north, the direction of Atlantis. Appropriate symbolism. Behind the northern horizon sat Callisto, the Atlantean volcano, preparing to spew destruction over Crete. Hidden behind the Bull Gate was the living symbol of that hideous power.

Staring at the Bull Gate was like looking down the barrel of a loaded gun. Behind the gate a passage led straight back to a pillared hall at the north entrance to the Labyrinth. The bulls were already in the hall. One would be chosen by lot, then driven down that dark passage into the light.

Jake hated these moments when he could only wait. When everything was out of his hands. Which bull would they get? Not even his compweb could say. Bodily inertia put his augmented brain into overdrive, frantically going over options.

What would he do if it was Snowball or Rusty? What if it was the Beast of Baal? The Bull Gate swung open. Silence gripped the court. All eyes fixed on the open door.

The bull burst out onto the Bull Court, like a racehorse bolting from the starting gate. Jake's corneal lenses gave him a couple of seconds' edge. Even as the bull thundered down the dark passage, he saw the reddish coat. It was Rusty.

A cheer went up, greeting the first bull of the day. Mentally Jake joined in. His worst fears were for naught. Peg and Anneke flashed him quick, knowing smiles. They had gotten the best of the bulls. Now there was no excuse to fail.

The brick red bull came streaking into the center of the court, head and horns high, looking about. Jake saw astonishment, and some annoyance, in the animal's eyes, finding himself in a human sea. Supremely confident, the bull did not seem angered, or afraid, merely surprised—wondering what these pesky, unpredictable humans would do next.

He did not have long to wonder. Anneke signaled briskly to the catchers, then led Peg and Jake toward the bull. She had told them that if the bull was a good one, she meant to begin with a leap, a dangerous crowd-pleasing gesture, gambling on speed and surprise.

As they danced forward over the flags, the bull pulled to a stop. Desperately trying to ignore the horns, Jake concentrated on the animal's stance—how the bull held his feet and head, what was in his eyes. He watched the beast's eyes go wide, then narrow in suspicion.

In the last moments Anneke kicked up her heels, sprinting straight at the horns. The bull's head went down, horns forward, ready to hook and gore. What happened next would have been impossible if they had not practiced it all spring. Peg and Jake put on a burst of speed. Diving at the bull's head from both sides, they each seized a horn and hung on, holding the head down.

Anneke went straight in between the horns, doing a handspring off the bull's thick neck. Rusty reared back, throwing his head up, trying to clear his horns. Peg and Jake kept him from hooking, letting the upward thrust throw Anneke high in the air, where she did a turn, landing on her toes.

A perfect opening leap. Jake and Peg broke in opposite directions, further confusing the bull. Rusty spun about, looking foolish, and not a little angry. But momentum was on the side of the dancers. Anneke had made her first crowd-pleasing leap. They were free to play the bull, dodging in and out, keeping him distracted, allowing them to wear him down.

When he was sufficiently tired and confused, trying to decide between Jake and Peg, Anneke jumped him again. This time from the rear, doing a handspring on his back, followed by a side dismount.

Cheering Cretans came to their feet, throwing flowers. Perhaps they had not expected much from mainlanders, and Anneke's mastery of the bull came as a welcome surprise.

Peg had a surprise of her own. By now Rusty was worn down, making it safer to take risks. Peg waved Jake and Anneke back, advancing alone. When she reached the edge of the bull's space, the territory he will defend with a charge—what Spaniards call his *querencia*—she dropped down to her knees.

Neither the bull nor the Cretans seemed to know what to make of this. Staying on her knees, Peg began to slide forward, using the side-to-side motion called the "samurai walk." The whole Bull Court drew breath as Peg crept up to the bull, in the most dangerous possible position, unable to run, her whole upper body exposed to the horns.

With Rusty's steaming breath in her face, Peg reached up, caressing his horns with her slim hands. Peg had done this before in mainland pastures, but the Cretans had seldom seen the like. Jake could hear the intake of breath. She did not dodge, could not run, but simply knelt there, near-naked before the towering bull, perfectly symbolizing the Sacred Marriage.

Tension became unbearable. People in the stands begged for her to back off.

Instead Peg responded with a swift fluid movement, ducking under the horns, provoking a charge. The tired bull hooked at her, trying to pin her. Cretans in the stands gasped, expecting to see her gored. But Peg just led him around her by the horns, caressing his crimson sides as he went by.

Gasps turned to cheers. Peg took three straight passes on her knees, gracefully wrapping the bull around her bare body. With each pass the cheering and stamping grew louder.

As Rusty took his third hook at her, Jake jumped in, seizing the outboard horn. Peg took hold of the one aimed at her, rising up as she pushed his head down. Anneke came bounding in for another forward leap over the horns. This time she added a complete somersault, ending in a handspring off the bull's back. A finale that made the stones of the Bull Court ring.

They backed off to thunderous applause, while catchers closed in with ropes, leading the exhausted bull away.

Jake was exhausted, too, wrung with exertion. When he rejoined the male dancers behind the Bull Court's wooden barriers, Enoch slapped his back, handing him a large blue body towel to wipe away the sweat. Saying he had set a mark to beat.

Jake laughed, mopping off the sweat. He had no illusions about his performance. Anneke's graceful leaps, plus Peg's sweet smile and horrifying courage, had shaken loose the Labyrinth. All he had done was duck and dodge, or grab a horn and hang on.

Now it was Enoch's turn to dodge and hang on. His team took their places. All eyes turned back to the Bull Gate. Of the two bulls left in the lot, which would it be? Snowball or the Beast of Baal? The bronze bound gate swung open. Jake gripped the barrier rail, seeing before everyone else.

The huge bull he called the Beast of Baal hurtled out of the Bull Gate, skidding to a stop on the stones, the black mound above his shoulders bristling with hate. The bull was enraged. Awesomely black and angry. A single narrow white streak ran down his back.

Jake thanked the gods his team had not gotten this monster, a fate they dodged by mere luck of the draw. He wondered how Enoch would play him.

They never found that out. The Beast of Baal did not wait to be played. Snorting with rage, he took aim at Enoch's team and charged. The team scattered, two to the right, one to the left. Catchers closed in, expecting trouble. The dance had barely begun and already the team was in disarray.

Instead of going bellowing through the gap, the bull spun to his left, incredibly light on his hooves, going for the lone man. A young Cretan.

And would have got him, too, if Enoch had not doubled back. The Canaanite came running up on the bull's left, waving his hands, desperately trying to distract the beast.

Enoch succeeded. The bull spun left again with blinding speed, tearing straight at Enoch. The Canaanite feinted left, then spun to avoid the horns. Going for the feint, the bull hooked left, then made an awkward jab to the right. If it had been Rusty, he would have missed, but the Beast of Baal had that dangerous outward splay to his horns. One tip stabbed straight into Enoch's thigh, just beneath the groin.

Screaming in pain, Enoch grabbed at the horn, trying to pull it out of his thigh. Catchers rushed to his aid. The bull jerked his head back to the left, and the horn ripped free. Bouncing off the bull's black flank, Enoch went down. Bright red blood gushed onto the stones of the Bull Court.

The Beast of Baal turned on the catchers, intent on claiming the whole Bull Court as his *querencia*, driving every human from it. And he had the strength and speed to do it. In nineteenth-century Africa, Jake had seen a single Cape buffalo take on an entire Zulu *impi*, killing a dozen armed warriors before being brought down by a mass of razor-sharp *assegai*. But none of these Cretans were armed. This bull was the God incarnate. There was no thought of spearing him.

Even as the veteran bull handlers retreated, Jake was already over the rail, clutching the big blue body towel and medikit, yelling for Peg to stay put.

Too late. He could hear her bare footfalls a couple of steps behind him. Nothing could keep Peg out of danger. Anneke leaped the barrier with her, yelling, "Look out, he hooks to the left!"

The bull turned, took one look and charged.

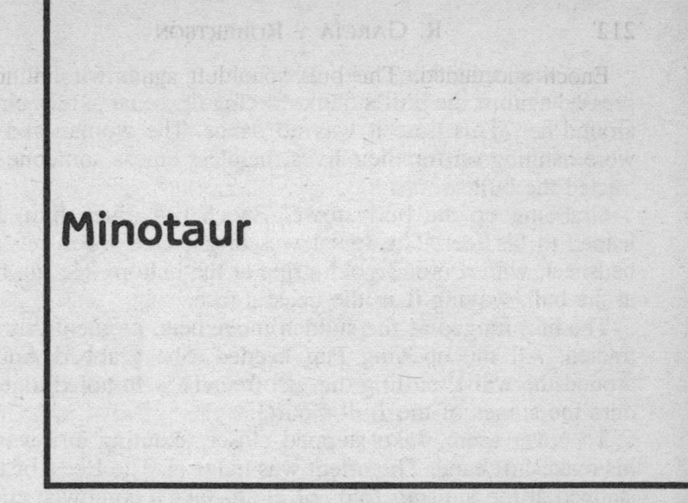

Minotaur

There is nothing he could do for Enoch. He had known that even before going over the barrier rail. Jake just hoped to keep Peg from dashing out onto the Bull Court. Fat chance, but he had to make the effort. The stones were slick with blood—way too much of it. The medikit announced that the femoral artery was severed. Strapped above the wound, the kit acted as a tourniquet, but demanded an immediate transfusion and transfer to an autodoc.

Not unreasonable requests. And there *was* an autodoc, not fifty meters away, aboard the *Atlantis*. Jake could see the bulk of the airship, rising above the west wing of the Labyrinth. But if Hera meant to save this Canaanite, she was showing precious little sign of it. And Jake could not approach the bogus goddess without giving himself away—which would not help Enoch any. The Canaanite was as good as dead.

Time to deal with the living.

Jake looked up, horrified by what he saw. The Beast of Baal was a stone's throw away, bucking and heaving. Somehow, Anneke had gotten on the bull's back—with her feet wrapped around the beast's neck, heels digging into his throat, a hand on each horn.

Peg was right there with her, holding on to the left horn, pressed against the bull's flank, forcing the beast to turn circles around her. This time it was no dance. The woman and girl were hanging on for their lives, helpless unless someone distracted the bull.

Grabbing up the body towel Enoch had given him, Jake leaped to his feet. The towel was bright blue wool, big as a bedsheet, with a broad gold stripe at the bottom. He ran right at the bull, waving it in the beast's face.

The bull lunged at the sudden movement, momentarily distracted. All the opening Peg needed. She grabbed Anneke around the waist, pulling the girl free. They tumbled together onto the stones of the Bull Court.

To cover them, Jake stepped closer, shouting and waving his makeshift cape. The effect was magical. The Beast of Baal stabbed at the shifting folds of cloth. Jake's compweb cut in, having his hands mimic the movements he had seen in Spanish *plaza de toros* three thousand years in the future.

But his feet were set wrong. His movements hurried and awkward. The Beast of Baal was only partly fooled, and not the least amused. He jerked his head up, smacking Jake hard with the flat of a horn.

Jake flew a couple of meters, then came slamming down on the stones, the wind whacked out of him. His compweb screamed, "GET UP!" It was death to lie there, however much he might need the rest.

Cretans shrieked as he scrambled to his feet, with the black bull almost on top of him. Enoch's wet blood gleamed on the bull's horn and side. Shaking his makeshift cape, Jake stepped toward the oncoming monster, shouting, "*¡Toro!*" at the top of his lungs.

The Beast of Baal lowered his horns and stabbed at him. Jake spun sideways, keeping the cloth before the bull. This time it worked. The bull went for the blue folds. Jake whipped the towel away as the beast thundered by, feeling hot breath on his bare hip. All the bull's anger had been transferred to the taunting fabric.

Shaking the cloth, Jake called the bull to him, "*¡Toro! ¡Toro!*" Timing his movements to the speed of the bull, he led the Beast of Baal through another pass. This one a perfect *veronica*. Followed by another. Then he switched hands, coaxing the bull through an improvised *natural*, bringing the left horn close across his body.

Cretan gasps turned into a resounding cheer. Not a proper "*olé,*" but the meaning was plain. Jake kept at it, as Peg and Anneke helped carry the dying Enoch back behind the barrier.

Now it was just Jake and the Beast of Baal, man and bull turning under the hot Mediterranean sun before a cheering throng. The passes grew more professional. Better timed. Even the bull seemed happy with this new dance, going eagerly after the shining lure. All they lacked was the music. This dance ought to be done to the brassy tones of a *corrida* trumpet. Jake had his microamps play a fast *pasodoble*, as he wrapped the Beast of Baal around him like a hairy black cloak. Cretans went wild.

Finally the catchers came to their senses. Bringing out their nets and ropes, they sneaked up on the tiring animal. Throwing a net over the Beast of Baal, they dragged him hobbled and helpless back through the Bull Gate.

Warm pats of rain fell out of the sunny sky. Jake folded the blue cloth over his arm, limping back across the slick stones to where the dancers waited. Cretans cheered each step, shaking the Labyrinth down to the deepest pillar crypt.

The day's dance was over. Snowball and the third team had to wait until tomorrow—weather permitting. Anneke had told Jake, "The dance ends whenever there is a blood sacrifice."

The morning left its marks on more than Cretan memories; Jake had a huge bruise on his ribs where the bull's horn had whacked him. And a matching welt on the rump where he hit the flagstones. Anneke had bruises on her hands from holding on to the horns. Peg was covered with blood, all Enoch's.

Shaken, exhausted, dirty, sweaty, banged in places, and scraped by the stones of the Bull Court, they still had to submit to enthusiastic acclaim. Cretans had never seen anything like Jake's cape work, or Peg's playing a bull on her knees. None of them suspected they were seeing the future of bullfighting. And martial arts. They marked it down as more mad innovation from the mainland, like two-horse chariots and an ever-living Zeus. Jake wearily accepted the adulation, and the invitation to lodge in the Labyrinth.

Priestesses led them down the Grand Staircase on the east side of the Bull Court, four flights of gypsum steps lit by a deep light well. At the bottom they entered the Hall of the Colonnades, supported by massive Atlantean-type columns, with round bulging tops and sides that tapered down instead of up. Corridors and staircases branched off in several directions, in keeping with the mazelike nature of the Labyrinth.

Two more turns took them into the Hall of the Double Axes, an elegant forest of piers and columns lit by an L-shaped portico. Wooden doors between the piers could be closed in winter to keep out the weather, but were all thrown open in the summer heat. The columned portico gave the room a beautiful view of terraced gardens. Thunderheads marching up the cypress green Kairatos valley.

Jake enjoyed the airy complexity of Atlantean architecture. The artful use of light wells and porticoes let the Atlanteans bring the outside in. The way they opened walls to reveal landscapes rivaled the best 3V effects of Home Period. Forests of columns, shafts of light, open colonnades, and labyrinthine corridors recreated the mysterious ways of nature, the heart of darkness that lay beneath the trees.

Another twisting corridor led them to a smaller hall, decorated in bright colors with pictures of dolphins, dancing girls, and flowery rosettes, beneath a spiral ceiling. There they were taken one by one into a bath, where women washed the dust and blood of the Bull Court from their bodies. As warm water cascaded over him, Jake began to shake—delayed reaction to the terror and ferocity of the Bull Court. The morning had been a microcosm of all he had been through in the Bronze Age. Warm willing service, intimately provided, combined with the gut-wrenching violence that had killed most of his expedition.

When Jake left the bath, groomed, perfumed, and wearing a clean tunic, he was given back his medikit—a sign that Enoch was dead.

There was one more death that day. They were led by a circuitous route to an outdoor tree shrine, decorated with the same art deco stone horns that rose above the Labyrinth. A tall double-ax stood before the altar. Beneath the blades of that ax, the final act of the day's Bull Dance was carried out.

The Sacred Queen herself presided, assisted by barefoot priests and priestesses dressed in sheepskin skirts. A eunuch played a large lyre, and pipers blew a lively tune to drown out the bellowing. The Beast of Baal lay bound upon a stone table, complaining mightily, beating his splayed and bloody horns against the stone.

Clouds closed in overhead. Prayers were said, then a priest in women's clothes raised an ancient flint knife with a fine scalloped blade. The black bull had proved himself too good with his horns, killing one man and tossing another. It had been a mistake to bring him into the Bull Court, and the Cretans did not plan to compound the error by letting him back into the herds to breed. He would be offered to Poseidon instead.

Taking care to avoid the bloody horns, the transvestite brought his stone blade down, severing an artery in the neck. The beating on the table grew weaker as blood drained into a pot on the ground. Ceasing to bellow, the beast started to cry. Tears rolled out of his big dark eyes. Then the eyes glazed over, losing their light. The dance was done. Rain began to fall in earnest around the Labyrinth, as though heaven, too, were weeping.

The sacrifice was followed by a beef banquet, but Jake did not eat any of his dance partner. Nor did Peg, a nominal vegetarian. Normally Jake enjoyed a good vat-grown steak—but these people lived closer to nature than he could manage, freely offering themselves and their animals to their gods. He stuck to the seafood, eating shrimp, shellfish, and raw octopus, along with wine, boiled chickpeas, grape leaves, honey cakes, and fried bananas. Atlantean menus could be an adventure.

Afterward they were lodged in a guest suite, near a southeast entrance to the Labyrinth, with a pair of rooms and a private bath. Jake collapsed in an alabaster-lined bedroom, exhausted by the morning. Listening to rain pour in through the light well, he readied himself for a night that already promised to be stormy.

He had his compweb wake him after midnight. Thunder rolled down the Kairatos valley. Lightning cracked. He reached over and woke Peg.

"This is it."

"Are you sure?" She did not sound the least sleepy.

"No, but we may not get another chance." The longer they waited, the more likely something would go amiss. The storm outside might even give them cover.

"I'll wake Anneke." Peg slipped off into the adjoining bedroom.

Jake lay by himself, listening to the thunder and going over options. He had risked his life in the Bull Court in order to get close to one of the airships. And now *Atlantis* was parked less than a hundred meters away, on the west wing of the Labyrinth. He hated to risk everything on a single roll, but when would he get a better shot?

Peg came back with Anneke, and they said their good-byes.

Any attempt to boost Hera's airship was bound to involve hijacking, sacrilege, and mortally offending a goddess. Heady crimes in that day and age. Anneke did not *need* to be included.

"We'll see you in Atlantis," Peg promised.

Anneke nodded, as confident as if Peg had been a prophetess. Jake was not so sure.

They dressed for action, Jake in a short-cut tunic and dancer's boots, Peg in her torso suit. He wished he had his sticky boots. And a neural stunner. Hell, why not wish for a couple of STOP teams and air cover? Peg had brought a climbing line, which would just have to do.

Their bedroom had a balcony, overlooking a terraced garden, that sloped down toward the Kairatos. Clouds hid the stars, leaving the Labyrinth in almost total darkness. A lamp or two in the Residential Quarters showed some people were up late. But no one was braving the storm. And no regular guards or sentries were set. Theft was rare. Armed enemies unheard of.

Edging out onto the balcony, Jake felt warm rain in his face. He tossed the climbing line onto the roof above, telling it to hook on. Each end of the line ended in a smart grapple, able to support half a ton.

He tested the line, then swarmed up, followed by Peg. Jake's lenses let him see like it was day, but Peg had to rely on the line and his terse warnings.

The porch above their balcony was empty. Jake told the climbing line to release. Then he repeated the process to get to the rain-spattered roof of the guest wing.

From there he could see the Labyrinth's roofline, zigzagging off to the north and west, half-hidden by the rain. Atlantean architects had built each part of the temple-palace as high as it needed to be. Flat expanses of roof rose to varying heights, and the breaks between sections were lined with windows, colonnades, and clerestory openings. Deep light wells threatened to drop the unwary roof walker right down to basement level.

Atlantis stood out above the west wing, swaying on her mooring lines, buffeted by heavy south winds. Between Jake and the airship lay the southern end of the Bull Court, a dark invisible gap that kept him from aiming straight for *Atlantis*.

Climbing over a rainswept battlement of stone bulls' horns, Jake set out. Almost at once he came on a yawning light well. He crouched in the lee of the Residential Quarters, waiting until Peg caught up. A cat with elegant Egyptian features padded across the little bit of dry roof to rub up against Jake's shin.

The rope slackened, and Peg appeared. Jake silently pointed out the light well, which to normal eyes was just a shadowy rectangle atop the dark roof. Peg nodded, and they shortened the rope, letting him lead by just a couple of steps, so there was no chance of falling in.

His compweb told him they were atop a long colonnade paralleling the south edge of the Labyrinth. The tops of tall cypress poked up twenty meters to the left, but so long as they kept inside the line of stone horns there was no danger of stumbling over the edge. Ahead he could see the wooden mooring pillar; attached to it was the massive prow of *Atlantis*, bucking in the storm. Only the pillar and ground-line grapples kept the ship from shooting off across the Cretan Sea.

The airship's forward gangway ought to be forty meters to the northwest, but this part of the up-down-roofline was particularly uneven. Rising between them and the airship was the roof of the Upper Propylon, with a wide light well in front of it. Jake took the long way around the protruding roof segments—running smack into trouble.

As he rounded the southwest corner of the Upper Propylon, a crack of lightning lit the roof. A guard stood by the airship's forward gangway. For a fatal instant lightning made it light as noon. Half-man, half-beast, the sentry was twice as broad as Jake, and much taller, but that was mostly due to his horns. From the shoulders down he was a man, naked, heavily muscled, nobly hung, and holding a long bronze sword. From the shoulders up he was a bull, with a massive head, flaring nostrils, and gracefully curving horns.

"MINOTAUR." Jake's compweb chimed in with a bit of unnecessary identification.

Jake was alarmed, but not particularly astonished. After seeing Pan, with his horns and goat legs, and nearly being a late-night snack for a two-headed tyrannosaur, anything was possible. The monster did not need night vision to pick Jake out, standing against the horned battlements, backlit by the bolt of lightning crashing into the hills behind him.

Spinning about, Jake ducked for cover behind the Propylon roof. Peg looked surprised. "What's happening?"

"Don't ask!" Jake slapped the grapple line onto the roof, telling it to grip. He tossed the free end of the line into the Propylon light well. Then he swung Peg over the side, shouting, "Down, fast." Gymnast training took over, and Peg disappeared into the Labyrinth.

The Minotaur came roaring around the corner of the roof, swinging his sword. Jake grabbed the line and swung into the light well. A bronze sword cut the night air centimeters above his head. The whoosh of air past his hair sent Jake sliding down the wet line to land on Peg.

They lay for a second in a tangled heap on the cold, wet flagstoned floor, between the Corridor of the Procession and the South Propylon Gate. A head and horns glared down on them from above, looking like the Beast of Baal come back to life, angry and ready for a rematch.

Jake did not mean to oblige. Scrambling up, he told the line to release, and hustled Peg into a pitch-black side corridor. It led to a large storage magazine packed with tall *pithos* jars. Jake threaded his way through them. But the far door was bolted on the wrong side. Rather than trying to break it down, Jake doubled back, hurrying past a grand staircase leading to the second-floor state apartments.

As he did, he heard heavy footfalls. Jake turned to see the Minotaur descending the monumental staircase. Somehow the man-beast had guessed where he was going and moved to cut him off. Jake dodged through an adjoining room, guiding Peg down a colonnade opening onto the Bull Court, now a huge black hole in the midst of the Labyrinth.

Atlantean architecture was utilitarian whimsy, in love with

the unexpected. Designers put things wherever they thought they were needed. Off-center doorways, rising and falling roof-lines, dogleg corridors, corner entrances, stairs appearing out of nowhere. Later scholars denounced the Labyrinth's floor plan as "incomprehensible, confusing, illogical, irrational, and primitive." Corridors turned back and forth upon each other. Walls and ceilings opened up to let in light. Rooms were sized and placed according to convenience. Storage closets and tiny shrines were squeezed between monumental staircases and grand colonnades. Labyrinth originally meant "Place of the Double-Ax" but it came to mean "maze."

What seemed to be an "insane jigsaw" must have made perfect sense to the Minotaur, who moved swiftly and easily to cut Jake off. So far only night vision and Jake's navmatrix had kept him and Peg a step ahead of their hulking pursuer. Jake did not have an entire map of the temple-palace in his head. There were big gaps in his 3-D floor plan, gray spaces where his compweb could only guess at layout and connections. But even this partial plan had better than a thousand rooms to get lost in.

Jake dodged back into the dark recess behind the Grand Staircase. Here a side hall led back toward the storage magazines. This time the bolt was on the right side. He stepped quickly into a long black magazine corridor.

And right into the path of the Minotaur. The monster had again outguessed him. Bounding out of the blackness, a horned terror etched in infrared.

Jake yelped for Peg to run, pushing her ahead of him down the pitch-black corridor.

Heavy footsteps gained on them. Theseus or Hercules would have simply turned around and made beefsteak of the bovine horror—but Jake was at his wit's end. Not at all feeling like a Bronze Age hero.

He decided to take a gamble in the dark. The magazine corridor ran straight ahead for almost the full length of the Labyrinth before turning back on itself. Twenty meters before turning back a thin wall divided the corridor in two—the left half stayed straight, the right half went up a small stairway. His compweb could not tell where the stairs went.

Pulling past Peg, Jake chose the stairs, bounding up them

two at a time, hauling her behind him. At the top was a door, latched on his side. He burst through.

Success. He was on the floor above. Just as he had hoped, the little stairway was a back entrance to the Upper Processional Corridor, and the main ceremonial reception halls, empty now because it was the middle of the night.

Lightning cracked outside pillared windows on the west side of the reception halls. Jake waved at the high windows, "Get up there."

Peg understood at once. Sprinting through the reception hall to the windows, Jake helped boost her onto the sill. Then she reached down and pulled him up. Swinging his climbing line onto the roof above, he told the grapple to grip.

The Minotaur appeared at the far end of the reception hall, looking about for his prey. It was too dark outside for him to see them so long as the lightning held off. Peg started up the slippery line. Jake held it taut for her, praying their luck would hold.

It didn't. Another flash of lightning lit the hall. The Minotaur spotted them, silhouetted against the suddenly bright sky. With an outraged bellow he came at them, sword in hand.

Peg pulled herself onto the roof above. That left Jake alone on the slippery sill, facing an enraged Minotaur—wishing to hell he had his adhesive boots. He dodged behind a window pillar. Bronze beat against stone as the Minotaur slashed at him. Jake clung to the wet edge of the Labyrinth's West Façade, trying to keep the window pillar between him and the blade, without getting punctured by a horn.

Suddenly a hand out of the dark gripped his shoulder. Peg was hanging head down from atop the roof. "Up," she shouted, shoving the climbing line at him.

Using her and the line for support, Jake ran right up the slick pillar, pulling himself onto the roof. The tail end of *Atlantis* towered above them, a black shadow on the storm.

His compweb gave the Minotaur an ETA to rooftop of about a minute. Finding the mooring line nearest the tail hatch, he pulled Peg atop the big grapple. Shouting, "Hang on," he told the grapple to release, and the mooring line to reel itself in.

In seconds they were swinging a dozen meters above the roof, right beneath the tail hatch. Night and thunder rolled around them. Jake had his compweb contact *Atlantis*'s onboard systems. Someone had altered the recognition codes, keeping him from giving flight commands to the ship, but he convinced the simpleminded lock controls to open up for maintenance.

The hatch swung open, still thinking it was closed. Jake boosted Peg aboard, heaving himself up after her. As soon as he was safely through the hatch, he ordered the rest of the mooring grapples to let go and reel in.

Lines whipping in release, the huge airship began to buck uncontrollably, held in place by the main nose grapple. Only the Helm could release that. But with the ground lines gone, the Helm had no choice. In this gale *Atlantis* would be ripped to pieces trying to hang on by her nose.

Atlantis let go, shooting skyward. Looking down through the tail hatch, Jake saw a furious Minotaur staring up at them, standing sword in hand on the rainy roof of the Labyrinth. Eight seconds ahead of his compweb estimate. Steadily growing smaller as they galloped off downwind.

Queen of Heaven

Alarms dopplered through the airship, responding to the mass failure of the mooring grapples. None of the onboard security systems suspected the ship had been penetrated. Jake had so confused the hatch mechanism that it had not reported their entry and no longer remembered being opened.

Atlantis had an auxiliary control station in the tail, a simple jumpseat and headset folded into the wall, with a security seal no smarter than the tail-hatch lock. In seconds Jake opened the jumpseat, again without alerting anyone. Reaching into the recess behind the seat, he removed the headset and put it on. It was an open circuit. There was no need to jack in. No telltale blip to warn onboard security that he was in the system. *Atlantis* was a research ship, designed for simplicity and ease of access. Whoever recoded the security systems did not realize how swiftly the codes could be bypassed.

The uproar over the mooring failure, and unintended takeoff formed a perfect cover. *Atlantis* wallowed out of control, headed for the coast of Crete. Commands raced through the system, accompanied by panicked demands for data. Pressure indications, wind turbulence readings, skin stress, trim and balance reports flowed into the Helm.

Jake had his compweb open a channel into the data stream, disguised as a damage report, inventing a stress fracture in the port rear stabilizer. This supposed fracture created an immediate demand for more data from the tail, giving him priority access to Damage Control.

Bit by bit his compweb inserted concealed commands into the data stream. Damage Control received orders to set up subroutines responding only to Jake's compweb, while sending soothing reports to the Helm. The fictitious damage in the tail spread to the security systems, forcing peripherals to shut down, without reporting their failure. Meanwhile the Helm continued to struggle with the "damaged" stabilizer, keeping *Atlantis* from returning to her dock atop the Labyrinth.

At best Jake had bought time. To take complete control of the ship, he had to break the security codes. His compweb settled down to the laborious task of weaseling out the new code keys, while *Atlantis* continued to run before the storm, crossing the coast, heading north over the Cretan Sea.

Peg signaled for his attention. "Someone's coming."

The pressure door to the tail section was cycling. Jake took a quick peek through the door security cam. It was Tyler, the female rigger's mate. He had last seen her aboard the *Argo*, when Artemis and Apollo were dividing up the spoils. She was undoubtedly coming back to work on the stabilizer, a rigger's job in an emergency.

He signaled to Peg to cover the door. She nodded, pressing herself against the bulkhead. The pressure door opened. Tyler stepped through. Her eyes went wide. Expecting a damaged stabilizer, she saw Jake seated at the auxiliary control station. Peg shut the lock behind her.

Tyler spun about, seeing Peg for the first time. "Where'd you come from?"

Peg smiled. "The Pleistocene."

"We're taking over the ship," Jake told her. "Want to help?"

"Of course," Tyler nodded eagerly. Rigger's mates were trained to respond immediately in a crisis, and Tyler was among the best. "I thought you were dead?"

"Not yet," Jake noted proudly. He aimed to show the gods just how alive he was.

"Who's aboard?" Jake needed a rundown of friends and

foes. Until he cracked the new security codes the airship's data banks were off-limits.

"Me. And DePala. She's at the Helm. And three of *them.*"

"Who are they?"

Tyler grimaced. "Hera, who runs the ship. And her son Hephaestus, who acts as crew chief. Plus this bull-headed brute charged with security . . ."

"Not anymore." Jake dismissed the Minotaur. "We left him behind."

"Excellent." Tyler was happy to hear the opposition had been cut by a third.

That left Hera and Hephaestus. But Jake did not plan to go up against anyone until he had control of the ship. "How fast are they expecting you to fix that stabilizer?"

Tyler shrugged. "I said I'd have to see the fracture."

Code solutions continued to cascade through Jake's comp-web. "Tell them you can do it—but they have to be patient. And hold this course." He did not want them getting back to Crete.

"Sure. DePala will understand. I don't think the others know what patience *is.*"

"We'll teach 'em." He told Tyler to keep reporting progress. "Give the impression that restoring the stabilizer is only minutes away. Do nothing that might attract one of them to the tail." He kept creating minor breakdowns throughout the ship. An auxiliary power shutdown. Gas vent leaks. Baffling turbine surges. Time-consuming glitches that had to be tested out, keeping Tyler from getting any "help."

In the meantime Tyler told how Apollo had traded her and DePala to Hera, in exchange for three surviving *Atlantis* crewmen. "Hera hates Apollo—but does not like being served by men. They cooperate if it's to their advantage."

From what Jake had seen these immortals were consummate egotists. Put any three of them in the same room for half an hour, and you were likely to have bloodshed. But they were bound to make common cause against him.

The storm abated, but the south wind continued to blow, driving them northward. Atlantis appeared to starboard, then fell steadily astern. They passed over Paros, Delos, and Tenos, then left the Cyclades behind, cruising through the gap in the Sporades, crossing the Central Aegean.

Codes began to break. Jake's compweb found a pattern of transposition keys susceptible to frequency counts. Strings of baffling nulls started turning into plain Universal.

In the midst of Jake's triumph, Tyler's face went white. "Hephaestus is coming back to work on the tail."

"Stall him," Jake suggested hopefully. He was seconds away from cracking the codes. "Make something go wrong with the door lock."

Tyler shook her head. "You don't know him. He's fiendishly smart and incredibly strong. His arms and upper torso are enclosed in some sort of mechanical exosuit. If he thinks I'm up to something, he'll tear his way in here."

Not very promising. Jake took a swift look at the situation. Too much was happening at once. Sunup was minutes away. His compweb had homed in on a code solution. *Atlantis* had passed Evstratios on the port quarter. Lemnos lay ahead. The keel slidewalk was running, carrying Hephaestus toward the tail.

Jake kicked open the hatch to the access tunnel that ran along the keel—the same narrow tube that he and Love and used to escape from the *Argo*. "Time to change shop."

They wormed their way into the tunnel, just as the pressure door started to cycle. This time Jake took the tunnel the other way, headed for the hangar deck. In a few moments Hephaestus would see that there was no damage to the port stabilizer, and no Tyler in the tail. That would mean a fight.

When he got to the hangar deck, Jake hardly recognized it. The deck was now an open flagged court in the Atlantean style. Large windowed bays were thrown open, letting in silvery first light. *Atlantis*'s pair of ultralight solarplanes had flown—heaven knows where. Replaced by a STOP hovercar. A fountain aft flowed into a shallow basin, forming a low grotto beneath a graceful stairway disappearing into what had been the repair shop.

As Jake looked about, his compweb broke the final codes. He had complete access to *Atlantis*'s controls and computers. Deck plans danced in Jake's head. He could see any circuit and move any microswitch on the airship. He grinned. "Got it!"

"Got what?" Peg looked at him.

"Everything." The whole ship was in his hands.

"It's about time." Waiting had worn on her. Peg was super in a crisis, but sitting in the tail of an airship while compweb ran numbers did not supply the proper mix of action and adrenaline. "What now?"

"We rock and roll."

"Shall I tell DePala?" Tyler was also ready to *do* something. Living at the mercy of the Olympians had given her a healthy head of anger.

"Not yet." Jake took another quick look around, matching what he saw against the deck plans. Main-hangar doors lay hidden and operational under the flagstone court. The repair shop had been turned into an armory and workshop for Hephaestus the Smith God. Hera's handyman son. Merely thinking of the shop produced a contents inventory. He called up "BOOTS, ADHESIVE." The answer came back, "THREE PAIR."

"First I want a pair of loose shoes." He took the stairs leading to the shop three at a time. Passing through the columned porch at the top of the stairs was like stepping into some surrealist Bronze Age armory-cum-netherworld. Presses were converted to turn out armor. Stands of arms hung on the wall, alongside bronze shields embossed with circles of dragon heads that snapped at Jake as he entered.

Women worked the laser forges, gold-skinned female robots with jewels in their spun metal hair. Those closest to Jake were turning out rock crystal cups, while others fixed gemlike microcomponents to the insides. Poison detectors perhaps? Three-legged smart tables followed the women about.

The inventory told Jake which cabinet held the boots. He thumbed the lock, telling it to open. None of the she-robots looked up from their work. Their eyes had microscopic lenses, shaded by lashes of fine gold wire.

As Jake pulled on a pair of boots, his compweb rang a warning. Hephaestus was coming back from the tail. Jake grabbed a shield and spear from the wall, then bounded back up the stairs, telling Peg and Tyler, "Trouble's on the way."

The moment he topped the stairs, Hephaestus emerged on the hangar deck, looking as formidable as Tyler said, his whole upper body encased in an armored exosuit, bulging with powered anatomy. He wore a helmet with a single cyclops eye slit, like an old time welder's mask.

"Come down," the Smith God ordered, hardly happy to have Jake raiding his armory.

Dawn broke, flooding the court with light through the high bay windows. Jake felt silly, standing at the top of the stairs, staring over his shield, hefting a spear. He had never thrown one in anger. What should he aim at? Head and torso were covered. That left the crotch. Unnecessarily vindictive, considering this god had done nothing to him.

"Come down," Hephaestus repeated his command.

Suddenly, Jake saw a better way. Handing the shield and spear to Tyler, he called out, "I'll be right down." Descending the stairs, he signaled Peg to hang back, using Lakota sign language, something a Greek god would not likely understand.

As he stepped off the stairs, he explained in polite proto-Greek, "Sorry, your Immenseness, but I am taking back this ship."

"This ship belongs to my Mother," Hephaestus replied. "Hera, Queen of Heaven."

Jake shook his head. "I suppose you have had it so long you think of it as yours. But it is not."

Hephaestus laughed.

Jake strode out onto the center of the hangar deck. "Is there no peaceful way I can convince you?"

"Absolutely not." Hephaestus flexed his augmented muscles, stepping forward. The exosuit gave him weight and reach, plus the ability to pull Jake's arm off and beat him to death with the soggy stump. His sole weakness was that he wore sandals.

Jake glanced over his shoulder, seeing that Peg was still on the stairs. At that instant, Hephaestus sprang, arms spread.

It was already too late. Telling his boots to grip, Jake ordered the main hangar doors swung open. The flagged court beneath their feet split along its central seam, each side pivoting outward into the rushing air.. The hundred-kilometer-per-hour slipstream nearly knocked Jake out of his adhesive boots, plastering him back against what had been the floor of the court—but was now a wide-open door, hanging vertically from the hull. His compweb identified the green-brown isle of Lemnos far below.

Hephaestus had nonadhesive sandals. When he came down

there was no deck to land on. What had been a flagged court was now cloud-flecked sky.

His holiness whipped past Jake, hit the slipstream, and started to tumble. Whirling end over end, he fell toward Lemnos, an irregular blotch on the sea over a klick beneath the keel.

Not wanting to see what happened when the god hit, Jake ordered the hangar to close. The flags beneath him swung back up, becoming a floor once more. A moment later he was picking himself up off the gypsum, surrounded by the dawnlit court. Everything as it had been. Only Hephaestus was gone.

Jake dusted gypsum off his hands. "Tried to warn him."

More warning than Emiko got anyway. And more of a chance, too. Apollo had sent Pan's dogs out to make sure she was dead. Half-encased in an exosuit, Hephaestus would most likely live. If he hit right.

Time to tackle the Helm. The same keel slidewalk that deposited Hephaestus on the hangar deck swept them up to the forebridge. Transparent bulkheads looked out on the isle of Lemnos, and the cloud-dotted sea beyond. DePala was at the Helm, seeming pleased and astounded to find the port stabilizer suddenly repaired, but puzzled by the way the ship insisted on flying herself. With hangar doors swinging open and shut.

Looking over DePala's shoulder was a tall goddess in sacral robes. She held a scepter in one hand, topped by a mechanical cuckoo, like the one that had spotted Jake in the grotto of the Hesperides. In her other hand she held a pomegranate.

She turned as Jake arrived. For a moment her face seemed familiar, then it dissolved into a queenly glare, becoming unrecognizable right before his eyes. A neat trick, even for a goddess.

"You," she sniffed. "Back already to bother us." Hera did not act the least surprised. She was supposed to have the gift of prophecy—an old time traveler's trick. Jake had used it often. "That little bitch Artemis and her bastard brother could not dispose of a rat turd if they had all day to do it."

Clearly there was no love lost between Hera and the Unheavenly Twins. But Jake wondered how real the hate was. Hera's actions all seemed stagey. Her anger for display.

Stepping forward, he held out his hand. As he was about to

touch her, Hera frowned and disappeared. A hologram goddess. Was she even on the airship?

Jake had his compweb race through the altered deck plans, tracing the 3V signal. Its source was in Officers' Quarters, which had been redesigned into a sumptuous private apartment. The "real" Hera had to be there. Jake ordered the area sealed off. He would deal with Hera later. In the meantime he did not want holos haunting the ship. Or messages going out to the other Olympians.

Atlantis obeyed, locking the surrounding hatches, shielding the windows, and shutting down communications within and around officers' country. Terminals went dead. Even the security cams shut down. Not so much as a cuckoo could get out.

Jake turned to DePala, saying, "Happy to see you."

The young helmsmate seemed to have aged a dozen years since he had last seen her. Being forced to fly for divine egomaniacs—who had murdered her lover and threatened to dispose of her without warning—must have been wearing. Worse even than what he had gone through. She stared back at Jake, as if *he* were the holo. "I didn't ever expect to see *you*."

Jake gave her a lopsided "not-dead-yet" grin, that acknowledged they were reuniting under desperate conditions. He wished he could say the worst was over. But most likely that lay ahead. Instead he told her to set course for Tiryns. To pick up Love and Hercules.

DePala gladly obeyed. Clearly pleased not to be flying for the enemy.

Jake could have set course himself. He *liked* to fly. Tackling the problems of trim, ballast, gas-cell pressure, static condition, angle of attack—all the minutiae of running an airship in flight—could be relaxing. Especially compared to battling semidivine psychotics. But he needed to have DePala running the ship. She was good at it. And if his plans even half succeeded, he would be way too busy to be piloting *Atlantis*.

And the flight from Lemnos to Tiryns would give him time to deal with Hera. Officers' country remained hostile territory, cut off from the rest of the ship. His own control codes were in place, and Hera did not have a micron's chance of doing what Jake had done. Jake had started with an auxiliary control station and an unsuspecting security system. The Queen of

Heaven did not even have a working terminal jack. But to get information out of Hera, Jake would have to go into officers' country—figuratively at least.

Sitting down at a secure terminal, he cautiously opened a sealed channel into Hera's quarters. Not letting so much as a blip get out. Two could play with 3V. Jake meant to send a hologram in to confront Hera, accompanied by all the sensing capacity he could muster. Sight. Sound. Galvanic response. Heartbeat. Brain waves. He badly needed information out of Hera. But he could not let her know what he was fishing for (having only a vague idea himself). People could fool a battery of sensors, *if they were prepared.* He hoped to catch Hera off guard, maybe startle some truth out of her.

When he was all set, he sent his holo in.

Jake was used to seeing himself in 3V, no longer finding the sight of his own back disconcerting. It was actually comforting to know that whatever happened to his image was not *really* happening to him. No matter how bad it looked.

Stepping inside Officers' Quarters was like leaving the ship. Bulkheads had been ripped out, replaced by a Sensurround setup converting officers' country into a wooded glen. Golden apples hung from the trees. Two small streams tumbled out of gray rock grottoes, running the length of the glen. One stream began boiling hot, the other ice-cold. Where they ran together a bather could find any desired temperature, just by moving up- or downstream.

Beyond the stream banks a mythical green landscape stretched off to merge with a blue 3V sky. Low sunlight precisely mimicked the angle of the real sun outside. A morning breeze blew out of nowhere. Flocks of winged horses grazed the hillsides, alighting, then taking off again.

Hera was standing hip deep in a warm part of the stream, stark naked. Not in the least pleased to have Jake suddenly appear in the midst of her morning bath.

She had the body of a goddess, full-hipped and high-breasted. Nor did she deign to cover herself. Jake felt like Prince Paris, for whom Hera stripped, insisting he examine her closely—offering untold wealth and the lordship of Asia, if only he would give her the Golden Apple of Discord.

Her frowning face brought Jake back to reality. It was not the hologram face she had assumed on the forebridge. Hera in the flesh had a face Jake had seen before. He zipped through his files until he found it. Eureka! His compweb came up with the match. Pieces tumbled into place. She was Juno, the senior FTL woman on the committee that interviewed him after the First Mesozoic Expedition.

Jake tried to cover his surprise with a joke. "Renewing your virginity?" The *real* Hera periodically renewed her virginity by bathing in a sacred spring outside Argos.

"That is hardly needed." She did not act the least perturbed at being caught naked by a hologram. Jake was plainly the one at fault, deserving divine punishment ASAP.

His mind raced. He had meant to surprise Hera; now he was the one taken aback. Here was a senior Faster-Than-Light time bureaucrat—in the nude no less—posing as a Greek goddess. He could come up with only one sensible reason for it.

Hera frowned, continuing to splash water on herself. "Don't make this any more a farce than it has to be. We both know we have met before."

"You were on the FTL committee investigating the wreck of the *Challenger*." Mundane duty for a goddess.

"I wanted to see you face-to-face."

"Why?"

"You are destined to cause us an immense amount of trouble." Veteran time travelers learned to accept things as they were—or as they will be. Not even a goddess could reorder events. No more than Jake could stop the Fall of Rome, or save Atlantis from annihilation. If you managed to "change" history—it merely meant history was not what you thought it was.

"What sort of trouble?"

Hera shrugged sculpted white shoulders.

"Like finding out that FTL's secret portal to the future is in the Bronze Age?"

Eureka again! Hera did not answer. She did not have to. Her leap in heartbeat and drop in skin resistance shouted, "Yes!"

Jake had been guessing. A calculated, educated guess. But it was clear that FTL was hiding something in the Bronze Age. Even killing to keep it secret. What could that be? He had started at the top. The biggest thing FTL could be covering up was its connection to the future. Jake's future. And what better place to hide a portal to the future than deep in the past?

"Is it on Atlantis?" Another guess.

This time Hera was ready for him. She shot back a counterquestion. "What have you done with my son?"

"Which son?"

"Hephaestus, of course."

Hera was a tough customer, using her mother's anger and concern to cover up her feelings, turning her grief and worry against him. Throwing off his readings. Lies were easily hidden behind legitimate concern.

Jake cut the holo, leaving her hanging. He reran Hera's last responses. There was a hint of reaction when he mentioned Atlantis, before she countered with Hephaestus. Right now he was not likely to catch her unawares again. But, maybe later . . .

Meanwhile he had plenty to do.

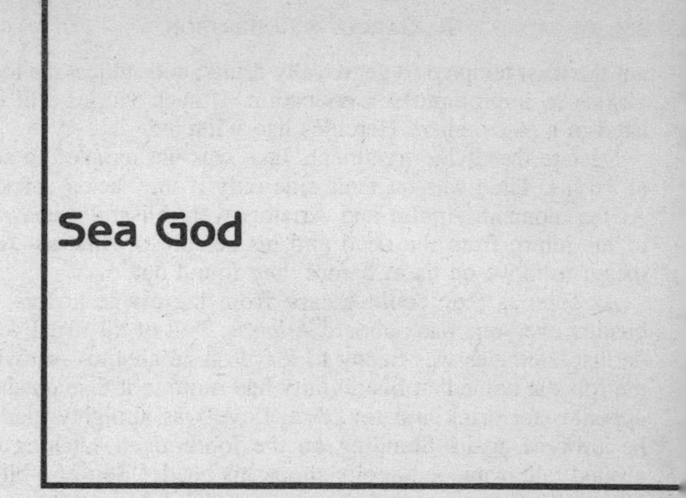

Sea God

They descended in triumph upon Tiryns. This fortress-palace guarding the sea approaches to Mycenae stood on the southern summit of an oval limestone outcropping. From the air it seemed to grow right out of the gray rocks, surrounded by a golden plain and green olive groves. Tiryns was Hercules's home between adventures, since he had been banned from Mycenae and worn out his welcome in Thebes.

DePala put *Atlantis* down on the flat northern slope just outside the walls. There was no mooring mast or ground crew, but the grapples were back in working order.

People threw open the citadel gates, welcoming them like gods. By now Jake was totally accustomed to being bathed by worshipful young women, then having his bogus heroics sung to him in primitive Greek, while some hapless beast turned on the spit. He indulged in some offhanded boasting about the Bull Dance, Labyrinth, and Minotaur. The bare facts sounded sufficiently impressive. He could afford to leave out details, like dropping Hephaestus overboard off Lemnos, or having Hercules' god-mother prisoner aboard ship.

And with Peg there to keep him on an even keel, he was

not the least tempted to get royally drunk, and subject the local virgins to impromptu sex education. If such virgins still existed in a place where Hercules had wintered.

Despite the divine treatment, Jake was not tempted to stay at Tiryns. Time was on their side only if they acted quickly. At the moment, Apollo and Artemis were blissfully unaware of his return from the dead and his seizure of *Atlantis*. Jake meant to move on them before they found out.

As soon as they could escape from the divine honors, he hustled everyone back aboard *Atlantis*. Full of his usual wanderlust, Hercules was happy to leave on an airship—showing the folks at home that his divinity had more to it than outsized appetites for drink and sex. And Love was almighty glad to be airborne again. Standing on the forebridge, watching the ground fall away, he happily shook his head. "Son-of-a-bitch. You did it."

"Impressed?" Jake asked.

"Man, when you left to dance with the bulls, I was givin' odds you'd come back punctured."

"Nearly happened," Jake assured him.

He told Tyler to make straight for Atlantis, planning to start his search at the center of things. If the time portal was there, the most likely place to pick up *Argo* was on a line running between Atlantis and Apollo's base on Delos. If that failed, he planned to execute a search pattern focused on Delos and Atlantis. Sooner or later *Argo* would turn up, hopefully before Artemis and Apollo found out what was afoot. Catch these gods off guard, and they proved all too human.

Winds were light and from the north, heating up with the day. To avoid updrafts that might drive the airship above her pressure height, Tyler stood out to sea, passing Nauplia, the main port of Tiryns.

Hercules pointed out Lerna, on the far side of the Gulf of Argolis—where he and Iolaus had killed the Hydra. Which by now had upward of fifty heads. "And breath so venomous that sniffing its tracks could drop you stone dead."

Beyond Hermione they were out over open water, leaving mainland Greece behind. Jake and Peg went to the upper deck to spot. In combination with her two ultralights, *Atlantis* was designed to cover three hundred klicks of clear air. But her ultralights were gone. And feathery clouds allowed only twenty klicks of visibility.

Jake saw nothing but open sea, until Melos hove into sight. Seeing that twisted, indented squiggle upon the sea made him think of Sauromanta, and their last night together.

By now Peg knew enough of the doomed chronology of Jake's original expedition to guess what Melos must mean. But she said nothing, just continuing to sweep the horizon with her maroscope. Peg could be *too* Zen at times. Jake *needed* his worries and misgivings. They gave his brain something to work on when he had nothing to do but wait.

Melos passed beneath them, leaving only Atlantis ahead. The wind from the north picked up, blowing a tall bank of clouds before it. Jake could feel Tyler fighting to hold the heading.

Callisto's volcanic cone poked over the horizon, topped by a wisp of smoke. Once this whole region, from Greece to Asia Minor, had been part of one great landmass—formed during the mid-Tertiary some thirty million years before. Faulting and subsidence broke up the landmass, letting in the sea. Lowlands were submerged. High valleys became bays and harbors. Mountain peaks survived as islands. The surrounding seabed concealed fault zones, tectonic trenches, huge gravity anomalies, and volcanic hot spots. The most volatile weak spot lurked directly ahead, beneath the island of Atlantis.

From a couple of kilometers up, Callisto did not look so dangerous. The lush green volcanic cone easily earned its title of the Beautiful One. On the northwest shore he saw Atlantis, her twin harbors looking like white-gold threads, reaching out to enclose the lapis sea.

Jake got his first good overhead look at the inner island. Behind the twin harbors, Atlantis proper was built on what had been low salt marsh and lagoon, formed by subsidence. A long sea canal connected it to the harbors, making the city into a sort of island Venice, ringed by the lagoon and a series of concentric canals, centered on a raised acropolis. A phenomenal piece of construction that must have employed the best Mesopotamian and Egyptian engineers.

Behind the city the entire volcanic cone was ringed by a huge cyclopean wall, built from giant blocks of colored volcanic stone. Inside the wall, on the slopes of the volcano, he could see the white Shrine of Callisto, looking down on Atlantis like a carved ivory temple. On the far side of the cone, was a newer, more monumental piece of construction, resembling the rock-hewn temple complexes Rameses II would use to decorate the Upper Nile in Nubia. Only bigger and grander.

"And this is all doomed?" Peg said it with a soft sense of wonder.

Jake looked over at her. Peg had made two long trips to the Mesozoic, her absolute favorite place in space-time. And she never once regretted that an arrant asteroid would one day demolish the entire era in a truly awesome cosmic traffic accident. To Peg the Mesozoic was a wondrous place, a great and glorious show with a two-hundred-million-year run. She was not about to cry because it did not last *longer*.

But Atlantis was different. It was a tragic *human* endevor. A civilization centered on art, beauty, and commerce, instead of war and conquest. Where women were honored, and men were their mates, not their masters. Where the God was in any man who strove for the good and true. And the Goddess could be found in a young girl, an aged crone, or a brave Bull Dancer.

All about to be blown to atoms in very short order. The volcanic pall already hung over the island. Cataclysm could come today, tomorrow, or twenty years hence. But it was bound to come. Despite all their foreknowledge and futuristic powers, there was nothing Peg or Jake could do about it.

Nor would Atlantis die alone. The eruption would level the Labyrinth and her sister places, drowning the prosperous island ports with a wall of water, and a suffocating rain of red-hot ash. Behind the blast, would come hordes of mainland savages, to lord over the rebuilt temple-palaces, until they, too, were drowned in a new age of blood and iron. A human tragedy that made the death of the dinosaurs seem pretty distant.

And the perfect cover for Faster-Than-Light's portal to the future. When Atlantis blew, it would take the portal with it. Jake had found no sign of the secret portal in Home Period—*since it did not exist then*. The portal only existed up through the Bronze Age, then it was blown sky-high in one of the biggest natural catastrophes of recent times. In theory the portal would still exist, but in practice it was nearly impossible to locate and map a spatiotemporal anomaly not attached to some material substrate. The portal could only be approached through the Bronze Age, and now the Bronze Age itself was sealed off to all legitimate exploration. The ultimate example of FTL's box-within-a-box security system.

"So what do you think?" Peg stared into the macroscope, never taking her eyes off the doomed island.

Jake had already gone back to sweeping the horizon. "I think we are seeing no sign of the *Argo*." As magnificent as they were, none of Atlantis's soon-to-be-detonated wonders looked like an airship. "We need to institute a standard search spiraling out from a point of maximum probability on a line between here and Delos."

Tyler took that as an order, putting the Helm over hard to port. The wind off the port quarter became a headwind, cutting sea speed in half. Low cloud cover advancing from the north forced them down to the wave tops, further reducing the search area. Atlantis sank into the sea behind them.

Sandwiched between the low clouds and the gray surface of the sea, they got a good look at what they did see, crawling along less than three hundred meters above the waves. An hour crept by. Ios passed below. Jake watched Paros rise up ahead of them. He would soon have to decide whether to begin the search spiral, or push straight on to Delos. Each option had advantages. Neither was a sure bet.

Suddenly the decision was lifted from him. Tyler called out from the forward observation post, "Submarine below!"

That had to be *Thetis*. Jake put on a headset, plugged into the upper-deck control station, allowing him to see through any macroscope aboard ship. The watery image of the minisub was unmistakable. Right beneath the airship, twenty meters down with no periscope showing, headed north.

He told Tyler to drop back and lower a sonar buoy. With luck they could fix on the sub's course, depth, and speed, without being detected.

Passing the headset to Peg, he dived into the midships lift. Heart pounding, he told the lift to take him to the hangar deck. He hated to rely on 3V when the real thing was anywhere near at hand.

By the time he reached forward OBS on the hangar deck there was nothing to see. The buoy was in the water, deployed in passive mode, picking up a strong sonar signal, along with weak wave turbulence. The sub was well ahead, continuing on course, plowing along at peace with the world, completely ignorant of her close brush with an airship.

Jake summoned up a nautical chart, having his compweb superimpose the sub's bearing. "She's headed for the gap between Paros and Naxos."

He told Tyler to take *Atlantis* up into the overcast. "But don't drop ballast." They must do nothing to alert *Thetis*.

Turbofans whined into overdrive, forcing the airship up into the clouds, flying several degrees heavy. As soon as the clouds closed in around them, Jake ordered Tyler to circle, waiting to see what the sub would do. Nearly invisible filament kept them in contact with the buoy.

Thetis held her course.

That demanded an immediate decision. So long as they stayed in the vicinity of the sub Jake's options were limited. He could neither drop ballast nor troll along with the buoy. Either would alert the sub's sensitive hydrophones.

He had to risk breaking contact to get ahead of the sub. Telling Tyler to reel in the sonar buoy, he set a course for the northern end of the gap between Paros and Naxos—they could pick up the sub there. Assuming she held to her course. "Drop ballast as we pass over Paros. Then wait in the cloud cover on the far side."

The silent stalk had begun. Over Paros, Tyler dumped water ballast without making waves. No longer flying heavy, *Atlantis* took up station between Paros and Delos. She hid in the overcast, with a spy-eye dangling out of the clouds, and the sonar buoy bobbing like a duck on the water.

Right on cue, *Thetis* emerged from the Paros-Naxos gap, still not knowing she was being shadowed. Bearing due north. ZERO-ZERO-ZERO. By now Jake guessed where she was going. Ahead lay Delos, and the sunken temple he had glimpsed from the hangar deck of the *Argo*—on the day Apollo and Artemis decided to defer his sacrifice.

As soon as they had visual contact through the spy-eye, Jake told Tyler to haul up the sonar buoy, then creep along after the sub. They followed *Thetis* all the way to Delos, seeing her dock at the submerged temple.

Jake called for Love, who had been keeping watch on Hercules, seeing the demigod did not damage or endanger the ship. "Want another swim?"

Love gave him a you-must-be-crazy look.

Jake explained that *Thetis* was in an underwater pen. "If things look right, I want to go in and get the sub." He had hoped to find *Argo* with Apollo, Artemis, and Sauromanta aboard. Most of all Sauromanta. But he could not pass up an opportunity to seize the minisub. Not while surprise was on their side.

"I told you, I'm a sinker."

"Good. Our run in has to be underwater."

Tyler took the ship north of the target, doubling back inside the cloud cover, drifting over Delos with the engines shut down. Through the spy-eye they saw Apollo's birth shrine, and the small harbor town where no one was allowed to be born, or to die. The pregnant and the dying were ferried over to the tiny islet of Ortygia—Artemis's birthplace.

Hercules said he had never been invited to Delos. "I scatter births and deaths too freely." A single visit, and Delos would never have been the same.

The Artemesion, Artemis's sanctuary and temple overlooking the Sacred Harbor, was bigger by far than Apollo's tiny shrine. Even on his own island, Apollo stood in his sister's shadow. She was the elder twin, and a manifestation of the Maiden.

Nothing on the island could have harbored an airship. Which Jake found irritating. Apollo *needed* something for *Argo* to shelter in. Something similar to the vast wooden hangar Wasserman had built in Hibernia.

As they passed over the Sacred Harbor, headed south and out to sea, the watery outline of a temple appeared, sunk in the shoals. Love ducked into Hephaestus's workshop-cum-armory, emerging with a sheaf of arrows designed for Apollo's silver-moon bow. He handed a half dozen to Jake. "Here, get heeled."

Jake looked them over. He was holding four flare arrows, and a couple of the gray-fletched hypodermic type. Paralysis arrows, like Artemis used on him.

"They got tanglefoots, too, and others with grapple points," Love informed him. "But they would be as useless as the bows underwater."

Jake nodded, tucking the ones Love gave him into his diving belt. "Let's get wet."

Descending from drop cables, it took only seconds to slip from the overcast to the sea surface. Jake got a quick impression of yellow-brown shorelines, white beaches, and an aqua-blue sea. Then he hit the water.

He instantly told his cable to release. Blood-warm waves closed over him. Love was in the water, too, descending in a cloud of bubbles ten meters away. Anyone looking out to sea would have gotten a quick glimpse of two figures dropping out of the sky to disappear beneath the waves. A pair of gods descending? Or two hapless humans falling out of heaven into the drink? Either way, a frightful omen.

His buoyancy suit was set for ten meters, dragging him down level with the temple. The water stayed marvelously clear all the way to the seafloor. Sea grass waved on the sandy bottom. Sponges, red-yellow coral, algae, and sea urchins clustered about the stone base of the drowned portico. Dogfish darted between tall slender columns.

The sunken shrine looked like a simple prostyle temple set in the sloping seabed, its rear buried under sediment drifting down from Delos above. Despite being half-buried, the temple seemed weirdly untouched by the sea. The marble pediment looked newly sculpted, showing the Rape of Scylla in vivid color, with Poseidon dragging the nymph aboard his golden chariot, accompanied by frisking sea monsters.

None of the colors had faded. No barnacles or yellow algae clung to the temple columns. The shrine should not even be there. There was no Ionic temple buried in the seabed off Delos. Not in the Bronze Age or in later times.

Love kicked past, headed for the temple entrance, swimming right through a fluted column. No wonder it looked so new. The temple was a huge holo. An illusion to awe the faithful and cover the entrance to the sub pen.

Heading straight for the back wall of the temple, Love swam through the stones and disappeared. Jake followed. On the far side of the hologram wall was a sub tunnel. Love lit a flare arrow, striking the point against the tunnel wall. Instantly it was bright as day for a dozen meters around them.

Jake swam after Love down hundreds of meters of dark

tunnel, until a great black hole opened overhead. Love turned upward. Jake kicked to catch up.

The hole grew lighter, turning from black to dull gray, finally showing a silvery surface. Reaching up, Jake caught hold of Love's flippered foot, signing for him not to break the surface. Love doused the flare arrow. The rebreathers gave off no bubbles to betray them. No sense tipping their hands until they had to.

Jake turned up the gain on his lenses, surveying the silver surface. A dark oblong hung on one side of the pen. The hull of the *Thetis*!

He swam over and made contact with the sub. There was no need for laborious code breaking. The minisub's operating system was hardwired to accept Jake's commands—no matter what was done to the software. One of many safeguards Jake had built into the expedition. *Argo* was similarly hardwired.

Jake ordered an underwater access hatch along the keel to open. So long as the bilges were sealed there was no chance of water rushing in. They slipped silently into the sub. Once inside he had the access hatch reseal itself, then opened the bilges. The command deck was deserted. Sitting down at the main control station, Jake flipped on the periscope.

Running lights atop the sub gave them a look at the low-ceilinged pen. Rough-cut rock surrounded flat dark water lapping softly against a stone dock. There were no guards or spy-eyes to be seen. Stairs led away from the dock.

"We need to see what's up those stairs," Jake decided. Now he wished they had brought bows to go with the arrows.

" 'Fraid you were gonna say that."

Jake told the hatch above to open, and hoisted himself up. "I'll lead off."

Love grinned. "Wouldn't have it any other way."

Swinging his legs out of the hatch, Jake slid down the hull onto the stones. Love came right behind him, striking a flare arrow. Crossing the dock, Jake crouched at the doorway and listened. His microamps picked up nothing but the faint dripping of water somewhere ahead.

Gingerly, Jake started ascending the steps. The stairs ended in a T. There was no way to know whether they should go left or right. Both arms of the T were equally dark and dank.

"Toss a coin," Love suggested.

"Can't. They haven't been invented." Coinage was many centuries in the future.

"Then maybe we just ought to go . . ." Love never finished. From the right arm of the T came the unmistakable sound of a bolt being shot. Followed by a door swinging open. Then footsteps. Lots of them. Headed their way.

Love doused his flare arrow. The soft yellow glow of lamplight showed far down the right-hand passage. Growing brighter, coming closer. Accompanied by an evil musty odor that they both instantly recognized.

"It's that goat dude." Love meant Pan. "We better damn well *dee-dee*."

Dee-dee they did, back down the dark steps, crossing the dock, then scrambling aboard the sub, the only hiding place in the bare pen. They crouched in the control cabin, watching through the periscope. Lamplight bobbed down the steps.

A bare foot with a woman's white leg attached appeared on the lamplit steps, followed by another, and another. A dozen lamp-carrying young women emerged from the doorway, dressed in skimpy linen robes embroidered with seaweed designs. Laughing and smiling, they spread out to completely illuminate the dock.

Pan came next, strutting down the steps on his goat legs, his erect cock proudly pointing the way. He strolled out onto the dock, turned, cocked his horned head, and surveyed the scene. Clearly he liked what he saw. The giggling young nymphs. Their scanty costumes. His dramatic erection. What could be better?

"God. If that goat guy comes aboard, we're gonna gag."

Love need not have worried. Pan ignored the sub, totally intent on a detailed inspection of the nymphs.

Last to descend the stairs was the Sea God himself, trident in hand, and stark naked. He wore nothing but a square-cut blue beard and a crown of golden seaweed. The face above the beard was a familiar one.

"Fuck," whispered Love, "it's Wasserman."

They had last seen the captain of the *Argo* over Africa. Despite the loss of his ship and crew, he seemed to have done very well for himself.

"What's the shit up to?"

"Look's like he's coming aboard." Jake drew Love back

into the aft cabin. They took up positions on either side of the cabin hatch. Love fumbled furiously through his arrows.

The Sea God mounted the sub. The upper control hatch swung open for him. Wasserman's bare leg appeared on the ladder. He paused, calling out to Pan. "Show restraint while I am gone. Don't make a complete goat of yourself."

"Oh, I will," Pan answered happily. The nymphs laughed.

Wasserman pronounced Poseidon's blessing on the upcoming orgy, then closed the hatch, jauntily descending the ladder.

Love did not give him a chance to turn. Stepping swiftly onto the control deck, he stabbed the Sea God in the thigh with a gray-fletched paralysis arrow. Poseidon gasped and crumpled.

Jake slipped a medikit around the Sea God's arm, to keep him breathing, at the same time ordering the sub to dive. A last glimpse of dock showed Pan enthusiastically rubbing on a nymph, not suspecting anything was amiss aboard the sub.

Clear dark water closed over them. *Thetis* began to thread her way out of the pen, then through the tunnel to the sunken hologram temple. Jake went to work on Wasserman. He did not need the array of sensors he had turned on Hera. A medikit could bombard you with data if you weren't careful. Nor did Wasserman need to answer. Paralysis made readings even more precise. Loss of conscious control let involuntary responses stand out. Wasserman could not use breathing tricks and muscle contraction to fuzz the data.

Jake started out with established facts, to set a base line. "Hello, Captain Asshole of the *Argo*. Did you have to kill Keane?"

Wasserman did not twitch, but the medikit registered anger and indignation, especially at the last part.

"Or did Dianna do the killing?"

That was the truth. According to Tyler and the medikit.

"You just let it happen."

More indignation, but basic agreement.

"Just to get your hands on this sub."

That was part of the answer.

"And to hide your portal to the future?"

Wasserman knew about the portal. No surprise there.

"The one on Atlantis. At the Callisto Shrine?"

Information confirmed, and added to. Now came the time

to slip in questions Jake had no ready answer for. "What about Sauromanta? Is she with Artemis?"

No response.

"Is she with Apollo?"

Still no response. Wasserman had no answer to Jake's most important question.

He shifted topics. "So where is the *Argo* now?"

No spike of recognition. Wasserman did not seem to know this either. Too bad. Jake would have to be more roundabout.

"Does *Argo* have a hangar?"

This time he had hit home. Wasserman reacted to "hangar."

"Where is it? Delos? Delphi? Atlantis?"

Atlantis drew the reaction. But where on Atlantis?

"Is the hangar in that new construction on the south side of the volcano?"

Bull's-eye! That had been a calculated guess. From the air that south temple complex was the only thing large enough to possibly house an airship.

"Is *Argo* there now?"

Wasserman honestly did not know. Which left only one sure way to find out.

Letting Wasserman lie there, Jake turned his attention to the sub, feeling like a juggler with way too many balls in the air. *Thetis* glided through the ghostly columns of the hologram sea-temple. As soon as they were properly out to sea, and out of sight of Delos, he told the sub to surface.

Somewhere above the murk, *Atlantis* was looking down on them through a dangling spy-eye. Jake got out on deck and waved, signaling the airship to drop a phone line. In seconds a light cable came tumbling out of the clouds overhead. Jake caught it and jacked it into the sub's onboard systems, giving them a secure comlink.

He told Tyler to execute a new search pattern, centered on Atlantis. "I'll take *Thetis* straight in and try to get a look at this hangar."

"What if we find something?" That was Peg, always practical.

Jake considered. It was hopeless to think he could give orders to cover every eventuality. "You'll have to decide. If you think you've been spotted, or you absolutely have to alert me, send a scrambled signal. Otherwise, keep communications silence. We caught Wasserman unawares. I want to do the same to Dianna and Apollo.''

He fervently wished he could be in two places at once—not at all impossible in a post-Einsteinian universe—but he lacked the proper equipment. Peg would have to do it on her own. She had the *Atlantis*. She had Hercules. Hopefully that would be plenty. He and Love would tackle Atlantis.

Jake rattled off a list of rendezvous points, each eight hours apart. Plus the equipment he needed—including his adhesive boots and a pair of silver-moon bows, along with their quivers and arrows. Once the package was lowered, he signed off. *Atlantis* reeled in the phone cable. Until they rendezvoused, his link with Peg was broken. He wished her luck.

For a long moment he stood on the deck of the minisub, surveying the low clouds and choppy sea. Somewhere out there was Sauromanta. Hopefully alive. So far—with the aid of the gods—he had made a total mess of this operation. At least he was beginning to get some of his own back.

Thetis ran at periscope depth all the way to Atlantis, letting Jake scan for *Argo* beneath the cloud cover, while Peg and *Atlantis* searched above the overcast. He saw nothing but sailing ships and fishing smacks. Finally the island's lush green volcanic cone came up over the southern horizon. This time he had no reason not to sail straight in, heading for the central gap in the great curving breakwater. A pair of tall ziggurat-shaped lighthouses flanked the entrance.

Atlantis did not need guard ships, or harbor walls. The great double port behind the mole feared no enemy. Not in an age when commerce hugged the coasts. And fifty heroes setting off in a single ship to steal a fleece was the stuff of legend. No one was going to come hundreds of klicks across the open sea in small boats, to storm a city protected by thousands of able-bodied citizens and otherworldly powers. The pair of Greek *pentekonters* that foiled their first attempt to scout the place had been a trap laid just for Jake.

Inside the mole, the twin harbors fanned out on either side of a double breakwater and central dock complex. The eastern harbor was the Phoenician one. Rows of round-sided, double-ended merchant ships sat moored at the docks, with big clay jars bound to their fore-posts. Curly-bearded sailors loaded cargo or lounged in the shade.

On the west side was the Greek Harbor, sheltering trading galleys with graceful curving sterns, and sharp cutwaters that carried the ship's all-seeing eye out over the waves. Jake's microamps picked up greetings and catcalls in Mycenaean as a thirty-oared galley from Argos arrived at the dock.

Quayside stalls offered food, wine, and bartered goods. The air smelled of fish and burnt spices. Twin breakwaters separated the harbors; between them a seawater canal ran inland, toward the circular city of Atlantis. Sonar reported that the canal had been dug deep enough for the biggest oceangoing ships, leaving plenty of room for the minisub.

The whip-thin periscope proved almost impossible to spot. It was eerie to sail invisibly past the dockside jugglers and market women hawking their wares. Knots of randy sailors sat atop bales of cargo, shouting bawdy comments at bare-breasted young women.

"Don't just stand there, lass, undo something."

"Need a hand to lift your skirt?"

Atlantean women laughed back. "Why? There's nothing here worth lifting it for."

Naked children sailing carved wooden boats in the canal spotted the periscope. Some went running along the canal bank, shouting and waving, keeping pace with the sub. None of the adults took notice.

Beyond the twin harbors, the canal cut through open cropland and salt marsh. Wood and stone bridges arched overhead. Half-naked huntsmen stalked waterfowl from small skiffs, aided by trained cats. As Atlantis proper approached, the canal widened to curve around the city. Jake took the western fork, picking his way between houseboats and pleasure barges, looking for a likely spot to land. On the port side, buildings adorned with bright frescoes came right down to the canal bank. Ornamental facades sparkled with mosaic glass and lapis tiles. On the starboard side fruit trees climbed the slope of the volcano.

Halfway up the cone, Jake could see the great cyclopean wall that ringed the volcano. Atlantis's only defense lay well away from the sea, enclosing not the city, but the volcano and the Shrine of Callisto. And *Argo*'s new hangar.

Finally Jake found a spot where a broad causeway crossed the canal. The shadowy space beneath the causeway was deserted, hidden from view by the central pylons and the causeway roadbed.

Pulling on his adhesive boots, he selected a moon bow, telling Love, "I'm going to get a look at that hangar, but it may take a while. Sit tight on the bottom. If I'm not back in forty hours, take the sub out and rendezvous with Peg."

"What about him?" Love nodded at Wasserman, still lying on the command deck.

"That medikit and glucose drip will keep him going. If you get kindhearted, throw a tanglefoot web over him and wake him up. But don't let him pull anything." Wasserman had betrayed Jake once, and did not deserve a second chance.

Love bent down to check the medikit. "Hey, his readings are going ballistic."

Jake took a look. Wasserman was having a silent seizure.

He looked back at Love. "We'd better wake him." Jake did not want Wasserman dying on them.

Love threw a tanglefoot web over the prone sea god, and Jake punched an antidote on the medikit. They watched as Wasserman came around. His eyes batted. His lips moved. Everything below the neck was wrapped in the sticky white web. Jake gave him water to moisten his throat, holding the cup to Wasserman's lips, tipping his head to let him drink.

Wasserman drank, sputtered, and spoke. "You can't leave me here!"

Jake set down the water. "Just watch."

"No!" Wasserman tried to lift himself off the deck, but the web prevented him, like a worm caught in a cocoon. "This whole island's going to blow."

"Sure," Jake tried to be soothing. "Someday. But right now it is just a calculated risk." The volcanic explosion would likely be preceded by bulging, tremors, massive outgassing. All the usual volcanic warnings.

"No! No!" Wasserman seemed about to burst. "It will happen *now*, if you tamper with the shrine's defenses."

"What do you mean?"

"There's an antimatter bomb buried deep down, atop the magma. It can be triggered anytime. If you get too close, she'll set it off."

"Who will?"

Wasserman struggled again to sit up, but the sticky web would not let him. "Artemis. Dianna. She thinks all cities are an abomination. If you get near to succeeding, she'll cheerfully blow us all to bits."

Wasserman's medikit indicated this was the absolute truth.

The Wild Hunt

Carrying his silver-moon bow, Jake emerged from beneath the causeway connecting Callisto volcano to Atlantis. Low clouds darkened the afternoon sky. The grassy bank felt insubstantial underfoot, despite the grip of adhesive boots. Jake knew that was illusion. There was nothing wrong with the ground. What made him feel shaky was knowing that at any moment a hidden antimatter bomb could trigger a five-hundred-megaton volcanic blast that would blow Jake, Atlantis, and most of the island to oblivion.

In fact he had the promise of Poseidon, Lord of Earthquakes and Tidal Waves—that this was exactly what *would* happen, if Jake pushed things too far.

Jake would have dearly loved to leave Poseidon/Wasserman lying in the *Thetis* at the bottom of the Grand Canal, forced to share the fate of the island. Making the bastard sweat. If Jake *did* trigger a volcanic cataclysm, he certainly wanted Wasserman there with him. Just for old times' sake.

But Jake had to forgo that bit of divine justice. Too much hung on every action. Right now Love was hustling *Thetis* back out to sea, carrying a warning for Peg. Wasserman went with the ship.

Despite cloudy skies and oncoming volcanic destruction, the people Jake saw did not seem doomed, or even discouraged. A loud and boisterous harvest procession came over the causeway, carrying sheaves of grain and winnowing fans. The men were stripped to the waist, wearing bulls' horns and singing lustily, led by a priest in a long quilted tunic. The women wore skins and animal masks. Everyone was having a time, swaying to the clash of cymbals, gulping wine from big clay jugs.

This was the High Summer Moon. Soon Bull Dancers from Crete and beyond would be arriving—Anneke included. A teenage girl wearing a fawnskin and a deer mask called for him to join them. "Dour bowman, don't stand there by the bank. Bonfires are waiting above."

They were headed his way, up the mountain. Jake joined in. He could hardly ask for happier company. Or better cover.

They climbed past rich volcanic croplands—grainfields, vineyards, and fruit orchards. Up into the olive groves. There Jake got an awesome view of the ivory white city, ringed by canals—then the long straight line of water connecting Atlantis to her twin ports. Beyond the harbors, wine-dark sea blended with violet sky.

Higher up, they ascended green goat meadows dotted with oaks, heading for the cyclopean wall ringing the volcanic cone. Neither the Callisto Shrine nor the smoking crater was visible. Both were lost in clouds and gloom. Toiling on into long summer twilight, they reached the base of the wall at dusk. There priestesses led them in a singing prayer to sunset, a red-gold stripe lighting the western horizon like fire on a molten sea.

Starless night descended. Bonfires flared up, brightening the dark volcanic slope. Celebrants settled down at the base of the wall to joke, sing, and pass the wine jugs.

Looking down on the lamplit canals of Atlantis, Jake could make out the moving lights of canal boats, like jewels rotating in their settings. Sad to think this would all be wiped out. Maybe before he got off the mountain.

Faster-than-light travel can be very distancing. Nearly everything that Jake had ever seen, from dinosaurs to Mississippi riverboats, was doomed to be destroyed—by cosmic collisions or civil wars. All cities, more or less, were marked for destruction. Troy was as doomed as Atlantis. Nineveh and

Miami both ended up in ruins. In Jake's own time, every city from LA to Bombay was consumed by the planetwide Megapolis. Astrophysics promised Earth herself would one day burn to cinders.

So why weep for Atlantis? Because she would go in a single blast, blown apart by the mountain he sat on, then to be swallowed by the sea? These people probably guessed that—maybe even expected it—yet they were laughing and singing.

Of course they expected some warning. Signs of the Earthshaker's displeasure. Maybe a chance to make amends. They could not know that an antimatter bomb with an electronic trigger was buried under the Callisto Shrine, set to hurry nature along. Only the gods had known that.

A lion called from the darkness beyond the wall. If Jake could get in and defuse the bomb, he might at best preserve the place for a natural death. Or perhaps his presence was fated to set it off. Not a happy thought.

The girl in the fawnskin and deer mask sat down next to him, offering a crock of unmixed wine. "Drink, stranger. High Summer is here." It sounded like a ritual invitation.

Taking the clay jug, Jake smiled and drank. The wine was sweet and heavy, but he could not afford much. From her voice and manner he could tell she was young. Though not that young. Rounded breasts showed beneath her fawnskin. He tried to hand the wine back. She would not take it. "Drink. Even a grim bowman can have a good time."

Maybe too good a time. Jake could hear giggles and murmurs in the dark, then a shriek of delight. He sipped again, trying to get her to take back the crock. She refused to touch it. The deer mask came down over her mouth, keeping her from drinking. Sex was taken as a matter of course, but removing the mask was strictly taboo. Laughing, she offered him goat's cheese wrapped in grape leaves to go with the wine.

Bronze Age morals no longer amazed him. This girl's mother had probably helped with her mask and costume, giving her the wine, and wrapping the cheese in grape leaves. Then sent her scampering off to have sex with the stranger of her choice. Teen pregnancy was still considered a blessing, not a calamity.

Gently, he gave back the crock, saying, "I'm on a quest." As much for his benefit as hers. The girl, the wine, and the warm fire were incredibly tempting. Compared to tinkering with megatons of explosive. They both might be dead in a couple of hours—making *doing the right thing* a ridiculous waste.

"What sort of quest?" She set down the crock, not the least turned off by the hint of heroics.

"I cannot talk about it here." Jake stood up, leading her away from the night fires and drunken singing, upslope toward the wall. Taking care not to tread on couples humping in the grass. It was easy enough to play the mysterious wandering hero. The Bronze Age was full of them.

When they reached the wall he ran his hands along the plaster white stonework. "How old is this?"

She laughed lightly. "Older than I am. It has been there ever since the new Ever-living Zeus seized the shrine." She made the Olympian Zeus sound like a new hyped-up late-model godling. Atlanteans still worshiped the Dying God, the divine child, born in midwinter, wed in the spring, dead when the earth grew cold. Child of the Mother, Groom to the Maiden, Husband of the Widowed Crone.

"Who built it?"

"Poseidon and Apollo, with the aid of Cyclopes." Gods and monsters were a natural part of her world.

"What is on the other side?"

"The Shrine of Callisto, the Beautiful One."

"What else?"

"No one knows," replied the girl in the deer mask. "There is a death curse on anyone who tries to climb it."

"Surely some must have tried." The lower courses were covered with plaster, but higher up Jake could see bare blocks, with plenty of hand-and footholds.

"Those that do, never come back." Already she knew what was coming.

"My quest requires that I go over." This seemed as good a spot as any. Jake went through his quiver and came up with a grapple-tipped arrow attached to a light climbing line. He fired it over the wall. The grapple caught on the far side and held. He turned back to the girl in the fawnskin.

Her deer face stared up at him. Away from the fires, and the couples thrashing in the grass, she seemed more daring. Slowly she reached around behind her head and undid the laces. If he was going to risk breaking taboos, she would too.

The mask dropped. Her uptilted face was full and strong, neither pretty or plain, merely young. She leaned closer, and they kissed. A simple, openmouthed kiss, with more feeling of the forbidden than if they had fucked all night.

When their lips parted he asked, "What is your name?"

She hesitated. That, too, must be forbidden. Which is why time travelers were told to leave their morals at Home. You could easily land in a spot where, "Hi, I'm Jake. Who are you?" was more insulting than, "Let's screw."

She summoned up her courage. "Pandora." It was the goddess name that meant "All-giving."

"Jake Bento." He-Who-Walks-Through-Winters, The Shatterer of Worlds, etc.

They kissed for the second and last time. Then he grasped the line, planted an adhesive boot on the stones, and walked up hand over hand. He paused at the top, looking down at Pandora staring up. Her eyes did not meet his. She had already lost him in the dark.

Jake turned his attention to the far side of the wall. The slope beyond did not look dangerous. Or much different. The only ominous sign was that on the inner side the smooth plaster surface extended all the way up the wall. Leaving no handholds between the stones—as though the wall were designed not to keep people out, but to keep something else *in*.

He let himself down, telling the arrow to release. He was in, surrounded by starless night, as comforting as a cloak of invisibility. His own eyes saw better in blackness than most people's did in daylight.

This was a primary recon. Poseidon had given up plenty of details. The bomb trigger was buried deep inside the Callisto Shrine, in a volcanic chamber accessed through the space-time portal. Actual penetration would have to wait until Love got back with Hercules. Jake was just going in to check on the opposition. To see if the *Argo* was about. And look for some sign of Apollo, Artemis, or Sauromanta. Especially Sauromanta.

First he had to check out the hangar. To reach the south side of the cone he crossed over the shoulder of the volcano. It took hours of climbing through rocky open country, scrambling over loose cinder piles, past twisted lava outcroppings.

Finally he came down on the far side of the cone. As he approached the tree line from above, he sighted the huge temple façade he had seen from the air. A grand ghostly structure shrouded in silent darkness. He did not need to touch it to know this was not a holo.

Up close he could see the monumental structure truly was a hangar. Hemispherical bronze doors towered over a wide, flat landing apron. Grooved tracks ran from the doors to the far end of the apron, to accommodate a mobile mooring mast. Another circular track ran around the edge of the apron, allowing the ship to take maximum advantage of the wind. Very neat. And well within the limits of Bronze Age artisans. In due time it would all be destroyed, but that was the price of keeping the place secret.

It remained to be seen if the *Argo* was in residence. Jake looked for a side entrance. Such a well-designed hangar would hardly rely on opening the huge main doors every time someone wanted to look outside, or take a leak.

He found a small subsidiary shrine set flush against the mountain. A stiff statue of Apollo looked out from between its pillars. Concealing himself in some brush, Jake released a bug he had brought with him from the *Thetis*. The little plastimetal insect scampered toward the shrine, trailing a microfilament line. Leaving his compweb and microamps to keep watch, Jake focused on controlling the bug.

He immediately got an insect's-eye view of the world. The steps up to the shrine became mountainous cliffs, stacked one atop the other. Slender columns became huge pillars holding up the sky. Apollo's statue was a colossus. The shrine itself became a great stone plain, with a maze of deep grooves running between the flagstones. Working his way through the maze, Jake guided the bug to the hangar side of the shrine, searching along the wall until he found a towering doorway. The door was closed and bolted, but the bug had no trouble climbing up to the key slot and slipping through.

There was no sign of the *Argo*. Humans find airship hangars immense, but the bug's-eye view is unbelievable. The hangar was like a huge empty world, twice as big as Jake expected. A pair of mobile mooring masts looked like twin Towers of Babel. It was a double hangar, built to accommodate both the *Atlantis* and the *Argo*. From the moment they hijacked *Atlan-*

tis, the god
were a step
Jake told
around the c
Callisto Shrin
thing he wante
a waste, if he
Recrossing t
roar. *Arraah-o*
from lower dow
out hunting. Or c
his medikit arou
Then he went on
It took him alm
Downslope from t canyon
in the side of the ggy oak grew at the
head of the cut. The branches would give him a good
view of the shrine, while the lower branches hung down into deeper cover. The base of the oak was scarred and scratched, but he found a broad strong limb hanging over the lower streambed. A perfect spot to stretch out and sleep away the day.

Dawn was coming and the clouds were lifting. The day ahead would be sunny and hot. Far below, Atlantis was just waking up. Jake could see smoke from breakfast fires, and moving pools of lamplight as people went about morning tasks. Slowly dawnlight worked its way down the mountain, touching the bronze temples on the acropolis, finally reflecting off the canals. Lamps dimmed, then went out.

He finished the cheese Pandora had given him, then went to sleep, leaving his compweb and microamps on watch.

Jake was awakened by goats bleating. It was late morning. The sun was already high up. His bones ached from having slept in the crotch of a tree. Silently he shifted position, staring upslope through the foliage. Goats were feeding beyond the oaks, a whole flock of them, cropping the grass, leaping rocks, jostling and complaining. Not caring that hungry lions had hunted over those slopes scant hours before. Dumb goats.

Reaching into his belt pocket, he got out some iron rations brought from the *Thetis*—synthetic jerky from ship's stores, vitamin supplements, plus a full meal tablet. As the tablet exgoats stagger on up the

boy, pitching pebbles to keep
, minus the smell. He had short
xie face, a smooth hairless chest,
d a shapely phallus long enough to trip
aving fun with biosculpt.
k to sleep.
akened by a warning buzz from his compweb.
was headed his way. He scrambled up for a look.
e topmost branches he could hear a terrible commotion
ing from downslope. The sea of treetops kept him from
eeing what was happening, but his microamps brought the unmistakable sounds of a hunt. A horn blared, followed by the thud of hooves, hounds baying, and a spirited view halloo. He hoped to hell he was not the quarry.

Sitting tensely in the treetop, he waited with bent bow. The hunt thundered closer. Suddenly the quarry burst into view. They were wild aurochs, *Bos primigenius*, the great black forebearers of the bulls of Crete. Six prime young males came crashing out of the thicket, bellowing in terror.

Who could be hunting them? Massing close to a ton, *Bos primigenius* had a trip-wire temper, and terrible spear-sharp horns that could uproot a tree. These six bulls would have made short work of the last night's lion pride. Only humans dared disturb them.

The hunting party burst from the thicket right on the last bull's heels. First came the hounds, big white beasts with red ears, living models for the plasti-metal hellhounds that Pan had "given" to Artemis.

Crashing behind them came Centaurs. For a moment Jake thought they were naked horsemen, then he saw they were fused to their mounts. Half-man, half-horse—human male bodies springing from the horse's shoulders, where the beast's head and neck should be. Shaggy manes hung down their backs. Each carried a long, four-meter pike, like the *sarissa* that armed Alexander's phalanx.

Here was biosculpt with a vengeance. Goat legs and horned brows were mere bone and muscle grafts. This was a melding of two mammals. One head controlled six limbs, two hearts and digestive tracts, two sets of lungs, plus a tail.

And clinging to these horsetails were women. Stark naked huntresses ran barefoot behind the Centaurs, bounding over clumps of brush and fallen logs, bows and javelins in hand, holding on to their partners' tails. A stunning sight.

As a bull turned at bay, the leading Centaur blew his horn. Hounds fell back, baying at the bull. Seeing his opening, a Centaur couched his *sarissa* under his armpit, the way a bull-ring *picador* held his lance. Charging straight at the bull, he drove his pike deep into the *morillo*, the lump of muscle above the bull's neck. Centaur meant "bull-stabber." Jake saw now where they got the name.

Blood spurted from the wound. But the bull did not seem to notice. Shaking off the *sarissa*, he drove the Centaur back, stabbing at the man-beast with his horns. The Centaur nimbly dodged this disemboweling stroke.

Women came panting up, letting fly with their bows. Arrows sang, and the auroch lurched off, bleeding furiously. His hunters sprinted after him. Since they could not graze, the Centaurs must have needed a lot of meat to support their horse bodies.

The need for the wall was explained. The "gods" had turned Callisto's green cone into a bioengineered playpen, complete with mythic beasts and maiden huntresses. With themselves lording over everything. Masters of life and death. Megalomania on a cosmic scale. And incredibly callous, since they *knew* it would all be destroyed when the volcano blew.

Jake climbed back down to catch some more sleep.

He was awakened again, late in the afternoon. This time by splashing and laughter. Women's laughter, coming from upstream. He crawled out on his limb to see what was happening. At the head of the draw, just before the stream plunged down into the gorge, there was a wide sunlit pool fed by the spring at the shrine. Nymphs were doing their washing, dumping armfuls of clothes into the wide clear pool. Pulling up their skirts, they waded in, stamping on the laundry to force it under, laughing and joking.

All of them seemed to be in their teens or early twenties. Older priestesses were no doubt excused from doing the washing, though the way these young women went at it was hardly like work. Clear water and warm sunlight made doing the laundry seem idyllic.

Jake lay back down on the limb. He was in no danger. More likely he was about to be entertained. The low-hanging branch was a perfect spot for observing the pool without being seen. Nymphs came out of the water, wet skirts clinging to their legs, laying their wash out on sunlit grass.

Thoughts drifted. By now Peg and Love should be winging his way, bringing *Atlantis* and Hercules. Tonight he meant to get a closer look at the shrine, then recross the wall and rendezvous with them tomorrow.

Shifting noiselessly, trying to get comfortable on the limb, Jake noticed little white tufts embedded in the rough bark. Picking up one of the tufts he examined it, switching his lenses to microscopic. His fingers grew to giant size, between their huge tips was a clump of little white hairs.

Cat hairs. His compweb recalled the deep scratches on the lower tree trunk. He was holding the white belly hairs of a leopard. *Chui* as he was known in Swahili.

Damn. His perch was *too perfect*. He was lying on a leopard tree. A big cat had lain up here during the day, waiting for some unsuspecting meal to come drink at the pool.

He had to shift his hiding place. No way was he going to wait for a leopard to come creeping up to share his perch. But not right now. Nymphs were moving about, spreading out the laundry. Some had disappeared into the brush. Others were standing hip deep in the water, looking his way.

One especially alert nymph with honey-colored hair looked right at him. He froze against the branch. Had he been seen?

Without taking her gaze off his hiding place, the nymph reached down, took hold of the hem on her chiton, pulling the fabric over her head. For a moment she stood stark naked, big almond eyes staring at the limb he lay on. Then she trod her chiton into the water.

Several others followed her example. Their sudden watchfulness was explained. Finished with washing, they had started to bathe. Yet another complication. Naked nymphs splashed and played. Sunlight glistened on wet bodies, gleaming in dark triangles of pubic hair. Jake hardly needed this. Just doing laundry had been a distraction.

One pair started to wash each other, stopped to kiss, then started again. Slowly lathering their bodies. Jake looked away toward the trees. Common prudence demanded he stay alert, and not get carried away "observing events by the spring."

Silent as a shadow, a speckled shape flowed down the back of a nearby tree, vanishing into the brush. The movement was so sudden Jake had to quiz his compweb—seeing it replayed—to make sure it had happened. It was the leopard. A big tom, more than two meters long, massing over sixty kilos. He had been lying up in an oak less than twenty meters away.

It was too much to hope that *chui* had been offended by the splashing and sex play, and was looking for a more decent spot to nap. More likely he meant to sample what he had seen. Jake slid his moon bow off his shoulder, praying he would not have to act. Lion prides like to specialize—going for the same game again and again, perfecting their technique. Leopards are more eclectic killers. Staking out a territory, then killing what comes along. Birds, goats, monkeys, even hairless apes—when they can get them.

For a dozen heartbeats Jake scanned the area, ignoring the frolicking nymphs. Just when he thought the leopard might have left, *chui* appeared again, closer to the pool. Visible for only a fleeting moment, the cat slipped through shadows beneath the brush. Floating collarbones let the beast belly along flat against the grass-roots. Dark rosettes on his light coat blended into dappled sunlight, making him invisible unless he moved. He disappeared into the rocks bordering the pool. Clearly he meant to kill.

Scrambling higher into the tree, Jake no longer bothered to hide. Shouting a warning would only make things worse. If the nymphs scattered, one was bound to rush right into the leopard. His compweb made the halfhearted suggestion that he wait, let the leopard make his kill, then slip off in the confusion. Such a course maximized mission secrecy.

But Jake was already frantically searching through his quiver for just the right arrow. He would have liked to use a tanglefoot, but he could not tell what sort of shot he would get. Instead he tore the cap off the tip of an armor-piercing arrow, to let the explosion expand in the wound.

Nocking the arrow, he stood up, his back to the trunk, the bow bent in front of him, covering the pool. Perspiration trickled down the curve of his jaw. He used the heel of his right hand to wipe at the sweat, then he pulled the nock all the way back to his ear—the way Sauromanta did.

The leopard appeared again. This time atop the rocks overlooking the pool. Jake homed in on him, blotting out the splashing and laughter from the pool, his arm humming with tension from holding the bow taut. Claws scraped on the rock. The big tom's shoulders tensed, ready to spring.

Jake released, telling his compweb to lock in on a single black rosette on the upper chest, right behind the neck.

The leopard sprang, sailing out over the pool. Guided by his compweb, the arrow met *chui* in midflight. The shaft sank smack into the middle of the rosette Jake had selected, triggering its armor-piercing point. A spray of blood and bone chips burst from the far side of the animal, blown out a hole bigger than Jake's head.

Nymphs looked up to see the big cat twist wildly in midair. Doubled in shock, the leopard plunged straight into the pool, leaving a spreading red stain.

Naked nymphs exploded out of the water like dynamited frogs. In seconds the sunlit glen lay still and empty. No sign remained of what had happened, aside from scattered laundry, bloody ripples in the pool, and the floating body of the leopard. The fletched end of the shaft showed in his speckled shoulder.

Jake dropped to the ground, and bounded downslope, his cover completely blown. Artemis and Apollo were not likely to give him a good-conduct award for saving a nymph or two, of which the gods seemed to have a goodly supply.

At the bottom of the draw he ran smack into the nymph with the honey-colored hair. She stopped wide-eyed—not bothering to cover herself. Sun-browned skin showed no trace of tan lines. She stared at him for several seconds, then turned and bolted into the brush.

No need to say thanks. Naked ingratitude was the least of Jake's worries. Spinning about, he headed the other way, determined to distance himself from anyone who might aid in tracking him. As soon as he was out of sight, he turned back downslope. The city of Atlantis was down there, below the trees. And before he got to Atlantis there would be villages, hamlets, and farmsteads. Like a book in a library, or a leaf in a forest, the best place to hide a person was among people. He had *seen* the wild hunt—with its hounds, Centaurs, and maiden huntresses. He did not doubt their ability to scour the mountainside.

Coming upon a shallow stream, he plunged in, running with the current, telling his boots to grip on the slippery rocks. It would help to cover his tracks, but in the end only speed could save him.

He stayed with the stream until he found a good spot to exit it, a scree slope that would not leave prints. He scrambled out onto the talus, scattering rocks. As he got his footing, he heard the first view halloo. It came from in front of him, followed by the baying of hounds. Dropping to one knee, he peered between the twisted trunks of ancient oaks. Farther down, between him and the wall, he saw a line of beaters. Centaurs and huntresses spread out to cover as much ground as they could, with dogs in front of them.

Damn. Some evil genius had the same idea he did. A signal must have come down from the shrine, telling them to block the direct line of escape. Now he was cut off from the wall, and the city below.

As he crouched there, digesting this latest disaster, a Centaur broke cover not twenty meters in front of him. It must have been the fellow who gave the view halloo.

Leveling his pike, the bull stabber charged, planning to spit Jake before his fellows arrived. Big mistake. The beast-man would have done better to keep watch until reinforcements arrived.

Drawing a tanglefoot arrow from his quiver, Jake aimed at the ground a couple of hoofbeats ahead of the charging Centaur, firing without thinking. One swift motion right out of *Zen and the Art of Archery*.

The arrow struck beneath the Centaur's forefeet, blossoming into a sticky white web. The Centaur went down, horse's ass over human head, his *sarissa* shattering against the ground. Attempts to struggle to his feet only entangled his rear legs, and one of his arms. Served the bastard right for being an eager beaver.

Having disposed of one pursuer, Jake spun about, retracing his steps. He had been thoroughly spotted, so there was no sense keeping communications silence. As he ran he sent out a long call for help—giving his position, and a summary of everything that had happened since he left *Thetis*. The message was scrambled, and there could be no reply without *Atlantis* revealing her own position. But the call might do Peg some good. And could possibly save his ass.

When he got back to the scree slope he turned the opposite way, away from the stream. When his pursuers arrived they would have two trails to follow, and no way of knowing which was the right one. His first dash for freedom had been turned back, and would now be replaced by a drawn-out duel of wits. If he could elude pursuit until dark, the night would be with him.

Beyond the scree slope, he struck a stretch of high moorland, dotted with oaks. Jake set out crosswind to confuse the dogs. Past the oaks, the moorland ended in a huge rockslide rising up toward the rim of the crater, a mad jumble of bare rock and lava flows, running smack up against the crater and the clouds. He scrambled up as best he could. Here his boots would leave no tracks. So long as he kept his head down he could not be seen from below. Nor would his odor stand out. Rocks stank of sulfur. Winds whipped around the crater, confusing his scent.

Hugging the rocks, Jake clawed his way across the shoulder of the volcano. He reached the top of the ridge, an uneven knife blade of piled boulders, with sheer drops on either hand. From this high shoulder he could see the shrine far below, and beyond it the wall, the city of Atlantis, and the twin harbors. A stately fleet was putting in to the west harbor. Cretan ships with white bulls on their black sails. The Bull Dance fleet, with Anneke aboard.

There was no sign of pursuit, until he looked up.

On the far side of the ridge swung the *Argo*. The airship hung just below the high clouds capping the cone. For a nanosecond he thought it might be *Atlantis*, come to save him. But his compweb supplied the differences. This was indeed the *Argo*, with Apollo at the helm.

Jake could have cried. He had beat back and forth between here and Delos, looking for this airship. He had climbed Callisto's mythic green cone, guarded by big cats and biosculpted man-beasts to look into her empty hangar. Just when he needed her the absolute least, *Argo* poked her nose around the volcano's cone, less than a klick away.

He ducked down. But it was clearly too late. *Argo*'s hangar doors swung open, and a bright spark streaked out. One of Apollo's godcopter hovercars. He had been spotted.

Jake could have dodged the airship, which had to be careful about coming near the cone. The hovercar was infinitely more deadly. Able to swoop down low, landing on the least bit of level space. Hovering where it could not land. He slid down behind a twisted lava outcropping, hoping for a miracle.

The hovercar did not bother to land. Swinging down, it hung like a fiery dragonfly above the ridge, disgorging plasti-metal dogs. Then the godcopter darted back toward the *Argo*.

That tore it. Jake skidded down the ridge, dodging between boulders, making for the next shoulder, putting distance between himself and Dianna's plasti-metal pack.

At thc top of the next ridgeline, he turned to look. He could not see *Argo*, or Artemis either. But the high-tech hounds were bounding after him, leaping from rock to rock, tracking him with chemosensors that could not be confused.

He was dead. He could not outrun them. He could not hide. His quiver did not hold enough arrows to fight them all. The lead dog was less than twenty meters behind him, red ears cocked forward, chrome claws ringing on stone.

Jake tried a tanglefoot. The dog went down in a struggling heap, jaws tearing at the white sticky web. But in less than a minute the plasti-metal beast was back on its feet, biting through the last of the web.

Making maximum use of the minute he gained, Jake hurtled downslope. But as soon as the ground bent upward again, he slowed and the hounds gained. He would never make the next saddle.

Turning, he loosed another tanglefoot, bringing down the lead beast. This time he followed the tanglefoot with an armor-piercing shaft. He had the grim satisfaction of seeing the dog shatter, its insides blown out by the arrow. But nine dogs were still on his trail, and he only had a couple of armor-piercing arrows left.

A volcanic plug capped the high end of the draw, a blunt pillar reaching toward the clouds that wrapped the cone. He got out a grapple arrow, arching it over the top of the plug, telling it to stick. When the first dog skidded up to the base of the plug, Jake was twenty meters up the shaft, pulling the line up behind him.

That stymied the hounds. Chrome claws could not compete with a climbing line and adhesive boots. But it did not stop them. Some started to inch up the shaft. Others bounded up the rock slope on either side.

As soon as he reached the top Jake flattened out, lying down to peer over the edge and take stock. His heart hammered against the rock. He had two armor-piercing arrows left to take out nine dogs. Not enviable odds. In fact it was heartbreakingly unfair. Had he been more callous, he could have slunk away, letting that leopard have a woman. Now he would die for showing mercy.

He could hear the hovercar's jet rotor, echoing off the rocks. The dogs climbing the shaft were halfway up. When they got a little higher he'd try taking them out with tanglefoots. But the ones scrambling up the scree slopes on either side were already level with the top of the plug. Soon they would be in position to leap down on him.

Something nudged his shoulder.

Jake squealed in panic, looking up, expecting to see chrome jaws gapping at him. Instead he saw a skyhook. One of those round horse-collar harnesses, hanging down on a line coming out of the clouds above him.

He could hardly believe it. Cut off, nearly helpless, backed into a corner, and suddenly someone was offering him a lift. Could it be *Argo* with Apollo at the other end? Or Artemis in her godcopter?

He did not much care. Anything beat waiting atop a stone plug for the dogs to rip him apart. He grabbed the harness, pulling in some slack, then looping it around his middle.

For a moment the line stayed slack. Then it snapped taut, jerking him off his feet. He was twelve meters up in the air when the first hound landed on the pillar. The plasti-metal beast sniffed about, getting his scent, but not seeing where he had gone. Then the dog looked up.

Jake waved a jaunty good-bye.

Chariots of Fire

Jake whirled up into wet foggy air. Clouds look fleecy white from the outside. Inside they are damp and gray as a dreary day. Up and up he went, watching the thinning mist turn from gray to white, with a sunny halo showing through.

Suddenly he burst into sunlight, seeing the volcanic cone for the first time in days, sticking up through the cloud layer, trailing a wisp of smoke. At the far end of his tether hung a silver lifting body hull, held aloft by concentric jet rotors cutting rings of fire overhead. He recognized the hovercar that had been aboard *Atlantis*. Peg's red-haired head peered over the side. She was operating the hoist. Love had to be at the controls.

Jake spun his hand rapidly over his head, signaling her to haul him up fast.

Peg obliged. Jake landed on the hovercar's mid-deck feeling like a sack of wet laundry, soaked with sweat, barely believing he was aboard—and safe for the moment. White clouds and dazzling sunlight seemed too shining bright. He gaped at Peg. She had a medikit out. Jake waved it away. He was not damaged, just dazed and confused. ''How? What happened?''

"We picked up *Thetis* at the sunset rendezvous," Peg explained. "And spotted *Argo* on the way in. Headed for Atlantis."

Thanks to communications silence, last night's stalking around Apollo's hangar had been pointless. When he had sent his bug in to search the empty hangar, *Argo* was already spotted and being shadowed.

"Then we heard your Mayday," Peg continued.

"And came gunnin'," Love added from his pilot's seat. They had separated from *Atlantis*, dropped through the clouds, tracked the action from a distance, then come up the back side of the volcano, passing just beneath the crater. Tearing through the clouds to get to him before the dogs did. A nice bit of split-second flying.

"Weren't nothin'." Love laughed. "I could have cut it even finer."

"It was close enough," Jake assured him. Way too close. His head was still spinning. "Make for the *Argo* as fast as you can."

"Don't you mean *Atlantis*?" Peg still had her medikit out, suspecting he might need serious attention.

"No!" He pushed the medikit aside. "We have to hit them before they realize what's happening." He meant to overwhelm them in one desperate rush. Before the Unheavenly Twins had time to regroup. While the hellhounds were still scrambling around on the volcano.

"Hang on to your lunches," Love called out, putting the hovercar into a high-g turn. Skimming low over the cloud wrack, closing in on the *Argo*'s position below. Quickly Jake cataloged equipment. He had his bow and a dozen arrows, plus his adhesive boots. Peg, too, had sticky boots, but never carried a weapon. Love had the hovercar. Not much. Surprise and audacity would have to make up the difference.

Love sang out, "Going down," then plunged through the cloud cover. Grayness closed around them, accompanied by a sickening "down-elevator" sensation. Harrowing seconds passed.

Suddenly they shot out of the cloud ceiling, with *Argo* a thousand meters below. Love made a perfect entrance. On the flat upper deck of the *Argo* Jake could see a pair of Hyperboreans staring up, openmouthed, clinging to safety lines. Beyond them lay the circular metropolis of Atlantis. Jake could see the ring canals and the temple-studded acropolis. The Bull Dance fleet from Crete was being hauled up the Grand Canal toward the city by throngs of citizens and countryfolk, all about to be entertained by an air battle.

Jake got out a grapple arrow, attaching the free end of the line to a recessed deck hook, telling Peg to be ready. "As soon as we board, I'm going to rush the upper bridge. There is a hatch at the base. I want you to sit on it. Keep it closed until I can . . ."

Love cut him off. "Heads up, gang. Copter coming on fast. One-five-niner."

Jake snapped his head about, looking aft. The hovercar's open rear deck gave an excellent view aft, blocked only by the raised twin-tailed boom. An angry spark of fire was roaring up from behind and below. He could see Dianna at the controls.

"Must have gone down to get her dogs." Jake shouted to Love. "Keep above her."

"Sure thing."

Height meant everything. Neither hovercar was armed. STOP had not anticipated the need for Bronze Age dogfights. Artemis would no doubt have her silver-moon bow, but so long as they were above her there was no way she could fire past her own rotors into a 300kph slipstream.

Love climbed. Artemis kept coming on, increasing her angle of attack. Love accelerated. "I believe the crazy bitch wants to ram."

It would be totally in character. For sheer guts, and an unwillingness to lose, Artemis was hard to beat. "Show her some evade," Jake suggested.

"No shit. Like I *really* want her running up my ass."

Jake shut up, leaving the piloting to Love. Ramming was not totally suicidal. Both hovercars had tilt-jets for maneuvering and double overhead rotors to keep them aloft. If Artemis could clip their rotors with her fuselage, she could knock them down, without doing fatal damage to herself.

Love put the hovercar through a series of high-speed turns. But Artemis stayed right behind him, barrel rolling to keep from overshooting, then closing the distance, threatening to clip Love's rotors or tail boom. Sticking to them like a heat-seeking SAM.

"She ain't givin' in to my evade," Love complained.

The avenging goddess had closed to within a hundred meters. Jake could see her face looking cool-as-be-damned, with the trace of a smile. Not in the least worried by the thought of a high-speed collision.

Putting aside his grapple, Jake got out his second-to-last armor-piercing arrow, crouching by the aft hatch, seeing if he could get off a shot. A gale of air tore at him, bent on sucking him through the hatch. Battling vertigo, Jake tried not to cough up his total breakfast. He wanted to tell Love to level off, but dared not interfere with the flying. Somehow he needed to get both hands free to shoot.

As he struggled with the bow, a firm steady arm wrapped itself tightly about his waist, holding him in. It was Peg, bracing herself against the bulkhead behind him, making sure the slipstream did not tear him away.

Distance dwindled. Jake bent his bow and fired, thinking, "Here's for Emiko." The shaft flew straight at Artemis's forward fuselage. A hit there would tear the hovercar apart.

At the last moment propwash from the lower rotor whipped the shaft aside. The arrow spun off toward the volcano below.

Love turned sharply to port. Artemis snap-rolled to keep position, then put on a burst of speed to close the gap, grinning in triumph.

Jake nocked his last armor-piercing arrow. Ignoring the body of the hovercar, he told his compweb to lock onto the port turbofan pod. Praying for someone, anyone, to guide his shaft, he fired again.

The arrow sped straight toward the portside turbofan. At the last moment the shaft wobbled in the propwash, starting to go wide. Jake swore at the wind.

Then the explosive arrow hit the torrent of air from the turbofan. Instantly it was sucked into the intake, disappearing inside the port turbofan. For a moment nothing happened. Then in a burst of flame the turbofan disintegrated.

Artemis's face dissolved in shock as the hovercar whipped to port, then flipped over. Plasti-metal dogs hurtled from the rear deck, spinning crazily in midair. Upside-down, with its main rotors windmilling, the hovercar whirled out of control.

Trailing smoke from the port side, the stricken ship spun out of the sky. Jake watched until it tumbled down, impacting against the green slope of the volcano a thousand meters below.

Love leveled off, smiling happily. "Can't say she'll be missed."

Jake nodded. Sick with vertigo, he clung to the hatch combing, held in by Peg, wishing he could puke. But there was no time for such luxuries. No time to nurse his shattered nervous system. Whipping the hovercar around, Love headed back for the *Argo*, aiming to settle with Apollo.

Love came at the airship from behind, matching speeds perfectly. Four times as fast, and infinitely more maneuverable, the hovercar had the bigger ship at its mercy. If they had just wanted to knock down the big airship, there were a number of ways to do it. But they were not just dealing with Apollo and his Hyperborean hard cases. There were innocents aboard. Survivors from the original *Atlantis* crew. Slaves, handmaids, bath boys, and whatnot. Jake had to take the ship intact.

He fired his grapple arrow onto the upper deck. It stuck. Love throttled back to keep the line taut. Snapping safety harnesses to the line, Jake and Peg slid down to the upper deck of the airship. As soon as their boots gripped, Jake ordered the arrow to release.

Blue-skinned Hyperboreans came running at them—tethered to the deck by long safety lines—screaming heathen war cries and swinging long-handled bronze axes about their heads.

Peg and Jake threw themselves flat, hugging the deck.

Love dropped the godcopter down to deck level, opened the throttle, and dashed the length of the airship, throwing a high decibel storm ahead of his hovercar.

Hercules might have stood his ground with two tons of metal and plastic hurtling at him in a hurricane of propwash, happily facing the howling avalanche with nothing but a bronze ax. These Hyperboreans were made of different stuff. Flying out of Love's path, they finished up at the far end of their tethers, hanging off the sides of the airship.

Nothing was left but a long sweep of light alloy deck between Jake, Peg, and the upper bridge. Dashing down the deck, they found the high bridge deserted. It was not a true command station, just an observation cockpit sheltered from the slipstream, with a small communications mast, and a hatch leading to the forward lift.

Peg sealed the hatch, so no one could get at them that way. Jake settled into the cockpit. His compweb had a program ready to convert the tiny cockpit into a control station from which he could run the *Argo*. Jacking in, he triggered the same hardwired override that gave him control of *Thetis*.

It worked. The Helm instantly answered his commands. He closed down the forebridge and the auxiliary control station in the tail, then shut off the slidewalks and sealed the lifts. With the airship's interior virtually paralyzed, he ordered the *Argo* to put about, making for a rendezvous with *Atlantis*.

No longer needing communications silence he punched through a call to DePala. The former helmsmate, now de facto commander of the *Atlantis*, was ecstatic. ''You've done it!''

''So far,'' Jake cautioned. Apollo was somewhere below-decks, no doubt hopping mad. Along with who knows how many Hyperboreans. Jake wanted Love and Hercules on hand when he confronted the maniac Mouse God.

Love flew top cover all the way to the rendezvous, making sure the Hyperboreans on the upper deck stayed hanging on their tethers. Twice Peg reported that someone tried to force the hatch she was sitting on, but she kept her hand tight on the manual override.

With the two ships running toward each other at 100 kph, range closed rapidly. As soon as they were close enough to transfer, Jake told Love to dock the hovercar. ''Have Tyler rig a sling to lower you and Herc to here. And bring more armor-piercing arrows.''

''Hope so,'' Love replied. ''A little AP goes a long way. I'll be bringin' the whole airborne brigade.''

Atlantis swung into position overhead, hangar doors open wide, her landing hoist extended. Love's hovercar slid up to the hangar, matched speeds, engaged the hoist, then cut her own engines. In seconds he was hauled inside.

Peg announced, ''We've got trouble.''

Jake looked back at the upper deck. A hatch had swung open. Apollo must have been waiting for just this moment. The hovercar had disappeared into the hangar overhead. Jake was totally occupied with keeping *Argo* matched with *Atlantis*.

The Mouse God vaulted through the hatchway onto the upper deck, armed with a long ebony spear, a gold-studded cuirass, and a round bronze shield. A sword and sheath hung over one shoulder. He wore his mouseskin cap tilted rakishly to one side. Otherwise, he was stark naked, smiling as he came on.

Peg abandoned her position at the hatch, leaping up onto the deck. Jake put in an urgent call to Love. "Get the hell down here. We've got big trouble."

"Hang on chief. Help is here."

A grapple line snaked between the two ships, connecting *Atlantis*'s hangar to the *Argo*'s upper deck. Jake maneuvered to keep the line taut—while winches reeled the two ships together.

But there was no chance of Love or Hercules getting down in time. Apollo sauntered forward, trailing a safety line, clearly meaning to spear Jake before help arrived. Only Peg stood in his way. The Mouse God nonchalantly waved his spear. "Stand aside, woman. I am taking my ship back. I'll attend to you when I'm done."

Peg did not bother to reply. Picking a relaxed stance, her right foot leading, she tested the feel of her adhesive boots against the deck. Unlike Apollo, she had no safety line. A thousand meters below lay the twin ports of Atlantis, dotted with shipping.

They were well away from the cloud cover around the cone. Sunlight spilled on the silver deck. Apollo must have taken that as a good omen, being the God of Light and Reason. He tried to temporize with Peg. "Be sweet, woman. Let me by. If you are lucky, I'll fuck you later."

She did not bother to comment on the offer, relaxing into *migi gamae*, the upright martial-arts stance. Her hands hung loose at her sides, her face clear and concentrated, centering her energy.

Love appeared at the hangar door above them, with Hercules at his side, snapping a sling onto the line. It was now or never.

Apollo shrugged, stepping closer, his shield slung on his left arm, holding the spear with both hands. "Have it your way. This death will not be on me." He lunged at Peg, stabbing with his spear.

Peg stepped into the attack, slipping past the point, seizing the spear with both hands. Not trying to resist his movement, she pivoted backwards, using Apollo's own momentum to swing him around in a smooth circular motion. Evasion, extension, and centralization. *Shiho nage.* Immobilization number 6. *Tenkan* variation. Her hips pivoted, her arms extended the spear, up and around, completing the circle Apollo had begun. He had no more chance of stabbing her than Rusty did. Or the Beast of Baal.

By the time Peg completed her pivot, Apollo was overbalanced, his back to her, with the spear high overhead. She continued the motion, bringing the spear around and down. Apollo was pulled over backwards by his own weapon.

He landed flat on his back on the deck, his shield pinned beneath him, locking his left arm. His right wrist was dislocated from holding on to the spear shaft for too long. He stared up at Peg. She had the spear tucked under her arm, pointed downward, the blade at his throat.

Jake called out a cheery warning. "Don't tempt her." He had never seen Peg slit a throat, but there is always a first time.

Love and Hercules came swinging down on the sling. As soon as they were safely tethered to the deck, Love told the grapple to release.

Seeing Apollo sprawled on the deck, Hercules congratulated Peg, saying he could not have done better himself. Sauntering over to where the Mouse God lay, the demigod reached down, helping his half brother up. "Don't feel bad. She has a spell on her. You can't touch her. I myself have tried."

Love was wearing a just-like-in-the-movies grin. "That about wraps up the ball game."

Just about, Jake agreed. They had both airships, plus the sub, and the worst of the Olympians in their power. Minus Artemis—who was, hopefully, dead.

Seeing Hercules, the Hyperboreans fell back, knowing they were thoroughly beaten. Hyacinth appeared, worried about Apollo, begging Jake to spare his godly bedmate.

Jake would just have soon have dropped Apollo overboard and been done with it. But petty revenge was not part of the program. Alive, Apollo might be worth something. And Jake needed every advantage he could squeeze out of the situation.

He had searched through *Argo*'s memory, getting an idea of what he had to work with. Chief Larsen and Bosun McKay were both aboard, along with a trio of survivors from the original *Atlantis* expedition—giving him the nucleus of a crew.

But the ball game would not be over until he found Sauromanta and defused the bomb beneath the volcano. Two extremely tricky propositions.

The Shatterer of Worlds

Artemis, Father Zeus has made you your sex's tyrant, a killer of women . . .

—*Homer,* Iliad, *Book XXI*

Jake descended on the Atlantis acropolis with his two airships and his prisoners. And got a divine welcome from high priestesses and the Sacred Queen. He never claimed to be a god, merely a heavenly messenger. Jake Bento, an avatar of Shiva—the Shatterer of Worlds.

The fiery conflict over the city—with a hovercar crashing into the volcanic cone—had let everyone know there was trouble among the immortals. Jake's cover story took it from there. He announced that there had been a revolt against Zeus. All the major Olympians were implicated—except for Hestia, the beloved Hearth Maiden. Hera was a prisoner in heaven—still holed up aboard *Atlantis*. Apollo and Poseidon were among the ringleaders, and would be punished here on Earth.

A plausible story, consistent with all the myths. Atlanteans were willing to believe the worst of Apollo. And Hera's hatred for her brother-husband was well known—he had raped her, forced her into marriage, then been breathtakingly unfaithful. Poseidon alone made them nervous—since the earthshaking Sea God had the power to swamp the island.

Neither airship landed. Jake brought his prisoners down to

the acropolis by hovercar, getting a dizzying view of the inner city, with its palaces, baths, racecourses, and temples. Until the antimatter bomb was defused, all this was at risk. There were not near enough ships to evacuate the island, but Jake let it be known that dangerous things would be happening on Callisto. Anyone planning a summer sea voyage would do well to take it now.

The Sacred Queen and her court reacted the way the Trojans did when Artemis showed up with Jake and Love—treating Jake with awe, tinged with fear. Accepting whatever he said as gospel, no matter how outrageous. Just so long as he did not ask too much from them.

All Jake asked was that Apollo and Poseidon be lodged in the Temple of the Dying Zeus until he returned for them. The Sacred Queen agreed. These were male gods, and men's business. She was happy to be as uninvolved as possible.

Jake had Apollo locked in the temple treasury, loaded down with electronic shackles, and a medikit lie detector. His first question for his prisoner was, "Where is Sauromanta."

"Where is who?" His medikit showed that the Mouse God was being evasive, giving Jake hope.

"The Amazon you fought."

"Doubtless she is with my sister."

"Your sister was alone when she crashed." Otherwise, Jake would not have fired on the hovercar.

Apollo looked coolly back at him. "You seem to know more than I do." The medikit said this was true.

Seeing he would get no information about Sauromanta, Jake changed his tack. "I'm going to defuse the bomb beneath the volcano. If you have any advice . . ."

Apollo shrugged. "Ask Poseidon. He's the Earthshaker. Just beware of Artemis."

"She crashed into the cone, along with her dog pack."

Apollo laughed. "And you think she is dead? You don't know my sister. If she were even hurt, I would know it. We are twins, linked at birth."

"If she's not dead, then where is she?"

Apollo shrugged. "Heaven knows. But beware, she hates all cities, and would just as soon see this one detonated."

"I'll be sure to let her know you're here."

The Mouse God grimaced. "That would hardly stop her.

She hates to lose. And she is the wild one. 'Nothing in excess'—that's my motto."

Jake said he would remember that.

Poseidon was shackled to the main altar—even more frightened by what Artemis might do. And very pessimistic about Jake's chances. "Defusing the bomb is nothing," Poseidon declared. "It is a simple lock—just remove the key. But you'll never get to it." His medikit said he absolutely believed this. "The volcanic chamber is deep down atop the magma. The only way in is through the portal. The way is guarded by a maze full of monsters, and Artemis will be expecting you."

Your typical heroic task. "I've gotten this far," Jake reminded him. "Any advice . . ."

"Yes, indeed!"

"What's that?"

"Get me off this island!" Poseidon pleaded. "I'll make it worth it to you."

Jake shook his head happily. "No can do." For a god of earthquakes Poseidon/Wasserman seemed terribly upset at the upcoming eruption.

Before going in, Jake had a scrambled conversation with Peg onboard *Atlantis*. She *wanted* to come with him. Down the throat of the volcano. Not your normal task for a paleontologist. Even one who had neatly handled Apollo . . .

"I need you to hold things together here," he told her. (And carry on if he did not come back.) There was no *reason* for Peg to come along. What she had done already was way "above and beyond."

"But what am I supposed to *do* while you're down there?"

"Find Anneke," Jake suggested. She was somewhere in Atlantis, with the Bull Dancers from Crete.

"Certainly." Peg acted like it was no problem finding one person in a strange city—possible the largest one on the planet. "Then what?"

"Get her off the island."

Right. Peg signed off. Without any elaborate good-bye. If he did not want her with him, then he had damn well better come back.

Jake had given serious thought to leaving Love behind as well. Going in just with Hercules. Aside from Jake, Herc was the only one who absolutely had to go. Hercules was Jake's ticket into Zeus's Shrine. Also his talisman—the only one of them guaranteed to be coming out. No matter how bad things got in the volcano, Hercules had to emerge alive. He still had one labor to go. He could not die until he had completed all twelve.

And the date and manner of Hercules' death were well-known. Fatally poisoned by the Hydra's venom, Hercules would mount and light his own funeral pyre. Having no particular reason to doubt the myth, Jake planned to cling to Herc like a shipwrecked swabby. As the Argonauts used to say, "Nothing without Hercules."

Soon as they crossed the wall, Jake went zipping to the crash site, setting his hovercar down next to the wreck of Dianna's. Mechanical dogs lay strewn about, smashed by the fall. But as Apollo had predicted, there was no body.

Jake was not much surprised. But very disappointed. He definitely wanted Dianna dead. Not because he hated her. Jake disliked a lot of people without wanting them dead. But seeing Artemis/Dianna's body, or some burnt approximation, would have made his job infinitely easier.

Nor was there any sign of Sauromanta. As Apollo said, he would probably find her and Artemis together.

When they got to the shrine, the Centaurs and Huntresses on guard drew back, letting the god-car land. Hercules hopped out, saying he had come to speak with his Almighty Father. No one lifted hand or hoof to stop him. Jake and Love entered in his wake.

Beyond the columned portico, the Callisto Shrine was a cave sanctuary, winding back into the volcano—part of the great network of sacred caves scattered across Europe. Where hunters and gatherers had worshiped, painting the walls with horses and bulls, long before there were ziggurats and temples.

Priests of Zeus welcomed them, taking Hercules aside for a private interview with the god. While waiting for the demigod to return, Jake went through a final equipment check. He had his adhesive boots, his climbing equipment, and the plastic explosive Peg had brought. Also a moon bow and quiver, with extra arrowheads. Love had found his stunner and flak jacket aboard the *Argo*.

Hercules came back in fine fettle, saying his heavenly father had promised to watch over him. Zeus swore his son would leave the volcano alive. Hercules had not asked how Jake and Love would fare.

The entrance to the maze was in the innermost reaches of the cave. Love lit a couple of flare arrows, handing one to Hercules, and they set out. The Cave of the Maiden above Amnisos—where Jake had been purified for the Bull Dance—had been a simple one-chamber cavern. But the Callisto Cave had a winding central passage, leading through a series of irregularly-sized chambers. Twisted lava formations resembled strange deities and wild beasts. The final chamber was cathedral-like, its ceiling soaring more than sixty meters above the cave floor.

In the center of the huge chamber was a wide natural shaft going straight down—a great ropy lava flue leading into the heart of the volcano. According to Wasserman, this shaft led to the portal. And Poseidon Earthshaker ought to know.

Leaning over, Hercules tossed in his flare arrow. Jake watched the arrow wobble a bit, then fall straight and true, illuminating the shaft walls. The arrow fell and fell, dwindling to a tiny spark that seemed to hang in the darkness. Eventually the spark faded to a glimmer. Jake's augmented vision followed it all the way to the bottom.

Love stared into the black pit. "God, I hate tunnel work."

Next to the opening was a great coil of rope, anchored to a lava outcropping. Hercules picked it up and heaved it in. "Let's get going."

They went down hand over hand, Jake's boots helping him keep position right behind Hercules. Love carried the light.

The opening above was soon lost in the glare of Love's light. Unable to see past Hercules, Jake could make out nothing but the lava tube's uneven walls, which kept lengthening as they went down. Long after they should have reached bottom they were still descending. The shaft, the rope, the descent kept getting longer. A 3V illusion. And a damned good one—though not good enough to fool Jake's navmatrix. Time and distance were being stretched to dramatize the descent, making the lava tube seem to be kilometers deep.

But it could not stop them from reaching bottom. Hercules landed with a triumphant thud. Jake and Love came down behind him. The arrow Hercules had dropped was lying at the base of the shaft, still burning. The floor around it was strewn with offerings tossed down the shaft—bronze figures, bracelets, gold rings, and sealstones.

Four tunnels led away from the base of the shaft, headed in four different directions. Only one of them was real. The others were as phony as the kilometers-long descent—3V illusions designed to send intruders in endless circles.

Nocking a tanglefoot arrow, Jake headed off in the only possible direction, relying on his night vision, navmatrix, and internal sensors. That meant walking point, a task he would have gladly left to Hercules. Or even Love. But he was the only one equipped for it.

Fortunately the way was simple. Despite the twisted tangle of illusionary tunnels and hologram walls, there was only one way to go. A head-high passage had been bored through the soft volcanic rock, presumably to connect the Callisto Shrine to the portal. What other reason was there to be digging around down here?

Jake was so busy ignoring illusion, he barely recognized the real thing. He stepped through a hologram wall, and came face to face with a lion.

Or what looked like a lion. A huge maned beast with sharp white fangs and fiery eyes. But rising above the mane was a second head, with the face and horns of a goat. "CHIMERA," his compweb informed him. A beast so absurd its name came to mean "nonsensical." Or "bioconstruct." The impossibility of it stunned him. His conscious mind insisted it had to be a holo.

Fortunately his internal sensors weren't fooled. Motion detectors screamed a warning. Muscles responded without thinking, pulling the bow and releasing, putting the tanglefoot arrow right between the beast's clawed forepaws.

It barely slowed the monster. With its rear legs still going, the Chimera bounded at him, both heads snapping, claws ripping the web to shreds. Bowled over by the tawny blur, Jake did not even try to draw another arrow. Jamming the moon bow into the beast's mouth, he fought to keep the heavy weapon between him and the fangs.

Pinned by the weight of the monster, Jake alternated between curses, and cries for help. Rolling back and forth, he struggled to stay away from the foreclaws, which were still gummed with tanglefoot web. At the same time pushing the moon bow deeper down the beast's throat.

He was still feeding his bow to the Chimera when Hercules came bounding through the hologram wall.

Hercules hit the Chimera like a blitzing linebacker, getting a stranglehold on the lion head. The goat head tried to butt him. But Hercules just laughed, digging his shoulder into the lion's throat. He buried his head in the mane, arms circling its neck, straining to snap its spine.

Unable to slash through Hercules' lionskin cloak, the Chimera twisted sideways. A venomous serpent-headed tail lashed out. Hercules stamped down on it with one foot, crushing the serpent head with his heel. Fortunately this biosculpted version did not have the mythical beast's fiery breath.

With a loud pop, the lion head went limp, its neck broken. So much for *Simba*. Hercules reached up to grab the goat head.

But the Chimera had had enough. Leaping backwards, it dashed down the tunnel, dragging its serpent tail, the limp lion head dangling between its legs. Glad to get away with its goat head still intact. That's what you get for taking on a true hero.

Hercules bounded off after the beaten bioconstruct. Not happy unless his foe was stone dead.

Love helped Jake up. "You still in one piece?"

"Hope so." Jake felt shaken, but semi-intact. His compweb claimed nothing vital was broken. They headed off after Hercules, fearing he would get lost in the virtual maze.

But the Chimera knew the way out. Dim light loomed ahead, growing into a gray circle. The tunnel exit. Jake put on a burst of speed, imagining he might somehow rein in Hercules. Getting back in charge of the expedition. A hopeless undertaking, but he had to try.

They charged out of a rock grotto, onto a gray shadowy landscape. Ghostly black poplars grew amid gnarled lava formations. Even the sky was drained of color, etched in grainy shades of charcoal. No wonder the light at the end of the tunnel had seemed so dim.

Hercules slammed to a stop, forgetting all about the fleeing Chimera. Strange behavior for a godling who never seemed to show an gram of caution—except for the time he refused to enter the Garden of the Hesperides. The Chimera limped off, thoroughly surprised to be alive.

Hercules heaved a sigh, turning to Jake. "I can go no farther."

Jake stopped, bent forward, hands on knees, gasping for breath. Trying to catch Hercules had been a gut-wrenching effort. Especially after having to wrestle a Chimera. Slowly he got his wind back. "Why?"

Hercules waved at the shadowy landscape. "This is the land of Hades. The Underworld. Unless properly purified, only the dead may enter."

Jake's navmatrix assured him that Hercules was mistaken. What Hercules thought was the Underworld, was a huge 3V illusion. The shadowy sky, gray hills, the dead trees, the shrine on the darkling plain—none of this was real. But he was going to have a hard time convincing Hercules.

Scanning the area with his compweb, he spotted a single blank spot. An especially dead area in the midst of a tiny shrine. The space-time portal.

Jake pointed out that they did not have to cross any pseudo-Styx. Where he wanted to go was just a few meters ahead of them. Hercules was not having any of that, saying he had come too far already.

Love shook his head. "Right. Perfect. Against the big guy's religion. 'Yea, though I walk through the Valley of the Shadow of Death . . . ' Damn. Don't he know he's the meanest motherfucker in the Valley?"

Jake shrugged. Mere fear was not holding Hercules back. When his own time came, Hercules would climb atop his funeral pyre and set the torch himself. The same taboo that kept people from raiding tombs held even greater force here at the Gates of Hell. Earth was for the living, this land was for the dead.

"So it's just the two of us?" Love clearly disliked going in without Herc.

Jake did not like it either. Herc had been his talisman. The one sure survivor he hoped to cling to. "No. Just the one of me."

Love gave him a sideways glance. "Why?"

"Lots of reasons." The portal looked tiny. Navigating a new spatiotemporal anomaly was never easy. Getting himself through would be hard enough. And if anything happened to Jake on the far side of the portal, Love would have no way of getting back. "Mainly, I need you to get word to Peg. If . . ."

Hercules had already turned about, headed back for the surface. Who knows what he would say when he got out, and how much Love and Jake would figure in it? Love was Jake's only sure line left open to the surface. If anyone was going to tell what happened, or return with a rescue party, it had to be him.

"Glad you ain't mad at me, or somethin'."

"No more than usual."

Love snorted. "How long should I wait?"

"I'll be back in a flash, or not at all." Even the longest faster-than-light trips caused relatively little time loss.

Love did not like seeing him go off alone. "Well, keep yer head low. Y'hear?"

"Sure." Jake started out for the shrine. If everything worked on the far side, he could be back out of the anomaly in seconds. And he hoped to keep Hercules in sight. At least until they regained the surface.

"Be sure an' come back alive," Love called after him. "I don't want to hear no sadass excuses."

Jake smiled and waved. Then he turned to face the shrine. It was a simple stone pen and altar, similar to the hundreds of wayside shrines he had seen since coming to the Bronze Age. Behind the altar stood a legless image of the Death Maiden, with a pot half-buried beneath her—home for the oracular serpent. The portal entrance showed up as a blank spot in Jake's navmatrix, a piece of dead ground right in front of the altar.

Jake stepped into it. The portal was tiny. Too small to take any heavy equipment. Whoever had opened it did not want to chance anything big coming back. That explained a lot.

Apollo and company had to be parasitic—they could bring virtually nothing from their own time. It helped to explain their extreme egoism. And their utter contempt for everyone else. They came with nothing but their wits and foreknowledge, and ended up owning everything. Immortal and all-powerful. Worshiped by millions through the ages. Virtually owning the Faster-Than-Light agency in Jake's own time. Every night an orgy, every meal a feast. Like Love said, "It messes with your head."

Otherwise, the portal was a fairly ordinary space-time

anomaly, hiding no unpleasant surprises for Jake's navmatrix. No more than any other strange portal. Only its beginning was special, reaching somewhere beyond Home Period—and blanked out for most of that time by the Atlantis eruption.

Fortunately Jake did not have that far to go. According to Poseidon the volcanic chamber containing the bomb trigger was just a couple of klicks beneath the surface and a hundred hours into the future. But those hours were crucial. By the time he got to the trigger, Hercules could easily be off the island, headed who knows where. There would be no guarantees Atlantis could be saved. Or that Jake would make it back.

He emerged in the Netherworld. Not just the Gates of Hell, but the undiscovered country itself. A broad gray River Styx divided the darkling plain in half. The near bank was dotted with burial mounds, and a small single-oared ferry was drawn up, ready to receive the grateful dead.

But what Jake wanted lay in the nearest burial mound. The *kurgan* stood open. A slab-sided earthen tunnel slanted down into the ground, paved with smooth river stones. According to Poseidon there would be at most one guard. The maze, the Chimera, the space-time portal, plus the forbidding locale, must have seemed like obstacles enough.

Jake nocked an arrow and entered the hot dark shaft, each step taking him closer to the magma. Dim light filtered down the burial tunnel from the shadowy sky. Jake would be silhouetted against the entrance, but that could not be helped. He picked an armor-piercing arrow, figuring he might get only one shot.

He had no hope of taking the guard by surprise. The sentry stood alert and waiting, holding her moon-shaped shield before her, spear arm cocked. It was Sauromanta.

Blue eyes fixed him from beneath her lynxskin cap. A disobedient blond curl hung down onto her forehead. Her arm stayed poised, her spear level—only her lips moved. "I wish to heaven that it was anyone but you."

Jake smiled ruefully. "Right. I'm happy to see you, too."

Weird to tell, he *was* happy to see her. He was always glad to see Sauromanta. Lately he only got to see her under trying circumstances. Like when he was hounded by a mechanical pack, or being sentenced to be sacrificed. But somehow that did not diminish the pleasure of just plain *seeing* her. Love is like that.

"I cannot let you pass," she warned.

"Of course not." That would have been too easy.

And he could not use his armor-piercing arrow. The AP point would blow through her shield and corselet. Almost anyone else, and he could have just pulled and released. One life to save thousands. But not her. Jake would just as soon have put the arrow to his own head. Too bad Sauromanta would not let him trade it for a tanglefoot.

Sweat trickled down his temples from the heat. He could feel the lava beneath his feet. There *had* to be another way. Lowering his bow, he let the arrow drop to the ground. It was useless to him anyway.

"What are you doing?" She looked for the trick behind his surrender.

"I cannot fight you." Slowly he unstrung the bow.

"You must." She stayed poised and ready.

"Why?" He made an elaborate show of setting down the bow, then unslinging his quiver. As he did it, he palmed a hypodermic point from among the spare arrowheads. Then he unbuckled his dagger—letting it fall—at the same time slipping the hypo behind his broad leather belt. Holding out his hands, he showed they were empty. "Can't we at least talk?"

"No," she answered, keeping her spear cocked.

"Why not?" He took a step toward her.

"Keep back," Sauromanta warned. She would kill him if she had to—but she clearly wanted some reason not to.

He took another step, hands still spread, looking into her eyes. Trying for a winning smile.

Bringing down the spear, she poked at him, to fend him away with the point.

That was the move Jake hoped for. He had his compweb replay the motions Peg made when Apollo stabbed at her. *Shiho nage.* Immobilization number 6. *Tenkan* variation. Reaching past the point, he seized the spear shaft, pivoting backwards, using Sauromanta's momentum to draw her to him.

He did not have Peg's smooth, easy execution—but he did not need it. He did not have to throw Sauromanta, just get her closer. Pulling the hypo point from behind his belt, he stabbed her in the arm.

The Amazon crumpled, dropping the spear. Jake caught her as she fell, laying her down on the smooth river stones, making sure she was not hurt.

Then he sat down beside her, shaken by the risks he had taken, letting his racing heart relax. He had found her alive. Half of what he needed to do was done. One by one Jake took her weapons away. The spear. Her dagger. Her double-bladed Saca battle-ax. She had lost her lynxskin cap in the tussle.

He brushed blond hair out of her face, staring at her calm sleeping features. Amazingly at rest. So much danger. So much beauty. For the first time since Melos he could just look at her. Without worry. Without fear.

Twice he tried to get up. Restringing his bow, he planned to go down the tunnel, disarm the bomb, then come back for her. But it was no good. He could not leave her lying there. Not after all that had happened. What if he came back and found her gone? He would always want to redo this moment—and faster-than-light did not work that way.

Whatever happened, would happen to both of them. Strapping his medikit onto her arm, he told it to wake her up. Putting distance between them, he nocked a tanglefoot arrow.

Her eyes opened, staring boldly at the bent bow. "You said you would not fight me."

"I lied," Jake admitted.

"You could never have won a fair fight."

"That's why I cheated. Now give me your parole. I know you won't *lie*."

"No," she shook her head. "You will have to kill me."

"That I cannot do. But I could drug you, and tie you, and haul you about. Be my prisoner. It is much more dignified."

She stared at him, clear blue eyes cutting through pretense. "I am your prisoner." She was stating a fact, not giving her parole.

"Then get up." Jake motioned with the bow.

She got up. Looking wary, ready for anything.

"Can I trust you?" he asked. "I mean not to put up a fight, or run off?"

Sauromanta's Homeric training showed. When asked a string of questions, she answered the last first, and the first last. "I won't run. But I will fight if I can. You can trust that."

Jake sighed. "That will have to do." He told her to go ahead of him down the tunnel. As they started out, he asked if she knew what she was guarding.

"Yes. The key to the Callisto volcano."

"Turn that key, and thousands of people will die." Jake very much wanted her to know the stakes.

She gave him a sober look. "So you have come to turn it?"

"Hell no!" He wondered what they had been telling her about him.

"Really?" Sauromanta raised an eyebrow.

"I've come to destroy the key," he insisted. Too bad he had already lied to her.

The tunnel widened ahead of them. Jake could see a dressed-stone chamber with an altar in the middle. Sticking straight out of the altar was a big Bronze Age slotted key. He motioned her in ahead of him. "After you, just don't touch anything."

Sauromanta obeyed, stepping into the chamber, then standing aside for him. He followed her in.

Motion detectors screamed in his head. A big bronze net came dropping down, tangling Jake in its heavy links, dragging him to the floor. The same sort of net Sauromanta saved him from in the Garden of the Hesperides. Through the links he could see her foot on a wooden treadle.

"I did not give my parole," she reminded him.

He stared at her. Hardly believing she had trapped him so easily.

The air between them flickered. Artemis appeared. She had the triumphant smile of a huntress happy to see her quarry netted. "Well-done."

Sauromanta thanked her. Glad to have done well by her goddess.

Artemis looked down at Jake, a bit of the old Dianna showing through. "I never, never dreamed you would get this far."

"Sorry to disappoint." He was talking to a holo. Always a fruitless exercise. But he had to draw things out, giving his abysmal luck a chance to change.

"Well this will be the last time." She turned to Sauromanta. "Go to the altar."

Sauromanta obeyed her hologram goddess.

"Now take the key and turn it."

"No!" Jake shrieked, struggling upright in the net.

Artemis gave him an arch do-not-contradict-me look.

"I am beaten," he reminded them. Talking more to Sauromanta than to Dianna. "There is no need."

"Perhaps. But you have shown amazing resource. This way is sure."

"But Atlantis. This island . . ."

"The world is better off without them."

"And your brother Apollo?"

"A true god will survive—I did." She turned back to Sauromanta. "Turn the key."

"Wait," Jake yelled. The doom that had hung over Anneke's people—ever since Jake dragged them into his conflict with the gods—was now too terribly real. Lifting a corner of the net he slid Sauromanta's steel ax clattering across the floor. "Take it. It's yours."

Sauromanta hesitated, staring at the ax at her feet. Her hands hovered over the key. Jake was helpless. Artemis was a holo. Life and death were up to her.

Jake knew that appealing to the Amazon's self-interest was worse than hopeless. That she would die if she turned the key meant nothing to her. Less than nothing. He had tricked and beaten her, forcing her to fail in a sacred trust. If death would redeem her, so much the better. They were in Hell already.

"Kill me if you must," he begged. "But there are thousands on the island. Women and children." Anneke was there. And Pandora. But those names would mean nothing to her. There was only one name that mattered. "Hestia, the Hearth Maiden, she would not have you kill them in their homes."

Tearing her gaze away from the ax, Sauromanta reached down and seized the key.

"Stop!" Jake screamed.

Slowly she drew the key out of the lock, then turned to face Artemis—ignoring Jake. "I am sorry. I cannot do it."

Artemis shook her head. "Then you are truly lost to me. Death alone might have saved you, erasing what men have done. You could have been with me forever. Now you are nothing." The angry goddess glared at Jake, flailing feebly in the net. "I hope you are happy. You have ruined her for me."

Jake was too shaken to admit he was pretty pleased.

"But I will win in the end," Artemis added primly. "None of you can escape death. No matter how hard you try." She flickered and vanished.

Sauromanta reached down and picked up the ax. She walked over to stand above Jake. Still holding the key.

"You scared the living shit out of me," he told her.

She smiled. "Good. You deserved it. Can I still kill you?"

"I suppose so," Jake replied weakly. It was not his first choice.

Setting down the ax, she grabbed the edge of the net, hauling it up, helping Jake wriggle out. He stood up, wringing with sweat, his chest heaving, barely believing he was alive, his heart pounding to wake the dead.

Letting the net drop, Sauromanta retrieved her ax, holding the big double blade one-handed in front of his face. Using it to emphasize each word. "Don't *ever* lie to me again."

"Never again," Jake shuddered. Not unless he *needed* to.

She handed him the bronze key. He held it, feeling its weight, remembering what she had said on that starlit run down to the Pillars of Hercules—"Trust me. I'll see we succeed."

He stared at her, shaking his head. She had done it, despite brain scrubbing, a brush with death, mythic monsters, and all-powerful enemies. Staying true to a vow she no longer remembered. What a woman. No wonder he had missed her so.

"Must we be enemies?" he asked.

Sauromanta tilted her head to think about it. Looking him over. "I suppose not."

"I'm going to put an end to this," he told her. With shaking hands, Jake rigged the chamber with enough plastic explosive to bring down the roof—setting a relay trigger. Hell outside might be 3V, but this chamber, the altar, the key—they were all too real. Once collapsed, the chamber could not be repaired. Not without heavy equipment, which would never fit through the portal.

When he was done, he thrust the key into his belt and took Sauromanta by the hand. She let him lead her to the portal, stopping only to stoop down and pick up her lynxskin cap. At the portal he had his compweb trigger the relay. They were gone before the blast came roaring out of the tunnel.

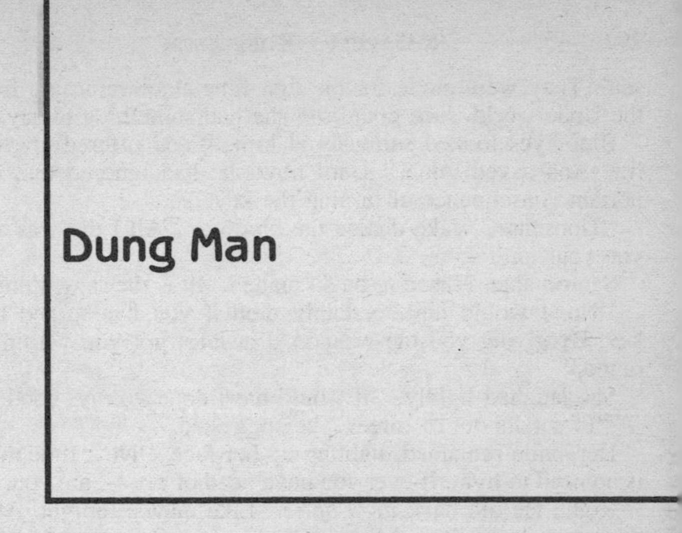

Dung Man

The Shrine of the Isthmian Maiden hove into sight, separating from the green-gold patchwork of the isthmus. Jake told the hovercar to aim for the bare flat spot by the altar of the peak sanctuary, setting the godcopter down right next to the hoof-marks Pegasus had made in the stone.

Nymphs and maidens came parading out of the shrine to meet them. Nausicaa led the procession, with Erin at her side. Followed by the *Wanax*. Some Bronze Age comnet seemed to have alerted everyone from here to Mycenae that they were returning in triumph from Atlantis. Medea and Jason had come up from Corinth. Iolaus was there. With him was a gent in white robes, with little gold caducei sewn into the fabric, carrying a herald's wand. Jake recognized Copreus, the Dung Man, the High King's Herald.

Anneke was first out of the god-car, eager to greet her family. Hercules was next. Then Love and Peg. Jake sat zeroing his controls. Sauromanta made no move to get out ahead of him.

They got out together and stood for a moment by the altar—where you can see both halves of Greece. And the two blue seas. They were alone for the first time since returning from the Underworld. Jake could see she had something to say.

Blue eyes looked seriously at him. "You offered up your life. And saved mine." Until now she had ignored that important consequence of turning the key.

"Nonsense," Jake denied the obvious. "All I did was toss you your ax."

Sauromanta refused to be dissuaded. "It is the same thing."

"No. I would have certainly died if you had turned that key. By giving you the weapon, I at least got you within ax range."

She laughed lightly. "It would have done you no good."

"Two falls out of three?" he suggested.

Her smile remained, lighting up her face. "Next time there is no need to fight. If ever you have need of me—I am yours."

Right. He did have *need of her*. Like maybe tonight. After the lamps were lit and the wine was poured. He could think of all sorts of uses for Sauromanta. And Peg as well—if she were in the mood. A dirty mind is a joy forever. But that was not what Sauromanta meant. She meant she owed him. And felt honor-bound to pay him back. A life for a life.

They were comrades in adventure. No more, no less. He would have to be content with that.

She turned and walked down the sacred hill. Jake watched her go, thinking of a little room on Melos with dolphins on the wall, and the starlit run down to the Straits of Hercules. He remembered all the way back to that caravanserai on the Royal Road east of Nineveh—where they would have their first talk, more than a thousand years hence. She had helped Hercules with his labors. Beaten back Pharaoh's army. Slept with one god and dueled with another. Died and come back to the living. And now she remembered none of it. While Jake was cursed with total recall.

Somehow, some way, those memories had to be unlocked.

Peg came strolling up, saying, "Come, join the party."

Jake nodded. Every night a party, every meal a feast. These people had plenty to celebrate. Hera, Apollo, and Poseidon were prisoners. Hephaestus was limping around Lemnos—no threat to anyone. Artemis was in the Underworld. The Olympians were put down for the moment. And the moment was all that mattered. Faster-than-light taught you that.

But Peg could see his heart was not in the moment. "It must be hard, her not remembering. But she is still young, brave, and alive. Thanks to you. That is something . . ."

Peg was always practical. Whether she was digging up dinosaurs, or wrestling demigods. And she had come tens of thousands of years to rescue him. That, too, was something.

Still, it *was* hard. Jake never knew what to do with the past. Not really. No matter how far you went—or how fast—you never escaped the present. In ancient times, or the far future, it was always here-and-now. Moment to moment, and nothing more.

He took Peg's hand and walked his wife down the hill, telling her again about the two-headed *T. rex*. Something she very much wished she had seen.

Hercules was in heated conversation with the Dung Man. He appealed to Jake as they came up. "Can you believe this bastard?"

Jake shrugged. After what they had been through, he was ready to believe anything.

"They think they have finally found a labor I cannot do. A place I am afraid to go."

"Where is that?" Jake already knew, but he had found it was better to let Hercules tell the tale.

"The High King wants me to go back to the Underworld. To bring him Cerberus, Hades's three-headed watchdog."

Jake could honestly say, "I have no doubt you'll do it."

"Of course I'll do it," Zeus's overblown son declared. "Once I am properly purified, the Netherworld is nothing. We've been there and back without a scratch. The dead cannot harm you."

Hercules clapped Jake on the shoulder, nearly knocking him sideways. "It will be nothing. Not compared to the Garden of the Hesperides. Remember? That was real adventure, not some land of shadows. Me, you, the African, and the Amazon. All the way off at World's End, by the Stables of the Sun. Where I killed that nine-headed dragon alongside the Ocean Stream."